'If poetry was the supreme literary form of the First World War then, as if in riposte, in the Second World War, the English novel came of age. This wonderful series is an exemplary reminder of that fact. Great novels were written about the Second World War and we should not forget them.'

WILLIAM BOYD

'It's wonderful to see these books given a new lease of life [...] classic novels from the Second World War written by those who were there, experienced the fear, anguish, pain and excitement first-hand and whose writings really do shine an incredibly vivid light onto what it was like to live and fight through that terrible conflict.'

JAMES HOLLAND, Historian, author and TV presenter

'The Imperial War Museum has performed a valuable public service by reissuing these absolutely superb novels.'

ANDREW ROBERTS, author of *Churchill: Walking with Destiny*

PAID TO BE SAFE

Margaret Morrison and Pamela Tulk-Hart

First published in Great Britain in 1948

First published in this format in 2023 by IWM,
Lambeth Road, London SE1 6HZ
iwm.org.uk

ISBN 978-1-912423-65-1

A catalogue record for this book is available from the
British Library.

Printed and bound by CPI Group (UK) Ltd, Croydon CR0 4YY

Every effort has been made to contact all copyright holders.
The publishers will be glad to make good in future editions
any error or omissions brought to their attention.

Cover illustration by Bill Bragg
Design by Clare Skeats
Series Editor Madeleine James

FSC
www.fsc.org
MIX
Paper | Supporting
responsible forestry
FSC® C171272

About the Authors

MARGARET MORRISON (1897–1973)
PAMELA TULK-HART (1918–2010)

MARGARET MORRISON (1897–1973) was a prolific writer of fiction in many different genres, with over 30 published novels. Many of these were written under the pen name March Cost, including one of her best-known titles *A Man Named Luke* (1932). Her interest in the subject of women in aviation was first expressed in the novel *Flying High* (1939, published under her real name), about a Dutch air hostess with KLM airlines. A sequel to this, *Wider Horizons*, was published in 1952. *Paid To Be Safe* (1948) continued the aviation theme, based largely on the experiences of her co-author, Pamela Tulk-Hart, but also drawing on her own wartime service as a medical officer with the Air Transport Auxiliary (ATA). Few sources of information on Morrison's life and work now exist, and her substantial literary output has for the most part fallen into relative neglect.

PAMELA TULK-HART (1918–2010) was born just before the end of the First World War, during which her father had served as a pilot with the Royal Flying Corps. Educated in England and Germany, she was working as sub-editor for a women's magazine at the start of the Second World War in 1939. Volunteering initially for war service as an ambulance driver, she signed up for the ATA in 1943 as a trainee pilot. She rapidly became adept at flying a wide variety of aircraft, including the Spitfire, and served as a ferry pilot until the end of the war, delivering her last aircraft in August 1945. Her ATA experiences directly informed much of the relevant content of *Paid To Be Safe*, which can in some respects be read as her wartime memoir.

Introduction

One of the literary legacies of the First World War was the proliferation of war novels, with an explosion of the genre in the late 1920s and 1930s. Erich Maria Remarque's *All Quiet on the Western Front* was a bestseller and was made into a Hollywood film in 1930. In the same year, Siegfried Sassoon's *Memoirs of an Infantry Officer* sold 24,000 copies. Generations of school children have grown up on a diet of Wilfred Owen's poetry and the novels of Sassoon.

In contrast to the First World War, the novels of the Second World War are often overlooked. Remaining largely unknown by today's generation of readers, Margaret Morrison has been variously called an author of romantic novels and a writer of lighter fiction. On a superficial level, *Paid To Be Safe* could be seen as a product of these genres. It features a glamorous heroine and is peopled with other glamorous characters who lead exciting wartime lives. There is plenty of action and romance, perilous aerial exploits and a generous helping of personal tragedy. However, Morrison was a more multi-faceted writer than this description would suggest. Her 1932 novel *A Man Named Luke* attracted considerable critical acclaim for its daring imagination and psychological complexity. Something of this is also evident in the portrayal of Susan Sandyman, the main protagonist of *Paid To Be Safe*. Behind the adventure, romance and pathos lies a powerful personal story, a compelling 'coming of age' tale amidst the turbulent and pivotal events of the Second World War.

The novel opens with Susan's harrowing return to England from Singapore, after the British colony fell to invading Japanese forces in February 1942. She is one of thousands of Europeans then living in South-East Asia who were forced to flee as Imperial Japan embarked on its conquest of mostly British, American and Dutch territorial possessions in the region – a campaign which opened in spectacular fashion with the surprise attack on the US Pacific Fleet at Pearl Harbor in December 1941. Susan's first tragic loss is that of her young daughter Felicity, who dies of a tropical illness aboard the ship taking them to England. She has had no news of her husband Frank, who stayed in Singapore as a member of the Malayan Volunteer Forces taking part in the desperate and futile defence of the colony. But we quickly learn that Susan is made of strong stuff, demonstrating a resolve to overcome even the most traumatic of setbacks that will become the defining trait of her personality as the novel progresses: 'Her memories and her sorrows lay deep. She would cherish them and they would inspire her to high endeavour'.

Returning to her childhood home in rural Hampshire, Susan is confronted with further family tragedy. Her father has died of pneumonia, contracted during Home Guard duties, and both of her brothers have been killed on active service – one while training with the RAF in Canada. Only her mother is left of the immediate family. Where others might have been overwhelmed and paralysed by grief, Susan interprets all of these ultimately incomprehensible losses as a direct personal call to action. She craves 'something that has danger' – 'Where I take all the risks a man would take. There is only me. The only one left to *hit back* – to fight for them all'.

Susan's grandmother provides a reality check and the wise advice to find a less dangerous occupation 'until your real job shows itself'. As a result, Susan starts her contribution to the war effort in the relatively modest but essential role of a Voluntary Aid Detachment ambulance driver (as did Pamela Tulk-Hart). It is, in some ways, a necessary and appropriate preparation for her later work with aircraft. The ambulance, a Ford Eight van, becomes her pride and joy, indeed 'her salvation'. The care and safe handling of an important piece of machinery becomes part of her redemptive mission. It is at this time too that Susan first encounters her future calling, when she strikes up a conversation with two Air Transport Auxiliary (ATA) pilots who have executed a practice forced landing in a local farmer's field. We discover that she used to fly a Gypsy Moth with her husband in Malaya, which had to be destroyed to prevent its potential use by the Japanese. The pilots allow her to sit in the cockpit of their aircraft, reviving a key memory from that time and fixing her resolve: 'It was the sudden familiarity. This was what they had planned. To fly home and land in this very field'.

So begins Susan Sandyman's ATA adventure. A chance meeting with a serving female ferry pilot in London provides her with a glimpse into this intriguing world of experience, and her application soon follows. She is encouraged and assisted by one of the male ATA pilots she had first met in the farmer's field, who refers to it as the 'silent service'. A civilian organisation under RAF control, the ATA performed the vital job of flying new aircraft from the factories to RAF (and Royal Naval Air Service) stations and frontline units. It also provided a 'taxi' service between air bases for RAF pilots and its own personnel. During the course of the war, some 1,154 men and 168 women flew over 300,000 aircraft to wherever they were needed. The ATA's task was in many respects as hazardous as that of the fighting units they supplied and 173 ATA pilots were killed in service. Aircraft losses and serious accidents were, however, remarkably few, considering that pilots often had to fly unfamiliar machines at very short notice to places they had never been to before. The daunting nature of the role was encapsulated in the ATA's unofficial motto: 'Anything to Anywhere'.

We follow Susan at a brisk and compelling pace through her initial training and first flying experiences. Like her, the reader quickly learns a great deal about how the ATA operates – the pressures, hazards, technical procedures and challenges, but also the sheer exhilaration of flying. It becomes clear that Susan is at last in her element and has found the war work that her past has been guiding her towards. She also finds a surrogate family in the close-knit and cosmopolitan ATA community, which included men and women from more than 20 countries. Some of the author's language around nationality, race and other issues would today be widely considered as offensive. For her readership in the late 1940s it would for the most part have been accepted as a feature of normal parlance.

Inevitably Susan also encounters prejudice and sexism from some of her fellow male cadets: 'Why couldn't they accept it as a normal job for a girl without thinking of her as something extraordinary, tough, or glamorous?'. The ATA became in fact one of the first of what would now be termed Equal Opportunities Employers, awarding women the same pay as men from 1943 onwards. Despite their crucial contributions to the Allied war effort, many female ATA pilots struggled to find employment in the aviation industry after the war.

The romantic attentions of men are also never far away, mostly unwelcome, with the exception of Australian bomber pilot Mark Cordner, an acquaintance from earlier in her life, who she meets again by chance and with whom a more intimate friendship develops. Traumatic personal loss again threatens to overwhelm Susan when Mark is reported missing during a bombing sortie over Germany, eventually returning to her after surviving being shot down over the Netherlands and sent to Germany for forced labour (having disguised himself as a Dutchman). He is subsequently helped back to England by Dutch locals who were part of an escape network for downed Allied aircrew.

As captured by Mark Cordner's bravery, the risk undertaken by bomber crew in particular was considerable; with 51 per cent of aircrew killed on operations, 12 per cent killed or wounded in non-operational accidents and 13 per cent becoming prisoners of war or evaders, there was a slim survival rate of just 24 per cent among Bomber Command. In total over 57,000 airmen were killed in action and more than 75,000 were killed, wounded or taken prisoner during the course of the war. Susan's best ATA friend Mandy's RAF pilot brother is one of these unlucky few, having been shot down and killed over the English Channel.

Suffusing the novel at regular intervals is the beauty of the British countryside, particularly as viewed from the aeroplane cockpit. The landscape and the people who inhabit it become an essential part of what Susan and her fellow pilots are determined to help defend. But the enemy is not confined to the forces of Nazi Germany. As Pamela Tulk-Hart had good reason to know, the British weather also poses an ever-present threat: 'Weather was the main danger. In spite of good Met forecasting, one often found oneself in cloud or smog. Bearing in mind that we didn't have radios and we had no "blind flying" training, this put one's navigational skills to the test!' Susan almost falls victim to this adversary when she embarks on a flight without the obligatory weather check and runs into trouble. As her superior tells her, 'the country cannot afford foolhardy ferry pilots; it wants every machine that can be produced, and it wants it delivered undamaged. [...] you are not paid to be brave – you are paid to be *safe*!' This last exhortation appeared in the 'Reminder Book' issued to all ATA pilots and became the service's watchword.

Just as Allied victory comes a vital step closer with the June 1944 Normandy landings, the other enemy has one last personal tragedy to inflict on Susan. Her mother is killed when a V1 'doodlebug' or 'buzz-bomb' hits her London flat, making her one of over 6,000 fatalities caused across England by the first of Hitler's so-called revenge weapons. Characteristically, even this cruel blow sparks in Susan 'the light of determination. The enemy should not take everything. They would not break her'. The novel draws to a close with the final months of the war, the capitulation of Nazi Germany in May 1945, the UK General Election in July (for which Susan flies to the polling station in a Spitfire) and finally the fall of Japan in August after the dropping of the atomic bombs on Hiroshima and Nagasaki. Susan learns that her husband Frank was killed during the defence of Singapore in February 1942, shortly after she left the colony. Her last hope and tie broken, Susan is free to marry Mark Cordner and move to Australia to start a new life.

As we bid Susan farewell, we can be confident in her readiness to take on whatever the next unwritten chapter will bring. In her own understated words: 'We all come to times when we think there is nothing left, but we re-adjust – it's the philosophy of life'. In the dark days of apparent defeat, Susan's triumph over shattering personal loss and wartime adversity was predicted by the ship's doctor who tried to save her daughter's life: '*The joy of victory will come, victory over our enemies. But it will be more glorious if we have also had our personal victories. You will have yours*'. This is the novel's essential message of hope, a message sorely needed in a post-war Britain struggling with austerity and facing new uncertainties.

Stephen Walton
2023

Dedicated to all who gave their lives while ferrying His Majesty's aircraft.

While the principal characters of this story are entirely fictitious, they move through the real circumstances and personalities of Air Transport Auxiliary.

In every case, wherever possible, permission to use their names has been asked and has been received.

To them all, and to my collaborator, I proffer my most grateful thanks and crave the indulgence of all for my omissions.

MARGARET MORRISON

BOOK ONE

ONE

THE DOOR OF the ship's surgery stood slightly ajar. The young doctor, busy at his desk with the various forms and indentures incidental to the ending of a voyage, had purposefully left it so. They were in the smooth waters of the Clyde and, when a sudden movement of the ship caused the door to slam, he arose from his desk and fixed it on its hook so that it remained firm, and more widely ajar. He was listening for a half-expected footstep.

Preparations for landing were in full swing. People came and went along the alleyway. They interrupted him and his work went slower in consequence, but he was fearful of appearing over busy, or that the door, closed, might act as a rebuff.

Almost an hour passed before, suddenly alert, he lifted his head and his eyes, behind their thick lenses, brightened. Only a moment elapsed before a light tap on the door and a question came simultaneously.

'Dr Jamieson! Are you busy? May I come in?' and before the girl had finished speaking, Robert Jamieson's fingers were unfastening the hook while he answered:

'Please do, Mrs Sandyman. Is there anything I can do for you?'

His voice and words gave no indication of the real state of his mind, but his tone was not formal. They had been through too much together. The girl – she was hardly more – had leaned on him through her hours of trial. She had not found him wanting; and she was quite unconscious that he was deeply in love for the first time in his life, because her own feelings were merely those of deep friendship and gratitude. She shook her head negatively as he added:

'Won't you sit down?'

'No, thank you, I mustn't stay. I am helping Mrs Lennox with her babies.'

Despite these practical words Robert saw the quiver of pain that passed across her face. He closed the door and, taking her bag, put it on the table before he turned about and took both of her hands

1

into his own, and his eyes glistened as he looked into hers and said:

'That's right.'

She gave him no opportunity to say more. 'Yes, you were right – but sometimes...' Her voice broke and the tears welled up in her eyes.

'I know. I know,' he answered, but she freed a hand to dash away her tears and hurriedly continued:

'There is such confusion on deck. I just had to come and risk disturbing you. I was afraid I'd miss you, and – and I – I do so want to thank you again – for all you did, and to say "goodbye".'

Robert Jamieson's heart missed a beat but he managed to smile as he answered:

'I should have found you.'

'Yes. In a crowd, and I should not have been able to tell you, again, that I shall never forget all you did for Felicity, and – and, sometimes, I feel I am breaking the last link with Frank and Felicity when I leave this ship, and *you*.'

Once more the tears welled up in her eyes, and once more Robert Jamieson possessed himself of both her hands; and there was more than professional sympathy in his voice as he answered:

'I shall always wish I could have done more—' His voice hesitated on the last word, but Susan Sandyman interrupted with a quick shake of her head.

'No, no! No one on earth could have done more; and I shall never forget our talks.'

She paused, while the silence within the cabin deepened. To Robert Jamieson it suddenly felt remote. As if he, and she, stood isolated from everyone and everything else. Alone as, perhaps, they would never again be alone. A thousand things he would like to have said flashed through his mind; but the time was not yet. Perhaps never would be. The realization gave him pain, pain he successfully disguised as he asked:

'Have you thought of any definite plan?'

'No. I am only remembering what you said, "No panacea like hard work." War is so awful. *We* may never meet again, but all my life I will remember and be grateful.' She paused again and the brightness of Robert Jamieson's dark grey eyes, as he looked into her blue-grey ones, was not wholly accounted for by his spectacles.

'I needed that pull up you gave me,' she continued. 'It is true I am young, I am strong, and I will put my back into whatever job comes my way. It isn't only what you did for Felicity that makes me grateful, it is also what you have done for me. Now, goodbye. I must go.'

A few more formal sentences passed between them, and then she was gone. Robert Jamieson stood in his surgery doorway and watched her retreating figure until she was out of sight. She walked firmly and swiftly down the alleyway, as if she had a new purpose in life. She did not look back, and he was glad. He felt, although he longed to see her smile once again, that it was indicative. She would not look back. Her memories and her sorrows lay deep. She would cherish them and they would inspire her to high endeavour. But he sighed as he closed his door and returned to his neglected papers. Absentmindedly he retrieved some that had fallen to the floor before he sat down and gazed unseeingly before him, deep in retrospection…

He had seen her for the first time when she came aboard at Colombo. 'Mrs Frank Sandyman and child.' He had read her name in the new passenger list, and afterwards, heard that she had escaped from Singapore in a little Dutch coastal steamer. She was just one of the many passengers who now overcrowded the already crowded SS *City of Truro*. Women and children, without clothes and without money. He had helped her, as he had helped others, and as impersonally, until he had fought with her, the twenty-four hours' losing fight, for her child's life. That was almost three weeks ago. The convoy had been slow, and they had come by the Western approaches into the Clyde. Their first sight of land after leaving Freetown had been the coast of Northern Ireland. Robert Jamieson sat remembering it all. Those hours of anguish had given him such an insight into the stability and courage of her character that the apathy into which she had sunk, and with which she listened to the service and watched while the tiny shroud of canvas slipped gently

3

into the sea, had puzzled him. For a few days he had left her to herself, then, being something of a psychiatrist as well as a physician, he had deliberately set to work to arouse her. He had, somewhat diffidently at first, taken what proved to be the right course. He had forced her to talk of her sorrows, of her child and of her husband left behind in Singapore, and of whose fate she knew nothing. He had called upon her for help with other sick children, and had kept her busy. He had reminded her of their country's need of every pair of hands, and had spoken, as he rarely did, of his own limitations, the defective sight that forbade his entry into either of the Services, adding ruefully:

'It isn't sufficiently dependable even to make me a really good surgeon, but I mean to be a good physician.'

Example and precept had done their work. Susan Sandyman did not know it, but she left the *City of Truro* that day with her loins girt ready to plunge into the fight.

At last the journey was over. The formalities of landing: the kindly Colonial Office representative who had met them all, and who had supplied the money for her journey south. The equally kind immigration officer who had produced clothes coupons and ration cards. The friendly people about the docks. The night spent in a Glasgow hotel with Mrs Lennox's obstreperous children, while their mother tried to get in touch with relatives. Her journey from Glasgow. The night in London when, although refusing to leave her bed, she could not sleep because the sirens wailed. It was all behind, and now Susan Sandyman stood on the corner of the familiar Hampshire common, watching the retreating bus. It was the familiarity that hurt. Everything looked the same. As if time had stood still.

Inside the bus it hadn't been quite the same. For one thing she had not been in the habit of using the bus all those years ago; but, now, for over half an hour she had sat penned closely in, so great had been the number of her fellow passengers, all anxious to get to one destination or another. The bus stopped frequently, and the atmosphere inside grew hot and disagreeable with the odour of wet mackintoshes.

She had sat, in her far corner, with her eyes closed, until she realized how she longed, and yet dreaded, to see a familiar face. But all had been strangers. Mostly women with baskets and bags, and babies and small children, returning from the market town with their shopping. She hadn't looked at the babies. That hurt too. Everything hurt. Everything exaggerated the pain within her breast – so poignant that it was physical. She had dreaded the journey's end. Now it had ended. At the bus stop on the corner of the familiar common.

The bus rounded the distant bend and disappeared. Slowly her eyes travelled back to that part of the village visible. The post-office with its white-painted bay window, and the clock pointing to twenty-past three. The bank, as usual, closed. It opened only on Tuesdays and Fridays for a few hours. Odd how one remembered, she thought. The butcher's shop and the grocer's. No customers coming and going. It had always been so. The village seemed to sleep through summer afternoons, and despite the persistently showery weather, this afternoon, late in May 1942, one could feel summer in the air. It was all so peaceful, so unchanged. Half unconsciously she noticed it all.

Then, suddenly, the air was filled with the roar of approaching machinery and she looked towards the corner where the bus had disappeared, wondering what was coming. Half a dozen tanks lumbered into view and the earth trembled beneath her feet as they rattled past. The first she had seen. Without moving she watched them.

She was wrong. Everything had changed. There was the proof. Nothing was the same. Nothing. Nothing could ever be the same. Quickly, as if shaking off her thoughts, she turned about and struck off across the common to where she knew the end of the King's Lane, her shortest way home, came out beside the church. A few steps and again she stopped. Under the trees at a little distance she could see row upon row, of Nissen huts and others grouped near the church and school. She walked on, passing them. Some soldiers were on parade where the children used to play, and a few others lounged about under the trees. They took as little notice of her as she did of

5

them. She only hastened to get into the lane. She had always loved the King's Lane. It would be peaceful there.

She looked lonely as she walked. Lonely and rather shabby. Her grey flannel suit needed pressing. She wore no hat and had no gloves and the coat she carried over one arm was somewhat crushed. One rather battered suitcase and a handbag comprised her luggage. The suitcase could not have been over heavy. She carried it easily, as she had carried it everywhere, whenever it had needed carrying, for almost four months. Ever since that awful day when Frank, her husband, had held her in his arms and said 'goodbye', while both knew, in their hearts, that this might be their final parting. She had got away. Frank was in the Malayan Volunteer Force. He had to go back. All he could do for her safety and their child's had been done.

'You must get home. Go straight to the shipping office. They should have a berth for you. If they haven't, get a passage on *anything* as far as Colombo. You can get money there.' Frank had repeated these sentences again, although they had already been said a dozen times. The parting was hard.

'If I am lucky, I will follow you as soon as the war is over. If not...' and oblivious of everyone in the crowded hotel lounge he had held her closely and their eyes, hers swimming in tears, had looked into each other's. 'We have had a wonderful time, Sue. *Always* remember that. You have been everything – just *everything*.'

'And you...' was all she had managed to say before her voice had broken.

Her eyes filled with tears again now as she walked on, remembering. Felicity, her child, who had died at sea. Frank had given her her name.

'Felicity – great happiness. That is what her coming means to us.' And so it had been, until a few months ago.

More memories crowded as she turned into the King's Lane. For a little while she walked swiftly. A few more houses had been built, but very soon she was beyond them, and the clump of hawthorn and larches, self sown, in the middle of the wide old road, hid them from view. Now she loitered, not noticing how the wet from the grass was soaking through her shoes, until she came level with the stile that led to the mushroom fields. She walked straight to it, put her suitcase on a step and, folding her arms on the top bar, buried her face in them.

The last time she had passed this way was on her wedding day, when, secretly, unknown to her mother and aided and abetted by her father and the old groom-gardener, she had driven to church through the King's Lane in her own shabby governess car, beloved from childhood, and behind the pony she had broken, trained and groomed herself. Her mother had been horrified, but Frank had been in the secret, and together they had gone back to the house in the same way. Less than five years ago – but – a lifetime!

Slowly memory produced picture after picture. 'This is a review,' she told herself heartbrokenly. 'I have to face up to things, but now, just here, before I go home…' She did not finish explaining to herself. She knew what she wanted. Just to be quiet and still and go through her memories. She was no coward. She knew she must play her part, must take up whatever war work she could, and she wanted to do it. It was all that was left for her to do. The only ways he could justify herself, and Frank's belief in her. So, leaning on the stile, she did not spare herself. Mentally she visualized every step of the way. Saw again the mountains of luggage that had made Frank gasp:

'Good heavens! Do we own all that?' and heard again her own laughing answer, '*More* than that!'

She moved her head and looked down at her one battered suitcase. All she had left – not even a garment of Felicity's. Other mothers' babies had needed those. She was not alone in her suffering. All over Europe, all over the world, hearts ached as hers was aching. All over the world women mourned their babies, or their husbands, or both. And not women only. This unholiest of wars had reversed the position. Men mourned women and children. There was only one thing to do. Robert Jamieson's advice had been right. '*Don't* give in. *Don't* stop to think. Get a job. Just as quickly as you can. There's no panacea like hard, interesting work.'

Mentally she shook herself and suddenly found she was staring across the meadows, beyond the stile, at a signboard, quite unaware that ever since she had lifted her head after that glance at her suitcase she had been staring unseeingly at it. 'Cultivated Mushrooms. Trespassers will be prosecuted. By Order.' She half smiled. These fields! Commercialized! Where all her childhood and girlhood she had searched for mushrooms. Her thoughts took a new turn. She remembered summer mornings while the shadows were still long. Naked feet in the dew-wet grass. Walking to misty September mornings. Her brothers; and the 'Come on, lazy-bones' of their voices as they roused her from sleep. Sometimes she was first and then it was her turn to call them 'Lazy-bones'; and the setting forth alone, a little frightened, as she crept through the still sleeping house, after they had returned to school. The dew-drenched garden; walking in their plimsolls until they reached this very stile. Thoughts that fell like balm, although for over six months she had no news and did not know what had befallen her brothers.

Suddenly, anxious for them, she lifted her arms from the stile and picking up her suitcase walking on more quickly, and now the lane was as she had always known it, wide and tree-grown. The giant oaks and beeches meet overhead. It was one of those old green roads of England, albeit more historical than some. Along this very way King John had ridden to Runnymede to sign that charter of all free Englishmen, now, for the first time over 700 years, in abeyance. For a moment her thoughts slipped back again to childhood, and her imagination pictured the scene as it must have been, as well as the way they had played it. She had always wondered if these old trees, as saplings, had seen him pass? Then, a great old road – now, merely a wide green lane, shady, and cool in summertime – a short cut by which a few dwellers at this end of the village reached the church, and school and shops.

Now she was walking where the garden of her own home abutted on the lane. She was nearly home. After all, she was lucky. Other women aboard the ship had no homes and no money. The thought hastened her steps until a rustle in the undergrowth as a golden retriever forced his way beneath the hedge and bounded towards her brought her to a standstill. One glance and she had dropped her suitcase, coat and handbag, and was on her knees embracing the dog.

'Jason! Oh, Jason! You *can't* remember! It's impossible!'

Impossible or not, the dog apparently did not agree. Voice or scent or something was 'family', and he knew it, and did not spare his satisfactory welcome. He licked her hands, licked the tears from her face, was boisterous; and then broke away, running towards the gate at the end of the garden, and then back again, to be boisterous once more, before settling down and trotting quietly as if to say 'Come along. Let's go home.'

Susan Sandyman once more picked up her belongings and smiled at the dog. Walking steadily, side by side, they went through the gate and across the garden.

She had reached home.

There was no one in the garden, no one on the veranda where the drawing-room windows stood wide open. Again the familiarity hurt. Susan dropped her suitcase and coat on the veranda and entered by the window. The room was deserted. She looked round. It was just as she always remembered it. As it had always been. The flowers and chintzes. No. There was an extra table beside her mother's favourite chair. A table that held photographs.

Frank's! Her own! A snapshot she had sent of herself and Felicity; but more. Her eyes took in their significance while her heart stood still.

Jack's! Her elder brother, with a medal ribbon pinned on top. Claude's, in a flying uniform. It hardly seemed possible. Claude was a schoolboy in his second year at Harrow when she went away. Then she became aware of a new photograph of her father, standing, a little apart, by itself. Before she had grasped the import of this she heard a door open and shut again with a bang, and a footstep in the hall. The drawing-room door stood ajar. Hastily she dashed to it, calling: 'Mother! Mother! I'm here! I've come!'

Her mother, apparently, had just entered by the front door. She carried a basket. Startled, she stared for a moment before ejaculating:

'Heavens, child! How you frightened me!'

'Did I? I'm sorry.' Their kiss was perfunctory.

'Nothing to be sorry about. When did you come?'

'Just this minute. I came on the bus and by the King's Lane. Jason met me. He seemed to remember.'

'Oh! He must have sensed you. That was why he suddenly dashed off. But—' she looked round. 'Where's the child? Where's Felicity?'

Susan caught her breath, as again that pain stabbed.

'She died, Mother. Died at sea. Poisoned by some awful insect. After – after we left Freetown. I couldn't – couldn't bring myself to cable. I thought I'd wait. Wait until I could tell you…'

For a few seconds her mother stared as if unhearing. Her face did not go white. It went ashen grey and twisted painfully. Susan, alarmed, sprang to her, throwing her arms about her. The older woman strove to speak; the words came in a whisper, with great difficulty. 'I'd – I'd borrowed a cot. I was trying to get a pram.'

It was too much for Susan. She could never remember any tenderness from her mother. If she felt any, she had always hidden it under a somewhat brusque manner. Now Susan's head fell on her mother's shoulder while a flood of tears had their way, but only for a moment. Tenderness there might have been, but her mother could not show it. Speedily she pulled herself erect, patted her daughter's shoulder and said firmly:

'There. There—' as to a child. 'Come. Crying doesn't help. Come with me. You may as well know it *all*, at once.'

Meekly, and amazed at her quick recovery, Susan followed her mother back to the drawing-room. There was no hesitation. Her mother almost marched to the table of photographs and stood looking down at them, and speaking in her own brusque way said:

'We haven't been bombed here; sometimes I wish we had been. One fell harmlessly in the woods. That was all. We are not an evacuation area because of the ammunition dump. There is nothing I can do except sew and knit. Father caught a chill while on Home Guard duty. It turned to pneumonia. That was in March. Claude was killed while training in Canada. Jack won the Military Cross and was killed the next week in Libya. I wrote to you.'

'Mother! Oh – I've had no letters – oh—'

'One – just – has – to make – the – best – of – it.' Her mother's voice went on speaking slowly, with a pause between each word.

'There is no one left but you. I had hoped—' She broke off and finished: 'I'll go and put the kettle on. I've only old Jane left, and she is out' and hurriedly left the room.

Susan stood motionless. The dog, who had been lying at full length in the patch of sunshine near the door, arose and slowly walked to her and thrust his nose into one of her loose-hanging hands. A deep silence fell on the room. After a few moments the whispered words, 'Oh, Daddy! I wanted you – just you,' hardly disturbed it.

Everything had changed.

TWO

'MOTHER IS LIKE an automaton, Grannie. I don't know what to do to help her.'

Susan was kneeling on the hearthrug beside her grandmother's chair and, now her greetings were over, warming herself at the acceptable fire. It had rained again, and the morning was chilly.

'I just couldn't bear it. I bolted to you.'

'I'm glad you did, child, but I am of little use to anyone now.'

'Dear Grannie!' Susan leaned forward and touched the old lady's hand. 'I was heartbroken when I heard about your stroke; and I did miss your letters.'

'Old and helpless,' murmured the other's gentle voice.

'You don't look a day older and your hair is beautiful. And you are younger than Mother in your mind. She is apathetic, while you are comforting and intensely mentally alive. But what am I to do, darling? Can you think?'

'Do you mean about yourself or your mother?'

'I mean both. I thought I'd have Father—'

'Don't talk of your father, if you would rather not.'

'I'd rather, really.' Susan spoke softly. 'I am all right *now*. I got all my crying over last night.' She flicked away a tear. 'At least, I did – nearly. I've faced up to it all. We had an awful evening. Poor Mother! If she could only let herself go, for *once*.'

'It's not her fault, Susan. She was brought up to restrain every natural impulse. To be very self-controlled. She does not lack imagination, but she was taught to be very material.'

'Yes, I know. Father told me. Of course we never doubted she loved us. That was his teaching, too, but Claude was the only one who ever got inside her shell. I know she is awfully glad I am back, but she won't show it. We had a ghastly evening. I had got myself firmly in hand before I arrived, but – those extra shocks…! Oh, Grannie! If only we could have talked and cried together! I had things I should have liked to tell her. Now it is too late. I *know* I *never* shall. She sat knitting and knitting until I could have screamed. We listened to the news, and then silence again. I sat, she knitted, until at exactly ten o'clock she almost jumped up, pushed her work away, she said, 'You must be tired: you will be glad to go to bed.'

'So I said "goodnight" and went. I know Felicity's death is the final blow. Poor darling! She had everything ready. Began directly she got my last cable. I sent it from Freetown. I'd said we both were well. It nearly finished me. I tried to thank her. The cot, and the blankets, and the big spare room all ready for a nursery...' For a few moments Susan covered her eyes and bent her head, leaning against her grandmother's knee.

The old lady did not speak, only lifted her one serviceable hand and gently stroked Susan's hair. After some minutes she said softly:

'Don't talk about it any more if you would rather not.'

Susan lifted her head.

'It helps me, I think.' She paused a moment before she continued: 'I'd pictured myself telling Daddy. Then – her face – when I told her about Felicity – it was dreadful – like being torn to shreds. If only she would let me *inside*. Let me help her. I feel I could, and she could help me. And yet, *even* of that I am not sure. It was terrible. To come home and hear what she had gone through – but, somehow that helped me. Her loss is the greater. I couldn't think of anything but how to help *her*, and she froze me. And I can't stay with her. I know I have to register and that means some job, and I must get a job as quickly as possible.'

'Do you mean you need money?'

'No. No. Not exactly. I owe the ship's doctor ten pounds. The Malay Bank stopped payment. I couldn't get any money in Colombo and I'd lost my coat. The doctor lent me enough to go shopping in Durban. I wasn't thinking of the financial side, but the other. I've got to be too busy to remember. That would be fatal. To come back – like *this*. I should keep thinking back – but Mother has really gone through more. I added to it.'

'Yes, darling. She was worn out with hidden anxiety. I shall never forget the day she rang me up to say you were safe and well in Colombo.'

'Yes. I got there in a little Dutch ship. Everyone – I mean all the women and children in Singapore – were just hustled into ships.

Any ship. Some people had only their evening clothes, and people in shops weren't allowed to go home. I was luckier. Frank warned me, and directly he left me I sorted out and put into the lightest suitcase just what baby and I *must* have, and what I could carry—'

'Frank left you?' Old Mrs Ledgard's voice was incredulous.

'Yes. Of course. He had to. The Volunteer Force. He joined it in '38, directly he knew he wouldn't be allowed to go home to fight if we had war.' Again for a few minutes Susan was silent. When she spoke her voice had sunk almost to a whisper.

'We drove and we drove. It's a nightmare to remember. At first we thought of flying, but things happened so quickly. The Japs had air superiority. Much better 'planes. If we had been shot down we were finished. I drove. Frank had the revolvers, ready loaded, and Felicity on his lap most of the time. He told me whatever happened to keep on driving. Not to stop. We took all the petrol we had – and just what clothes we could, and we set fire to everything else, the house – the 'plane...'

Again she paused while memory looked back. Those clouds of rolling, billowing smoke! Would she ever forget? Or how Frank had taken the child from her saying, 'She is safer with me.'... "Safer with me!" Memory gave a jolt. Abruptly she said, 'I *know* Frank is dead.'

'My dear! I did not—'

'No. I haven't heard anything,' Susan interrupted. 'Only the night Felicity died I heard *him*. Oh, I know it sounds silly, perhaps unbelievable, but very soon after we started that day Frank took Felicity from me – I had her in my lap – and he put her on the floor under his legs where he could shield her – we had the hood down because of keeping watch – he said, "She is safer with me." Then, the night she died, I felt he took her again, and I heard his voice, "She is safer with me." It was quite close and plain – so – I just *know*. I told the doctor. He is a Scot, like you. He helped me so much. He believes we do hear sometimes – in moments of great emotional stress. Says nothing else explains it – and it's been such a comfort.'

Susan's head went down again while she fought back her tears, and, again, the old lady gently stroked her head, murmuring, 'My darling – my darling,' over and over again. 'Let the tears come. They ease one's heart.'

Susan choked down a sob. 'So you see, I *know*. I know there will be no wonderful cablegram. No long watching and waiting and hoping. His name will be among the missing. I shall probably never know how he died, but I know he is safe. Nothing can hurt either of them any more. Nothing can hurt Daddy. Nothing can hurt Jack, or Claude. Not again. So, the responsibility is on me.' Again she paused, but now she held her head erect and gazed into the fire while her grandmother looked puzzled.

'You mean – to avenge, darling?'

'No! Oh no! That is impossible.' As she spoke Susan rose to her feet with an abstracted air, and dragged the fender-stool forward, placing it so that she could sit facing the old lady and yet close to her. 'Impossible!' she repeated as she sat down.

'The whole thing has grown too vast, too colossal for individual vengeance. But I think of all the girls who were born about the time Felicity was born. It was so wonderful. I was so happy. I hardly dared breathe. That happiness is not unique. It should be every woman's lot. Those girls will grow up. The doctor and I talked about them one night at sea. It stimulated me. He was a moral support.'

Again she was silent a moment. The old lady watching her knew it was not the moment to speak. Quietly, firmly, Susan's voice came again.

'I saw my bungalow – I was so proud of it – my treasures, my wedding presents, the piano you gave us, the things we had bought, and you had all sent for Felicity, the 'plane – we loved it – we'd had such a wonderful time in Sydney learning to fly – I saw it all go up in flames. Then I lost them both, Felicity and Frank. Those girls – and the men they are to marry. The responsibility that it never happens again, that they will get the chance to rebuild what we were forced to destroy, is mine as much as anyone's. So Grannie' – Susan twisted round again on her stool and looked into the old lady's face – 'help me. *What* can I do? What job can I *best* do? I don't care for nursing, but if it would be *best* – only I'd rather be out of doors. There is ambulance driving, but older people can drive ambulances – I wish I knew.'

For some moments the old lady did not answer, but Susan's next remark, said half under her breath, 'Something that has danger,' made her look at her granddaughter as if appraisingly, a look that grew more intent as Susan added: 'I don't mean something with merely a modicum of danger, but *real*. Where I take all the risks a man would take. There is only me. The only one left to *hit back* – to fight for them all.' Her voice died away. The old lady waited another moment. Then she said quietly:

'Susan, believe me, I understand, and I think you should, a little later on, join one of the women's services. But, for the present, if you can find some job that brought you home at night – for your mother's sake...' She hesitated and stopped. Susan was silent, but in a moment or two she took the old lady's hand between her own and looked up, but, before she could speak, the words, 'She, too, has to make her readjustments,' fell softly on her ears.

'Yes, Grannie. I know. Now, without Felicity, she doesn't know what to do. Felicity meant – everything. She had it all thought out. No. She did not tell me – but that room did.'

Again silence fell and, when Susan spoke, there was an undercurrent of fierceness in her tone.

'It's difficult. I'll do my best. But I feel I want to hurry into something arduous. Where there is movement and excitement. I'm in a way itching for battle. I don't want to think, or to remember too much. But, Grannie! *What* can I do?'

'Mark time a little, darling. Try to be patient. There is plenty of work locally. Hazlewood House has recently been taken over as an Auxiliary Hospital.'

'Has it? I didn't know. But – *nursing*! It's – it's so *tame*.'

Mrs Ledgard smiled and answered:

'It has its moments.'

'For the trained nurses, yes. But I can't see myself as a VAD,' Susan answered dryly. 'Susan, my dear. Just for a while. Until your real job shows itself.' Susan looked up, and meeting her grandmother's eyes looked straight into them and asked:

'You think it will?'

'I know it will. It is going to be a long war, darling. There is much to do before we are ready to invade Europe.'

'All right, Grannie, and I'll try the petting way with Mother! Perhaps we shall get a bit closer. That's what Daddy used to do, and Claude succeeded.'

Old Mrs Ledgard half smiled, and immediately she said:

'There is no time like the present, Susan. Ring up now. The telephone has been moved to the pantry. Rose knows the number. The Commandant is a Mrs Knaggs.'

Susan rose to her feet.

'All right, Grannie,' she repeated. 'But what about registering and the Labour Exchange?'

'Quite simple. They won't have to find you a job.'

Susan was gone some little while. She was obliged to talk a moment or two with the elderly parlourmaid, whom she had known since childhood, and then, while the maid got the number, with the equally elderly cook; but after a somewhat prolonged conversation she ran excitedly back to the drawing-room to fling herself on her knees by her grandmother's chair and exclaim impetuously:

'Grannie! You are a genius! You said no time like the present! You made me catch *the* moment. What do you think? Someone, up in Scotland, had given them a shooting brake to use as an ambulance. It's all ready – petrol – everything – and the girl who was to fetch it has jibbed. Ill or something. So I am going, next weekend, and Mrs Knaggs wants to see me *this* afternoon!'

THREE

INTERVIEWS WITH THE commandant of the hospital and with the Labour Exchange were all behind and, within a week of her arrival at Hazeley, Susan was en route for London and Scotland.

The train was so crowded that, although she had been successful in securing a corner seat, she had no space in which to open out her newspaper, so, instead, she gazed unseeingly out of the window and reviewed the past few days.

It had seemed incredible that the classes on 'Home Nursing and First Aid', which she had attended during the winter before she went abroad, could have proved so useful. About those Susan really felt a little conscience-smitten. She had attended them with no other thought than that 'it might be useful to know how to adjust a bandage', and that 'we may be far from a doctor'. 'Selfish motives, absolutely,' she told herself, but they had landed her with her first war job.

She had been very frank with the hospital commandant. 'Yes, I have my certificates, but I was very young when I took them, and I don't like nursing, and I loathe housework,' but Mrs Knaggs had merely sniffed, in a way Susan was later to find characteristic, and lifted her somewhat bristling eyebrows, and explained:

'That is all right. What I want is someone capable of fetching that car and looking after it,' and she had gone on to further explain that they were not an hospital, but a convalescent home: that the patients were not the helpless or the very ill. 'Just sitting cases, and some are coming or going almost every day. There is a lot of station work and the shopping to fetch. That brake will be invaluable. And our Quartermaster has no assistant. Shall we make you the Assistant Quartermaster? Of course you must join the detachment and have your uniform.'

That had been the preliminary, but things had also gone very smoothly at the Labour Exchange. Contrary to the expectations aroused by her fellow-passengers, Susan had found sympathy and interest. She was thanked for reporting so promptly and her plans were instantly approved. She was surprised by this and said so, only to meet with a smile and an approving nod from the registrar, who answered:

'It's a relief when anyone has a useful job, or a special training. It's the undecided, untrained, lazy people who make all the trouble,' and Susan had left the Exchange marvelling within herself. These were people she would not have known, never have encountered, in her former life, and yet here they were equally full of purpose, as she was herself. All they apparently thought about was their job, and how best they could fulfil their appointed duty. And she did not realize how soothing was the influence of the calm woman to whom she had spoken. It helped her to be patient. Only she herself knew how she longed to get away to work among strangers. Poignant memories seemed to lurk in every corner of her home. They haunted her and shook her determination of closing the door on what had been, and of taking up life anew.

The population of the village she found much changed. Only the elderly people and the very young were left. Those more or less of her own age, boys and girls with whom she had played, were scattered far and wide. Her own home was not the only one that mourned its sons, or its daughters. She hadn't, she found, to walk abroad to gather this information. Her mother had it all tabulated and seemed to know the details of every tragedy. She was surprised, too, at her mother's attitude. Felicity was not mentioned again. Neither were her brothers, or her father, except about matters of finance, a conversation that seemed to come about naturally and spontaneously.

It arose over clothes. On the second evening Mrs Ledgard's grey sock had disappeared and some soft-looking yellow wool had taken its place. Susan's offer to hold a skein made her ask, 'What is it for?'

'For you. A jumper.'

'Oh, Mother! Thank you, but don't bother. I shall be in uniform. Make it for yourself.' 'It is too bright. Father disliked mourning of any sort, but – I don't like bright colours, and you must think about clothes.'

'I suppose so – but my uniform will help. Mrs Knaggs seemed to think I could get some ready-made.'

'But you need other things. You can afford them.'

'Can I?' And it was with surprise, mingled with pain, that Susan heard of her financial independence. The thought, although she realized that Frank's income had ceased, had not occurred before, and having relinquished her own allowance as unnecessary, upon her marriage, she now learned that it had been saved for her, and that her brother's allowances were now hers. For a few moments she had been too overcome to speak and her mother had continued:

'Some day you will be very comfortably off. Grannie is not poor.

It was all overwhelming, and they, both Grannie and Mother, had been adamant about her clothes. Both had presented coupons and Grannie a cheque, and Grannie had made Susan sit down and make lists.

'No, my dear,' she had argued, waving aside Susan's protests, 'to begin with you *need* new shoes, and a smart mackintosh. I may sit here day in and day out, butat least I can see the weather,' and she had glanced towards the window where, yet again, a heavy shower splashed down against the panes. 'And I still have a little common sense. One could afford to despise umbrellas and thick shoes from the comfortable protection of one's own car – but, nowadays—'

'Grannie! You are incorrigible!' Susan had tried to interrupt, but was not allowed.

'Clothes coupons!' The old lady's voice was indignant. 'At my age! What do I need with clothes coupons? My cupboards are sufficiently well stocked to see me out. I do not like to be told what I may buy.'

At this Susan had laughed outright and pulled the fender-stool nearer the old lady's chair.

'Darling! All my life, ever since I can remember, you have tried to find excuses for giving me things. The nicest parties, the nicest toys, the nicest clothes. We always knew where to come when pocket-money ran short. But, now, it isn't really necessary. Mother's cleaning and pressings have made me quite presentable – and – I can't be bothered. I truly am not interested.'

'That is a bad beginning,' and now old Mrs Ledgard's voice was stern. 'It is all nonsense to think that one's appearance does not count. It does, and very much so – and that applies even more in uniform.'

'All right, all right. I give in.' Susan had laughed as she spoke, and, now, she sat and conned her lists, and tried not to think of that hectic, exciting time and the thrill of her final shoppings, in London, during the last days of her honeymoon, before she had sailed with Frank for Malaya; days when the luxuries of the world could be bought within a stone's throw of Piccadilly and which, when recalled, only added poignancy to her unforgotten memories.

The rain teemed down when Susan reached Waterloo and she had to wait some time for a taxi. Taxis were difficult to get and uniforms were everywhere. She queued, like everyone else, and waited, and when her turn came refused it for the sake of a young naval officer, who, minus a foot, hobbled across on his crutches with his escort, a smiling VAD nurse. She even felt a pang of envy at the other's efficiency, and her thoughts flashed to the possibilities of her own job. She was still thinking of this when the other girl, now in the taxi, leaned forward, and said: 'We are going to Paddington. Can't we drop you somewhere?'

'Can you – in Vere Street – at the Bank?'

'Easily. Of course. After all, it was *your* taxi.'

Susan got in and for a few minutes, until they turned into York Road, they merely smiled at each other and looked at the weather.

'What a day!' said the girl.

'It changes so quickly,' said Susan. 'I left in sunshine.'

'And so did we,' said the young man, and again they all smiled and Susan, glancing at both, noticed the similarity of colouring and smile and thought 'brother and sister', and another pang of envy, of a different sort, stabbed her. She looked quickly away and watched the rain; but the sight of the bomb damage to St Thomas's Hospital made her lean forward and ejaculate:

'Oh...!'

'Hadn't you seen it before?' asked the girl.

'No,' and, for a second, overcome by a reluctance to speak of her own affairs, Susan hesitated before she repeated, 'No – I only got back a few days ago.'

Two pairs of very similar hazel eyes looked questioningly at her and the girl said, breathlessly:

'Back. Where? Have you been abroad?'

'Yes – I escaped, from Singapore—'

'Oh – so did David – my brother.' She made nod of introduction then, with a quick glance at Susan's ungloved hand and her wedding ring, asked impulsively, with quick sympathy, 'Your husband?'

Susan shook her head. 'I don't know.'

'One minute' – and now it was the young man who spoke and he dived in his pocket and produced a notebook. 'Look – I keep a list. It's – it's perhaps rather futile, but one never knows. Tell me your name and when you left your husband. I send all the names I hear to my elder brother. He's in the Navy too. One never knows what may happen. Chance is a funny thing. He might hear something.'

'Or,' added the girl, 'might even be taken prisoner and get into the same camp. John never forgets names or where he heard of a person.'

Susan was overcome and her eyes were bright with unshed tears as she gave her name. They were so young, so eager. The girl only about eighteen, the boy perhaps two years older. It was the first happening that made her realize the real war fraternity of youth. Ordinarily this girl, at her age, would be thinking merely of her pleasures – dances and parties – but they had reached Vere Street and there was no more time for anything else but swift handshakes and goodbyes and thanks, only Susan's hand lingered for a second in the young man's and she said:

'Please tell – tell your brother that my baby died at sea.'

The girl's startled eyes gazed at her.

'Oh! Oh – I'm so sorry. Our name is Verner – V-E-R-N-E-R – don't forget – David and Dorothy.'

'I won't,' said Susan, 'and thank you again.'

Susan stood on the steps of the bank to watch the taxi out of sight, her thoughts with the two inside. How could England lose the war when her boys and girls were like that? But she had a lot to do; with a little sigh she turned into the bank. It was also Robert Jamieson's bank, and she was anxious to repay her debt.

* * *

Susan was still hatless and, although she wore her mother's shoes and stockings and the yellow jumper, her grey suiting was the one she had travelled in – so it might not have been difficult for Robert Jamieson to recognize her at a distance; but as she left the bank they almost collided on the steps.

'Mrs Sandyman! Good morning!' The words were joyous, but for a second, until his hat was off, Susan stared at the rather nondescript figure on the lower step. He looked much smaller in civilian clothes.

'Dr Jamieson! What a pleasant surprise!'

'Yes. Isn't it?' His eyes behind his thick spectacles showed how the word expressed his feelings. 'But why in mufti?'

'Everything at the cleaners. I join ship again on Saturday.'

'Where?'

'Where we landed,' he answered rather pointedly, and suddenly Susan remembered the posters admonishing caution in speech that adorned railway carriages and the walls of the bank. She nodded and dropped her voice.

'I'm going north too. I've got a job.'

'Have you? What?'

'The last thing I expected to be. A VAD. I've a car to fetch from Scotland.'

'When do you go?'

'Saturday. By day. I couldn't get a sleeper.'

'Oh – dash it! I go up Friday night. You can have my sleeper. I'll sit up.'

Susan shook her head and answered: 'No. I wouldn't dream of it. Besides, I've more to get through in this next forty-eight hours than I know how to do – uniform and shopping, lawyer, et cetera.'

'Oh, dear. That's bad luck for me.' Robert Jamieson glanced at his watch. 'I've also a heap to do. An appointment round the corner in ten minutes, and I must be at home tonight. Sister's twenty-first – but tomorrow. I'll come up early and take you out to dinner. Can you?'

'I'd love it.'

'All right. Where are you staying? I'll call for you,' and as he

23

noted the address of Susan's club he asked almost casually, 'Did you find all well at home?'

'No,' and the gravity of Susan's voice startled him, and his eyes gazed into hers as she briefly recited the triple tragedy that had bereaved her home.

'Oh, my dear – I *am* sorry. I wish to goodness I could spend today with you. You ought not to be alone – but—'

'No, no! You must go, now. Till tomorrow – about six thirty? Goodbye,' and without even a handshake Susan dived across the road and left Robert Jamieson staring after her.

FOUR

'YOU LOOK LIKE a million dollars!'

There was admiration in Robert Jamieson's eyes. He saw at once that Susan's face had lost its strained expression and her hair its dullness. He did not say so, but he liked her new frock of soft brown, with a gleam of gold trimming about it, and her short jacket of soft fur.

'Do I? That is Grannie's doing. She was firm with me as you were! It must be your nationality. She also is a Scot.' Susan smiled as she spoke and Robert was happy. He felt this was his evening and he wanted to make the most of it.

'Is she? How nice! Then, you are, partly?'

'Yes, I am; but not through Grannie. She was my father's stepmother, only no one ever knew it.'

'Well, tell me presently. It's raining again and I've got a taxi waiting.'

'Where are we going?'

'I've booked a table at the "Coq d'Or".'

'Now – *who* is behaving like a million dollars?' laughingly questioned Susan.

Susan's club, of which she had kept her membership while overseas, was in Halkin Street, so it was merely a matter of minutes before they were in Stratton Street. That Robert kept possessions of her hand throughout the short journey she scarcely noticed. She was glad to be with him; he was her one link with the past and had been kindness itself.

'You don't mind about music, do you?' he began. 'If you'd rather—'

'No. No. I want to talk.'

'That's good. I'm longing to hear all you have been doing.'

'Are you? There really isn't much to tell. This isn't a cleaned uniform, is it?' She broke her own sentence irrelevantly and touched the braid on his sleeve.

'No. It's my best one!' Robert laughed light-heartedly. 'Kept for special occasions! Such as this!' He gave her hand a light squeeze, but there was no time to say more. The taxi drew up and the commissionaire flung open the door.

Susan looked about her with interest. They were early and as yet there were few people in the dining-room, although the bar and lounge seemed rather crowded. She was glad Robert had, by accident, chosen a restaurant that had no association with Frank, and, as they found seats and ordered cocktails, she found herself thinking that this was the first time she had dined alone with any man except her father or Frank.

For a moment a sadness over swept her, but she shook it off, telling herself that was Robert's evening: she must make it a happy one. A memory for him to cherish in the midst of many and great dangers. She lifted her glass and their eyes met over the rims, and they smiled.

'Success to your ventures!' said Robert. 'Safe journeyings to you!' said Susan. Conversation for the next ten minutes was casual. People were coming and going and looking for seats, and after smoking one cigarette she readily acquiesced when Robert said: 'Shall we move? It will be more comfortable in the dining-room,' and nodded agreement and picked up her bag and gloves, and only remarked as they crossed the hall:

'Reminiscent of a country house, isn't it?' and again looked about her with interest as they took their places. She liked the long 'L'-shaped room with its tables separated just far enough to allow conversation to be quite private, and she liked the way they sat side by side on the comfortable seat behind the table.

'I like this,' she remarked. 'It is nice to see the room so comfortably – only it's a little like sitting in a railway carriage! Do you often come here?' she finished.

'I like it, too,' he answered. 'Perhaps they haven't altered the seats since they called the place the something or other train. No, I've only once before been here – then it was to celebrate my brother's wedding.'

'So it *is* an "occasion"?'

Robert leaned slightly forward and turned his head to look her more squarely in the eyes.

'Yes. It is. A very great occasion—' but the wine waiter interrupted and, a few moments later, Susan gasped and her eyes met Robert's in horror and reproach, while his danced with joy.

'You wretch!' she exclaimed under her breath. 'Champagne! At *that* price! And that man aided and abetted you!'

'Good for him!' answered Robert. 'I told you it was an occasion. A *great* occasion! Besides, I'll tell you a secret. Someone yesterday repaid a debt of ten pounds and I'm going to "blow" it before I sail.'

'Oh—' began Susan and stopped short. 'But haven't they all repaid?'

She knew there were others who had gone shopping in Durban with Robert Jamieson's money.

Robert shook his head.

'No. Not all, and no one is under any obligation—' and he immediately changed the subject and said, 'Tell me about your doings,' only to break off to discuss the menu.

'Now,' he said, when the waiter had left them.

'There really isn't a great deal to tell,' answered Susan, and as she spoke she was thinking, 'I have only sad things to tell about and that seems too bad, this evening. What a blessing I met him yesterday. I needn't talk of Father and the boys. I'll have to make the most of Grannie and going to Scotland as topics of conversation; and how different people are these days – that woman at the Labour Exchange – those two in the taxi – what darlings they were—' but Robert was smiling at her.

'A brown study?' he questioned.

'No. I was only thinking—' She smiled in return. It was rather a ghost of a smile.

'Doctor!' she began, but he stopped her.

'Couldn't you drop that?'

'Drop what?'

'The doctor.'

'And what, instead?' she questioned gently.

'My name is Robert.'

'Only if it is *quid pro quo*!'

Robert nodded. 'I'd love to – now, go on, Susan.' But another interruption came. The champagne arrived, and Robert tasted and approved before Susan's glass was filled, and directly they were again alone Robert lifted his glass and bending forward, so that he could look into Susan's eyes, he said:

'To our lasting friendship, Susan!'

'And to my eternal gratitude, Robert,' and their meal was served before their conversation continued, and then Susan's was, as she had decided, of her home and surroundings, and she suddenly found herself summing up the two relations left to her in a new way – almost as if she were an outsider looking at them.

'It isn't easy to understand my mother. She just goes on with practical detail. What she thinks, one can never know. Whether embittered and resenting, or resigned, she gives no clue, and she is so full of surprising activities. That first evening she said there was nothing to do but knit – but she is never still, never idle, just as if she was determined to find things to do, and do them with all her might.'

'And your grandmother?' questioned Robert.

'Quite different. I have always wished I was properly related to Grannie. I'd like to look as she does when I grow old. She sits in her drawing-room looking like the most exquisite portrait, in her soft silk frocks and lace and pearls – a picture of daintiness – so is her drawing-room, all soft greens – and masses of flowers – and she is so human. Occasionally we all got scolded – even the Almighty. She fights, and she denounces God for allowing war. She says it isn't her idea of being "all-merciful and all-powerful".'

Robert Jamieson laughed aloud. 'We all feel like that at times but feel too timid to say it! I'd like to know her,' and Robert in his turn told of his home. There was nothing exciting or romantic about any of their conversation. They sat rather close together, absolutely unaware of their absorption, or of the many interested glances cast in their direction, and talked of themselves and their upbringing and childhood's surroundings. Merely getting to know each other.

'We are a family of doctors,' Robert told Susan. 'I'm the youngest but one. My brother is with the Eighth Army and my eldest sister is with the ATS. in Scotland. I saw her in Edinburgh.' His father, although getting elderly, was still practising in the outlying Surrey suburb where they had all grown up, and would have already retired but for the war.

'I've said goodbye this afternoon,' he finished, and he dropped his voice. 'I wish I could meet you tomorrow – but I have to be aboard quite early. I suppose it means we are sailing.'

'Oh—' Under the tablecloth Susan's hand unconsciously caught his. 'It's sweet of you to give me your last evening, Robert.'

It was a dangerous remark. The moment it had passed her lips Susan regretted it. She had guessed, very accurately, what he was feeling by the expression in his eyes when she left him so abruptly on the previous day. A moment only and her regret passed and she was glad. Glad, without analysing why.

Robert's hand closed over hers and his eyes were luminous as he answered, whimsically:

'Will you believe me when I tell you that there is no one else I'd rather spend it with?'

Their eyes held each other's. Once again Robert's revealed much, and Susan understood, and knew that he understood also. Life was too short, too uncertain for anything but truth. She had nothing to give but her eternal gratitude, and friendship.

She had not encouraged him. What had happened was inevitable – but Robert was speaking, softly, under his breath, with his head bent towards her.

'It's a strange place for a confession of love, and I thought I was too shy – too diffident ever to tell you – and you'd think it presumptuous, anyway; but it isn't. It's – just – *there*, Susan. You understand...'

'Yes – Robert – I understand.'

After that the evening seemed short. Although they had talked and talked, sometimes hardly noticing the hovering waiter or what they were eating, it seemed to Susan no time at all before they were again in a taxi, and Robert was taking her back to Halkin Street, although they had sat until almost ten thirty when, in common with most other restaurants, the Coq d'Or closed.

In the streets it was not yet quite dark. There was no moon, but the rain had ceased, and Susan had suggested that they walk.

'No, better not,' said Robert. 'It's easier to get a taxi here, and I want it to take me on to Euston.'

So, in the taxi, they sat close together, and Robert put his arm gently across Susan's shoulders and slipping it down until it was round her waist drew her closer. His shyness had completely vanished. For a moment only Susan was fearful. She hadn't imagined that he could ever be like this. That he could not test her loyalties she knew, but she wanted nothing that could in any way smirch the memories of her perfect married life. Frank had been her all in all as she had been his.

She did not stiffen; only kept quite still, and as Robert turned his head she knew she had no cause for alarm. Almost immediately he began to speak and his voice was tender, and she could see his eyes, again with their curious quality of luminosity in the darkness. It might have been a luminosity due to the spectacles, without which he was so helpless.

'It's a dear little coat, and so soft!' He stroked her sleeve with his free hand. 'I shall always remember you just as you have looked this evening. It has been so different to what I had pictured. I never thought I could so easily tell you how I love you. I hadn't thought you would ever know. But I *do*, Susan; so much – and it's love with the best part of me. You are enshrined. I don't even want a picture of you. It is too deep and too secret and – precious. I'm not envious of what your husband had. I'm a little chap and very plain and you are – different, lovely – and he was grand-looking. I know by that photograph you showed me. I wish I could find him for you. If I go East again I will ask everywhere. Someone may know something. I worship you. I know I can and ask nothing, and I know, too, that you don't mind and neither would he. I have you enshrined in secret and no one will ever know.' A lump was rising in Susan's throat and tears in her eyes. She could not speak. Robert leaned forward and tapped the glass in front of them and spoke to the driver. 'Just tootle round for ten minutes or so, will you?'

The driver nodded and Robert, turning to look at Susan, saw her tears. In a moment his handkerchief was out and he mopped her eyes, saying: 'There! There! I've made you cry and I can't have my beautiful evening spoilt. I am so happy!'

Susan, half laughing, half crying, perhaps feeling a little hysterical, took the handkerchief from him and quickly used it to good purpose, saying, as she did so, in an effort to be practical: 'It's *your* fault. You know, Robert, you must not waste all that loving on me. It isn't fair. Sooner or later you will meet the right girl, and then – then you'll be sorry.'

'No.' Robert uplifted a warning finger. 'You know, and I know, that is highly improbable. I think – I can't help it – I think, when the war is over, I shall not be here.'

'You mustn't—' began Susan, but again he stopped her, gently, reproachfully.

'Don't – don't spoil it. I love the way I live. I hug each glorious, precious, uncertain day as if it were the last, and, don't you see, *you* are *part* of it. It's been more glorious lately—'

Susan half turned on his arm. Their eyes held each other's in the and darkness. Robert's head fell forward and rested on her shoulder, Susan's hand came up to caress it. For several moments they sat thus; then Robert straightened up and said very simply, 'Thank you.'

'And I thank you, Robert.'

Whimsically he answered:

'My mother called me "Rab" or "Rabbie" – always. Could you?'

'Of course, Rabbie. I like it.'

'And you will write me, sometimes? Not very often. Just to tell me all you are doing?'

'Of course,' said Susan again.

'Address them to the company. They will know best where I am.'

'And you will write to me?'

'Equally, of course. I want to. I couldn't bear not to.'

The taxi drew slowly into the kerb and Robert called 'All right' to the driver, but before he moved he lifted Susan's hand and turned it palm upwards, and pressed a kiss on it and closed her fingers over it. Susan did not speak until they said goodnight and goodbye in the shadow of the doorway, but with tears brimming in her eyes she stood and watched the taxi out of sight, wondering if they would ever meet again.

In the taxi Robert sat bolt upright. He could not have put his thoughts into words, any more than at that moment he could think of Susan as a woman. All he was doing was saying over and over to himself:

'I've told her. She knows... I've told her. She knows. Now it doesn't matter *what* happens. She knows... It doesn't matter what happens. She knows.'

FIVE

IT WAS A MONTH later, and her journey to Scotland and back merely a memory, before Susan stopped to reflect and take stock, or to think of her future. The days had flown past, and, in retrospection, it seemed that not since those hours spent in the train between London and Glasgow had she thought of any but immediate things.

Old Mrs Ledgard had been right. Susan had found plenty to occupy her time, and life had been full of surprises.

The first had been what Mrs Knaggs had described as a 'shooting brake of some sort' turned out to be a Ford Eight 'station' van, practically new. Susan had been delighted. In some queer way it was a sort of compensation. She determined to lavish on it the same care that Frank had taught her to take care of their own car, and their 'plane. She felt it had to be her own.

She had arrived in the early afternoon on Sunday, by the one train of the day, to find her elderly host deliberately painting large red crosses on either door of the car. For a moment her heart sank. She had intended motoring back to Glasgow that same evening and spending another night at the Central Hotel. Also she had engaged her room and left a message for Robert Jamieson – just in case. But when her hostess remarked with Scottish sagacity, 'To telephone is cheaper than paying for a room,' and her host explained, 'The crosses are an afterthought, and you have to stay the night, and we want a fish for supper. So – come along, we'll away fishing, despite it being Sunday,' she found herself happy to agree and stay. After all, she reflected, the chances of seeing Robert again were extremely remote and that one evening had been very satisfactory. It had cleared the position and made Robert happy. It was little enough she could give him, but perhaps another meeting would be unwise.

What her kindly hosts knew of her own circumstances, Susan did not discover. They just accepted her, entertained her, fed her on freshly grilled salmon steaks, and, in the end, Susan enjoyed her brief stay and left with a promise to return some day.

The long journey back had been delightful. She had started early and done it, as the days were long, in one day, and was rather proud of the achievement. It had been an enlightening day. 'Pick-ups' and 'hitch-hikers' had enlivened it. She had travelled very little of it alone. At every stage soldiers of varying nationalities had signalled and, as long as there was room, and she was not taken out of her way, Susan picked them up; and they all talked until she wondered if camps were exempt from those posters, concerning discreet conversation, that she seemed to meet with everywhere. She listened to them all and heard much of personal histories, of life in camps, and of events that had already made history. More than once she had to stop to draw the car into the roadside, while she looked at photographs of wives and children and sweethearts. It was a wonderful day. She picked up her first hiker and dropped him in Glasgow, and her last she turned out on the Southampton-London road, a mile or so from Hazeley. Her mother, still knitting, and Jane both awaited her when she arrived home, tired, triumphant and hungry, just before dusk, and put the car into their own garage for the night.

'Supper and bed, miss,' said Jane, who could never remember to call her anything else.

'No, Jane, not until I've 'phoned a telegram,' and she turned to her mother and asked: 'I may 'phone it, mayn't I? It's to Mr McRae. He was so anxious to know how the car behaved, and it's been *glorious*!'

Susan did not realize it, but that car was her salvation during those first weeks. Her one regret was that she was not allowed to garage it at home. The possibility of its being required during the night was the one snag. She grew to hate the thought of anyone else driving it, and 'your car' was the designation by which it was soon known. The daily shoppings, the Red Cross supplies, the patients and nurses – as in those days the staff were allowed transport – all kept her busy and there were few days when she was not on the road between Hazeley and Basingstoke, the nearest town and station, several times. Also she learned to appreciate her stout shoes and mackintosh as she bicycled backwards and forwards the two miles between home and hospital in all weathers.

Perhaps even then Susan would not have stopped to think had

she not been forced to take 'days off'. In vain she protested and pleaded that she did not want them, that she was not tired, that she would much rather go steadily on. Mrs Knaggs insisted and tried to be playful, but only succeeded in being thoroughly irritating.

'I know what it is! It's that car! Someone else *might* have to drive it.'

'Well, it's bad for a car to have all sorts of people driving it,' Susan had answered; but she was obliged to give in and found herself faced with a long weekend and nothing to do.

On her first free morning she started off after breakfast, with Jason, intending to take a long walk, only to meet the postman bearing Robert Jamieson's first letter and to sit on the stile to read it. She sat some time and Jason grew impatient before she opened it.

Dear One. She liked the beginning. Simple and satisfactory, personal, but not possessive. He would, she felt, *never* be that. It was addressed 'From a northern port where we await another convoy,' and it was dated three weeks previously. Before she read further Susan found herself reflecting that Robert might be anywhere ere this. It was a quiet letter. He merely spoke of the great pleasure she had given him and then went on to encourage her in whatever she was doing. He did not speak of his love until nearly at the end, when he wrote:

> *I hope you are satisfied with your job. That you feel you are doing good work. Remember whatever you are doing I am, in spirit, with you. In that way I shall try to help you. To remind you that there is so much in life which is worthwhile. The joy of victory will come, victory over enemies. But it will be more glorious if we have also had our personal victories. You will have yours. Be assured of that. I am.*

It was a strange letter. Despite its quietness it disturbed Susan. She gazed across the fields remembering the many times they had talked – short conversations mostly, at odd moments. Robert had had little spare time. She felt strangely detached, and, for the moment, her idle day hung heavily upon her hands. Almost she wished she had decided to go to London, but there was nothing she wanted to do, no one to meet and nothing to do at home. Later she was to lunch with, and read the newspapers to, Grannie. Jason whimpered, arresting her attention, and she answered: 'All right, Jason. We'll go in a minute,' and she made to get over the stile. But the dog flopped down in the lane, refusing to move, and Susan, fearing he was ill, turned back and bent over him, just as a small aeroplane came low down over the trees.

That in itself was nothing new. The village, situated as it was between two aerodromes and two tank-testing grounds, saw plenty of 'planes, and was shaken and racked by noise at all hours of the day and night as the tanks rattled through, or the 'planes, taking off and then returning, flew low over the houses tree-tops. But there something different about this one. With her hand on Jason's collar, Susan stood by the stile and watched.

The mushroom field was large and although the wooded lane, with its gigantic old trees, bordered it on the lower and north side, the other sides boasted only low hedges. This year the field had been laid up for hay, but now the hay had been carried. Only a few mornings previously Susan had lain in bed and sniffed as the light breeze carried the scent of new-mown hay to her nostrils, and she had expected, this morning, to see the young cattle already turned in to graze.

The little 'plane circled and turned into the wind, as if coming in.

'Heavens!' ejaculated Susan, with a catch of her breath. 'A forced landing,' and in a moment she was over the stile and running across the field. She could see someone in it peering through the opened window over the side, but, before she could reach it, it was down, and she stopped and waited because the pilot began immediately to taxi towards the far side of the field, into position for taking off again, before she hurried towards it. Apparently all was well, for she heard a laugh as two tall men, dressed in what appeared to be naval uniforms, climbed out.

Susan was puzzled. She recognized the machine as a 'Fairchild', but it was painted yellow, and she had thought all machines of

Coastal Command to be white painted.

Jason trotted sedately at her side. Suddenly she stooped and patted him and said:

'Good old boy! How on earth could you know they were coming in? We might have been frightfully in the way,' and then looking up and finding she was within earshot, as the two tall men came towards her, called out:

'Good morning. Is anything wrong?' while at the same time she gave a puzzled glance at their uniforms. They must be Naval Reserve – but no wavy braid, and pilot's wings, and a badge she did not recognize. There had been so many new uniforms in the years since the war started. The thought passed swiftly through her mind as she repeated:

'Is anything wrong?'

'Good morning,' both answered and saluted simultaneously, and the taller and seemingly older, added: 'No. Nothing wrong, thank you. Are you the owner of this field?'

Susan shook her head. 'No, it belongs to a farmer. But why?' She looked questioningly at the 'plane, and again the same pilot answered, this time with a laugh:

'Last year I was obliged to make a forced landing in this field. This year we have practised one. The reason is – mushrooms!'

'Oh—' a long-drawn 'Oh' – and Susan glanced about. 'I haven't seen any yet. It's been its season for hay. They carried last week. But you are trespassing, you know. The farmer sells his mushrooms nowadays.'

'So the elderly gentleman I met last year told me, but we did pretty well in spite of that – and – by Jove! That's the same dog!'

'Jason!' Susan exclaimed, and she glanced from the man to the dog. She was thinking quickly. 'Daddy! He was the only man Jason could have accompanied'; but the repetition:

'Jason! That's it!' interrupted her. 'Jason of the golden fleece! I remember,' and he stooped as he spoke to pat Jason, and questioned:

'Remember me, old man?' But Jason's answer was a low growl, and the tall man straightened up and laughed while Susan apologized.

'Oh, I'm sorry. I've never known him do that before.'

'A bit bad-tempered, isn't he? Doesn't approve of me or my trespassing, that's obvious.'

'No. He is not bad-tempered.' Susan's denial was stout and, as she spoke, she slipped her fingers through Jason's collar caressingly. 'It's probably the 'plane he doesn't understand. But – who are you?' and her puzzled eyes looked directly at their badges, and again the elder man answered, with an exaggerated bow.

'The very silent service. Air Transport Auxiliary, alias Ferry Pilots, alias ATA.'

'Oh—' said Susan. 'Thank you. I know very little about it.'

'I told you silent – very silent.'

Susan decided she did not like him, but she was fascinated by the little 'plane. She wanted a closer look. The younger man remained silent while his companion still talked.

'My name is John Potts and my friend's John Pitts. Potts and Pitts. Not much to choose.'

'I am Susan Sandyman. Mrs Sandyman,' answered Susan. 'May I look at your 'plane while you look for mushrooms? It's a Fairchild, isn't it? I'm not very up in 'planes.'

'Right, first time. Pitts, you do the honours. Excuse me – there's my first one!' and John Potts moved away a few steps and stooped. Jason growled again, and John Pitts smiled as he called out:

'*That* is to teach you manners!' and without another glance at his companion he turned to Susan and with another smile asked, 'Would you like me to show you the 'plane?'

'Yes, please,' and as they walked towards it Susan found herself recalling all she had ever heard about ferry pilots, and after a moment's thought, said, in a puzzled tone, 'I thought ferry pilots were women.'

John Pitts laughed.

'Lots of people do. They got into the limelight when they first began, but the men do outnumber them.'

'And are silent, I suppose?' but by this time they had reached the 'plane, and John Pitts' only answer was a laugh and the question: 'Ever flown?'

'Yes.'

'In a Fairchild?'

'No. I learned on a Tutor and we had a Gypsy Moth.'

He stopped short with his hand on the door of the 'plane.

'You mean you had your own?'

'Yes. In Malaya. We burned it before we ran away.'

She tried to speak lightly, and fortunately her companion was sensitive. He did not ask her any more questions, but held open the door and asked:

'Would you like to get in?'

'May I? I'd love to,' and she climbed into the cockpit and, while he ran round to get from the other side, was, for a moment, alone.

'There we are. Nice little machines, aren't they?'

Susan nodded in agreement and after one glance at her face John Pitts fell silent. He wondered of what she was thinking, and watched her while she apparently studied the several dials and looked up at the compass above her head. She had slipped into the pilot's seat, and he sensed that something had made speech impossible.

It had. It was the sudden familiarity. This was what they had planned. To fly home and land in this very field. They had talked of it so often, and planned, like two children. Herself, Frank and Felicity. Counted the cost over and over again, just for fun; and part of the picture she had imagined was true, spread out there before her eyes, just as she had known it would be. The tall trees, the stretch of green grass, the low hedges, the church tower standing upright and solid, as it had stood for centuries, on the crest of the slope, and there where the trees were their thickest, was her childhood's home and her beloved father and brothers. The whole picture of their arrival, just as it might have been, passed swiftly through Susan's mind as she looked fixedly ahead – 'and the wind today just right.'

Unconsciously she said the last words half aloud, and just at that moment John Potts, walking slowly and carrying his forage cap carefully, crossed her line of vision and with a jerk she came back to the present, and remembered she was not alone. But her first thought 'John Pitts must think me a half-wit' died on her lips as her eyes met his, serious and questioning, and she found herself saying:

'Forgive me. I was reliving a dream. We had planned, someday, to fly home and land just like *this*. That elm, in the corner, is the snag, isn't it?'

'Yes, but Odiham is only three miles away,' answered John Pitts. 'It would be easier. We may have just come from there.'

'That was part of the plan.'

'And now?'

Susan shook her head. To explain meant speaking of personal affairs, and to change the conversation she remarked:

'This machine looks even simpler to handle than the "Moth". Have you flown much?'

'Yes. I was in the RAF,' and before she could ask more John Pitts leaned forward and began to explain some of the points difference, and Susan again noticed the very narrow gold stripe on the shoulder of his tunic. John Potts wore a wider one. She felt curious about him and realized that, although a little shy, he was at heart a very friendly person. Also it was suddenly borne in upon her mind that she really, and very urgently, wanted to know more about ferry pilots. But she waited and listened and asked a few intelligent questions before she touched the braid on his should and said:

'Tell me. What does this mean?'

'That!' John Pitts glanced sideways. 'Oh – I'm merely a cadet – a pupil.'

'But – the RAF? Were you a pilot?'

'Yes. Spits. Spitfires.'

Susan's bewilderment showed in her expression.

'But I don't understand. *Why* have you left the RAF? And how can you be a ferry pilot when you are no longer an RAF one? Forgive me if I am curious. You see, I'm only just home. I don't know much about these things.'

'There is nothing to forgive. I always feel I need explaining. I had a crash.'

'Oh – I'm so sorry.'

'Nothing to be sorry about. I broke a few bones, and there is a bit of doubt if I'll ever get back – so – this.' He waved his hand.

'I'm still curious,' said Susan. 'I'm sorry about the crash. But—' she hesitated.

'But what? Don't be afraid. Ask anything.'

'Thank you. Well – why have you got to be a pupil *now*, when you've flown with the RAF?'

'That's simple to explain. I was in a Spitfire squadron. Trained to fly a Spit. In the ATA we have to be able to deliver any machine.'

'You mean – women do too? Bombers?'

'Rather. And they are just as good pilots as men. I say, why don't *you* come along? They mostly are women – ladies, who belong to flying clubs and a few who had their own 'planes. Some of them are celebrated. You love flying. Why not?'

'Because,' began Susan, and shook her head and eyes, looking into his, clouded. 'Because—' she repeated and broke off. 'It never occurred to me. I was in a Voluntary Aid Detachment before I was three days at home.'

'You mean they didn't give you time to think?'

'I didn't want time to think. I'm – I'm afraid I am a widow, and I've lost my father and brothers – all within six months—'

'Oh – I say. I am sorry.'

'It's difficult. I've signed on for a year – and I couldn't leave home until Mother has re-organized.'

'No. I see. But perhaps later?'

'Yes. Later,' said Susan, but it was a fact, not an idea, that registered in her mind. 'Until your real job turns up.' She remembered her grandmother's words. She turned impulsively to John Pitts and repeated: 'Yes. Later. Thank you.'

Susan watched the Fairchild out of sight before she called to Jason and repeated to. herself: 'Yes. Later… Come, Jason. We will go and pay for those mushrooms. I know Daddy did last time.'

SIX

OVER AND OVER again as the weeks passed Susan thought of that meeting with John Pitts and of the questions she wished she had asked. She felt she had wasted an opportunity. Flying! That was what she wanted. She knew now; but, curiously, not even on that first morning did she mention either her encounter with the two ferry pilots, or her new ambitions, to her mother or grandmother. The little 'plane seemed to have arrived and departed unnoticed. Even the farmer, when Susan tried to insist on paying for the mushrooms, stared incredulously and ejaculated:

'Well – that beats all! Shows what we are coming to. Getting so used to them, I suppose. But that one could come down and go off again from any part of my farm and me not know! Well...'

Susan smiled and continued her walk.

Later, when reading to old Mrs Ledgard, her thoughts wandered and occasionally she broke off and stared out of the windows, at the sky, with unseeing eyes. If the old lady wondered where her thoughts were, she made no comment. Only once, when Susan apologized for her abstraction with the words, 'Sorry, Grannie. A thought intruded,' she smiled and said, questioningly:

'You are finding what a lot there is to do, and think about?'

'That is, exactly, it!' answered Susan.

But as the summer passed into autumn Susan found that the longing for wider spheres made the daily round of hospital life irksome. She could not dismiss that meeting as accidental. She looked upon it as a guidance which, in part, was due to Frank's undying influence, and as she came and went up and down the long two-mile slope that led to Hazlewood House, and journeyed to and from the station, she grew to watch wistfully for the 'planes taking off and coming in to either aerodrome.

Her work being more or less routine left time for thought. The van was her one responsibility. For some reason she did not like Mrs Knaggs and felt no companionship for her fellow Quartermaster, a woman of very ordinary education and upbringing. She was not young, but looked older than her years. Her name too was considered a joke by the younger VADs. Mrs Scragg. Soon, too soon, someone thought of the sobriquet of 'Scrag-end', and, to the recipient's annoyance, it stuck. Susan especially was amused, because so often 'See if you can get some scrag-end' was the final suggestion on the butcher's list when supplies ran short, and 'Bony, like herself,' the observation of a flippant junior added spice to the appellation.

After that one day Susan took her times off regularly, and throughout the summer visited the mushroom field frequently, hoping that the Johns, Pitts and Potts, would again descend on another quest. But it did not happen again. Also on her rare journeyings to London she found herself watching for that blue uniform, with its decoration of the golden wings and the 'ATA' of the ferry pilots. Sometimes she saw it. Once, when lunching at the Dorchester with her mother, at tall girl with a mop of fair hair sat at a table just sufficiently far away to make it impossible for Susan, try as she would, to catch any word of what appeared to be a gay conversation. During that summer also no mention of the Air Transport Auxiliary Service in the newspapers escaped her notice. Early in the autumn she saw the announcement of John Potts's death – 'killed while ferrying His Majesty's Aircraft' – and for a moment her heart stood still. So accidents did happen, she reflected, and her purpose grew stronger.

Christmas came and went. The hilarity of an hospital Christmas helped Susan through. As long as she was busy all went well. She tried to persuade her mother to spend Christmas Day at the hospital, but Mrs Ledgard only shook her head.

'No. Grannie has asked me to a midday dinner. We shall be quiet, and remember, together.' But on Boxing Day, when Susan returned home somewhat earlier than usual, she found her mother had made a few preparations; but the sprigs of holly and the decorated table only accentuated the sense of desolation Susan felt within. She made no comment and futile efforts at conversation soon petered out. Mrs Ledgard was apparently not interested in hospital life and answered in monosyllables, until, suddenly, in her brusque way, she said:

'A pretence – all a pretence.'

Startled, Susan looked across the table at her mother, but before she could speak Mrs Ledgard, with a quick movement, arose and pushed back her chair and, as if continuing her sentence, added:

'Come. We have finished, haven't we? I want to talk to you.'

Wonderingly, Susan followed to the drawing-room. 'Pretence', of course, it was. She had been aware of it all Christmas Day. Mrs Ledgard sat herself by the fire and immediately, as if she had nothing further to say, drew her work-basket towards her and commenced to sew as if her life depended on it. Susan needed no prompting. She knew exactly how her mother was feeling. Boxing Day, her father's birthday, had always been a gala day of the holidays, and, as she busied herself with the coffee, she thought of the happy, carefree Christmases of her childhood, when the house overflowed with noise and gaiety. With a faint hope of restarting some conversation, she remarked:

'Yes, Mother. You are right. Except, perhaps, for some of the younger men with crushes on some of the girls, I felt, yesterday, even when the fun was at its highest, that there wasn't a soul there who, if they could have had their own way, would not have been elsewhere. I found myself wondering "Suppose the war ended and everyone was suddenly free? How many minutes it would take to clear the buildings, and what a clamour there would be!" Christmas would be paled.'

As she finished speaking Susan carried her mother's coffee cup to her and, clearing a small space on the low table, placed it carefully. Mrs Ledgard glanced up and for a fleeting second their eyes met. For the first time Susan saw torture in her mother's eyes. But, by the next second, Mrs Ledgard had looked down again and her needle might have been an instrument of vengeance. Susan retreated to the other side of the fireplace and sat down.

Mrs Ledgard's work-basket had been one of the surprises of Susan's first weeks at home. She had gasped when she saw it, piled high with men's underwear and khaki shirts. Her puzzled glance had brought the explanation.

'It all began with the searchlight unit. They were just over the hedge in the field across the road, and it has gone on ever since.

You just happened to arrive during the hiatus, when the troops were changing over. They pass each other on. Always a dozen or so bring their clean washing along, and Jane and I air it, and mend it, and then it is ready when they come for their baths. That's all.'

'Can't I help?' Susan had picked up a grey sock and drawn it over her hand as she spoke.

'If you like,' answered her mother, and then with a catch of her breath, she added: 'Someone, in Canada, did it for Claude. It's – it's the only way I can repay her.' Susan had been standing, and, for a second, she was silent. Then, suddenly, she stooped and kissed her mother's cheek, and, for a moment, let her own rest against it, before she straightened up again, and said:

'Mother – you are wonderful!' She paused. There was no answer, only Mrs Ledgard seemed to pull her needle more briskly through the button she was sewing and she gave her head a slight jerk. Susan wondered if it was to shake away a tear and sighed within herself. 'If only' If only she could get below that brusque exterior! But at the moment there was no more to say, and so, with the remark,

'Grannie told me that the next troops to come in are Canadians,' she had sat down and selected a needle.

Tonight Susan put down her empty coffee cup and waited and wondered until she thought that, perhaps, if she made some movement it might help her mother to get started, so, with the remark, 'I'll take this out to Jane,' she arose and began to collect the coffee cups.

'That is, if you don't want any more?'

'No. No, thank you,' answered her mother.

The silence in the room seemed deeper when she returned. She had found Jane sniffing and mopping up an occasional tear as she washed up and so had lingered a few moments, consoling and wishing she could do something about it. She knew her mother and Jane never stopped working; but there were days like this when no amount of work drowned memory. Of herself she dared not think. She must not look back and, in a flash, it came to her as she walked the few steps across the hall, how much she thought of a future with the ferry pilots was bolstering her up. Somehow she would get there, of that she was certain, and once there, there would be no looking back.

With the remark, 'I'll do socks', she picked up several and re-seated herself. For what seemed like a long time Mrs Ledgard did not speak. Susan was acutely aware of small sounds, the occasional rustle in the work-basket, the snipping sound of scissors, the crackle of the logs as they burned, and the ticking of the clock, and of Jason's soft snores; also, although she did not look up, she was aware that from time to time her mother looked at her, but whether questioningly, critically or appraisingly, she had no way of knowing. She darned and waited, knowing that nothing she could do would precipitate matters, and indeed might only retard them.

Nine o'clock came.

'Shall I turn on the news?' she asked.

'If you like.'

'I don't care really. I listened at six.'

'Then leave it.' Mrs Ledgard let her hands fall into her lap, and with the air of stating a fact said: 'You are not satisfied at Hazlewood. You don't like some of the people.'

Susan smiled.

'Have I given it away? I've tried not to.'

'Tell me about them.'

'Well—' Susan answered slowly. 'To put it briefly the donning of a uniform doesn't make a woman a commandant. I think it is an unfortunate name. Gossip says this one is there because she happened to know someone in authority and her husband found her carrying on with someone else. Of course that may not be true, but the gossip and possibility undermine her authority, and that spoils everything. A commandant, like Caesar's wife, should be beyond reproach. Some of the VADs are so very young. Darling girls, mostly.'

'And that Scragg person?' interrupted her mother.

Susan gave a little laugh.

'That exactly describes her. Scraggy and petty. She has a husband and the photograph she keeps on her dressing table makes him looks years her junior. She has two nicknames. "Baby snatcher" and "Scragend". I put my foot in it one day. She called me to her room –

she wasn't very well – about shopping, and I thought the photograph was of her son. She hasn't forgiven me.'

'Then you won't mind if I let or sell this house, and you have to change your hospital? Perhaps a flat in London would be a more convenient home? I could then work with the "Women's Voluntary Services". We both could.'

'But – Mother – should you?' Susan began to protest.

'Why not? Are you thinking of my age? Do you know it?'

Susan shook her head.

'You were born before I was twenty-one. Forty-six is not old these days. If you would rather remain at Hazlewood, Grannie will, I know, be glad to give you a home, and a second home in London may be useful.'

In spirit Susan got closer to her mother that evening than ever before. For a moment or two she was silent before she said:

'Put your work away, Mother, and I'll tell you what I want to do. It is true. I am unsatisfied, and, in consequence, I magnify the petty annoyances. The van is my salvation. I couldn't be anything but mobile...' and, in a short time, Susan was telling of the mushrooms and of the Johns, Pitts and Potts, and all she had managed to discover of the ATA.

'It's true,' she finished. 'It *is* a silent service. It's awfully difficult to find out much about it. I buy odd flying magazines when I see them, which is seldom, and always there is something, and, that day at the Dorchester, I just longed to go and talk to that girl. One of them, at a table close by. The uniform is inconspicuous, among so many. I noticed when she put on her coat. It covered the "wings". Then it might have been just anything. There is danger, too, Mother. I've seen several deaths. John Potts – and some girls. One was only twenty-two.'

'There is danger everywhere,' said Mrs Ledgard. 'Safety and peace have vanished. Very well. We will let this house furnished. It is overcrowded with furniture. I can take enough for a small flat without its being missed. Jane will go with me.'

'Brave Jane. You both are – going to London,' said Susan.

Mrs Ledgard shook her head.

'It grows harder to believe with so much death around us that no one dies before his time. Yet I still do believe it. And now, while we are talking, I think you should know exactly how things stand. You may be left, I may be left, or we may both be left. Or neither of us. One never knows.'

It was midnight before Susan went to bed. Everything had been discussed and her mother's goodnight kiss was the first really affectionate one of Susan's remembrance, and her final remark was:

'Make your plans and as soon as you are free I will carry out mine. There are shadows and memories in every corner of this house. One must break away before they overcome one.'

Impulsively Susan threw her arms round her mother's neck. 'Mother! You are wonderful. I didn't know, until tonight, how much I love you.'

SEVEN

THAT WAS THE beginning of a real *camaraderie* between Susan and her mother. It lightened everything. Susan looked forward to her homecoming at the end of each day and found herself talking over the day's happenings exactly as with her grandmother.

Things slipped into their proper perspective. Slights and indignities mattered less, and then towards the end of the winter things began to happen with extraordinary rapidity.

It was Susan's habit every morning directly on her arrival at the hospital to walk straight through the long back corridor to say good morning to the cooks, and to put her head round the surgery door to speak to the VADs on duty, busy, at this hour, getting ready for dressings. Commandant and Matron being still at breakfast, a sense of freedom pervaded. Susan, nicknamed 'Sandy', was a great favourite with all the young VADs. She was always in request to buy oddments and stamps, and usually this walk through to the office was the favourite and most convenient time to press these small commissions, or beg a lift on the van.

On a bright morning early in February Susan proceeded, just as usual, to be greeted in the surgery with: 'Oh, Sandy! Do come in. We've such news for you! We've been aching lest you'd be late.'

'Why? What?' began Susan.

'Cheer up. You are going to London,' the elder of the two girls answered.

'London!' ejaculated Susan, looking from onto the other.

'Yes, London—' broke in the younger girl, while her eyes danced and she pushed back a falling lock of hair. 'Yes, and, Sandy! Angel! Pet! I've got my three hours, my half day *and* my day off *all* together, so, if I manage just nicely to miss the bus, and you see me weeping, forlornly, by the roadside, you will pick me up, won't you, pet? By the first bus stop.'

'Of course!' laughed Susan. 'But tell me some more. What has happened? Who is going?'

'It's Harris,' answered the elder girl. 'He has to go for some special medical board. I couldn't exactly hear what.'

'She eavesdropped! In the lav!' the younger broke in again.

The elder girl's fair face flushed.

'Well, I couldn't help it. I'd slipped into the cloakroom and Knaggie left the door to the office open. I couldn't get out without being seen. Matron and Knaggie were on the verge of a row royal – at least it would have been, with anyone but Matron.'

'Quiet insistence wins the day,' interrupted the other. 'She's always like that.'

'Yes. Go on,' said Susan.

'Well, I heard Matron go in and say: "Yes, Mrs Knaggs. What is it?" and then Knaggie in a sort of off-hand way: "There is a message. Private Harris has to go to London tomorrow. I will order Mrs Sandyman to take him for the ten o'clock train." I couldn't catch what Matron said, but Knaggie said: "Oh nonsense! The doctors wouldn't have asked for him if he had been unfit to travel." Then I could hear. Matron's voice would have cut ice, let alone one door; and she said, "I did not say unfit to travel, I said, unfit to travel by *train*." Then Knaggie again. "But the petrol! Where?" and I heard her jump from her sofa – you know how the springs creak. Then Matron again. "It is for patients like Harris that the Red Cross supplies petrol." Of course, by this time, I was behind the cloakroom door with both my ears sticking out, but Knaggie banged her door so I made my escape. But quite early this morning Matron went into Harris and told him. He's that nice quiet fair man who had an emergency op. Perforation. He's been in bed all the time he's been here.'

Susan listened and nodded and, not for the first time, felt herself to be the perfect liaison officer. She was the junior of the officers, and yet so much more in sympathy with the VADs, and ignored when possible by the office staff.

'Of course,' continued the younger girl, 'I know what it is. It's her hair morning. We'd see the grey if she missed it. She wanted the van herself.'

'What matter?' said the other. 'She'll take her own car *plus* Red Cross petrol and be gone at least two hours! I bet she prayed for fog!'

Susan laughed and went her way. Perhaps they were a bit disloyal to their commandant, but that was Mrs Knaggs' own fault. The VADs came from many different divisions and were intensely loyal both to the Red Cross and their own especial commandants, a fact which Susan had found seemed to escape the notice of *this* hospital commandant. She dismissed their own commandants as of no consequence. Was superior and offhand when they called, and apparently quite oblivious to possible criticisms and comparisons that might be made. The hurried conversation had also reminded Susan of her own annoyances. She was heartily tired of finding that, no matter how well she had planned and put the van away, clean, before her half-days and days off, there seemed so often to be some reason why Mrs Knaggs must take it out; and Susan hated a dirty car; also, try as she would to keep them straight, always there was a deficiency between her mileage and her petrol returns. Susan had no illusions about herself. To cherish was second nature. She had loved and appreciated her own household gods in just the same way. It still was agony to look back and remember how, with Frank, she had set them ablaze, and it hurt her to see anything roughly used. She could always see the care and thought expended behind the most inanimate objects. She had been born so, and could no more help it than she could help breathing.

Now it was with a feeling of elation she made her way to the office for her day's orders. A feeling of elation of which she gave no outward sign. As she entered her heart sank. Mrs Knaggs, seated at her desk, was writing, signing the men's passes as if her life depended on doing them speedily. She was dressed for out-of-doors. Susan's first thought was, 'Could she be going herself to London?' Otherwise she knew the frantic, self-important signs. The pretence of the thousand and one things with which only a commandant's authority could deal. She smiled inwardly as she said 'Good morning.'

But Mrs Knaggs was too busy to answer. Susan walked over to the fire and stood waiting.

It was easy to see that the Commandant was annoyed. Her red cheeks were more red than usual. After a few minutes she looked up, as if only that second had she become aware of Susan's presence.

'Oh, there you are! I was afraid you'd be late and I've such a lot to do.'

'I am never late,' answered Susan.

'Oh no. I suppose not – but so many people *are* I quite forget *who*. You have to take a patient to London. I suppose you know your way about London?' She shot the question at Susan.

'Perfectly,' fibbed Susan, and thought of her maps. 'Where have I to go?'

'Charing Cross, I think. Matron will tell you. She is afraid the patient will collapse on the journey, so you'd better see her. It's very tiresome. I have an important appointment and I must go to the Red Cross office. I suppose you couldn't do the shopping first? They want him at twelve o'clock.'

'I could, but the butcher doesn't get his supplies very early, and the fish is never in until ten,' Susan reminded her.

'Oh well – I always say it's the people at the top on whom the extra work always falls.'

Susan made her escape.

Peace reigned in Matron's office. It was like another world. A polite greeting. Papers and instructions ready and the explanation:

'I'm afraid it means a little hanging about. You will have to find out whether, or not, Harris is to return with you. And, if you can, there are some stores ready at Headquarters. I should be glad to have them. I have telephoned. They will be ready. The orders are "before twelve". That means the earlier the better. By the way, Harris has driven a lorry about London for the last two years, so you won't lose your way.'

The last words were accompanied by a smile which Susan returned. The wordless understanding was perfect. 'And two men have passes for Staines, so drop them off,' continued Matron. 'They are *not* to go to London. They will try, I know.'

'Yes, Matron. Is that all?'

'Yes. Sister is getting Harris ready. Don't let him have anything to eat. They may want to X-ray.'

By nine o'clock Susan was on her way. It was a lovely morning, heralding spring. This was lovely, she thought, and the patient, a quiet young man, seemed as delighted. A long run to charge up her batteries. And Nurse Robinson waving frantically at the nearest bus stop. A car-load of happiness, spoilt for a few minutes at Staines by the two patients, who thought they had wangled a trip to London.

'Matron would have given it you if you'd been honest,' stoutly asserted Nurse Robinson, and all the blandishments of:

'Oh, be a sport, Sister,' failed to move Susan.

'Buck up. There's a bus to take you back. Serves you right for being deceitful,' was Harris's contribution, and then the trio went lightly on their way with Nurse Robinson singing happily to herself in the back of the van.

'And where do you want to be dropped?' asked Susan over her shoulder.

'Any tube station. Hammersmith is a good one.'

'Where are you going?'

'Home! Richmond. Won't "me mum" be surprised to see me so bright and early? I'll be home before twelve.'

Not since she was a young girl, in the days before her marriage, had Susan driven a car in London – but she had no fears. She knew the way to, although not about, London. Even had the signposts still been there, she would not have deigned a glance; also, when they left the Great West Road, the boy at her side knew every twist and turn, and took charge, with the result that, a little before eleven o'clock, Susan deposited him at his destination, and by twelve she was free. Harris was not returning.

It was a wonderful feeling. In London! The sun shining and the journey back ahead. She made quick plans.

Fortnum first. Some coffee, and get a few things for her mother. It was all on her way to Belgrave Crescent. Then her stores and lunch. Then – well, a leisurely journey back; perhaps, as before, a few entertaining hitch-hikers would enliven it.

But it all took more time than she had allowed. She reached Belgrave Crescent only to find she would have to return 'after lunch'. 'Well, anyway,' she reflected, 'a Red Cross car should be safe outside HQ, and Halkin Street and lunch aren't far away,' so she immobilized and locked the car and sauntered off with still that sense of complete freedom and of a red-letter day.

And so it proved. Just before three o'clock, her stores loaded, Susan pushed up the tailboard of the van and carefully let down the glass upper part and locked it. Then dashed round rather impetuously to the front and immediately collided with a woman dressed in Red Cross uniform. At a glance Susan saw she was one of the nursing sisters. They both laughed and the nursing sister glanced at Susan's van.

'Hants,' she said. 'Why aren't you Kent? I'd beg a lift.'

'Sorry,' answered Susan. 'I'm afraid my petrol won't run to Hants via Kent,' and again they both laughed, and the nursing sister went her way leaving Susan regretfully wishing she could have given her a lift.

'Now it's up to you, St Anthony! You always find things. Find me just the right travelling companion.' As she spoke the words to herself she manoeuvred the car and turned to get into the stream of traffic at Hyde Park Corner. She was held up at the end of the Crescent and was just thinking that she had to get into the middle of the road when a hurrying figure caught her eye. Surely she knew that blue uniform? And a flying cap? Susan's heart missed a beat. It was a girl. One of the ferry pilots. The girl stopped on the island in the middle of the road. She looked straight at Susan and then stepped forward.

'I say, you aren't by any chance going to Marylebone, are you?'

Susan shook her head and leaned forward. 'No, straight back to Hazeley. Can I give you a lift?'

'Can you go to Maidenhead?'

'Maidenhead!' Susan thought of Mrs Knaggs. An extra fifteen miles at least – but thought and decision were one.

'Yes! Yes! Quick! The traffic is moving.' The girl needed no second invitation. Despite her rather heavy suitcase she was a moment only in dashing round the front of the van and, a second or two later, flopped into the seat beside Susan.

'Thanks,' she said. 'Thanks awfully! You are heaven-sent! I must get to White Waltham before five, and I've been over half an hour trying to get a taxi, so have missed the train I intended to catch. Are you really going to Maidenhead? It's incredible that I chanced on you!'

'Well, perhaps I wouldn't be, if I did as I should.' Susan gave her new acquaintance a sidelong glance. More was impossible. She was just entering the park. She turned left. 'I'm going to be the girl who took the wrong turning.'

'For me? How nice of you.'

'Not really.' The lights of Knightsbridge were against them and Susan seized the opportunity to explain. 'You see, I'd just been asking St Anthony to find me the right travelling companion. He finds things, you know, if they are findable.' The other girl nodded. 'I'm not RC,' continued Susan as she let in her clutch and the car sped forward, 'but ever since I was knee-high to a grasshopper I've appealed to St Anthony.'

'Well, I'd better let you know who St Anthony's pick-up is! My name's Diana Barnard. Spinster – as yet!' She waved a hand on which gleamed a large sapphire ring. 'Now, tell me why I am an answer to prayer?' She looked curiously at Susan.

'I expect I sound crackers,' Susan began, and she could not have explained why, suddenly, she was constrained to speak flippantly. Perhaps it was because the girl at her side wore the air of one to whom life had been very, very kind, or, equally perhaps, it was due to some inner prompting which guided her as to how best she could appeal to her unexpected companion.

'I recognized your uniform before you spoke to me. The ATA. That is what I really want to do and I've been longing to meet one of you to ask more about it.'

'But why *this*, if you want *that*?' broke in the other. 'Have you ever flown?'

'Force of circumstance,' answered Susan. 'And, yes, I have flown. We had our own 'plane in Malaya.'

In half a dozen sentences Susan outlined her own position, told her name and then told of her meeting with the two Johns, Pitts and Potts. Diana laughed amusedly at the episode of the mushroom field, but added:

'They took a bit of a risk – but Potts always did. Well, he was foolhardy once too often. You knew?'

Susan nodded.

'But Pitts – he is a nice little chap. Awfully disappointed not to get back on active service, but he is going back to the RAF for instructing in Canada. I don't know if he has gone yet. Now tell me what you want to know.'

'How? Where? When? *Where* do I apply? How long does the training take? And when? Any special times?' Susan's questions came in a rush.

'I'd better settle down to it, I can see,' laughed Diana.

'Is it all right?' Susan's voice was anxious. 'Not hush-hush?'

'Some things, of course,' said Diana. 'Names of places where we collect the machines are, and we mustn't talk to the press – but the preliminaries aren't. Give me your address first. I'm sure to remember something I've forgotten that may help you. "Hazeley" – she repeated – 'I know where that is. Flown over it lots of times. Let's think. If you take me to White Waltham you'll be quite a bit out of your way.'

'Yes – but think I can find it all right.'

'Can you? With no signposts? And what about petrol?'

'I haven't wasted a spot of petrol in eight months,' asserted Susan, 'so' – she paused – 'I've stopped being over conscientious. They've *made* me.'

'OK by me!' laughed Diana. 'I'm not arguing – but have you got your map?'

Susan nodded. 'Yes, thank you, and, you know, along those roads they hide masses of ammunition. It's everywhere – and soldiers. I expect I'll be accosted by hitchhikers. It isn't above fifteen extra miles, after all.'

'OK,' said Diana again. 'Would you like me to tell you exactly what happened to me?' 'Thank you. Do, please,' and both were silent for a few minutes while Diana seemed to be arranging her thoughts.

'I'd flown so little,' she began. 'Only a few hours. I thought I hadn't a chance – but, here I am. It's unbelievable. And the days I first flew alone up and down the country, getting to know it – cross-country flights we call them – they were the best of all. Up in the sky all alone! It was wonderful. It's just up to yourself, then. We don't learn blind flying and we don't carry radio – just sheer, visual map-reading. Not so simple as it sounds when you're cruising at over two hundred in bad visibility. Another amazing thing is, that it's said to cost the ATA three thousand pounds to turn out a good pilot, male or female.'

'Gosh!' said Susan. Her eyes were shining. 'Please go on. I could listen for hours.' 'I'd better give you the address first. Do as I did. Write to Miss Gower. She is our commander.'

'Do I call her that?'

'It doesn't matter. I didn't. Now – there it is.' Susan slipped the scrap of paper into her pocket and, for a moment, noticing some distant lights were against her, slowed down. Diana looked ahead, wondering.

'If you handle a 'plane as well as you do a car—' she commented.

'I'll try, but how long does the training take? How long before they let one fly? I'm *aching* to fly again.'

'You fly, but with an instructor, of course, from the beginning – but the actual training never stops. Single-engine types first – then twin engines – then four. One goes back and back again for different "conversions". One is learning all the time. Must – because different machines are coming along all the time. I'm longing for my first big bomber. I'll tell you exactly what happened to me. I began in November '41. I don't know what changes there have been, if any. I applied, as I told you, to White Waltham where one is interviewed, vetted and given a test flight. Then days passed, and just when I had given up hope I got a chit and reported to Luton. That is where one begins – or did. Now, I hear, it will be Thame. That is quite a sizable airfield, but the one where we train is at Barton, and small. It's so pretty, just beyond the last spur of the Chilterns. It's such a good landmark, the spur with the wood on its top, but you will see for yourself.'

'I hope so. Go on. I'm listening with both ears and all my heart.'

'I can see you are. Well, we started with "Maggies". Magisters, to be correct. With an instructor, of course. First dual, then solo, although I already had an "A" peace-time licence, just as you have. Then came cross-country flights. One does twenty-five of those, going everywhere. Getting to know the aerodromes and the landmarks. A first officer was in charge of cross-countrys. Oh – it's a lovely time! I got it just as spring was beginning, and I was beginning to feel I was worthwhile and that I was in the war. I suppose, because one feels in the know. Sometimes one flew Tigers and Tutors, but usually "Maggies". By the way, my first delivery was a Tiger. That was a day! Well, after cross-countrys we had a check up with the same first officer in something one has not flown before. I had a Fairchild. Do you know a Fairchild?' Diana broke off questioningly.

'Yes. Pitts and Potts,' answered Susan. 'I got in and I had a good look-see.'

'Good show. No opportunity missed, but you know, Susan – I call you Susan, don't I?'

Susan nodded. 'Of course, Diana.'

'You know you will find you have a lot to unlearn. One flew for pleasure before. One's instructor buttered one up. The ATA is, no matter how it is glamorized, damned hard work. It exists to deliver the 'planes. Let me see – where was I? Oh yes! The Fairchild! Then I got my wings! I shall never forget *that* day. I had thought I was wonderful! Terrific! That there never had been such a pupil. I don't know what I expected. Some sort of ceremony, I think. Like Prize-day at school. But to be given them so casually, with the remark, "Here, Miss Barnard, are your wings, but because you have your wings it doesn't necessarily mean you can fly." It took all the wind out of me.' Diana laughed at the remembrance and Susan uttered a sympathetic:

'Poor you – but do go on. I'm getting more and more thrilled and determined. I do hope they'll take me.'

'Well, there's no harm in trying, is there? When can you give this up?'

'About May, I hope,' answered Susan. 'Perhaps a bit earlier. I'm leaving my holiday until the end of my year.'

'Then get your application in right away.'

'I will. I'll write tonight.'

The Great West Road was clear that afternoon and the days were drawing out. The sun was still shining and there was no threat of fog when they reached what Diana called 'the parting of the ways'.

'That, m'dear,' she said, smiling and pointing, 'is really your road.'

'I know,' said Susan and her chin was firmly set. She swung the car round the roundabout and on to the Bath Road.

'Luckily White Waltham is on your way from Maidenhead,' said Diana.

'Yes, Now go on. There is so much more I want to know. What happened after you got your wings?'

Diana settled down again to her story.

'I was seconded, as a junior taxi-pilot, to Hamble for three weeks. Just a stooge, taking a Fairchild and bringing back pilots – one picks up, but is a passenger coming back. The most experienced pilot takes over the 'plane. You go all over the place, to pick them up from wherever they have delivered machines. That gave one twenty or thirty hours' flying – about sixty in all. After that one really has learnt that part of the country. Next I was sent over to Thame for four days, and I had to take a "Maggie" to Scotland. That was my first trip to Scotland. I was very slow, got lost and was gone four days. It was bad weather. Kept closing down. However, I got the machine there.'

'How did you get back?' interrupted Susan.

'By train. They give you railway vouchers and pay expenses, of course. After that I was sent back to White Waltham again. Class Two conversion. Harvards and Masters. Then I had a crash. Nothing very serious and luckily *not* my fault. After Harvards and Masters I did about three hours' "circuits and bumps", which means taking off and landing, in the old "School Hurricane". There is where one needs extra care. One would never live it down if a school Hurricane got broken. Then I was put in the Training Pool, still at White Waltham, and not until I had delivered about a dozen Hurricanes did I get my first Spitfire. After that I was let loose on all single engines.'

'And where next?' asked Susan.

'Posted to Hamble, where I am now, flying everything in Class Two.'

'And what is Class Three?'

'Twin engines – the easier types – Oxfords, Ansons and Dominies. I shall be sent back to White Waltham for that. It takes about two years to get into Class Four, if all goes well. One goes ahead pretty fast. I had a spot of bad luck and lost some months when my mother was ill, else I'd be farther on. However, I'm catching up.'

'So am I!' Susan's tone was very cheerful. Diana's chatter had heartened her. She felt things were moving. 'I've felt all wrong ever since I came home. Hospital isn't my sphere. I'm a square peg. St Anthony has done me very good turn this afternoon.'

'Well, St Christopher hasn't done me a bad one,' laughed Diana.

EIGHT

PAST SKINDLES, WHICH hotel Susan did not know until Diana pointed it out, over the bridge, where, so Diana chirruped, William the Fourth and Mrs Jordan had their final parting, straight through Maidenhead, little dreaming how well she would come to know that town, Susan drove, until Diana said:

'Steady! We are almost on the turning. Here we are! That lane to the left. Now we've only a mile or two. D'you know, we've only been just over an hour! Some driving! Congrats! I've oodles of time. I'll be at Hamble almost as soon as you are at Hazeley, and you'll be there long before dark.'

Susan's only word at that moment was a questioning 'Which?' She had slowed for the turn and now looked at the two lanes opening out beyond the triangle of grass and trees.

'Over there, by that house.' Diana pointed and her tongue ran on. 'I'm not a scatter-brain really; but there's a party tonight and the boyfriend suddenly 'phoned. I was frantic! Said I couldn't possibly make it by four thirty; and here I am, thanks to you, with time to spare! Look! See that house on the left? That is Altmore.' Susan slowed to look. 'Where we go first, when we join. Not to stay – but to forgather and be collected.'

Susan nodded and accelerated. 'Thanks. I'll remember and I shall always think that finding you today was too wonderful!'

'And this lane, m'dear, is called "Cherry Garden Lane". By the way, have you got your Red Cross identity card handy?'

Again Susan nodded. 'Yes. Of course.'

'That's good, The airfield cuts across this lane. It ends nowadays at the airfield; and your shortest way, to save going back to Maidenhead, is round the perimeter. I'll show you.'

'But – shall I be allowed?'

'Leave it to me. Only smile. Here we are. The railway bridge – then we are there! Can't think why the railway people never made a station here. It would be *so* useful.'

By this time they were on the bridge. Still talking, Diana leaned forward.

'I just want to see... oh, it's all right.' Her tone was satisfactory, but her words conveyed nothing to Susan, who was gazing ahead at buildings that looked like temporary ones, and at the flag-staff, with the ATA flag fluttering in the breeze; but she had little time. Diana, still leaning forward, was speaking to the policeman on the gate, and the sentence Susan next heard was:

'I've got some luggage—' and Diana gave a half-glance at the cases in the back. 'May my friend drive me round to the tarmac?' The policeman followed Diana's glance and looked at the cases, but his eyes came quickly back to Susan, and then he stepped backwards and looked at the inscription on the car, and then back at Susan.

As usual, Susan's cap was off. She made a quick grab and smiled as she dragged it on. The policeman smiled back.

'Got your identity card, miss?'

'Yes – of course. I've two...' she produced them. Her personal one and the green one showing she was Red Cross Service.

'That's all right.' He waved them on.

'Goody!' said Diana. 'Now you are all right. Wish I could take you in for a cup of tea – but I haven't the time.'

'And I couldn't stop,' answered Susan. 'Which way?'

'Oh – bear to the right.'

Susan did so and found herself between what appeared to be long rows of offices and canteens. She had no time to look and Diana was gazing intently, upwards, through the windscreen.

'That's the Anson! Just come in!' she exclaimed. 'Oh – I'm so grateful to you. Round to the left. We're there!'

'The Anson? Where?' Susan was longing to ask more.

Ahead at first, now to her right, lay the expanse of the airfield. It was tantalizing to have no opportunity to see it properly.

'Stop opposite the steps, please,' said Diana, who at first appeared not to have heard Susan's questions. Susan did so and noticed a group of girls and men on the steps, and she could hear laughter and someone called, 'Hi, Diana!' as Diana flung open the door and began to drag out her suitcase. One of the men came forward to help, but Diana made no attempt at any introduction. She stood on the step of the car and pointed.

'See – there it is – taxiing in! There are half a dozen of us here from Hamble. It's come to take us all back.'

Susan looked where Diana pointed. A smallish twin-engined 'plane with one girl pilot inside came to a standstill at a little distance.

'Thank you. I'm so glad we met.'

'And I'll never cease to be grateful. Goodbye. Just follow the perimeter. The gate is the only one – it's on your left, of course. Turn right when you get out.'

'Yes, I know, and thanks.' Susan waved a hand in farewell. There was nothing for which to linger. She suddenly felt flat, but reflected she had been very lucky, and she drove very slowly for the mile or so to the White Waltham Gate, looking, this way and that, at the various 'planes parked on the edge of the field. There seemed a good many. Some she recognized. She stopped once to see one big one land, guessing it to be a Wellington bomber, and she watched the solitary pilot climb out dragging his parachute, and stride away over the grass.

'Well, one day—' she comforted herself, and suspecting another policeman would be on duty at this gate, had her identity cards ready. She met only a smile, and an 'All right. They 'phoned round about you,' and surprised, she said:

'Did they?'

'Yes. Regulations. Goodnight, miss.'

'Goodnight,' and a moment later Susan was on her way home.

'That was extraordinary,' she reflected. 'I thought Diana had half sneaked me in and I was sneaking out the other way. But, of course—' Then she suddenly thought of the Anson and the flight back to Hamble and stepped on her accelerator. 'Perhaps I'll see it. There's over an hour of daylight yet.'

Susan did see it. She came out on the high ground at Crowthorne about twenty minutes later just as the 'plane came overhead. She stopped the car and got out, and something that might have been a handkerchief, or a bit of white paper, fluttered for a moment and then floated down. She waved back and watched until the 'plane passed out of sight, hidden in the sunset haze which was beginning to overshadow the wide valley. Then with a feeling of contentment she got back into her seat, and, a quarter of an hour later, arrived at Hazeley.

Susan was late that evening. First she had had to search for the odd man, who should have been on hand to help unload the cases and was nowhere to be found. Then she had to appeal to Matron for a patient sufficiently well enough to do the job. All took time. But, eventually, it was done. The car washed and put away. Her reports made and as, after refusing supper, she mounted her bicycle for the two miles' run home, Susan realized she was a little tired and gave thanks that so much of her short journey was downhill. Eight o'clock, to suit her convenience, was dinner-time at home.

Her way led out from the old stable-yard and round past the front door. Just as she was passing the door opened suddenly and someone dashed out, calling her name. A moment later she saw it was the Quartermaster, Mrs Scragg. For a split second Susan was tempted to pretend she had not heard, and to hurry on, but she jammed on her brake and put one foot on the ground.

'Oh, Sandyman! I was afraid you'd gone. There was a message. I thought Madam had told you, and she thought I had.'

'A message? What? A 'phone call?' With a rising sense of irritation, which was betrayed in her voice, Susan continued:

'I looked on the board. There was nothing there.'

'Yes. But it's not *my* fault. I didn't take it and we don't usually put Officers' messages on the board.'

Susan curbed herself. She longed to answer, 'It would be better if you did.' People were so casual about messages. Not that she had many, but – perhaps Grannie was ill?

The sudden anxiety put impatience and fear into her voice.

'Well, what was it?'

'Oh! Only your mother. She wanted to know if you could get home a bit earlier. She 'phoned about six.'

'Did she say why?'

'Some unexpected visitor I think, to see you. Well—'

The last long-drawn word was uttered as Susan disappeared, and she had dashed off with such speed that her perfunctory 'Thank you' was lost to Mrs Scragg.

A visitor! To see *her*! Someone from Malaya? Was it possible? Her pulses throbbed. 'If only—' Resentment at the delay over the delivery of the message was lost in anticipation. Who could it be?

Afterwards she had no recollection of the short journey that evening. She did it in record time and pedalled, in the darkness, up the drive of King's Lane House ringing her bicycle bell vigorously to announce her coming. She dropped off, on the front doorstep, just as Mrs Ledgard opened the door. Her bicycle, for convenience in the morning, spent the night indoors.

'Oh, Mother! *Who* is it? I didn't get your message until just as I was leaving and I was late already. *Who*? *Mother*!'

'Didn't they tell you? My dear – I said Mr Pitts had arrived and to ask you to try to be a little early.'

'Oh—' there was agony in Susan's tone. 'Oh – and I've imagined a thousand things! Someone to tell me about Frank, someone we knew – or Dr Jamieson—'

Susan's head drooped and for a second, her self-control at low ebb, she rested it on her mother's shoulder, and the action was expressive of the softening of Mrs Ledgard's character. Her hand came up caressingly; for a minute or two she held Susan's head pressed closely.

'My poor child. I am sorry. It would have been better not to have phoned… But come. Dinner is ready and we have a guest.'

'All right—' Susan lifted her head. 'It's all right, Mother. I'll just run and wash.'

'But how on earth did you find us?'

They were at dinner, Susan and her mother at either end of the diminished dining-table, with Jane hovering in the background, and John Pitts between them. Jane had evidently thought it an occasion. She had laid the table as of old and 'let herself loose', to use Susan's unexpressed thought, in the store cupboard.

John Pitts laughed.

'By a process of deduction. It was quite easy. I knew your name. Knew your people must have lived here for some time because not only did Potts know this fellow' – his hand fell caressingly on Jason's head – Jason, perhaps remembering the Air Force blue, having attached himself firmly to John Pitts since the moment of his arrival – 'but, don't you remember, you said the top end of the field had always been the best for mushrooms?'

Susan shook her head.

'No. I don't remember.'

'Then the rest was easy. I got a lorry, coming this way, to drop me off at the post-office, and, do you know, when I asked that nice postmistress you have where I could find "Mrs Sandyman and Jason", she said, "If you'd said Jason only it would have been enough!"'

'Well, everyone knows him and he *never* forgets people. I was away five years and he gave me a wonderful greeting.'

John Pitts nodded and put down his soup spoon.

'That's the kind of dog I like.' He patted Jason's head again and a contented thump-thump of Jason's tail answered him, while the same thought passed through the minds of both Susan and Mrs Ledgard:

'Just so had he always sat by his master.'

A momentary silence fell, broken when Susan asked:

'How long do you expect to be stationed at Odiham?'

'Two or three weeks. Then I go to Canada.'

'So I heard today.'

John Pitts raised his brows and looked puzzled.

'Today! How?'

'Picked up Diana Barnard. Broke all the laws of the Medes and Persians and took her back to White Waltham. She is a dear.'

'She? One of the best!' supplemented John Pitts, and he turned to Mrs Ledgard. 'She *is*!'

'Five foot nothing, if she's that. As rich as Croesus. Engaged to a chap equally so. Awfully pretty. Almost too favoured of the gods, and without one atom of conceit or side. Pretty good pilot, too...' and for the rest of dinner Susan's day, and the ATA provided the entire conversation.

It was over coffee in the drawing-room that Mrs Ledgard made her suggestion. She had disappeared for a moment towards the kitchen and Susan had given no thought. She was busy with question after question, getting more of the information she longed to possess.

Mrs Ledgard spoke quietly and Susan, after one glance, showed no surprise.

'Mr Pitts. Would you like to make our home *your* home, until you go to Canada?'

'Like it? I say, do you mean it? *Real* home?'

'Of course. We should be very pleased.' Mrs Ledgard paused a second. 'And – there's a bicycle in the garage if it's any help. Your room is ready, if you like to stay – tonight.'

'But – but I've no things—'

'There are plenty of things...' answered Mrs Ledgard.

NINE

THE ADVENT OF John Pitts into her home, coming, as it did, immediately on top of her talk with Diana Barnard, only served to strengthen Susan's resolve.

About ten o'clock that first evening Mrs Ledgard, as usual, folded her work and departed to bed, leaving Susan and John Pitts bent over the composition of Susan's letter application, only to return after a few moments and open the door, just sufficiently wide to be heard, and say, 'Jane has left the cocoa ready, lest you stay late,' before she shut the door again.

Startled, Susan straightened up and stared a moment at the closed door, while John Pitts stared at her. Then, her blue-grey eyes widely open, she turned her head and, looking straight into John Pitts' blue ones, said:

'What have you done to my mother? She spoke exactly as she used to do. It was like an echo down the years. She used always to go off to bed – after we were big, I mean – and leave us to finish our games, and Daddy to shoo us off later, and, always "the cocoa in the kitchen".'

'I like your mother,' she answered John Pitts. 'She is *real*.'

'Thank you. But what, exactly, does that mean?'

'I suppose I mean a *real* mother.'

Susan dropped her pencil and half turned in her chair. For a moment she looked more puzzled before her face cleared and she nodded gravely.

'Yes. You are right. I see – only when we were all at home – I mean before my marriage – Claude, my youngest brother, was the only one who – penetrated.'

'Penetrated? Now what do you mean?'

'Exactly that,' and for a few minutes both pencils lay neglected while Susan briefly told of her childhood and finished: 'It isn't until *now*, after all this trouble, that I've really got to *know* my mother. I am so glad you came. Do you know, you have made her laugh this evening, and she hasn't done *that* since I came home.'

'But I loved her at sight.' John Pitts coloured and quickly added:

'Now let's finish this. Just the rough. I'll take it and get it typed in the office tomorrow, then you can get it off tomorrow night.'

Susan smiled and agreed, thinking, 'I'll spoil it if it makes him self-conscious.'

The swiftness of the reply to her letter amazed Susan. She expected at least a week to elapse and resigned herself to wait. To her astonishment a mere forty-eight hours elapsed before a letter inscribed 'On His Majesty's Service' arrived.

It was still quite early in the morning and her day off. She intercepted the postman, while taking Jason for his morning run, at the end of the Green Lane. It was the only letter addressed to herself. She stood still where she was to read it, and then, calling excitedly to Jason, ran back through the lane and across the garden.

'Mother! Mother! Where are you! I've got my letter!'

'Bring it here,' her mother's voice answered from the kitchen. 'Read it to me, dear.'

So while her mother turned the breakfast bacon Susan read aloud:

'*Dear Madam,*

'*With reference to your application for a position as ferry pilot in this organization we shall be glad if you will please report to the undersigned any day, except Saturday, Sunday or Monday, convenient to yourself, arriving here not later than 10 am for an interview and possible medical and flight test.*

'*Kindly let us know beforehand the date of your visit.*

'*Will you please bring with you the enclosed application form duly completed with your certified log book.*

'*Presentation of this letter will be necessary for admittance to the airfield.*

'*Yours faithfully—*

'And it is signed by someone who calls himself "*Chief Instructor*". Oh, Mother! I do feel I am getting on! Won't John Pitts be pleased?'

'I am so glad, child. But what is that about a log book?'

'Mercifully I have that,' answered Susan. 'I kept it – all I could keep. We started them in Sydney when we learned to fly. Both of us. I have only about fifty hours. Frank had – has' – she corrected herself without noticing her mother's quick glance – 'much more. I didn't fly while Felicity was coming.'

'Come and have breakfast.' Mrs Ledgard led the way with her laden tray. 'Then you can run over to Grannie. She will want to know.'

Susan hardly heard. She was studying the 'enclosed form', but she followed, and as she sat down said:

'This looks hopeful. They want names and address and telephone numbers, and ask them to be such as to enable urgent communications to reach me.' Susan passed the form to her mother as she spoke.

Mrs Ledgard adjusted her spectacles, saying: 'So tiresome. I can't see to read without these.'

Susan reread her letter while her mother studied the form.

'It is very business-like,' commented Mrs Ledgard. 'Nationality. Date of birth. Married or single' – stopped at 'children' and then went on – 'Licence number – what does that mean?'

'It's my "A" Licence. If you look below you will see "B" Licence. That is a commercial pilot's licence. I have, of course, only my "A".'

Question by question Mrs Ledgard read the whole form, stopping only to ask if Susan had ever flown any other 'plane than her own. And 'All very satisfactory,' was her comment at the end.

'Such a pity it is Saturday. I'd like to go straight away,' said Susan. 'I shall go on Tuesday.'

'I think you had better say Wednesday. You cannot possibly get to Maidenhead from here by ten o'clock in the morning, and "Saturday, Sunday or Monday" looks as if your Chief Instructor likes his weekends. Better give him time to read his letters. He won't be ready for you at ten o'clock on Tuesday. Why not telephone to a Maidenhead hotel and get a room for Tuesday night? Then you will be fresh for your flying test.'

'That is sense,' answered Susan. 'But isn't it stupid? It's only about twenty miles. If only Mrs Knaggs would let me have the van, plus some of the petrol she annexes – but it's of no use to ask...'

An hour later Susan hastily returned from her visit to old Mrs

Ledgard, left her bicycle on the veranda and rushed to find her mother, calling at the top of her voice:

'Mother! Mother!'

'Here – in the store cupboard—' her mother's voice floated down from the top landing.

'Mother! Can you hear? Grannie wants us all, you and me and John Pitts, to go to dinner tonight. She's got "an animal" – at least it's a chicken or an old hen, but enough for four – and she is going to give us champagne, to drink to my new career!'

Mrs Ledgard hurried down from the top landing.

'How kind of Grannie! That will be very nice. I'll just tell Jane. The casserole will keep for tomorrow.'

She broke off as the telephone pealed.

With a laugh at the intricacies of wartime housekeeping Susan answered, 'All right – I'll answer it,' and a minute later she was listening to Robert Jamieson's voice.

The voice gave her a momentary shock. She had written, as she had promised, occasionally, and had had two letters from Robert, but the last was several weeks old. She did not know what ship he was in. That he had left the *City of Truro* was her one item of information concerning him.

Now the call was from Scotland. After greeting her and congratulating himself on his luck at finding her at home, he spoke quickly: 'I am just leaving for London. Have to re-kit. Could you meet me? Tonight? Is it possible?'

'Oh dear! I'm so sorry,' and so far had he been from her thoughts that Susan had slight struggle with memory before she could recall which diminutive of his name he had asked her to use. 'I can't – Rabbie. I've just this minute arranged sort of celebration.'

'Celebration?'

'Yes. I'm hoping to get a new job.'

'Oh – I'm so sorry. But what job?'

'Can't tell you now. But I'll be in London *next* week. Is Wednesday any good?'

'Rather. I'll make it. Susan! I say, wear that same dress. Will you? *Do.*'

Susan laughed. 'I'll have to! I haven't any other suitable. Did you get my letters? Where have you been?'

'I've only had one letter—'

'I've sent *three* – but *where* have you been?'

'I think I'd better not say – but not where I could get any news for you. Have you heard anything?'

'No – Rabbie! Why the re-kit?'

'Will you please terminate your call?' A cold expressionless voice broke in.

'All right, Rabbie! Where shall I write?'

'My bank. I'll keep in touch. Goodbye.'

'Goodbye,' and Susan almost added, 'I'm sorry about tonight,' but the words died on her lips. They would not, she felt, be quite true. Slowly she replaced the receiver and moved to the window to stare across the garden at the budding trees and the newly opened daffodils, deep in thought. A sense of disappointment was uppermost. She had clung to the hope that Robert Jamieson had been East. India, perhaps? Somewhere where he would have gleaned *some* news. Susan was perfectly conscious that she was hoping against hope. The conviction that Frank was dead was very strong – but – sometimes, as this morning – something would rekindle the faint hope that she might be mistaken. Then the remembrance of the Verners came back. Chance, passing acquaintances of a few moments – but, perhaps, a purpose to fulfil. A soft sigh escaped her just as Mrs Ledgard entered the room.

'Who was it, dear? They don't, I hope, want you at Hazlewood today?'

'No. Oh no. It was Dr Jamieson, Mother. 'Phoning from somewhere in Scotland. He says he has to re-kit—' Susan stopped short.

'Re-kit? That means—'

'Yes, but the wretched operator cut us off just as I was about to ask. I think I'll go for a walk, Mother. That is, unless I can do anything for you?'

'No, darling. Go for your walk.'

For a moment Susan hesitated, then, as her eyes met her mother's and she saw the light of understanding, she moved the few steps across the room and the same words rose to her lips.

'Mother – you are wonderful. You *always* understand. It's – it's anything – even a voice connected, ever so remotely, with *that* time—'

A swift embrace and a moment later Susan had called to Jason and was striding across the garden.

TEN

WHITE WALTHAM AGAIN! Susan felt on familiar ground. After all, the journey had presented no difficulties. John Pitts had attended to that and one of his colleagues, going on leave, had been persuaded to arise early to give Susan a lift as far as Maidenhead.

That they had entered Maidenhead at the wrong end of the town mattered not at all. He had obligingly made a detour and dropped Susan, plus her large suitcase, at the station; and wished her 'all the luck in the world' before he left her. Even a taxi had been immediately procurable and Susan arrived at the main gateway of White Waltham airfield well before ten o'clock with an air of general wellbeing because, so far, all had gone well. She had recognized the turning, felt she knew every inch of Cherry Garden Lane and craned her neck to scan Altmore as she passed.

Unfortunately it had been a wet morning, but when Susan had regretted this her companion had assured her it was going to clear, and when Susan had looked doubtful he had laughed cheerily. 'You are thinking of your test flight? Well – there's nowhere in the world where the weather closes in, or clears as quickly, as in England. You'll see.'

He was right. As Susan showed her letter and listened carefully to the directions of the police constable on duty at the gate – who was not one of those she had previously seen – the rain ceased and a moment later a burst of sunshine made shining reflections on the concrete roadway, while every raindrop hanging from the nearby buildings and shrubs glistened and glittered. It seemed to Susan such a good omen that it lit up her smile of thanks, and the constable's 'Best of luck, miss,' cheered her, just as she was beginning to feel a little nervous. So much depended on this morning. The three people who made up her present world would be so disappointed if she failed. Perhaps just to see her smile again the constable repeated his instructions.

'The Chief Instructor? That's along there,' and he walked with her a few steps to point out the doorway. 'Then you'll be sent to see the doctor. That's there – just opposite. Walk in – you'll find one of the nurses there.'

He was rewarded. Susan smiled once more and renewed her thanks, then, remembering the solid rubber soles of her new shoes and the slovenly look of splashed stockings, she picked her way carefully along the roadway between the buildings she had driven through before with Diana. Offices and canteens. She had been right, and a strong smell of coffee made her suddenly realize it was some time since she had breakfasted. It was amazing, she reflected, how much she had seen on that previous visit, although Diana had been too much absorbed in her own affairs to point out anything. This morning everything looked new and clean and rain-washed. Suddenly a loud-speaker blared. Several names and ranks were mentioned. The ranks did not surprise her. She knew now that the ATA followed the ratings of the Merchant Navy; but the sudden outpouring of a dozen or so men and girls, from a doorway at the far end of the roadway, did surprise her. She stood still to watch. All dressed exactly alike, only their slimmer figures and their hair showed which were the girls. Some ran, some hurried, some walked nonchalantly, but their voices came pleasantly as they called to each other and laughed. A moment only and all had disappeared through an opposite doorway on the other side of the roadway. The explanation came to Susan. Pilots! Going on duty! The weather had cleared. She glanced up at the sky. A perfect morning. For a second she felt envious. They were going to fly! Over England. In the sunshine. It was wonderful. Wonderful to feel close to the greater work that was being done. Susan's pulses throbbed and her pace quickened. She gave a glance at the airfield beyond the roadway, took a deep breath and turned to the doorway the police constable had indicated.

Susan did not know it, but she made a good impression on the Chief Instructor that morning. Her interview was not long. She was surprised at its brevity. Questions were tersely put and she answered them as directly as possible. He shot them at her as he examined her log book, and then asked more about her instructor in Sydney. Susan summed him up as rather a martinet, but with the qualifying statement 'just and fair'. She liked him and, perhaps because he was so practical, her nervousness vanished. She was surprised when he suddenly rose to his feet and bowed her out with instructions to go for her medical.

The high-spot of Susan's day was her flight check. She wasn't sure if the slight trepidation she felt beforehand was due to excitement, fear that she might not acquit herself well, or merely to hunger. Later she decided that it must have been a mixture of all three, but it was a fact that as she walked out across the airfield it suddenly left her. Analysing it afterwards, when talking with Robert Jamieson, she said:

'Oddly, for a moment I was back in Australia and Frank was beside me. I could hear him saying, just as he used: "Don't be nervous. You are going to be a jolly good pilot. As good as any man," and there, in front of me, was an old "Tutor"! It's a biplane, you know, a replica, believe it or not, of the one we had our first lessons on in Sydney! I could hardly believe my eyes, and the next second I was back, as it were, in myself, and the instructor was asking how long it was since I had flown.'

That short first flight over England was unforgettable. Whether she did well or ill, Susan did not know, and neither did she care. She was once again in a 'plane taxiing out, waiting for her signal to take off, with the wind in her face, all else forgotten and her spirits soared with the machine as the ground fell away below and ahead she saw a wide park, and a moment later they were over an old Tudor mansion and circling a tall slender church spire. She even remembered afterwards that the main building of the house sprawled out like a huge, stumpy letter 'H', and her mind registered the fact that it must be of Henry's and not Elizabeth's time. It was all so typical, so English, and even while her attention was riveted on her instruments and the handling of the 'plane she was subconsciously taking in the whole picture. The church so close to the mansion. The trees, especially a great chestnut, its blossoms faded now, but which must, a week or two earlier, have looked like a huge cauliflower. She was quite unaware of how acutely the instructor was watching her, noticing everything as she obeyed his directions. The expression of her face and the clearness of her intelligent eyes. There was nothing tense in her attitude. She sat at the controls as if perfectly used to handling a 'plane, and he was satisfied.

Susan sighed as they left the machine. Her companion heard her and asked: 'Sorry that is over?'

'Yes. Very.'

'Satisfying, isn't it?' was his next remark. 'Sort of shakes things into their right perspective. You feel that?'

'Always, and when I land I feel about the size of a sixpence.' She smiled and glanced at him.

'One is. Just that – only the size of a sixpence,' he repeated, 'compared with *that*...' and he glanced upwards before their eyes met in a friendly smile. 'Know what you do next?' he asked.

'Yes. They told me. An interview with Miss Gower.'

'You won't see her today. She is away.'

'Oh – then who?'

'I don't know who is stooging for her.'

'Who is – what?'

'Stooging. Aren't you up in flying slang?'

'I'm afraid not.'

'You'll soon learn. Goodbye. That door, and upstairs. Go along the corridor. It's on your left.'

'Goodbye – and thank you.' He nodded and was gone.

Rather more than half an hour later Susan again sought the friendly policeman. By now she was desperately hungry and feeling rather flat, and, as she walked towards the gate, she was wondering what bearing half-an-hour's conversation, chiefly about skiing, could possibly have on her future career. She hadn't skied since the winter before her marriage, when she was nineteen, well over five years ago, and had said so. She had loved it, of course, and had been pretty good at it, then. Her father had also loved it and had taken her to Switzerland every winter since she was fourteen. Their family programme had never varied. Switzerland in winter and Scotland in summer. She wondered, too, what impression she had made on the various people who had interviewed her. Except for that casual 'you'll soon learn', which might mean just nothing at all, no one had vouchsafed other than formal words. Her last dismissal, 'OK,' was not however exactly formal, she reflected. Its brevity was casual in another way. Casual, non-committal and extremely modern. Did it epitomize the attitude of mind expected in the Air Transport Auxiliary? Would she ever find out?

* * *

'Lunch, miss?' The policeman looked sympathetic at her enquiry. 'These canteens are for all the personnel. Somebody could take you as a guest. Nobody asked you?' He questioned, and Susan shook her head. 'That's too bad. Now, one of the nurses—'

'No. No. I couldn't ask them.' Again Susan shook her head. 'What about a taxi?'

'No good, miss. There's only a taxi if someone comes up.'

'Oh – I thought I might get one to Skindles.'

'There'll be a bus going down in ten minutes. It takes you to Maidenhead, but not as far as Skindles.'

'Thank you. I will wait. Where do I go?'

'Just wait here. It'll be along in a few minutes.'

Susan waited and looked about her, noticing everything. She saw one of the doctors leave his office and dash for his car and watched it swing through the gates.

The policeman noticed her glance. 'No good, miss. He's only going down to the Senior Officers' Mess.' So, apparently, were others, The policeman saluted more than once as cars and bicycles passed out.

Susan noticed the uniforms, and her knowledge of the Merchant Navy gave her a clue to various identities. There were other girls wearing slacks and again she appealed to the policeman.

'Transport drivers,' he told her. 'They all wear trousers.'

Then, a moment later, a big bus drew up on the opposite side of the road. 'There you are – be quick! It soon fills up.' Susan thanked him and made a dash for it, and very soon had paid the threepence demanded and was on her way to Maidenhead. She looked at her fellow travellers and thought, 'all sorts and conditions.' The only two to wear wings sat and talked quietly. Two men, one wearing the badge of Poland on his shoulders, but it was some minutes before the other moved and she saw his. He was dark-skinned and his shoulder-flash said 'Jamaica'. John Pitts had said her co-pilots – were she lucky – would be of varying nationalities. A group of girls and men sitting nearer the door, which opened at the far end, and whose conversation seemed entirely banter, she thought must be office-workers, or from the hangars. She spoke to no one, but noticed several curious glances in her own direction. The bus driver made short work of the three miles and before Susan realized it they were in Maidenhead, near the centre of the town, but, she thought, still a good distance from Skindles. She got out with the rest, but went straight round to the front of the bus to ask the driver.

'This is as far as I go,' he answered. 'An' if you want to go back you'll find me there.' He pointed to the opposite side of the road.

Susan shook her head.

'No. No, thank you. I am not going back today.' Then, remembering the one hotel Diana had pointed out, asked: 'Exactly how far is it to Skindles? I have only driven through Maidenhead.'

'It's a goodish way, but straight on.' He was not, evidently, interested as to how she got to Skindles, or elsewhere. Susan repeated her 'Thank you', turned away and walked on. Her high hopes of the morning suddenly seemed very remote. No one, except the pilot who had taken her for the test flight, had given her one grain of hope or encouragement, or apparently cared whether she succeeded or not. What she had expected she hardly knew. Susan completely forgot she was hungry. It simply did not occur to her that the wave of self-pity which, at this point, overwhelmed her, was due to nothing but the relaxing of tension of the morning and her need of food. She only knew that she felt desperately lonely and longed for Frank. The tears of self-pity were welling up when the roar of a 'plane overhead made her look up. Her tears dried as she gazed. She recognized it. The Tutor in which she had flown barely an hour ago. Only a moment or two and it had passed out of sight over the houses, but it had given her thoughts a new turn. Only an hour ago, up there, feeling untrammelled as she always felt when flying. No. She must not look back, not to mourn and regret. Memory must be her spur. But – how hard it was. This morning, for a few seconds, Frank had felt so close, and now she was lonely and hungry in a strange town.

Suddenly she shook herself free of her gloomy thoughts, called herself an idiot because the hunger could be remedied, and there must be places nearer than Skindles, and nearer the railway station, too, if she guessed rightly. She began to notice the shops, looking for a restaurant, when a voice behind her – a girl's voice with a Canadian accent and a laugh in it – said, almost as if answering her thoughts:

'Well – what's wrong with Bovril sandwiches and coffee?'

'Sounds good to me!' answered another Canadian voice. 'There's a cosy little place close by. Come along.' That was the first voice again.

Susan glanced round. Three girls of just about her own age, dressed in the smart uniform of the Canadian Nursing Service, were close behind. Susan recognized the uniform. Privately she thought it the smartest she had seen. And, as on several occasions she had been deputed to take patients from Hazeley to the Canadian Hospital at Taplow, she knew at once where they belonged. So, feigning to be attracted by something in a shop window, she stood and gazed blankly at the window until they had passed and then followed. Nothing at that moment was more desirable than Bovril sandwiches and coffee.

Half an hour later, refreshed in mind and body, Susan left the little restaurant and made her way to the station. She had been unable to secure a table within earshot of the Canadian nurses, but she had sat where she could see them. Apparently some very good joke was afoot. Susan watched and wished either of them had been one of those she had met when escorting her patients and she could have claimed acquaintance, until a sudden stampede, after an exclamation of 'Oh gosh! That bus! We'll miss it!' swept them from the room. They passed close to Susan's table. One tall girl, slender and pretty, smiled as her eyes met Susan's. Susan longed to know her.

If there had been time she would have spoken, but a hasty 'Come along, Isobel' interrupted, and they were gone. Susan sat a moment longer before she followed, thinking of them.

They looked so gay and untroubled. So attractive – their make-up so beautifully done – from top to toe their uniform perfect. Evidently the girl at the desk shared her opinion. As Susan paid her bill the girl soliloquized. Perhaps she had noticed how Susan had watched them.

'Smart, aren't they? Them Canadian nurses. Come down from Taplow-Lord Astor's place. Number Five Canadian General, they call it. In and out here a lot. The station? Oh yes—' she broke off to answer Susan's request. 'Up the next street to your right. Turn left as you go out. Sorry. Can't tell you about trains.'

That short impersonal encounter had given Susan new food for thought, and suddenly she was glad she had an appointment with her hairdresser before meeting Robert Jamieson. Grannie was so right. Small things did count. She smiled to herself. Grannie's maxims rubbed home by a trio of Canadian nurses.

Robert Jamieson arrived, as he had said, early. They met as old friends meet: friends of long standing, steadfast, proved and reliable. Susan was surprised at herself, at the deep emotion that shook her, as Robert Jamieson came towards her across the room. They had arranged as before. Robert called for her at her club.

'Rabbie! I didn't know how badly I wanted to see you.'

'I did,' and a whimsical expression crossed his face. ''Specially when I was afraid I wasn't going to have the luck.'

'When was that?' Susan caught her breath.

'About the third day in the drink. Let's forget it. Are you ready? We are going to repeat our programme,' and he tucked her hand, which he still held, under his arm.

'But,' protested Susan. 'It's *so* extravagant!'

'That is where you are wrong. *Nothing* is extravagant anymore. Besides, you are dressed for it. Thank you. That is how I always see you in that frock and the little fur coat.'

Susan made no further protest, but accepted, without comment, the best the 'Coq d'Or' had to offer, and once when Robert said:

'D'ye know, I thought I'd had the best evening of my life – but I hadn't. *This* is it,' she felt the hot tears spring to her eyes. Robert did not look like the stuff of which heroes are made, and it was difficult to make him talk of his adventures. She gathered he had had them and that it was only a fortnight since he had spent several days in an open boat. He revealed a lot when he said:

'It does me good just to hear your voice. I think I shall never forget the eternal sound of the sea. That will always be in my ears. That swish-swish – thump-thump against the side of the boat. We sang and we sang. Taught each other all the bits and pieces we knew – but it made us thirsty—'

But he smiled as she gripped his hand under the tablecloth and said, 'Oh, Rabbie!', and he quickly began to talk again of her doings.

'You haven't told me about your test flight yet. Where did you go this morning?'

'Nowhere, really. It was just a sort up and over – I mean outskirts of Maidenhead, and the instructor pointed out the house where the Queen of Holland is living. We went over her garden. It's lovely country all round—' and, again remembering, Susan's voice took a deeper tone and her eyes brightened.

'Robert! You remember – the night Felicity died?'

Robert nodded gravely and watched Susan's face.

'How I thought… I thought I *heard* – Frank?' She broke off with a questioning look, and again Robert nodded. 'Well – this morning – I thought – no, I *felt* him beside me… It was – wonderful. You do think so? It could be?' Her voice lingered on the question.

'I *do*, and I am so glad. That means you are going to succeed.'

'Oh – I hope so!'

At intervals as their meal was served Susan told her impressions. Robert did not question over much, and she completely missed all reference to her 'medical' until he asked:

'You haven't told me yet about the doctors. What sort of chaps?'

'Just – doctors!' Susan laughed. 'I'm sorry, but I did not notice very much. One was rather dark and very nice. Oh – he wore a medal ribbon – a new one to me – little stripes. I think red and blue.'

'Sounds like the George!' commented Robert. 'He must have had a lucky chance. Did you see only one?'

'No, two. I hate medical examinations. They are so intrusive.' Susan laughed teasingly. 'You all ask such impertinent questions. I was 'one hundred per cent fit' in my school report, and when Felicity was coming, and I was never ill in Malaya, so all that bores me.'

But Robert was insistent, and for two reasons. One, the paramount, his dissatisfaction and the longing to be of more use in this national emergency. The other, a new one, if he could serve with the 'ferry pilots' he might see more of Susan.

He had been bitterly disappointed to be turned down for the RAMC and the question that now arose in his mind was, did this medical service, of which he knew nothing, offer more opportunity? He put the question to Susan, who considered for a moment before she replied.

'I should think there was no comparison. What you are doing is far away a better job. You wouldn't change, would you, just to do medical examinations?'

Robert shook his head.

'No, I wouldn't. But there must be more to it than that!'

'I don't think much. The little nurse was talkative. She said there was no *real* nursing in it, and she had come into it hoping to fly on an ambulance. She was a bit disappointed, and, I think, wishing she were an applicant instead of me. Their chances of flying are so few.'

The evening sped even faster than before. Once again Robert was catching the midnight express to the north. Susan begged to be allowed to see him off, but Robert would not hear of it.

He insisted on taking her back to her club and, as before, sat with his arm round her. He also gave the same command to the taxi-man, 'Tootle round for a few minutes,' and it was only then he referred to his love.

Picking up her hand he bent over it, kissing it softly over and over again, saying in his own whimsical way:

'Being allowed to love you makes me very happy.'

'But it's such a waste,' Susan began to protest, but he interrupted her.

'No. No. That is where you are wrong. Just as you were over extravagance. These things don't matter anymore. When there is no personal future for which to plan, every glorious day has such a finish that it is incredible. It's so – so joyous and so perfect.' And to this statement Susan had no answer.

He left her as before under the shadow of the doorway. But she moved to watch the taxi out of sight. For quite a little time after it had disappeared in the darkness she still stood, watching. She could not have adequately described what she felt. Something, she knew not what, had gone, but something that blessed her remained. She could not feel that she might never see Robert Jamieson again. If it should be so, he had left something of his presence with her. She sighed softly as she entered the darkened hall of her club.

But there was another reminder.

The porter stepped forward to give her a small package.

'The gentleman left it, madam: To be given to you when you came in.'

In her room Susan opened the package. A pasteboard box containing a jewelled badge, a brooch of the Royal Merchant Navy, and a note in Robert's small, crabbed handwriting.

I want you to have something I gave you. Goodbye. Rabbie.

ELEVEN

'I QUITE UNDERSTAND. There is no need to say any more. If your heart had been in this...' Mrs Knaggs sniffed and broke off with the air of one who utterly fails to understand.

It was Susan's last day at Hazlewood House. The evening of her last day. Her year, minus the two weeks due as holiday, had ended, and only she herself knew how long it had seemed, especially these last few weeks while she waited to hear of her success, or non-success, with the ATA. Now the suspense was over; and, tucked safely away in the inner pocket of her tunic, was her 'chit' to report 'at Altmore House on May 31st at fourteen hundred hours'.

From the first she had made no secret of her intentions and had punctiliously obeyed every order concerning her departure; but that made no difference to Mrs Knaggs, and what the younger VAD members called 'Knaggie's Griselda mood' was much to the fore this evening.

Susan looked at Mrs Knaggs across the desk. She was her Commandant, and one did not reprove people twice one's age, or one's superior officer; but she wondered what would happen if she answered:

'Yes, I agree. My heart has not been in this job. But partly it is your fault. You are not a leader and you cannot inspire.'

The reflection caused a moment's pause, just sufficiently long enough to enable Mrs Knaggs to follow her remark with another, an even more tactless one.

'You cannot deny *that*.'

Susan was nettled, and without thought her answer came.

'I am not attempting to deny it. I came to say "Goodbye", but, I do *know* how very much more I want to be a ferry pilot than an ambulance driver,' and she managed a smile.

'Oh yes! I understand. Glamour! Everyone wants glamour!'

This time Susan almost bit her tongue in an effort to keep back the words she longed to speak. It was better to part harmoniously, and she was aware of a slight sympathy. One by one the more reliable workers were disappearing; some to other services and some back to their own particular units. There was no team spirit between officers and members, and it was getting harder and harder to replace people. Even herself. The van had been looked after as well as she knew how. It had never let anyone down, and had been ready for the road at all hours of the day or night, and *never* once had she, no matter how tired she had been, put it away dirty. Also Susan felt she had been a pretty efficient Assistant Quartermaster, and no job had been too menial for her to lend a hand in an emergency. Also she knew that, so far, no one had been found to take her place. Poor Mrs Knaggs. Such a square peg.

Susan's sympathy and reflections quickly dispersed her anger as Mrs Knaggs continued:

'But I must grant you one thing. You have been quite frank over your schemes. But none of you seem to realize how difficult you make it for me. Those new girls! They know nothing.'

'I do understand and I am sorry. Goodbye. Mother will be expecting me,' and at last Susan made her escape, and her thoughts were busy as she made her way upstairs to Matron's office. She had no conceit about her own work, but she had a pretty clear knowledge, after a year's experience, of the varying motives that prompted, and influenced, her fellow-workers and shirkers, as she privately called them. Some of them did scheme – and Susan was wondering why it was that Mrs Knaggs so persistently used the wrong words. She hadn't schemed – perfectly open plans were not 'schemes'.

But comfort awaited in Matron's office. Matron looked up and smiled.

'Well, Susan! Come to say goodbye? For my own sake I am sorry you are going. I shall miss you. Bless you, child. I know you will succeed, because you cannot be second-rate in anything. Now, give me a kiss and run along. The "children" are all awaiting you in the surgery. It's all right. They have my permission.'

'I wondered where they all were,' said Susan. 'Oh! One thing more. You said your mother was giving up King's Lane. Give me an address that will always find you.'

'Yes. Mother has let the house. She leaves on Lady-Day, but Grannie's and my bank will both find me. Shall I write them for you?' Susan scribbled both addresses, made her farewells and then betook herself to the surgery.

Absolute silence reigned in the little corridor that led to the surgery, only a light showed from beneath the door, but pandemonium broke out as soon as Susan appeared. Shouts of 'Sunny Sandy' and 'Here she is. At last!' greeted her, and Nurse Robinson seemed to be the ringleader in what was a little ceremony. Susan found herself pounced upon by a dozen hands. They were all there, day and night nurses, and the kitchen staff. They crowded round her, and in a moment Nurse Robinson was standing on a chair and calling for silence.

'I can't make a proper speech – but we're all going to miss you horribly. Our 'Sunny Sandy!' You've been such a brick and we want you to remember us, so we've clubbed together to buy you a memento and now we'll put it on you. Hold out your arm and shut your eyes.' With the arms of several girls round her Susan was propelled towards the speaker. 'Shut your eyes—' the command was repeated. 'Your left arm.' Laughingly Susan did as she was told, and felt her wristwatch pushed up little and something clasped round her wrist.

'There! *Now*, you can look! We didn't know *what* to get – or when we'd got it, what to put on it. It's only your name and your identity card number.'

Susan looked. A strong-looking little gold chain encircled her wrist. Her identity disc. 'How darling of them!' was her first thought. She knew that none were well off. That most of their allowances from home had been curtailed – that some even depended entirely on their Red Cross pay – which was mere pocket-money. For a moment she had no words – then one thought expressed itself.

'It's perfectly darling of you.'

'But Matron and Sister are in, too – only Knaggie and Scraggy haven't been asked, because they wouldn't let us have a party! It's too bad. Other hospitals do it. It's only a matter of saving the nicest things you have and eating it together and decorating the table.'

Although late, because of double summertime, it was still broad daylight when Susan left that evening. She had stayed and had 'second supper' with the day staff. They had insisted and would have been disappointed; and, when she had said she must telephone home, they had assured her:

'Oh! We've done that already. Your mum said it was all right. There's no party at home tonight.'

Susan was touched. She stayed and they made it a little 'occasion' – but, for fear of interference, were very quiet. 'Such a pity,' thought Susan, who had exactly the same sensation she remembered from the unauthorized 'feasts' of school days. 'These hospitals shouldn't be like this – they should have a fraternity second to none. They are all doing the same job...' But there was not time for much thought.

She had to promise to fly over one day.

'Circle round, Sandy! When you see us sitting on the roof!' and Susan promised. The roof being the favourite sunbathing and resting-spot, whenever the days were warm enough, throughout the summer.

Even when she left she had an escort across the bit of heath that cut a corner to the main road. They wheeled her bicycle and carried her belongings and clung to her arms, chattering like magpies. Very young, most of them – girls like Dorothy Verner of the taxi incident, who ordinarily would hardly be out, and most of them came from very aristocratic homes, and, while they mostly behaved as if still at school, they also fully realized the gravity of their position and the country's position. They came from homes where politics and the international situation were topics of ordinary conversation. They had fathers who were in the Army or Navy, or had been in the 1914–18 war. Most had brothers in the Services. More than one had already lost brothers, as had Susan.

At last they let her go, and when, from the bottom of the hill, Susan looked back, she could still see their waving hands and the glimmer of white aprons and caps through the dusk that was beginning to fall.

She sighed. 'Well – that is over. Another chapter. I'm twenty-four and I feel I've lived three lives already. Perhaps I'd better go and see Grannie.'

BOOK TWO

ONE

AS THE PRINTED slip in her pocket ordered her, Susan reported on Monday, May 31st, at Altmore House, Cherry Garden Lane, at fourteen hundred hours exactly.

She was, as a matter of fact, a little ahead of time, although today there had been no kindly friend of John Pitts' to bring her across country. John Pitts and his friend were both already in Canada, and John's first letters were beginning to arrive; and Susan's reflections, as her taxi made short work of the three miles from Maidenhead station, took a humorous turn. She really began to think about her journey to keep her thoughts off whatever might lie ahead. She was, she knew, very excited. It was all too wonderful. Just a year since she had arrived back from Singapore and now she was well on the way to fulfilling what had at first seemed an impossible ambition. So, switching her thoughts from the near future, she found herself smiling at the exigencies that made a twenty-mile journey take at least four hours – four and a half, to be exact – and cover at least eighty miles, as well as costing rather a lot of money.

'After all,' she thought, 'although it doesn't strike me as a war economy, perhaps it is. I am not overburdened with luggage. I could have zig-zagged between trains and buses; but one can't depend on buses these days, and here I am, on time, and that is all that matters.'

But Susan was to find that being on time seemed not to matter over much, because when she presented her printed slip to the policeman at the door he merely pointed to the hall and asked her to sit down and wait.

She glanced at the wooden bench indicated. Already two men occupied it. They sat staring into space, apparently, with their suitcases beside them. 'New recruits also', she guessed.

Both heads turned as she entered and one of the men, who wore the uniform of an RAF officer and the shoulder-flash of Poland, sprang to his feet, while the other's yellowish face creased in a friendly grin which caused his somewhat oblique black eyes almost to disappear. 'A Chinese man! How odd!' The thought flashed and for a split-second Susan was back in Malaya.

The whole thing began to take on an unreal atmosphere – 'Alice in Wonderlandish', Susan commented to herself, and after a moment or two she thought that the Mad Hatter had himself strolled down the stairs, or walked out from any one of the numerous doors which gave on 'to the hall, she would not have been in the least surprised.

'Plees – vill you seet down? You are a new student? No?' The Pole's manners were charming. His English not so good. Susan sat down and immediately the Pole placed himself between her and the Chinese. He turned a pair of large grey eyes on her, piercing as a couple of searchlights.

'You are marreed, no?' he asked. Rather taken aback by such a leading question from a complete stranger, Susan answered, a little weakly:

'Yes.'

His face fell, but a second later a happy thought caused it to brighten again.

'Your husband, he is not in England, yes?'

'Yes, he is in England.' Susan lied in self-protection. This was becoming overpowering and she wanted to take stock of her surroundings, not to talk about herself. However she was temporarily saved by the entrance of another girl, a tall blonde with strong features and an assured manner.

Again the Pole rose, took her suitcase and sat himself down beside her on the opposite bench. A moment's pause and Susan heard him ask, 'You are marreed, no?'

'Sure, Babe,' came the answer in broad American. 'Three times.'

Susan was glad that a bunch of chattering pilots came into the hall at this moment, for she desperately wanted to laugh. They burst into a room marked 'Private', the door slammed behind them, and a few seconds later gusts of laughter were shaking it on its hinges.

Susan sat and wished herself on the other side of that door. She could not, of course, hear anything that was said – only an occasional shout of 'No. *No*' came clearly. Well, with luck, she told herself, she would be one of this useful band of men and women – trained, sure of herself. Beginnings were inevitable. She loathed them. She wanted to plunge right into the middle of it all, and not have to go through the stage of not knowing and not quite belonging.

'Patience', she told herself stoically. 'They had to go through it.' But it was difficult on such a day, and time dragged. Machines roared overhead continually as they took off or landed on the airfield a few hundred yards further down the lane; pilots came and went through the hall of the big Georgian house, now taken over by ATA as its Headquarters; typewriters clicked busily behind closed doors; cars drew up at the front door, decanted their passengers and drove away again. Susan felt idle, inactive – useless.

She lit a cigarette, and immediately wished she had not, for a tall, grey-haired officer appeared out of a door marked 'Adjutant' and approached the new recruits, three more of whom had arrived by this time. She hoped he would not speak to her, for she felt it was 'not done' to smoke whilst talking to a senior officer, and she had no wish to create a bad impression at the outset.

With a typewritten list in his hand, he peered at the seven new pilots through thick-lensed horn-rimmed spectacles; then, bringing the paper to within an inch of his nose, he pushed up his glasses and blinked below them. He looked so odd, yet again so in keeping, Susan felt she must laugh.

'In this house,' she thought, 'it *would* be someone who looked odd!'

'Flight Lieutenant Zamboiski?' He began to call the roll.

'Plees, sir.' The Pole stepped forward and clicked his heels.

'Mrs Cushing?'

The blonde American half raised a strong brown hand.

'I'm here, sir,' she drawled.

'Miss Dalrymple-Ducane?'

'Yes, sir,' answered a clear English voice, and Susan turned to see a copper-haired girl, with striking grey eyes, behind her. She was already dressed in the navy-blue uniform of the ATA, but wore no rank stripes on her shoulder, nor wings on her jacket. For a fleeting moment their eyes met, then Susan heard her own name called.

'Mrs Sandyman?'

'Yes, sir,' she said, and in her turn was uncomfortably aware of six pairs of eyes focused upon her. 'Flight Lieutenant Cherry?' Another officer in RAF uniform stepped forward and saluted smartly. 'Sir,' was all he said.

'Mr Reid?'

'Here, sir.' The answer came from a dark-haired young man, who Susan judged to be in his early thirties. He wore glasses and had a slight stoop, and in the two word she spoke she could hear all the burns of the Highlands.

'Mr Fang?'

The voice of the young Chinese was quiet and cultured.

'I am here, sir,' he said, and was apparently unaware of the curious glances of the other recruits.

The Adjutant became brisk.

'The bus is waiting outside to take you over to Thame. The School Adjutant and the Billeting Officer will tell you what to do when you arrive. Thank you.' He disappeared into his office, and the seven embryonic ferry pilots were left staring at each other like children at their first party.

* * *

In the bus Susan found herself sitting next to the copper-haired girl, and soon noticed that she had no suitcase.

'What about your luggage?' she prompted, thinking that it might have been left in the hall.

'My luggage? Oh! I got one of the boys to take all my stuff over to Thame and dump it with the Adj. on Saturday. He was flying an Anson over, so I thought he might save me some arm-ache.'

Susan wondered how this girl knew her way around so well, and how she dared to dump her luggage on an unknown adjutant at an unknown airfield, and feel it safe for a weekend. Such casual confidence was enviable.

The girl settled herself more comfortably, and then smiled as she asked: 'What is your name? I couldn't hear a word that old buffer said just now.'

'Susan. Susan Sandyman. What's yours?'

'It's rather unfortunate really – especially over the tannoy.' Tannoy! thought Susan. Thanks to John Pitts she knew it to be the airfield loud-speaker. 'Amanda Dalrymple-Ducane! But don't attempt the whole thing – *ever*. It's too awful. Just call me Mandy.' She smiled again, and Susan thought she had never seen anyone with such beautiful eyes, nor yet anyone who could wear such silky hair so straight and get away with it. She was about to ask her why she was already in uniform when the driver started up the bus, and the occupants were forced into a mental coma, for the noise, the jolting and the heat defied thought or speech.

However, several times during the hour's drive through the hilly, wooded country between White Waltham and Thame the radiator boiled over and the old bus had to be given a rest, so before long Susan's question was answered. She also discovered that for the last year Mandy had been working on the ground staff in Central Ferry Control at Andover, and so already knew most of the pilots by name, while many of the Operations Officers were firm telephone friends.

'Took me a year to wangle my way over to the flying side,' she told Susan. 'I thought I never should get out of that damn' Control Room. I only hope to goodness I make the grade now!'

Susan's heart sank.

'Why?' she asked. 'Do they fail many pupils?'

'God, yes! About fifty per cent, I believe.'

Susan did not speak; she was watching a Spitfire racing across the cloudless sky. John Pitts had not depressed her with this information.

'Please, God, let me pass,' she prayed.

The bus started up again and soon swung off the main Oxford road to the right.

'Not far now,' Mandy said. 'Only about nine miles. I had a look at the map. The airfield isn't at Thame at all. It's in a village called Haddenham, about three miles beyond.'

Susan decided that she liked Mandy, liked her direct, almost abrupt, way of talking. And the fact that her beauty had not spoilt her. There was a certain tomboyish confidence about her that Susan found as infectious as it was unexpected.

The bus rattled on through the lazy summer's afternoon, leaving deep tracks in the melting tar of the road's surface. Mandy's map reading proved correct, for after driving down Thame High Street and past its famous Spread Eagle Inn they turned off down a side road and bumped out into the open country once again, and for the next ten minutes the bus continued to stay and rattle along what at times seemed to be little more than a lane.

Suddenly Mandy spoke again, this time a little excitedly.

'Look! There it is!'

Susan hastily turned her head. She had been looking in the opposite direction. Over the hedge indicated by Mandy she could just see a row of propeller tips, while beyond stretched a big grass airfield. A current of excitement swept through her as she stood up to see better. Huts and blisters hangars at the far side came into view. She stared speechless. So she had arrived at last. Memories of the past year fell away almost as if they had never been. This, she felt, *was* her arrival in England. This was where she would again pick up the threads of her own life.

Suddenly she realized something was odd. This was no hive of industry. Not a soul in sight! The whole place seemed deserted.

'Why? What has happened? Where is everybody? Shouldn't there be people about?' Her puzzled eyes met Mandy's.

'School's long weekend,' Mandy explained briefly. 'Friday night till Tuesday morning every three weeks. Not bad! They'll all be back at the streak tomorrow. Give us a chance to settle in.'

Susan was thankful that Mandy knew some of the ropes; it was going to make things much easier, and she felt instinctively that Mandy would not mind how many, or how ridiculous, were the questions she asked.

'The Training Pool works differently, of course,' Mandy continued. 'They have three days every fortnight in the summer, and two in the winter. But they are probably all out ferrying still. I heard there was a general flap on at White Waltham this morning.'

As the bus drew up at the Guard Room gate a twin-engined

machine came in low over the hedge and landed softly as a feather half-way down the field.

'That's an Anson, one of the taxi machines, I expect,' Mandy said.

'Been on the milk round.'

Susan laughed. 'And what, may I ask, is the "milk round"?'

'Well,' Mandy began, 'to start at the beginning, every night, at Central Ferry Control, poor suckers like myself have to work out a plan of campaign for each Ferry Pool for the following day, and I may tell you there are fifteen Ferry Pools in the British Isles!' she added.

'We allot the aircraft to each Pool, then ring the programme through to their Night Duty Officers, who copy it down – sometimes incorrectly – and then leave the headache for the Operations Officer to cope with next morning.' She paused.

'But where does the milk round come in?' Susan persisted.

'Patience – patience,' said Mandy with mock severity. The guard at the airfield gate had by now passed the bus through and they were driving slowly round the perimeter track. Mandy was watching the pilots pile out of the Anson which was ticking over outside some long low huts.

'There's old Fritz,' she said, pointing to a short, tubby man with an incredible shock of red hair. 'Wizard type. Nutty as a fruit cake – you'll love him.'

Susan's mind was reeling. Milk rounds? Wizard types? Fruit cake? It was crazy and she wished that Mandy would explain the whole thing to her in words of one syllable. She nudged Mandy gently.

'Go on,' she urged. 'What happens then?'

'Oh yes!' Mandy had a faraway look in her eyes. 'The milk round.'

'Yes,' Susan prompted her, afraid lest she should strike off at another tangent before the whole story was told.

'Well, then the Operations Officer has to allot the aircraft to the pilots who can fly those particular types, allot the pilots to different taxi 'planes, and taxi pilots, who drop them at the airfields where the machines are awaiting collection. Later in the day the old taxis stooge round and pick up the pilots when they have delivered their goods. Got it?'

'Um.' Susan nodded. She was still very puzzled and her mind seemed to contain one large question mark, but by this time the bus had drawn up outside the group of hutments, long wooden buildings – the 'School', Susan supposed – and they were all getting out.

She was right. The School Adjutant was waiting for them. He introduced himself as Flight Captain Markham. He was round and Falstaffian, and his bushy white eyebrows jutted out alarmingly over a pair of kindly blue eyes, his thumbs were tucked into the belt of his straining uniform, and his little hands rested comfortably on his stomach. Susan's thoughts flashed back to Altmore. This surely was 'Tweedledee'.

On learning Mandy's name he tried to look severe, failed completely, and ended by laughing fatly.

'So it's your luggage that has been cluttering up my office since Saturday, is it? You artful little minx!'

'Yes, sir.' Mandy smiled disarmingly. 'I knew you would not mind.'

The Adjutant did not have time to comment, for at this moment the driver of the bus came up to ask if he were wanted any more, as there were some engineers over at the Ferry Pool waiting to be taken back to White Waltham.

'No, you can go now.' The driver saluted and left, and the Adjutant half turned and called over his shoulder to a girl driver who was standing by with a camouflaged shooting brake. Susan noticed that she wore exactly the same uniform as the pilots, except that she sported no wings and no rank stripes. 'Take these pilots down to the Billeting Office. I think they can all fit in at a pinch.' Then, turning back to the new recruits, he continued: 'You will be. shown your billets and the canteen. Report here, to my office, at nine o'clock tomorrow morning. And your luggage, young lady' – he added, looking at Mandy – 'has already been sent down to your billet, which is a deal more than you deserve.'

'Thank you, sir.' Mandy's eyes were downcast in mock repentance.

* * *

'Quite a reasonable collection this time,' thought Captain Markham, as he went back to his office. 'Hope they do better than the last lot!'

Of the last batch of recruits only two out of ten had soloed, the other eight having failed to make the grade in the maximum twelve hours allowed.

* * *

Much the same thought ran through the mind of First Officer Bartlet when, a few moments later, the same 'collection' came into the Billeting Office.

'You four,' he addressed the men, 'are in Number Two site. The driver will take you down, and on the way ask her to show you the canteen.'

He opened a ledger on the desk in front of him. 'Now will you sign here, please, for the keys, and then you can be off. Five shillings a week will be automatically deducted from your pay for the use of your rooms, and there is a man in charge of the huts who will clean them for you.'

The Pole, the young Chinese, the Scot and Flight Lieutenant Cherry all signed their names and were given keys. As they went out to the car the Flight Lieutenant looked at Susan.

'So long, girls,' he said cheerfully. 'See you later!'

'Now—' the Billeting Officer turned to another page. 'The girls!'

When they, too, had signed and been given keys he offered to run them down in his own car.

'I am just shutting up shop for the day and it really is quite a step to Hopefield House. I can drop you first, Mrs Cushing, as you are in Yelsom House, and that is at this end of the village.'

'Thanks,' said the American girl. 'Suits me.'

As they came out of the Billeting Office an ancient sports car rattled past with two pilots in the dark blue uniform, a man driving and a girl beside him.

'Are we allowed cars?' asked Susan hopefully.

'Not until you are out of the School, and then only for billeting purposes, of course. Have either of you girls got bikes? Unfortunately it's quite a step to Hopefield House, but we simply couldn't find anything nearer the airfield.' He sighed. 'This billeting question certainly has been a headache!'

Mandy answered that she had a bicycle at home, which she could bring back after her next weekend, and Susan echoed that she could do likewise.

At the main gate the policeman saluted, and a few hundred yards down the road they pulled up outside a modern red-brick villa.

'This is Yelsom House. You are in Room Three, Mrs Cushing. There is a housekeeper, who will be sleeping in tonight, so you won't be alone, and anyone in the village will tell you where the canteen is. You can get a meal until eight o'clock.'

'OK, sir, and thanks for the buggy ride.' She climbed out, heaving a well-filled grip after her.

First Officer Bartlet smiled. He was used to the informal language of the Americans, for there were quite a number of them in this cosmopolitan corps.

'That's all right. And if there is anything you want to know in the billeting line you know where to find me.'

They drove on through the village and turned into its square, with its white-thatched cottages and warm Elizabethan brick houses, rubbing shoulders with an occasional Victorian villa. Old-fashioned and lovely, but there seemed to be only two tiny shops, and Susan realized that she would be completely cut off from what is termed, rightly or wrongly, civilization. However, she told herself that as long as she was allowed to fly she did not care where she lived – did not care if she had to sleep on a straw mattress in a bare room.

Five minutes later she discovered that this was exactly what she was going to do!

Hopefield House was a rambling old Georgian building set in an overgrown garden behind a high mellow wall. Once it may have had its attractions; undoubtedly an atmosphere of gracious living still lingered there, but it had long since lost any appearance of comfort. The floors were covered with shiny, brown linoleum, there were no pictures, no rugs, no welcoming flowers now in the large rooms, which were empty except for the bare necessities in the way of furniture. Long blackout curtains flanked the tall windows, and with the tropical Sun still warm in her memory, Susan noticed with a shiver that there was no central heating.

'Well, here you are,' grinned their escort. 'Not exactly a luxury hotel, but it's only five bob a week out of the old pay packet, and there are only three of you in your room. Let me see,' he said, referring to a list in his hand, 'Number Seven, I think. Yes – that's it. Can you manage?' He nodded questioningly at Susan's suitcase.

'Oh yes, and thank you.'

'All right. So long.'

Mandy and Susan watched him out of sight, and then each turned to the other and laughed before they entered the house.

'It's all so – so comical – so different to what I expected,' said Susan.

'Let's explore,' said Mandy. 'There seems no one about.'

Upstairs and downstairs they wandered from room to room.

'Well, at least we only have three beds and all the others have four or five! I can't bear a mass of bods in the same room.' Mandy's voice was consoling. 'I wonder who the third is?'

The evening sun was streaming in through the two long windows, and, although the room merely contained three narrow beds, three deal chests of drawers and one built-in cupboard, it was not in any way depressing.

Mandy flung herself on a bed, only to leap up again as suddenly as if she had sat on a pin.

'Heavens!' she gasped. 'Feel that!'

Susan tried another and had to admit that it was harder than she had imagined any bed could be. Mandy started to pull hers to pieces.

'Look!' she said. 'No springs – Army blankets like boards – *and* biscuits! I ask you!'

Susan had never heard of a biscuit mattress before, and was amazed by the three straw-filled objects on which she was, apparently, going to sleep for the next few months.

Mandy looked at her watch.

'Only half past six, but I'm famished!' she said. 'What about finding this canteen?'

By the time they did find it both girls quite understood the Billeting Officer's suggestion of bicycles, for it was almost a mile from Hopefield House.

At this hour the long Army hut, with its rows of linoleum-topped tables, was almost empty, with the exception of a few mechanics, who apparently also shared the Pupil Pilots' Mess.

Susan discovered from one of the maids serving behind the long hot plate that there was another mess-hut next door which belonged to the Ferry Pilots from the Pool, and that there they had tablecloths, glasses instead of tin mugs, and other such refinements. It was slowly dawning on Susan that there was little glamour about the life of a pupil pilot, and as they were finishing their meal Mandy put words to her thoughts.

'I can see that they don't mean us to become soft with luxury!' she said. 'What do you say to a drink, or do you think a mere pupil is denied the pleasure of a quiet noggin? I saw a pleasant-looking spot just along the square.'

'I don't see why not; after all, we're not officially on duty until tomorrow,' Susan pointed out.

As Mandy had surmised, the 'Crown' was a pleasant spot: clean and whitewashed outside, cool and fresh within. Little did Susan dream that evening of the many hours she would spend in that cosy bar-parlour in the future, in friendly discussion or hot argument with other pupils, or listening to and learning from older and wiser pilots after the day's work. She did not know how restless she would become, or how difficult pilots find it to settle down of an evening and concentrate on book or hobby, and how much more likely they are to forgather in just such a cheerful den as the parlour of the 'Crown'.

'What's yours?' Mandy asked.

Susan thought a moment. 'Beer, I think. I'm a dry as a desert.'

The landlord, later to be known as 'Bert', looked at the two girls with undisguised interest.

'New pilots?' he asked, having taken their order.

'Correct!' Mandy admitted. 'How did you guess?'

He put his shirt-sleeve to his damp brow. 'Easy,' he said. 'I've seen 'em come and I've seen 'em go, and I can tell 'em a blooming mile off. Now you look at me—'

'Evening, Bert!' The landlord's speech was interrupted by the arrival of a tall, bearded ATA pilot.

'Shooting a line as usual?'

'Evening, old man!' Bert greeted him. Evidently, Susan thought, they knew each other well.

'I was just telling these two little ladies that I know a pilot when I see one.'

The bearded man smiled at them. 'Don't take any notice of Bert,' he warned them. 'He's a shocking type.'

Bert grinned delightedly, obviously taking this as a huge compliment. 'What are you having ?' he asked.

'Six pints of bitter' – then, as Bert's eyes opened wide in protest – 'five others just coming.'

They had arrived before Bert had drawn the pints – five hot and exhausted-looking pilots.

Susan looked at them with great interest, wondering who they were, where they had been that day, and what machines they had been flying. She longed to ask, but her eyes caught a poster on the wall warning her that 'Careless talk costs lives', and she refrained.

One of them, a tiny, dark girl with close-cut curly hair, asked Mandy how she came to be in uniform already, and on learning that she had been at the Central Ferry Control, plied her with questions about the work other Pools were doing.

'Nobody ever tells the poor pilots anything,' she complained. 'We just do the work.' Mandy laughed. 'They are not exactly idle at Ferry Control,' was her comeback.

Gradually Susan and Mandy were drawn into the general conversation, and by the time she attacked her third half pint Susan knew a little more about the workings of a Ferry Pool, and a lot less about how to fly an aeroplane. She became quite dizzy, listening to discussions on booster pumps and feathering, single engine approaches and the merits of various RAF messes, prospects of summer leave and brake pressures.

At half past nine the bearded pilot said he must be off as he had a date at Thame.

'Can I give you two girls a lift?' he offered. 'I pass the "Cloister".'

Susan gathered that this was the name given to Hopefield House owing to the fact that no male was allowed to pass the threshold. She and Mandy accepted the lift gladly, as they were both feeling weary.

However, when Susan finally got into bed, she knew she was tired but could not sleep, and lay awake for a long time thinking. In any case she doubted if she would ever be able to sleep in this narrow cot with no springs and board-like bedclothes. Mandy, too, was obviously finding sleep difficult to achieve, for Susan heard her tossing and sighing many times.

High in the clear night sky some bombers throbbed over, and Susan could see their navigation lights crawling across the window-pane.

'God be with you,' she said softly under her breath, and suddenly wished fiercely that she too were a man. Consolation came, however, with the thought that in the none too distant future she might be flying those very machines, helping in some small way those same heroic men; and by the time the last bomber had crossed the Chilterns into the silver valley of the Thames, Susan slept.

TWO

THE FOLLOWING MORNING Susan and Mandy reported to the Adjutant at nine o'clock, and together with the other recruits, gave him details of their home addresses, next of kin and religion. They were told that their first day would be spent in collecting flying equipment and maps, and that they would not actually start their flying tuition until the following day. 'When,' continued the Adjutant cheerily, 'you must be ready with your kit outside the canteen at eight thirty sharp. The bus will be waiting to take you over to Barton – that's where you do the first part of your training. In the same way you will be brought back at about seven thirty every evening.'

They were then presented with a list of equipment which they must draw, that day, from the stores, and finally the key of a locker in which to keep it, for the time being.

Susan looked at the list in amazement. What was a 'CDC' – and what might 'One Sidcot, inner', look like?

She appealed to Mandy, but Mandy's answer was a negative shake of her head, and a practical suggestion.

'I haven't a clue. Let's go and have a coffee in the snack bar before we tackle it. If we go to the stores now, in the ugly rush, we shall only have to wait hours.'

This sounded logical enough to Susan, and it was here in the little wooden hut on the south side of the airfield, between the School buildings and the Ferry Pool, that Susan became further initiated into the ways of Ferry Pool Pilots.

Several pilots from the Pool, who had no machines to deliver until later in the day, and a few Ground Instructors, whose lectures had not yet started, were also wandering in and out of the snack bar, and each in turn, while waiting at the serving counter, looked over his shoulder at the new arrivals.

They certainly made a striking couple. Susan with her fair curly hair and her clear blue-grey eyes set off by the egg-brown tan of her skin, and Mandy with her burnished copper head, violet eyes and well-bred beauty. There was something of the gloss and grace of a young racehorse about Mandy which made it impossible for her to pass unnoticed.

Yet she seemed completely unaware of the stir she caused.

One of the younger pilots – a rosy-cheeked boy, whom they had met the previous evening, brought his coffee over and joined them at their table. Then an instructor followed and, with his eyes wandering from Mandy to Susan and back again, said:

'Hullo, George. How's it going?'

'Fine, thank you, sir,' and the colour rose in the boy's cheeks and flushed his forehead. 'Odd,' he commented when the instructor had left them, 'that chap hasn't spoken a word to me since I left the School!'

Suddenly Susan felt very old. It was obvious that the boy, like Mandy, did not yet know the score between man and woman. Perhaps, she thought, it was because for the last three years, when normally they would have been completing their education, they had not been 'brought up', but literally 'forced up' by circumstances, and now, although they both possessed the assurance of youth, yet they lacked the insight which enables one to judge the motives of others.

On the way back from the snack bar to the equipment stores Susan asked Mandy how old she was.

'Nineteen. Quite an old hag, really!'

Susan laughed. 'I'm just twenty-five, so I suppose you would say I have had it!'

'Well, it *is* getting on!' Mandy's smile flashed. 'Not that you look twenty-five,' she added kindly. 'By the way, where is your husband?' and a moment later, after Susan's brief explanation, she was apologizing.

'I *am* sorry, Sue. I am a fool to have asked. Those sort of questions are silly nowadays.'

'That's OK. Don't worry. I should have told you sooner or later. Now,' and abruptly Susan changed the subject, 'where are these stores?'

A few enquiries sent them in the right direction, and they found the stores tucked away at the back of some hangars, a tin-roofed building with a portly sergeant in charge. Behind the wooden counter he looked to Susan far more likely to be serving groceries than helmets, goggles and flying clothing. He was, however, very efficient, and within half an hour had fitted the girls up with leather gauntlets and their silk linings, helmets, waterproof Sidcot suits and thick quilted 'inners', which Susan thought must be converted eiderdowns. Then there was a large white canvas kit-bag with a blue line round it, some navigation instruments, the use of which were an added bewilderment, a pair of goggles, and 'One pair glasses anti-glare, air-crew for the use of'.

'Rather like learning German,' laughed Mandy. 'None of the words the right way round!' Lastly the sergeant issued each of them with a pair of lovely big flying boots, brown suede outside, rubber-soled and fur-lined.

'Not permitted to be worn before October the first,' he added, as if he were reading out a proclamation.

'Aren't they heavenly?' remarked Susan. 'Roll on October!' The sergeant and his corporal assistant helped the girls stow their kit in the kit-bags, but Susan thought it could not possibly all fit in, and said so.

'Go on!' said the sergeant. 'That's nothing; there's more to come in there yet. You'll be drawing your maps next.' He was right, for as Susan plonked her kit-bag in her locker she heard the tannoy in the pupils' rest-room confirm it.

'Attention, please,' a man's voice commanded. 'Will all new pupils report to the Maps and Signals Office at Number Five Ferry Pool immediately, where they will be issued with maps. Thank you.'

There was a loud click as the instrument was switched off; the voice stopped, yet Susan felt that an invisible pair of eyes still watched her, and she recaptured the sensation of her schooldays, of being under observation, a mere pupil.

By now the sun was hot in the flawless June sky, the School was in full swing and a variety of training machines were in the air. It was so difficult not to stand still, just to watch. Round and round they flew, practising the endless circuits and bumps, circuits and bumps. Hawker Harts, Harvards, Miles Magisters, and with a quickening pulse Susan saw a Spitfire taxi out to the take-off.

'Do we fly Spits in the School?' she asked eagerly.

'Yes, eventually, but it takes months to reach that stage. That comes at the end of Class Two.'

'What do you mean by Class Two?' Mandy seemed to know so much, while Susan's mind was a turmoil of newly learned facts, new words, new names and faces. She knew that she must learn all she could as quickly as possible; must get an idea of the pattern her life was to follow. Mandy was certainly at an enormous advantage knowing the 'form', as she called it, and as she was willing to impart her knowledge Susan felt herself more than willing to learn. Now Mandy explained to her that pilots were divided into six classes. Those qualified to fly light aircraft, such as Moths, and Magisters, Harts or the little taxi-craft called Fairchilds, were in Class One.

'When we are ready to ferry this small stuff we shall be seconded to another Pool for a month or so, maybe two, then we shall, I hope, come back here to convert on to Class Two types. That includes all the single-engined fighters – we train on Harvards for that.' She pointed out a yellow trainer that was just landing. 'One of those.'

Susan watched while the machine touched down, bounced, swung slightly and finally came to rest.

'Pretty ropey!' commented Mandy laconically, and continued with her explanation. 'Just before we are checked out on Class Two – should we ever reach those dizzy heights, that is – we do a couple of hours in a Spit, and then they pack us off to the Pool here to do some real ferrying. They even raise our pay,' she added gaily, 'and make us Third Officers. They only keep us a week or two and then post us out into the big wide world to a pukka Ferry Pool.'

'Oh God!' – and Susan, for the first time, copied Mandy's way of speaking. 'Don't tell me any more today! My brain is reeling and I shall only forget.'

Mandy laughed. 'You'll soon get the hang of it. Now for those maps.'

They had reached the wooden buildings which belonged to Number Five Training Pool, and which also housed the Station Met Office and the Maps and Signals Office.

Susan looked round in amazement at the maps covering the walls; they seemed to her to be one mass of red chalk-marks, flags, and different coloured pinheads. She was about to ask Mandy the reason for this when the five other new pilots came in, followed by the officer in charge of the section.

'Well, now that you are all here,' he began, 'and before I issue you with your maps, I might as well explain the significance of this place.' He sat himself informally on a high wooden stool. 'The information in this office is exactly the same as you will find at any other Ferry Pool, so if you know your way about here you know all the others too. But remember,' he impressed on them, 'this information changes from day to day, and before you ferry a machine, or start off on a cross-country flight, it is up to you.to come and find out what the latest 'gen' on that particular route is. For instance' – and he pointed to a red circle on a map on the wall – 'that airfield, which is Hawker's factory at Langley, is surrounded by barrage balloons, and there is a different route in and out of it every day, so that, before you land there, you must come and find out which plan is in use; then we ring the factory for you, tell them what time you are coming, and they haul down the necessary balloon to allow you to land. And that is only one of hundreds of hazards to the unwary pilot at the moment; but we are here to help you, and to help you deliver the machines safely. Take full advantage of us and you will have a much better chance of surviving. This afternoon you will be marking on your own sets of maps the permanent barrages, firing ranges and other prohibited flying areas which are scattered about the country, but that is not enough! There are such things as nomad balloons, whose positions change from day to day, airfields with temporarily unserviceable runways, or which in winter become waterlogged and unsafe. New airfields open daily, others are closed, and these things must be continually watched and checked on. It is up to you!'

He paused to allow his words to sink in. 'And now for work.'

Some minutes later Susan found herself with an armful of twenty-eight maps covering the British Isles, one set of which was on a small scale, the other on a much larger scale and suitable for reading when cruising at higher speeds.

'One more thing before you go, and this is very important. These maps are marked with highly secret information, so that should you lose one you must report the fact immediately. There are many people in this country at present who would give a great deal to get hold of them, so look after them well.'

'What a lot of hot air!' said a voice behind Susan as they filed out, and she turned to see Flight Lieutenant John Cherry at her heels.

'Worse than the RAF – if that's possible!'

He attached himself to Susan for the rest of that day. She found him sitting next to her in the lecture room in the afternoon when they marked their maps, and he sat himself down with Mandy and herself in the canteen at supper, then insisted that they both have a drink at the 'Crown' with him afterwards. He sat on the arm of Susan's chair.

'Well, honey,' he said suddenly, 'and where are you going to next weekend?'

'Home, of course,' she answered. 'Hampshire.'

John's pale blue eyes, eyes that Susan thought a trifle too close together for her liking, widened in surprise. His tone was bantering.

'Why "of course"? Does mother's little girl always go home for her weekends?'

'Yes,' she repeated shortly. 'Of course.'

Susan did not mean to be rude, but there was something about John Cherry's attitude that was irritating and slightly possessive. However, her coolness seemed to pass him by.

'Well, what about changing the routine?' he suggested. 'I'm not living in those filthy Nissen huts. I've got the CO's permission to live out at Aston Clinton at my brother's place. Fixed the Adj. for petrol, too, so how about coming out there next weekend?'

Susan drained her glass before answering.

'Thanks very much for the invitation,' she said, 'but I'm afraid it can't be done. And now, if we are flying tomorrow, I think I'm for bed.'

On the way back through the quiet village streets Mandy remarked:

'That chap loves himself rather a lot, doesn't he? Wonder why he is out of the RAF?'

'Something wrong with his eyes, he said.'

Mandy thought, 'Strange he doesn't wear glasses,' and in the same moment told herself 'not to be such a bitch'.

'He certainly is very good-looking,' she conceded, 'but, boy, does he know it!'

Susan made no comment; instead she looked at the sky. 'I'm longing to get over to Barton and start flying,' she said. 'Hope this weather holds!'

It did. The following day dawned fresh and clear, a perfect June morning.

Almost before Susan opened her eyes she was conscious of a feeling of excitement, and this feeling had not grown less when, a couple of hours later, the bus carrying the twenty-five ATA pupil pilots jolted down the last long hill from Luton into the little village of Barton-in-the-Clay.

Having passed through the main street, the bus unexpectedly turned into a narrow, high-hedged lane, passed a farm, rounded a sharp corner and there, suddenly, Susan saw the tiny grass airfield before her.

Immediately she fell in love with it, and it seemed to her that it possessed an atmosphere of friendliness foreign to Thame. This sensation grew on her, and, as the day progressed, became a certainty. Even the feeling she had had of being back at school dropped away, and Susan felt as if she were once more a member of a private flying club.

The whole place consisted only of one large public rest-room, which also served as a dining-room and lecture-room, one for the instructors, a locker-room, cloakrooms, a kitchen and a small room at the end of the building for the nurse, who was always on duty when flying was in progress. There was also a tiny office marked 'CO's office', and an even smaller cubbyhole where the parachutes were kept.

That was all. As soon as they were inside, the Adjutant, First Officer Ellis, called the new pupils into the CO's office, allotted them each a locker and gave them a key.

'Now, if you wait in the rest-room your instructor will come and find you in due course,' he said. He was tall and fair, a man of few words, but what he did say was always to the point.

'Pleasant type,' murmured Mandy, as they left the room.

To Mandy, who at Ferry Control had lived in the middle of an RAF Group, everyone was a 'type', and Susan already found she was using the expression herself. She only hoped that she would pick up the knowledge that mattered as easily.

In the rest-room John Cherry came up to her. 'Seems a nice little dump,' he said, then, passing her the *Daily Express* from table, 'Seen the paper today?'

Susan sat down. 'Thanks,' she said. The paper remained unopened in her hand. John went on talking to her, but Susan did not hear what he said, for she was far too intrigued with her surroundings.

Out of the window she could see the little Magisters, most of them dispersed round the field, some of them parked under the opened tin blister hangars near the mechanic's hut. A few fields beyond a beechcrowned hill rose sharply, and Susan guessed correctly that this must be the far end of the Chilterns; and she remembered John Pitts' description, 'The wood on the top'. Her attention was brought sharply back into the rest-room by a sudden lull in the buzz of conversation.

The door into the Instructor's Room had opened, and several men in dark blue uniform came in. They were not all as young as Susan had expected, and some of them, she thought, looked old enough to have fought in the last war, but their eyes were keen and their faces deeply tanned by many hours' flying in an open machine.

Quickly they singled out their own pupils, told them what times they would be flying, the numbers of their machines, and to those who were going solo what exercises to practise, or which cross-country route to take. As the pupils dispersed, some to don their flying kit, others to sit in the sun and wait their turn to go up, Susan caught snatches of their conversation.

'Where are you going, Tom?'

'Bedford, and then—'

'Me? Oh, aerobatics in the Tiger—'

'Thame for the post again, Hill—'

'God It's my check with Timber—'.

Until only the new pupils were left in the room.

Three instructors came over to them. One, a fair, slight man, wearing RAF uniform and a long, wispy moustache, spoke to John. 'Are you S. Sandyman?' he asked.

'No,' and observing the other's rank to be the same as his own, John Cherry purposely omitted the 'sir'. 'This is Mrs Sandyman.' He turned to Susan.

'You are to be my pupil, Mrs Sandyman,' said the instructor. 'And now, which of you is G. Reid?'

Susan pointed him out, and then, without wasting time, her future instructor introduced himself as Flight Lieutenant Adamson, announced that he would not be able to take her up until after lunch, as he was busy with another pupil, and told her to be ready by two o'clock.

'In the meanwhile,' he said, 'I have told another of my pupils to show you round a Magister. Max Roskoff is his name – you can't miss him – he is the tall, dark chap with glasses. Ask him any questions you like, then read this and learn it.' He handed her a printed sheet headed 'Magister Type Technical'.

'And you, Reid,' he said, addressing his other pupil, 'be ready at three o'clock. You will see me land with Mrs Sandyman in Number Six.'

'Yes sir.'

Susan and Gavin Reid went out together to find Roskoff, who had already settled himself outside with a book in the sun.

'OK,' he said, when they approached him. 'No peace for the wicked, I suppose, so let's do it now and get it over.'

He took them to a machine which was not in use at the moment, and for the next half hour showed them the ins and outs of the Magister. Good-naturedly he answered all their questions, and Susan was glad to find the little Miles trainer much the same type of machine as that in which she had first learnt to fly.

'You'll like Flight Lieutenant Adamson,' Max said, as they walked back to the hut. 'He's a good scout. He was instructing with the RAF until recently, and has only been lent to the ATA. By the way,' he advised, 'I should learn that Type Technical thoroughly – it's worth it.'

Susan took his advice and went back to the rest-room, where her attention would not be distracted, and by twelve o'clock she had it by heart.

Going out into the sun she found Mandy surrounded by three men, still struggling with it.

'Hullo, Sue!' she said, looking up. 'Do you know this horror yet?'

'Just about. Do you?'

'No. I'm a fool at learning things like this. And these three types aren't helping a bit!' She indicated the young men, who took it as a huge joke.

'It's about lunchtime,' said one, 'and as I'm going up at one thirty, I want mine early. What about you?' He looked at Mandy as he spoke.

'OK. Come on, Sue,' and they all went in to lunch together. Although the food was good, Susan could not eat very much; the day was too hot and she was too excited.

By a quarter to two she was ready, helmet on, parachute collected, and every time the Instructor's Room door opened she looked up expectantly.

It was then that she saw the CO, Captain Twigg, for the first time, whom she had heard referred to all the morning as 'Timber', when, for about the sixth time, she looked up as the Instructor's Room door opened, and her eyes met a pair as blue as her own.

He was a thick-set man, with iron-grey hair, a determined chin and a network of small lines running round the corners of his eyes – lines that came from laughter. For a moment he looked straight at Susan and she knew immediately that here was a man who would be utterly fair, and she also knew that it was he who was responsible for the friendly atmosphere which had struck her so forcibly all the morning.

He turned and spoke to a pupil near the door, and at the same moment Flight Lieutenant Adamson came into the room.

For Susan the next hour passed all too quickly, and because she was completely absorbed in what she was doing she was happier than she had been since the day she had parted from Frank.

On learning that she had already done fifty hours' flying, and finding that what she had learnt had not been forgotten, her instructor took her quickly through the most elementary exercises such as taxiing, straight and level flight, shallow turns and climbing turns, then, landing the machine himself, even let her try to 'take-off'.

When they had landed for the last time and she got out to let Gavin take her place, Flight Lieutenant Adamson shouted to her above the noise of the engine: 'That's not too bad, Mrs Sandyman. I'll have a chat with you later.'

Instructors, Susan was to learn, rarely use superlatives in their praise.

For the rest of that day Susan found her thoughts continually with Frank and she wished most desperately that he could be with her. She felt closer to him than she had for sometime, and supposed it was because the last time she had flown had been with him. And this sensation of 'closeness' continued during the next two days, but it was so precious she could not have mentioned it to anyone, not even Mandy, although she found herself longing to tell Grannie.

She progressed steadily and, because Max Roskoff was away with a bad attack of hay fever, her instructor was able to devote more time to his new pupils.

On the second day she quickly re-mastered steep turns and managed some passable forced landings, so that, by the Friday, Flight Lieutenant. Adamson was able to spend two hours with her practising nothing but take-offs, circuits and landings. At first she found the ATA circuit difficult to remember, for it was very different from the one she had been taught in Australia, designed, as it was, not only for light aircraft, but for ferrying the most advanced and complicated types. However, by the Friday evening Susan had it well under control, and her last three landings had been safe, if not yet polished.

The weather continued fine and clear, and early on Saturday morning her instructor again took Susan up for an hour of concentrated landings and take-offs. Afterwards he called her aside.

'I have told Captain Twigg that you are ready for your check,' he said. 'If he has time he will take you this afternoon. Now remember – open up slowly and you won't swing; and when you are landing none of that pump-handling down to which you seem rather attached!

'Let her float a little, wait for the stall, then bring the stick right back *and*' – he emphasized his last words – 'keep it there!'

'Yes, sir,' said Susan doubtfully. She was taken completely by surprise, for she had not thought she would have her solo check until the following week. As yet it was only John Cherry and Flight Lieutenant Zamboiski who had soloed, for they both already had several hundred hours' flying in their log books.

The hours dragged by and Susan sat in a fever of impatience, first out in the sun, then in the rest-room, then back again outside. She saw Captain *Twigg* take off with Max, now recovered from his hay fever, for his final cross-country check out from Barton, and although they were gone little more than an hour it seemed an eternity.

She tried to read a book, turned several pages, but at the end of the chapter realized that she bad no idea what she had been reading about. Fang, the young Chinese, sat down beside her and expounded his theory of life at great length, which would, normally, have interested her enormously, but now it seemed boring and unimportant.

It was about five o'clock before the CO sent for her.

'Get Number Twenty-Six, Mrs Sandyman,' was all he said. Mandy met her in the locker room. 'Good luck, Sandybags!' she said. 'Don't ruffle the old boy's temper and you'll be OK. I'll be watching.'

'Thanks.' Susan smiled. 'Hold thumbs!'

As she walked out to her machine, her parachute humped on her shoulder, her knees shook and she felt cold beads spring out on her forehead. 'If only Frank were here,' she thought, and quite suddenly felt much calmer. 'Ass!' she told herself. 'It's not as if you had never flown solo before and, after all, Timber can't eat you!'

Once in the air, with Captain Twigg's solid frame in the cockpit before her, all Susan's nervousness dropped away. As she took off she thought once of Frank, and then her whole attention became focused on the little Magister and a curious sense of control came over her. The machine almost seemed to be flying itself, her hands to be moving the controls before her brain ordered them, and she surprised herself as much as Captain Twigg by the perfection of her first landing.

Three times he made her take off, complete a circuit and land, but each time there was very little criticism to be made.

'Taxi over to the petrol bowser.' The words came down the intercom after her third landing, and for one awful moment Susan thought he was going to tell her to refuel and put the machine away without sending her solo.

She saw him undo his Sutton harness and parachute as they approached the corner of the field by the bowser; the brake went on in the front cockpit, and they came to a standstill. His voice came gruffly to her ears down the rubber speaking-tube.

'All right, Mrs Sandyman. Off you go – one circuit!' and climbing out of the cockpit he pulled his parachute after him.

All trace of her previous nervousness vanished now, as Susan taxied round to the take-off position. She turned cross-wind, looked all round her to make sure no other machine was coming in to land, went very deliberately through her cockpit check, then turned the cheeky little nose of the Magister into the light westerly wind and slowly opened the throttle.

Faster and faster the wheels spun over the dry grass until they gently unstuck and the tiny monoplane climbed steadily over the trees. There was a great singing in Susan's ears, and of the rest of that circuit she afterwards remembered very little, but having landed again safely she was conscious of a great peace engulfing her, something deeper than mere relief at having soloed. 'Thank you, Frank,' she whispered. 'Don't worry about me any more now, darling. I shall be all right. Bless you – wherever you are…'

Having parked her machine, Susan went into the locker room, which was in the usual state of upheaval before the weekend. Suitcases everywhere; pupils stuffing things in at the last minute; shouts of 'The bus is waiting!'

John Cherry's head popped out from behind his locker door. 'Pansy landings, honey!' he congratulated her. 'Can't think why the old buzzard didn't send you solo!'

'He did,' said Susan briefly, and before John could answer she had passed quickly on into the ladies' cloakroom. She did not want to talk to John just then.

'Wizard landings, Sue!' Mandy greeted her.

'Why didn't Timber let you go?'

'But he did,' Susan answered again. 'Weren't you watching?'

'Yes, of course! We all were!' Mandy grinned. 'So you can't pull that one, Sandybags! And, by the way, why hadn't Timber got his helmet on the last time you landed? Did he fling it overboard in a rage?'

'He didn't, because he wasn't there,' Susan insisted again. Out of the corner of her eye Susan saw Mrs Cushing tap a meaning finger on her forehead, but suddenly she did not care... she remembered that Frank had always refused to wear a helmet! It was confirmation. Frank was safe. Felicity was safe. It was up to her.

THREE

ALTHOUGH NO ONE mentioned it to Susan, Mandy and John Cherry were not the only ones who saw her 'passenger' that day.

The story passed into legend. To Susan it was a precious and sacred memory which would persist as long as she lived.

She felt warmed all through, and knew that she had been vouchsafed a moment given to few mortals.

Her weekend was already arranged. She was spending it with Grannie. Mrs Ledgard and Jane were in the throes of the move to London – Mrs Ledgard having found an entirely satisfactory flat in South Kensington – and Susan's personal belongings had already been moved to Grannie's.

Now Susan thought of this with joy. Grannie knew about these things. Grannie understood. She felt impatient to tell her, and the journey to Hazeley seemed long that afternoon.

Mandy, watching her, was silent. She knew Susan had married at nineteen, her own age, but today had emphasized the six years between them in a new and unexpected way. 'She looks,' thought Mandy, 'like someone who has lost a treasure and found it again,' and so, each busy with her own thoughts, for once there was no shouted chatter between the two girls as the bus rattled along to Luton Station.

It was not until she flopped into a corner seat in the carriage which Mandy managed to get to themselves that Susan realized just how exhausted she was. Her mind seemed full to bursting point, yet she was unable to focus it on anything, and the sense of peace which had come over her after her solo flight had, in the end, been dispelled by the noisy bus ride. Now the continuous drumming of the train's wheels had the same effect. The morning already felt far away.

Mandy, sitting in the opposite corner, was apparently reading, but after a while she suddenly closed her book, and threw it down on the seat.

'It's no good,' she sighed, 'I simply can't concentrate. Funny, I love reading, but in the last few days I haven't been able to settle down to it at all. Richard said he found the same thing as soon as he joined the RAF.'

'Who is Richard?'

'My brother. My twin.'

'Oh! How nice! Are you the onlys?'

At this moment Susan was relieved to talk about someone an something other than herself, something completely detached from the events of the past week, so she led Mandy on to tell her about her family and home.

Mandy smiled and dug her hands deep into the pockets of the old corduroy trousers she wore when flying.

'Oh lord, no! There's Tony and the Babe as well. Tony's a Brown Job, he's five years older than we are, and the Babe is still at Eton – he's only sixteen.'

Susan was genuinely interested. There was something about Mandy, perhaps in the casual way she wore her rough riding jacket, or the friendly way she chatted with everyone, or maybe it was just imagination, but Susan felt she could paint a pretty accurate background to Mandy's nineteen years. There would most certainly be a Nanny in a white starched cap and apron, ponies, dogs, children having tea in the shade of a tree on a wide lawn, an old grey house beyond, and two gongs for dinner.

Not that Mandy had mentioned her family during the past week, beyond saying that she was going home to Sussex for the weekend, yet Susan felt instinctively that her picture was correct.

'What's the Babe's real name?' she asked.

'Jeremy – but somehow he has always been "the Babe", and I suppose he always will. He's hopping mad now that he is not old enough to join up, in fact he ran away last half and tried. Daddy was furious, though I really think he thought it was a good show, so now he lets him join the Home Guard in the hols.'

Susan took a long shot. 'What has Nanny got to say about that?'

'Oh, Mummy says she is in a very bad mood nowadays, but I think it's only because the Babe refuses to let her wash his back in the bath any more.'

So she was right. In Mandy's world there was always Nanny; in her experience there always had been, and she took it for granted there always would be. She was not even surprised when a comparative stranger referred to her out of the blue.

'Where is your twin stationed?' Susan asked. She was trying to picture a male edition of Mandy and finding it difficult.

'Hornchurch. He's on Spits – the lucky devil – Sixty-four Squadron,' and from the tone of her voice Susan knew immediately that they must be very close twins.

'He's a darling – you would love him. What about coming down one weekend, say the one after next – that will be a long one. Richard said he might make it, too.'

'I should love to, but are you sure your people won't mind? Wouldn't they rather have you to themselves? And you know how tricky it is with rations – no maids and things now,'

Mandy quickly brushed her doubts aside. 'Oh no, there's still old James, and Nanny and Cook. We only live in one wing of the house now, the Army have got the rest – Canadians at present. It's rather amusing. *Do* come!'

At this moment the train roared into a tunnel, and as there were no lights in the carriage Susan waited silently in the noisy darkness. It would be fun to meet new people; go into an atmosphere through which, as yet, death had not stalked, and for one weekend shelve the memory of the tragedies of her own home, She was certain her mother would understand. In fact, both her mother and Grannie would: approve. By the time the train had emerged into daylight again Susan had decided, and so repeated, 'I should love it, but do ask your mother first, and make certain.'

'Oh, that'll be OK,' Mandy laughed. 'Mummy hardly notices we are there. She's a darling, too, but she simply hasn't got a clue about the war. She can't take it in, somehow it's just nuisance value to her. You will die laughing at the things she says about aeroplanes. She's certain Richard and I are mad to want to fly. You see she wanted Richard to go in the Scots Guards with Tony, but then he always has upset her plans from the moment he appeared unexpectedly after me! It's odd, really, because Daddy was in the RAF in the last war, so she should understand.'

Susan smiled. With Mandy's words she could now see her background taking shape. 'Anyway, I'm longing to meet them all,' then, looking out of the grimy window, she added, 'Oh – we are just about in, aren't we?'

As the train drew in to the platform an air-raid warning blared, loud and insistent above the noises of the station. 'Damn! That means we shall never get a taxi,' Mandy said. 'What a bore!'

'Where are you making for?' Susan asked.

'Victoria. What about you?'

'Waterloo. Let's get an Underground.'

Together they pushed their way down the crowded passages, and just managed to jump a westbound train as the doors were closing. At Piccadilly Circus they parted. Mandy slipped out to change for Victoria, and, in a moment, was lost to sight amid the crowd of people who swarmed over the platform. At Waterloo Susan found the same state of affairs. Soldiers, sailors, girls of the ATS, girls of the WAAF, and WRNS and civilians, were everywhere. Absolutely no chance of a cup of tea if she were to get her ticket, she reflected.

Her suitcase grew heavier each time she had to lift it as she moved up in the queue to the booking office. A friendly, very young sailor behind her came to the rescue. When she asked for her ticket he remarked:

'I'm going that way. Wait a minute. I'll carry it for you.'

Susan was surprised at his tone. An AB and a gentleman. What oddities war produced!

Later, standing shoulder to shoulder in the crowded corridor of a train packed to what was almost beyond capacity, and watching countryside familiar from childhood slip past, she heard a little of his history. He grinned down at her from his extra eight inches.

'Couldn't even pass common entrance. Couldn't pass exams – even my mother said I just hadn't the what-nots. But I love the lower deck. They're all such good chaps. It's – it's like seeing the world sitting on a rainbow.'

He did not look stupid, thought Susan, but at Woking, when a few people left the train, and he stooped to move her suitcase so that, upturned, she could sit on it, Susan saw the scar of a mastoid behind his ear, and as he lit her cigarette, a similar scar behind the other ear.

Perhaps that was the reason. They talked of sport and horses. He loved games and riding, and was overwhelmed when she spoke of the ATA. He wished he could do likewise. Desultory talk that was friendly and, in the end, conveyed little.

At Hazeley he helped her out, regretted she was leaving the train and wished her 'good luck' and 'happy landings'. As the train moved off Susan was forcibly reminded of the two Verners. It was odd how people shot in and out of one's life in wartime.

It was late when she arrived at Grannie's. The wait for a taxi, 'phoned for after she arrived, had been long. She sank on the fender-stool as soon as she had greeted her grandmother, and ejaculated:

'Oh gosh! Travelling by train is the limit. Gets worse and worse,' and plumped for sherry when Grannie said:

'Tea or sherry, Susan. Which?'

Perhaps the sherry – two glasses – on an empty tummy helped, but perhaps it was just the atmosphere. Susan all her life had brought her joys and sorrows to Grannie. The old lady felt the heat and looked more frail than usual. She held Susan's hand while Susan sat on the fender-stool and told the experiences of the week, and her eyes never left Susan's face. When all was finished she was silent, and Susan, looking up, saw the gleam of tears.

'Oh, Grannie!' In a moment Susan's arms were about the old lady. 'I've made you cry.' 'No, darling. They are tears of joy. You are happy again. Happy and content. I know what a trying year it has been – but now—'

'Yes.' Susan loosed her arms as the old lady sought her handkerchief. 'Yes, Grannie, I am.' She sank back on the fender-stool to await her grandmother's next word.

'And, my darling, you will find that the moments in life when we come close to the unseen are the happiest, the most blessed, of all.'

'Yes, Grannie.'

'And now you must go and change. Mother is coming to dinner.'

FOUR

THE FOLLOWING WEEK was uneventful – that is to say, the weather was good; only one 'Maggie' was damaged when a pupil overshot and ran into the far hedge, and only two pupils, both of the course ahead of Susan, were failed.

By the middle of the week Mandy, having taken her full twelve hours, had also gone solo. Susan was not altogether certain that the full twelve hours were entirely Mandy's fault, because it was obvious, from his attitude towards her, that her instructor – who was one of the older men – thought she had joined the ATA more for the glamour of the job than anything else, and, in order to remove any false illusions, had made it rather harder for her than for his less attractive pupils.

The hours in Susan's own log book crept slowly upwards, and by the time the weekend arrived she had flown six hours solo and twelve dual. She was progressing now on to the more advanced exercises, and it irritated her that the weekends seemed to come round so quickly; but it irked her even more when the following Monday dawned wet and misty, with the clouds down on top of the hill, making it impossible for pupils to fly.

Most of the morning was taken up with a lecture by Captain Twigg on parachutes; how to look after them, and how to use them should the necessity arise, but after lunch, as the weather was forecast to remain bad, all pupils were released.

'What about a flick?' John Cherry suggested on the way back to Haddenham in the bus, for he had again manoeuvred himself into the seat beside her. '*Mrs Miniver* is on at the Astoria – ought to be good.'

'Lovely idea,' she answered, then turning to Mandy who was in the seat behind them: 'What about you? Coming to a flick in Aylesbury?'

Much to John's annoyance, for he had wanted to take Susan alone, the subject became open to general discussion. He had intended asking her to dine with him at the 'Bull' afterwards.

It was not difficult for Susan to sense John Cherry's irritation, and she had purposely turned to Mandy, for John had already tried to make love to her one evening when he had given her a lift back to Hopefield House; and, although in many ways she liked him, for he was amusing, good company, and good-natured in a crowd, there was also a lot about him that she definitely disliked. She disliked the way he referred to girls he had known as his 'Popsies', or 'Nice little pieces', and the frequency with which he disdainfully ran down the ATA. 'Think they can fly! They haven't a b— clue!' However, because as yet Susan had little knowledge of ferrying, she did not argue with him and let him criticize. Sometimes it was on the tip of her tongue to say if he thought that way why had he left the RAF? But somehow she guessed it to be a sore point and charitably refrained.

The party now grew to a fivesome, for not only Mandy but also Mrs Cushing and Fang decided to go to the cinema. Fang and the Pole were devoted to Mrs Cushing.

John's irritation grew, and Susan overheard him muttering sanguinary remarks about 'Yanks' under his breath as he got out of the bus at Aylesbury's market square.

Mrs Miniver proved to be, as advertised, an outstanding film; but Susan did not enjoy it. It was too poignant. She was several times moved to tears. It was, she decided, a film for America; for those who had not lived through bombings, or had to run for their lives. It left her depressed and with a slight headache. John Cherry was dismayed when she refused dinner and elected to go back to Haddenham and the canteen. Even there supper was a farce. He could just not understand. He drifted off to the 'Crown', and Susan spent the evening domestically. She washed her stockings and did some mending, and went early to bed. Still lying awake she feigned sleep when Mandy returned after closing time.

At Hopefield House Susan always awakened to the same sounds. Those of engines turning over, warming up on the airfield. The Harvards, the Harts and the Ferry Pool's Ansons, for, although they were more than a mile away, the air was still at that hour in the morning, and the village only just stirring.

For some time she would lie and listen, and let her thoughts run idly on to many things in the future when she, too, might be flying those machines; then she would doze off again and half dream, half day-dream herself in the cockpit of a fighter, with England spread as a map beneath her wings. Then Mandy's alarm clock would bring her sharply back to reality, and she would spend the next quarter of an hour persuading Mandy that it really was half past seven and that her clock was *not* fast. Mandy loved her bed, and had become used to the 'biscuits' surprisingly quickly.

About a quarter to eight she would pull her long legs from under the blankets, leap up, dash along to the bathroom, wearing neither gown nor slippers, fly back and fling on her clothes, bang a brush through her silky copper mane, pull the bedclothes up without making the bed and be ready for the canteen as soon as Susan.

Susan could not help laughing; there was so much of the child in Mandy still, such a quantity of animal spirits that sometimes it made her feel quite maternal.

'Don't forget you are coming home with me tomorrow night,' Mandy reminded her as she rushed back from the bathroom on the Friday morning. 'By the way, have you got a bathing costume? The Canadians have been clearing the weeds out of the lake, and it's quite good now. Hope I have letter from Ric today; he promised to let me know for certain if he could get away.'

Susan nodded. 'Yes, I have,' and she thought of her swimsuit, a beautiful white lastex model, patterned with large vividly splashed flowers. Frank had bought it for her on their last visit to Rangoon and it was still almost new. She had kept it: perhaps because it was Frank's last gift.

She was looking forward to the weekend in Sussex: it would be a complete change, and amusing to meet Mandy's family. Besides, she had really visited very few private homes since she returned. Her girlhood friends were scattered far and wide, and she had lost touch with most of them after she married and went to live in Malaya.

On Saturday morning all seven pupils who had come with Susan, and several from the course ahead, were told that they were to report at Thame on the following Tuesday morning, where they would start a fortnight's Ground Course on Navigation, Meteorological and

Ferrying Procedure.

By three o'clock both Susan and Mandy were released, as they had both flown two hours that day, and, in any case, there would be no free machines for them.

Susan had had an hour's dual with Flight Lieutenant Adamson, and had then practised her circuits and bumps solidly for an hour solo. It had been a wonderful day, hot yet not oppressive, and she had flown in her shirt sleeves. The countryside had lain drowsing beneath her, the beechwood on the hill spreading in full foliage, motionless, enchanted, and only the droves of heavy bombers, droning occasionally back and forth into East Anglia, reminded her that not so many miles away across the channel the most frightful crimes in history were, even now, being perpetrated.

At lunchtime, when she drew her week's pay packet which amounted to some three pounds odd, Susan could not help thinking how extraordinary it was to be paid for doing something one enjoyed so much.

And now the weekend! Quickly Susan changed out of the corded slacks she wore flying into a lavender blue tailored linen dress, which matched her eyes exactly and set off her short golden curls to perfection, and she thought of Robert Jamieson, and wondered where he was, as she pinned on his brooch. Mandy stayed as she was, in her somewhat grubby corduroys, open-necked shirt and riding jacket. Mandy believed in travelling light, and so her clothes were at home.

Together they trudged off up the lane to the main road, taking it in turns to carry Susan's suitcase, for it was still very hot and the case heavy.

Having discovered that there was no bus for another hour, they decided to hitch-hike into Luton, and soon were ensconced in the back of an empty sand lorry. Luck was with them, for a London train pulled in just as they arrived on the platform, and taxis seemed more plentiful at Euston than usual. It was barely six o'clock when they reached Victoria.

'There's a six-four – if we are quick we shall catch it. You take the case and I'll dash and get the tickets. I wonder if Richard will be on this train?' and Mandy dashed off.

At Falcombe, although Mandy waited expectantly, looking wistfully up and down, she and Susan remained the only two passengers to get out of the train, and the only person in sight was an ancient porter bumbling busily up and down the little wooden platform.

'Evening, Miss Mandy!' he said, touching his cap as he took their tickets. 'Surely you be not goin' to carry that thar case all way up to the Manor?'

Mandy assured him that she was not, and asked him to look after it until it was fetched. 'The Canadians always have a truck running up and down to the station,' she explained to Susan. 'We'll get them to collect it.'

As they walked up the hill and through the village Susan became more and more convinced of the accuracy of the mental picture she had painted for herself. Opposite the old Saxon church stood the 'Cat', and on the benches outside sat a few old men, one or two Canadian soldiers and some villagers in Home Guard uniform. Each had two things in common: a pint of beer, and a determination to fight for this way of life which allowed him to relax in his own way after the day's work, and say exactly what he liked without fear.

When they passed there was a general chorus of 'Evening, miss', and Mandy, smiling, returned their greeting.

Further on she stopped to have a word with a nut-brown, wrinkled old woman, who was leaning over her cottage gate. 'How are you, Mrs Botting?' she enquired. 'Any news of Jim?'

'Oh, same as usual –'e's still a pris'ner. I only 'ope those Jerrys is feeding 'im proper; 'e always was delicate like, and kinda fussy about 'is food.' Then her face brightened. 'Mister Richard was over yesterday dinner-time. Lord save us, 'e near took the steeple off, 'e did! 'E's a one!' and she wagged her silver head knowingly.

'Do you know if he is home yet?' Mandy asked eagerly. 'He is meant to be on leave this weekend.'

'No, miss, 'e's not back yet – only the little un. 'E's been out 'Ome Guarding with yer Dad.' From the vigils at her gate Mrs Botting kept an eye on all the comings and goings in Falcombe. She knew exactly who was 'going with' who in the village; she could watch all the weddings and funerals down at the church, and it was said she could usually tell you what was for lunch at the Manor!

At the end of the street, where the cottages petered out, Mandy suddenly said, 'Let's take the short cut through the fields – it saves at least half a mile,' and so Susan, at this first visit, did not enter Mandy's home by the great iron gates, wrought and fashioned by the old Sussex iron-workers three and a half centuries before. Instead she approached Falcombe Manor from the west, across a spacious parkland, and her first view of the house brought her to a standstill. For a moment she just stared before she exclaimed:

'Mandy! How beautiful! Why didn't you tell me?' The sun was low by now and its rays, reflected in the ancient leaded windows, turned them into a blaze of glory. The house itself, built on a gentle slope, was of grey, mellow stone, the roof of heavy Horsham slab.

'"S'pose it is quite a pile,' agreed Mandy nonchalantly. 'Goodness knows how much longer we shall be able to hang on to it, though. Still, a Dalrymple built it, and I think it would break Daddy's heart to part with it.'

Between Susan and the house lay a broad strip of water, and as they drew nearer she saw a canoe moored in the reeds, with someone sitting in it. At the same moment Mandy saw it too, and waved. 'Hullo, Babe!' she shouted.

When they reached the bank Susan saw a brown-faced boy, with Mandy's eyes and a mop of fair hair which stood up in an unruly tuft.

'Hullo, Sis! How many prangs have you had this week?' The full effect of this truly brotherly taunt was somewhat lost owing to the fact that the speaker's voice was in the process of breaking. As he caught sight of Susan he looked a trifle shy.

Mandy, completely ignoring his crack at her, introduced Susan.

'This is Mrs Sandyman – Susan to you. Caught anything lately?'

'Two pike yesterday; nothing today, worse luck. Any idea what time it is?'

Susan looked at her watch. 'Twenty-past seven.'

'Good lord! I shall be late for dinner again,' and he started pulling in his line. 'Mum's in a pretty chivvyish mood, I can tell you. Major McCracken's upset her again, and I forgot all about dinner last night. You go on, and I'll catch you up.'

Mandy laughed, and as they walked across the lawn she explained to Susan that there was one Canadian officer, a certain Major McCracken, who annoyed her mother intensely, chiefly because he would call the house 'a cute little place', and she had once seen him spit on her favourite rose-bed.

Lady Dalrymple-Ducane was a tall, graceful woman, with vague, dreamy blue eyes, and an air of complete preoccupation. She welcomed Susan in a distant sort of way, and then seemed to forget her existence.

'I've had the most ridiculous telegram from Richard,' she told Mandy. 'He says he won't be here until after dinner and that he is bringing his WC with him, and he hoped it will be OK. Now, what can he mean? We've six of those in the house already!' Mandy collapsed on the sofa in a fit of helpless giggles.

'Oh, Mummy, you are a scream! He means his Wing Co! Wing Commander Dundas.'

'Well, why doesn't he say so then? And your father is just as bad nowadays; he is out somewhere in the woods at this moment playing at soldiers, and Cook can think of nothing but that awful sergeant, so goodness knows what time we shall have dinner.' And so saying she drifted from the room.

'You mustn't mind Mummy,' said Mandy, still giggling. 'She just doesn't understand. We've all tried – even Daddy – but it's no good. She still lives in an age that is gone, and wonders why everyone else doesn't do the same.'

She wandered over to the window as she spoke. 'Good!' she exclaimed. 'There's a truck in the drive. I will show you your room and then fix someone to fetch your case.'

Susan found that she was to sleep in an old four-poster bed, hung with white chintz curtains sprigged with rosebuds, and she was so enchanted with the room and the view from her window, stretching as it did away to the South Downs, that she did not hear the door open and the entrance of Nanny.

'I have just come to see you are all right, miss – ma'am,' she corrected herself. 'Miss Mandy is a wee bit scatterbrain at times.'

'Oh yes, Nanny. Thank you, I was just admiring your view. Mandy is trying to get my case fetched from the station,' she explained. Nanny was a Scot, and had been under nurse when Sir Francis was a baby, and now in her own quiet way she ran the household. She washed and mended for everyone, made beds, filled hot-water bottles, looked after anyone who had a cold, and fussed over her old charges when they were at home.

She still wore her starched apron, and little white cap was perched on her silver hair. Susan loved her at sight.

'M'lady will be changing for dinner, but I am sure Miss Mandy will not, so there will be no great hurry for you. Would you like a hot-water bottle tonight? – you'll find it comforting in a strange bed.'

'No, thank you, Nanny,' Susan answered 'It is really very warm and I am not used to such luxuries.'

'Puir wee lambkin!' Susan heard her murmur as she left the room, and knew immediately that Mandy had already told Nanny her story.

When eventually her case did arrive, Susan had a wash and changed into a little pair of white, high-heeled sandals. Mandy, whose bedroom was next door, put on a green and white silk afternoon frock, and Susan thought she had never seen her look so lovely.

'Let's go down,' said Mandy. 'If Daddy is in, there will be a drink waiting for us.'

They found Sir Francis in the study, a tall, middle-aged man, still wearing his Home Guard uniform, who greeted them cheerily, and, as Mandy had predicted, a tray of glasses and bottles stood on the table beside him. A big golden labrador sprawled at his feet, and, as the girls entered, the dog raised his head and thumped his tail on the floor.

'Hullo, darling!' Sir Francis kissed Mandy affectionately, and then looked questioningly towards Susan.

'Daddy, this is Susan Sandyman – Mrs Sandyman. She is the star turn of our course. She soloed in five hours. Hullo, Jackie, old boy!' she exclaimed, stooping to pat the labrador.

'That isn't exactly true, Sir Francis,' said Susan, as she put her hand into his, and felt the warmth of the greeting. 'I had flown before. I learnt in Australia.'

'Now that's one of the places I've never been to. When were you there?' and not awaiting an answer he turned to the table, and his next question was: 'Sherry, or gin-and-it? I'm afraid there is no other choice.'

As soon as the drinks were distributed he turned to Susan with a merry smile, and said:

'Now, Mrs Sandyman, you can give me the low down on this brat of mine. How is she doing?'

Unlike his wife he seemed genuinely interested in what his children were doing, and was always ready to welcome their friends to Falcombe, and he awaited her reply with genuine interest.

But Susan was given no opportunity to speak. Mandy's voice broke in reproachfully.

'Oh, Daddy! I've told you *heaps*. Don't you even read my letters? I've been solo! But now, damn it, we've got to do a fortnight's ground course. How's the Home Guard going, Daddy?'

'Oh, ticking over! Tomlin at last knows which end a rifle goes off; Rush is almost safe with a hand-grenade, but that old poacher Cyril beats them all – he gets bull's-eyes every time!'

While they were still laughing and talking Lady Dairymple-Ducane came into the room. She was wearing a long grey chiffon dress, which made her appear more dreamy than ever. Susan thought she looked quite lovely, and wished, more than ever, she had had her suitcase in time to change more than her shoes.

'Where is Jeremy?' she asked. She was the only member of the family who always called the Babe by his proper name.

'Last seen playing poker with the batmen in the pantry,' Mandy answered. 'If James rings the gong he'll come.'

As they sat down to dinner in the library, which they now used as a dining-room, the Babe entered.

'Just had a straight flush!' he announced triumphantly.

'Young man, you're late again,' said his father.

'Sorry, Dad.' The Babe looked anything but sorry. 'By the way, the

Colonel says will you all go and have drinks with him in the Mess tomorrow evening?'

'Why my drawing-room must be referred to as a "mess" I simply cannot imagine. Is that terrible Major still there?'

'Yes,' the Babe winked at Mandy, 'and I saw him spit out of the window!'

'I don't think I shall go, then,' Mandy's mother announced. 'Francis, I wish you would speak to the Colonel about it!'

'Yes, my dear,' said Sir Francis, and continued to talk to Susan who was sitting on his right.

As they were finishing dinner there was a roar in the drive outside, and both Mandy and the Babe leapt up and ran to the window.

'It's Richard!' Mandy got the words out first as she rushed for the door.

'He's got a tall, dark chap with him!' The Babe proceeded to give them a running commentary. 'He's got bags of gongs – and a wizard car! It's boiling too – gosh, they must have been moving! And there's a dog – a bull-terrier. Hope it doesn't fight with Jackie! No – all OK. He's a bitch!'

'Jeremy!' Lady Dalrymple-Ducane's voice was reproving. 'Such language.'

Further conversation was cut short by Mandy returning with Richard and his Wing Commander. Susan stared. It was incredible that two people of different sexes could be so alike. Richard was some inches taller than his sister and his features more pronounced, but his colouring, eyes, hair and complexion were amazingly similar.

It was Michael Dundas's first visit, and in the midst of all the greetings and introductions he appeared somewhat bewildered, and his eyes kept returning to Mandy. 'I just can't get over the resemblance,' he said to Lady Dalrymple-Ducane.

It was just on nine o'clock, and as the newcomers had assured their hostess that they had already dined, Sir Francis's voice broke in, 'Well, if you honestly have, come along; it's time for the news,' and a general move was made to the study. Lady Dalrymple poured out the coffee while her husband turned on the wireless.

The King safely back from Algiers. Heavy bombings of the Ruhr.

The Africa Star. The 1943 Star for all Services in other theatres of war. As the news finished Mandy turned impulsively to Michael Dundas.

'You'll come in for that, won't you? The Africa Star?'

Somewhat to Susan's surprise Michael's face lit up, until it dawned on her that Michael's eyes had hardly left Mandy's face since he arrived, and this was the first time she had taken any real notice of him. What answer Michael made she did not hear. Her thoughts suddenly went to her brother, killed in Libya. He, too, would get the Africa Star. It would mean a lot to her mother. And then another thought flashed. 'Medals are not so much for the men that win them – but for the others – mothers – and others.'

At ten o'clock the door opened and Nanny appeared.

'Now come along, Mister Jeremy. Remember you're a convalescent, and it's high time you were in bed.'

'Oh, I say, Nanny! I'm not a baby!'

'Yes, you are! Off to bed, Babe!' jeered Mandy.

But Jeremy did not hear this last jibe. He lifted his head. He had caught a distant sound. The next second he shouted: 'Bombers! I hear them! Let's look!' and he made a dash for the window. In a moment everyone was outside on the lawn, gazing upwards. Only Nanny lingered. She walked across the room to switch out the one shaded light, and then busied herself with the blackout curtains.

Jeremy, his head thrown back, was continuing excitedly: 'Gosh! Ten, twenty! No – there are more coming!' In his eagerness he caught Michael's arm. 'And that won't be all, will it, sir? I wonder what target they are making for? D'you know, sir?'

'No. I don't know. But I expect it's the Ruhr.'

'I expect so.' Jeremy's voice was as serious as if he were sixty instead of sixteen. 'We must keep their heavy industries slowed down, mustn't we, sir?'

'Now, Mister Jeremy—' Nanny's voice called from the window.

'Jeremy!' It was Sir Francis who spoke. 'You're keeping Nanny up.'

'Oh blow!' But the words were said under Jeremy's breath, for discipline ruled in Sir Francis's household. The good nights that followed might have been a trifle sulky, but Jeremy disappeared after Nanny through the blackout curtains, followed by Lady Dalrymple.

The others drifted slowly back; Mandy, with her arm through Richard's, and closely followed by Michael Dundas; Susan and her host bringing up the rear. A belated bomber passed over and they both turned to look. Very soon it was out of sight, and as Sir Francis held back the curtain for Susan to enter he said:

'If it does not distress you to talk about it, I would like to hear the story of your escape from Singapore.'

But Sir Francis was fated not to have his question answered. Mandy turned to him as he entered, exclaiming:

'Oh, Daddy – come and hear about this! Richard has a gong!'

'What? What's this?' Sir Francis stared at Richard, who blushed and mumbled:

'Oh, it's nothing.'

It was Michael Dundas who answered him. 'It's a DFC, sir, actually. Confirmed just before we left.'

'Good show, Richard.' Sir Francis was beaming. 'Where's Mother? This calls for a drink. Fetch her, Mandy. I'd like to hear more about it.'

'Ah! State secrets, Daddy!' said Mandy, as she hurried to the door.

Michael's eyes followed her, and Susan noticed and felt sure that, given the chance, Michael would tell Mandy anything within his power.

The evening was made. Susan was swept along in the general gaiety of the family, and was happier than she had been for months. Even the Babe, reappearing in pyjamas and dressing-gown, was allowed to remain. They were all so natural that by the time they all departed to bed – the Babe making conscious efforts to show he was tipsy – she felt she had already known them for years.

* * *

The house was quiet. Silence reigned within and without. A deep brooding silence. Then something ruffled it and Susan, lying awake, lifted her head to listen. From somewhere came the muted sound of a clock striking. It was not within the house, and before the reverberation of the last of its twelve strokes died away Susan had located it as the stable clock.

'Odd,' she thought. 'It must have struck three or four times since we arrived and I haven't heard it.' She dropped her head again and cuddled Nanny's hot-water bottle closer. 'How nice of Nanny.' Even a hot-water bottle was company of a sort, and she felt lonely. The sound of voices in the next room had ceased. Mandy's room was next. She and Richard had been talking. Richard must have gone very quietly. There had been no sound of a door either opening or closing. Susan's thoughts went back to where they had been when she had heard the clock.

'Of course I ought to go to sleep, but... Yes, tomorrow, perhaps, Sir Francis will ask me again. I could talk to him. I like him. He makes me think of Daddy. Poor Mother! Is she more lonely or less lonely than I am? Do the years make any difference? I think about her so often. How will she feel when Jack's Africa Star comes? Anyway, it's general. She won't have to go to Buckingham Palace for it,' and for some moments Susan's thoughts drifted back to that wet day the previous summer when she had accompanied her mother to receive Jack's decoration. From that Michael Dundas slipped into her thoughts. What a row of ribbons! He must have faced many dangers and had many escapes, but, tonight, life had changed for Michael. 'It won't be easy. Mandy has a brother complex. That's obvious! I had been in love with Frank for months, and we were married when I was Mandy's age. Oh, Frank!' The last words came as half a moan. Susan crept deeper into the big bed and the soft pillows. 'How am I to get through the years without you? They – are – so – long—'

* * *

Mandy, too, heard the stable clock. She was not undressed and was still sitting on the side of her bed. Richard had only just left her. They had been making plans. Every spot of leave they could they would spend together, and they had drifted into more serious talk when Mandy had said:

'I don't know if it's because I am flying – I s'pose it is – but Ric darling, I am so much more conscious of your risks than I was.' And Mandy had heard details of Richard's 'gong', known to no one else.

'I was scared stiff, Sis – thought I'd never do it, and, before I'd got over the scared feeling, and while the sweat was dripping down my back, it was over! Incredible! I didn't care about the flak. Felt nothing could get me – and – that's all.'

'Oh, Ric!' Mandy hugged him. 'But you will be careful—' she began, but Richard interrupted.

'But that's just what we *can't* be! You do see, don't you?'

'Yes, I do,' Mandy answered. 'But I am growing a "safety first" spirit. It's the ATA. One can't help it. "The 'planes *must* be delivered, and must be delivered *whole*." That's what they train us for, and din it into us on every possible occasion. "To take no unnecessary risk—"'

'But there are always risks,' interrupted Richard again, 'and you take off in new machines. There is always the thousandth chance – plus the human factor – and – Sis, promise. *If* I go you won't make any fuss, will you? I—'

'Ric!' It was Mandy's turn to interrupt. She hugged Ric more closely. 'Don't!' Her voice was agonized. 'You mustn't even *think* such a thing. As if I could *live* without you!'

'You may have to face it, Mandy. Better do it now.'

'Oh, Ric!'

For a little while Richard had reasoned, and finished, 'It's only a question of what courage you bring to it, and you have courage.'

'Courage'. Mandy repeated the word. A little later, staring out of her window into the summer darkness, and with the darkness behind her, she clenched her hands and vowed to keep her promise.

* * *

Richard stood by his window. It was wide open and nearer the stable yard. The sound came more clearly. He, too, counted the strokes. It was the earliest-remembered sound of his life. Tony had been born before Sir Francis inherited Falcombe, but Mandy and Richard had been born there.

That old clock! Its notes were interwoven with every remembrance of home. Richard loved Falcombe. Now he stood by the window and, as the last note died away, he heard the shrill cries of the moorfowl from the lake. That was another sound familiar all his life. How many more times was he to hear them? With that question in his mind he drew the curtains closely, turned from the window and unerringly crossed the room to the light switches. His room. His, since nursery days. He looked round. His books. His stamp albums. His collection of birds' eggs. School photographs. Photographs of Windsor and Eton. The boats! None of university. Those would come after the war. Richard sat on the side of his bed and mechanically kicked off his shoes. After? But – *his university?* No. That would never be.

* * *

And Michael Dundas? In the old downstairs schoolroom, in a small bed pulled across the open French window and his head almost under the stars, Michael Dundas lay wide awake and listened, every thought of his work and career obliterated by a woman's face. It had come so unexpectedly. He liked Richard. Liked what he could feel behind him: That long line of fighting ancestors, but now he knew. The attraction of Richard – it was all destined to lead to this. But would Sir Francis and Lady Dalrymple frown on him? Mandy was their only daughter. He was well off, but, despite his good name, knew little of his ancestors. Nowadays his family was in trade. Would they consider the third generation of hats, caps and waterproofs good enough? Michael's eyes closed. Mandy's face – the way her hair grew and glowed – her eyes so like violets. Flying homewards – after sunset – he'd seen the sky deepen to that violet blue – so lovely... Michael slept.

* * *

The Babe, curled up, lay sound asleep, one hand thrust deeply under his pillow to clutch a silver teaspoon which had lain warm in his pocket for some hours. He had dived straight for it when he returned to his room. A chap couldn't trust Nanny. She'd be brushing his slacks and turning out his pockets. One never knew where she would snoop. It would make such a jolly good spinner and, tomorrow, Susan was going with him. She was a sport. She'd promised. She knew about fishing. Perhaps they'd catch that pike. Gosh! It was a big one. What luck he'd had that cold. Pity it hadn't turned to German measles. He'd have had longer at home... That pike! Pop was sure it was the same one that had eluded him when he was boy...

The Babe was asleep almost as soon as his head touched the pillow. The clock did not disturb him.

* * *

Sir Francis counted the strokes and sighed contentedly. What a wonderful evening it had been! He was proud of Richard – and of Mandy. Good stuff. Twelve strokes. What would they have been like if he and Althea had had twelve children? Thank God they hadn't. There was a time, just after Dunkirk, when he'd almost wished they hadn't had any, but even now the outlook wasn't a bright one for the young. Money would be tight for God knew how long – if not for always. It was pretty worrying for a father of a family. What hell wars were! And yet he had enjoyed the last one in lots of ways – yes, and this one, too. It was the comradeship, of course. Why did it take a war to make real comradeship between one's fellow-men in different walks of life? All those good chaps in the Home Guard. Even the old poacher! A good chap. Those Canadians were such good chaps, too – so was their whiskey! It wasn't every day one's son got a DFC. He'd just had to go and tell them in the mess. They crowded things up, of course – one had to double up a bit. Did Althea remember? This was the room they had occupied on their first visit to Falcombe after they were married. He snuggled down still more contentedly with the last moment of consciousness. He was back in the same room – in the old double bed.

* * *

Althea Dalrymple lay very still. Francis was evidently already asleep. She must not disturb Francis. He must be tired after struggling with the Home Guard. It was a trial, being short of beds. This was the one they had used on their first visit to Falcombe. She wondered if Francis remembered. It would be much more restful for him in a single bed, and all those things – ARP and Home Guarding – were too much for these middle-aged men, most of whom worked all day and frequently had to give up their nights to it. Still, all things were passing. It had been a happy evening, and now, probably, everyone in the house was asleep, except herself. She thought of Jeremy, her youngest. She hoped the war would be over before he was a man. He was just at the stage which must give all parents a pang – that cracking voice, and his grown-up ideas – and so very much a child still. Perhaps she really should have said something about that silver spoon? But he thought she had not noticed, and it was giving him great pleasure, and, after all, did material things matter any more? Had they ever mattered very much? Yes, of course they had. Not in themselves, perhaps, but in the leisure they provided; the time for thought; the possibility of beautiful surroundings; circumstances favourable to a graceful life.

Graceful! What a charming, but what a strange, word. Would it become obsolete? Graceful... Beauty in movement... That did not apply to the young girls of today. A picture rose in her mind of Mandy, in corduroy slacks, hands in pockets, new words and phrases on her lips. 'Richard's got a gong!' Just a repetition of the young in the last war; it came and went – an endless circle. They meant very little, these assumed mannerisms. The young people of today were, surely, even more splendid, more full of purpose, with a deeper sense of responsibility, braver – in fact, *full* of grace. And now she remembered! In the middle ages that word had meant just that – graceful – full of divine grace. No, it was not growing obsolete... Dear Richard! How glad she was he had that DFC. It made Francis so happy. These things meant much to him. For herself, she knew what Richard was, and no DFC could make him of more account in her eyes. He was proving himself to be of the same worth as her first born – and he was most like Francis.

Poor Francis! He worried so unnecessarily about what would happen to them all, although he put a cheerful face on it. Had he noticed that that young man that Richard had brought home with him had fallen head over heels in love with Mandy? He was covered in 'gongs'. (Was that the right way to use that new word, or was it one of those things which would make the young people laugh at her?) Wars came and wars passed. They always would. Fourteen known civilizations were already extinct...

In Mandy's vocabulary her mother 'hadn't a clue', but in reality she accepted human destiny with a high tranquillity of soul, born of some inner conviction that she had experienced it all before, and that such things, in themselves, were not of paramount importance. This detachment, which her children accounted as 'vagueness', was a never-failing amusement to them, and she entered into the part with good humour. It made them laugh – in a world in which laughter was none too plentiful. She was like a woman who possesses a jewel so rare and precious it is kept in-some hidden and unassailable safe, and very especial must be the occasion that brought it forth as an adornment for its owner. Few, perhaps only the most intimate, or those selected ones who shared some high occasion, knew of its existence, but consciousness of its possession gives an unconscious dignity and a feeling of assurance.

'No,' she thought dreamily, 'Francis shouldn't worry. Time will bring full circle again. He doesn't mind for himself – it is just for us.'

Very gently, lest she awaken him, she sought his hand. The old stable clock struck one. It was a new day.

FIVE

SUNDAY PASSED VERY swiftly. From the moment Susan opened her eyes to see Nanny, so immaculate that she looked as if she hadn't been to bed, standing beside her with a tea-tray, until almost midnight, the day alternated between the age-long pattern of English country life and the exigencies of the life of the moment.

Mandy had appeared before Susan had finished her tea, and a few moments later they were racing across the park to overtake Richard and Michael, and plunge into the ice-cold water of the lake.

A lovely morning and a glorious swim, then back to find Nanny waiting to take possession of wet bathing clothes and towels, and her bath ready. Then the settled decorum of breakfast, and a walk across the park to church, where the whole seven of the house-party filled the family pew, and khaki-clad Canadians in other pews sang lustily and brought back the atmosphere of war. Then a family lunch with the OC and two young subalterns present, and, afterwards, catching the Babe's eye and slipping away according to promise. The serenity of the afternoon until they were discovered, and the water churned by Mandy and Richard and Michael Dundas in the bigger boat. Races on the lake. Tea on the terrace. Cocktails in the mess. Dinner and the departure of Richard and Michael immediately afterwards, and later a quiet talk with Sir Francis, made up the day that occasionally, Susan thought, took on the aspect of the unreal, so conscious was she, even while the frequent 'planes crossed the sky and khaki-clad figures came and went through the great nail-studded open front door and the rattle of despatch-riders' bicycles rent the summer air, of the underlying fragrance of centuries of peace, and luxury, and ordered living still clinging to the very walls of Falcombe. Of tranquillity and assurance; nothing could or would disturb that. It was like one's religion.

Susan thought of it again when, so soon it seemed, she found herself once again in the train, en route for London and Thame, on Monday afternoon, but she did not speak of it. She might have done so had she and Mandy been alone, but Jeremy, having utterly failed to persuade his parents that he was of more use to his country in the Falcombe Home Guard than at Eton for the short remainder of the half, accompanied them, accepting his fate, once he found it inevitable.

Mandy was quiet, and Jeremy's talk being mainly of fishing, Susan found herself telling the story of her journey to Scotland to fetch the Red Cross van, and of Mr McRae. Much to her amusement Jeremy made a note of Mr McRae's address, remarking sagely:

'Perhaps I'll get a chance to look him up. Perhaps when I'm in training. I shall be, you know, in about two years. The war won't be over in two years. Major McCracken thinks so, anyway. And you are coming again, aren't you? Often – to Falcombe. You see, I know *you*. It's an introduction.'

'Yes. She is coming – often.' It was Mandy's first remark for quite half an hour.

But it wasn't until she and Susan had left Marylebone in a train that would eventually deposit them at Haddenham that she turned to Susan and asked:

'The Babe didn't worry you, did he? You will come again, won't you? You did like it – at home – didn't you?'

'Three questions,' answered Susan, 'and the answers are "No. Yes. Yes." The Babe makes me think of Claude. He was younger than the Babe when I went to Malaya—' and she gave Mandy no time for comment, but went straight on, 'and I love your home, and I hope you will ask me to come again.'

'You heard what Father said. Whenever you like. You can always be squeezed in somewhere.'

'Yes,' agreed Susan. 'He is very kind. They both are – but, Mandy, I haven't much to offer in return.'

'Shucks,' said Mandy. 'As if that matters.'

'But Grannie may be useful at times,' continued Susan contemplatively.

'She wants to know you, and she said that if either, or both of us, ever got stranded at Odiham or Black Bushe, or any other convenient airfield, we were to go to her for the night.'

'That is worth remembering. How nice of her.' Mandy's tone was enthusiastic.

'And there's Mother's flat, my second home. Mother says we may find it convenient. She has taken two beds for her spare room. It is often very difficult to get into hotels. I say, Mandy, let's run up one day when there's a wash-out?'

'Good idea! Let's,' said Mandy, and her thoughts wandered.

'Wonder what that ground course will be like? Can't bear to think of it. No flying for a fortnight. Long enough to forget all one knows. It will seem ages.'

It did. For Susan, as for the eleven other pupil pilots, the fortnight's ground course seemed an eternity. Not that the lectures lacked interest. Far from it. But she found it incredibly difficult to keep her attention fixed on *terra firma*, when every few minutes she could hear machines taking off and roaring into the summer sky. Involuntarily in her mind's eye she followed them round the circuit and away over the English countryside. North, south, east and west, to their ultimate and exciting destinations.

Vividly she recaptured the feeling of acute impatience and frustration she had known when, as a child, her governess had kept her at lessons throughout the length of a summer afternoon.

But, at last, it was over. 'Now,' she thought, 'thank goodness that's over, and I can get on with the job again, out of the lecture room into the air,' and in a few minutes she was on her bicycle, and with her suitcase wobbling precariously pedalled furiously after Mandy, who was already disappearing by the ash path at the Haddenham end of the airfield. But Mandy, with one backward laughing glance flung over her shoulder, pedalled more furiously, with the result that Susan did not overtake her until they both were in the canteen. Mandy was in the wildest spirits. She was going to Hornchurch, where Richard had secured a room for her in the nearest 'pub' and was feeling a little sorry for Susan with no one but a 'dull old grandmother' – the designation was Mandy's – to visit.

Susan loved her weekends with Grannie. It was there she felt as if she slipped back to make her readjustments. It was there she had time to think about this new life, the new life, with its hard work, its excitements and dangers; with its strange people, their courage, their sophistications, the pretence of 'I couldn't care less'– which seemed a sort of catch-phrase coined to cover the fact that they did care, and care very much – the indefatigable diligence and perseverance of one's instructors; and the opposite, the casuistry of John Cherry, everlastingly quibbling against the rules he was obliged to obey. This new world which had opened up. It was good to go back sometimes; but, always, Susan felt she was growing a dual personality. Growing flippant – but not really. Flippancy was an armour – that was all.

But this particular weekend she wished with all her heart that there was no weekend leave, so that she could go back to Barton on the morrow and fly.

There were three letters awaiting her at Grannie's. She opened her mother's first, and stood aghast – Robert Jamieson! Dead! Mrs Ledgard had seen it in *The Times* and written very sympathetically. How could she herself have overlooked it?

The other letters were a very belated one from Robert himself and one from his father. His father wrote *all we know is that he died at sea, of wounds 'received in enemy action'.*

Susan was more emotionally disturbed than she had thought possible. Robert's letter she could not bring herself to open until she reached her own room for the night. Then she sat by the open window until the summer twilight deepened to darkness and the stars came out. She had a feeling that a door had quietly closed, and she found herself comparing her sorrows. Robert, at once, felt remote. He had loved her, but she found herself thinking, 'I did not love him – perhaps that is why? I feel he has gone so completely, while Frank is never far away.' After a while she moved and wrote to Robert's father, and with the sealing of her letter she knew an episode had closed.

On Sunday morning very early, before the household was astir, Susan quietly rose, and as soon as she was dressed called softly to Jason, now firmly installed as the pet of Grannie's household, and without any very definite idea of how she had got there found herself in the churchyard beside her father's grave. He, too, was remote. Had she held Frank back? The mystery of the reality occupied her thoughts for a long time – but was Frank as present as he had been? Since that day of her solo, when she had told him, 'I shall be all right'? Food for thought, and no conclusion to the thought.

Susan sat, once again, until Jason grew impatient and whimpered. She had sunk down, sitting on her heels, beside the grave – and a wordless prayer went upwards as she arose. She had her chosen work, and one's own particular troubles and emotions did not affect one's fellow-pupils. Neither must they affect one's work. But Susan, unconsciously, was graver.

Two people noticed. One was Commander Twigg. Very little passed those shrewd, kindly eyes. The other was the Nursing Sister-in-Charge of the First Aid Post. Not over young, quiet, with a sense of humour, dignified and friendly, she had more influence than was generally supposed. To the OC she was invaluable.

At Barton it was the custom, weather and work permitting, for everyone to sit outside to watch the comings and goings on the airfield. Occasionally the OC was to be found there, and it was on one of these rare occasions, about the middle of the following week, that he watched Susan as she walked out with her instructor to the waiting 'plane.

He turned to Sister, who occupied the next chair. 'Something has sobered Mrs Sandyman this week, Sister. Have you any idea?'

Sister shook her head.

'No. But I had noticed. She is very reserved about her personal affairs.'

'Yes, and I like her for it.' The OC watched a few moments longer and, as Susan took off, made a rare comment.

'Have you noticed the way she walks, Sister? One can tell a lot by the way they walk.'

Sister looked up with a smile.

'Well-balanced? Body and mind—'

'Exactly! Well – back to it—' and Commander Twigg disappeared. But, before the week ended, Sister was destined to know. A tiresome mosquito bite took Susan to the surgery. She felt a little foolish and apologized for being fussy.

'I'd like it to be disinfected, please, Sister. Don't think me stupid – but – my baby died of an insect bite.'

'They can be tiresome.' Sister's quiet serenity was impressive. 'We will disinfect and cover it. Tell me about your baby. I've been married years and years. It's a great disappointment that I never had one.' Something clicked. Perhaps it was maternal instinct, and Susan spoke easily. The story came in few words while Sister's fingers were busy, and then Susan found herself, without thought, telling of Robert Jamieson.

'I heard,' she finished, 'only last weekend. He, too, is dead – died of wounds – at sea.'

SIX

THE NEXT WEEK, the first in August, was to stand out in Susan's memory for the rest of her life.

In every way it was a week of contrasts. Brilliant sunshine and fog. Acute, almost painful, happiness, followed by hours of deep depression and doubt of her own capabilities. A growing friendship with Mandy, offset by a blinding jealousy on the part of their room-mate.

From the moment she opened her eyes each morning Susan was aware of every nerve in her body. The days held for her so many possibilities, so many unknown quantities, both human and mechanical. Even the hour's bus ride in the old Black Maria, immediately after breakfast, from Elms Site Canteen over to Barton, was to her full of interest, while for some others it just meant a period of acute indigestion.

For one thing the bus stopped in Aylesbury market-place to collect the newspapers from a little tobacconist's shop, and Susan spent the next half hour combing *The Times* from cover to cover for any small scrap of news of Malaya.

She could never quite understand Mandy who, with two brothers in the forces, promptly turned over the war news and dived straight for a comic strip called 'Jane'.

'Oh, you *must* read "Jane"!' Mandy giggled. '*Do* look – she is actually wearing a leaf today!'

But Susan had never heard of 'Jane', and it was only after a number of such small and apparently unimportant topical references that it dawned on her that five years away from England had left many gaps to be filled.

During the break in lectures the previous week she had sat spellbound while John Cherry had told her about the Battle of Britain, for although in Malaya news of it had eventually filtered through by the press and radio, Susan discovered that she had had little idea of what life had really been like at that time in southern England.

One morning she asked her instructor what she should do if she were to meet a German machine during a cross-country flight.

'I don't expect he would even notice you crawling round the sky in a Maggie,' was his reply, and Susan felt rather damped, as the hundred-miles-an-hour cruising speed of the Magister seemed very fast to her.

'Well now, Mrs Sandyman, I think it is about time we got you started on those cross-countries. Let me see' – he said, apparently concentrating only on refilling his pipe – 'you have practised turning on to course, haven't you?'

'Yes, sir,' Susan answered, her heart tight with excitement.

'And we have done a fair amount of forced landings this week.' He walked over to the door and gazed thoughtfully across the little airfield to the hills beyond, which, in the haze of midday heat, appeared to be moving gently up and down.

'Yes,' he said, suddenly brisk. 'I think we'll do a cross-country this afternoon. Get me your Sheet Eight, will you?'

Susan was glad that her maps were all in order and her locker tidy, because her hands were trembling so much that she was sure that she would never have found it otherwise.

'And I think Sheet Nine, too,' he said, when Susan returned.

Back she went and fetched the map covering East Anglia.

Flight Lieutenant Adamson spread them both on the locker-room table. 'We'll go out to Newmarket,' he said. 'Then out west to this little town here – Olney, it's called – and the third leg back here. I think you can ignore the wind, it is dead calm, so you should have no difficulty in working out the courses. Have an early lunch,' he added, 'and we will take Number Twenty-five. Be ready out here at one thirty.'

It was now about twelve o'clock. 'An hour and a half,' thought Susan, and so anxious was she to have everything worked out in time that she ignored lunch altogether.

John Cherry sauntered up, idly swinging his helmet.

'What's all this?' He gazed with uplifted eyebrows at Susan's maps, ruler, protractor and computer. 'Going on a round trip of the British Isles?'

'Don't be so *blasé*!' Susan removed a pencil from between her teeth. 'It's my first cross-country, and I don't intend to lose myself.'

'Where are you going, honey?' He peered at the map over her shoulder, and Susan could feel his breath on the curls at the nape of her neck.

She told him her route.

'My sweet Sue,' he said patronizingly, 'from a thousand feet you can almost see the grandstand at Newmarket today! It's the proverbial "Piece of Cake"!' He lowered his voice. 'What about having dinner with me in Aylesbury tonight? We can drop off the bus on the way back, and as I left the car in a garage there this morning to be greased, I can run you home afterwards.'

Susan wished he would go away. At this moment she wanted to be left alone to work out the courses and concentrate on the job. For John, with several hundred hours already behind him, a flight such as this was probably childishly simple, but Susan realized that navigation over the wide open countryside of Australia, with its few clearly marked railroads and rivers, was a vastly different matter to finding one's way across the innumerable little fields, patches of woodland, network of railways and criss-cross of streams that was England.

Frank would not have been so selfish, she thought; he would have known just how much it meant to her to do this job well, and he would have encouraged and helped her. He would not have tried to distract her.

Susan was beginning to realize that most of these men who were training with her refused to take the women pilots seriously. Also she found that there were two attitudes, both of which she found equally annoying: either they said, 'I think you girls are quite wonderful!' or else, 'Flying! Why, there's nothing to it! A child could do it!' Most irritating! Why couldn't they accept it as a normal job for a girl without thinking of her as something extraordinary, tough or glamorous?

In that moment it came to her clearly that there was going to be a great deal of male prejudice to overcome from time to time in this game, and, as yet, she had not sorted her thoughts out clearly enough to cope with it.

For the present, and because she did not want to be distracted for the next hour, she gave in.

'OK,' she answered, and immediately her thoughts returned to Sheets Eight and Nine.

By the time she had it all worked out to her satisfaction it was one o'clock, and Susan went to her locker for her helmet and goggles, gauntlet gloves and scarf.

'Hullo, Sue! Been up yet today?' asked Mandy in passing.

'No. First cross-country in half an hour. What about you?'

'Just had my first check with Timber. The old boy was in a marvellous mood and passed me this time – thank heaven!' Mandy looked relieved; her lovely face was flushed, her burnished hair standing on end. Sitting there on the edge of the table, her hands in her pockets and not a spot of powder on her nose, Susan thought she looked more like a slim, handsome young man than a girl.

They went into the cloakroom together. Mandy turned to the mirror. 'What a mess! I shall never get a comb through my hair. Where are you going on this lark of yours, Sue?'

Susan was busy pulling on her helmet.

'Newmarket, Olney and back,' she said. 'Thank goodness you can see for miles to-day. Isn't it a bore – I've let myself in for dinner in Aylesbury tonight with John – can't think why I did it.'

Mandy was tugging a small and useless piece of comb through her head of tangled silk.

'Oh, I don't know. You might have quite fun – he's not as bad as I thought at first. Bit conceited, perhaps, but I have a hunch that is an inferiority complex rearing its head. Anyway, he is mad about you. Now I think I shall celebrate my advent to Thame with Pete and Russ and Co. in the "Crown". Come and join us if you get back in time.'

Susan said she might, and went off to collect a parachute from Dick, the boy who looked after them, and so out into the broiling August sun to the bay where Number Twenty-five was dispersed. She climbed into the rear cockpit and strapped herself in. One of the mechanics came over to her.

'Ready to go, miss?' he asked pleasantly.

'Yes, all set,' said Susan, pulling her goggles down from her forehead.

The mechanic put his hand on the propeller.

'Switches off,' he called.

'Switches off,' repeated Susan.

He gave a few turns.

'Switches on.'

'Switches on,' she answered.

'Contact,' and with a splutter the little Gipsy engine burst into life.

While it was warming up Susan went through her cockpit check, tested the trimmers and throttle-nut tension, mixture and petrol, flaps and gauges, and finally, as she taxied away after running up and flicking her magneto switches, she tried her brakes. All was well and she felt confident.

As she waited, with engine ticking over, outside the window of the Instructor's Room, someone taxied past her, and behind the disguising goggles she recognized John. He gave her the 'thumbs up' sign and her heart warmed to him, but it was of Frank she thought as she turned finally into wind for take-off.

'Come with me,' she asked. 'Help me find the way, darling.'

The take-off was perfect, and climbing gently round the circuit her instructor did not say a word. At fifteen hundred feet he said, 'All right; level off now and set on to course.'

Susan obeyed. How she wished that wretched compass needle would keep still for a moment instead of swinging and hunting like a mad thing.

'Don't chase the needle,' came the voice down the intercom.

'Make use of a check point.'

There was a church steeple which should have been dead on track, but now it had vanished, and Susan looked wildly round for another landmark to check on. She pulled out her map which she had wedged in the cross-straps of her Sutton harness. It was upside down.

'Keep your revs up to nineteen hundred,' came her instructor's voice, and Susan was horrified to see that they had dropped back to sixteen fifty while she had taken her hand off the throttle to get out her map. It was some minutes before she managed to sort it all out, and each minute seemed a year.

'I've got her,' came the voice from the front, calm as ever.

'You've got her, sir,' Susan answered, as she had been taught.

The instructor took her back into the circuit.

'Now, try again. What is your course?' he asked.

'O six O,' Susan replied, and out of the corner of her eye she saw the illusive church steeple.

'You've got her.'

'I've got her, sir.' Away they went, dead on track, and at last the compass needle was steady. After ten minutes or so Susan managed to relax a little; the aircraft perfectly trimmed, the next check point came up according to plan, and slowly confidence returned.

'What is the town to port?' Flight Lieutenant Adamson asked presently.

Susan did not hesitate. 'Cambridge, sir.'

'Good,' he said.

Next Susan looked out on to the wings to check the petrol, for the fuel gauges were set one in each wing-root, and she had been taught to check up on the contents of the two ten-gallon tanks at frequent intervals.

'Port tank full, sir,' she reported. 'Starboard tank seven gallons.'

Presently the grandstand of the Newmarket racecourse came up to port – to Susan's amazement just at the moment she expected it – but instead of the cheering crowds and strings of thoroughbred horses she automatically connected with the very word 'Newmarket', Susan saw that it was now watched over by a squadron of great sinister-looking bombers, and that one of the racecourses had been turned into a huge grass airfield.

'We are now over Newmarket, sir,' she said as soon as they were in the circuit.

'Righto! Changed a bit, hasn't it? Now what is your course to Olney?'

Susan told him, and this time she managed to set off correctly. The visibility was wonderful, and Susan had to admit to John later over their dinner in Aylesbury that her cross-country had been almost as simple as he had predicted.

For the next two days, however, the weather was hopeless for flying, at least as far as the beginners' cross-country flights were concerned, for although it was hot and cloudless there was a thick industrial haze and the visibility was down to a few hundred yards.

Susan became restless. She was longing to be off on a solo cross-country, and while this weather persisted it was hopeless.

Susan found herself spending more and more of her time in John's company. He saw to it that he always sat next to her in the bus; he bought elevenses for her and brought them out to her if she was sitting outside studying in the sun, and then he would continually interrupt her work by telling her that it was no earthly use reading about flying because you could learn more about it during one hour in the air than in one year with books.

'Talk to me, honey,' he would say. 'I can teach you far more than that old book – it's just a waste of time.'

But Susan found that the conversation would all too frequently drift from flying to more personal subjects, and instead of John explaining how to do a cross-wind landing he would be far more likely to tell her how blue her eyes were, or how mad he was about the curling tendrils at the nape of her neck. So that when Friday dawned clear and sunless Susan was more than thankful, and her hopes rose.

It had rained hard during the night, and the whole world smelt fresh and sweet. She got up early and was already dressed when Mandy awoke.

'What's up?' asked Mandy sleepily. 'Why all this energy?'

Susan lied. 'Because that bed was so hard that I could not stay in it another minute. Come on! Get up and walk up to breakfast with me.'

'OK,' Mandy yawned. 'What about you, Jane?' she asked of the figure humped under the bedclothes of the third bed.

'Don't want any breakfast,' was the muffled answer. 'It's too revolting to eat.'

Jane Pritchard had arrived the week after Susan and Mandy, together with a dozen other girls who were also billeted in Hopefield House, but from the beginning she had been difficult and seemed to regard her room-mates with deep suspicion.

'Who are the glamour boys?' she had asked, picking up the folding leather frame on Mandy's chest of drawers containing photos of her two brothers, both in uniform, and scrutinizing them minutely. 'Greedy with the boyfriends, eh?'

There was a certain harshness in her voice and ungraciousness in her manner that grated on Mandy, and for that reason she had not satisfied the other's curiosity.

'Could be,' she had said vaguely, and went off to her bath. Then a week or so later, when they had been going to bed, Susan had enquired: 'How's it going, Jane? Soloed yet?' Jane had suddenly turned on them; her little eyes, which were sunk deep in fat, had flashed, her sallow skin had become blotchy with anger.

'If I looked like either of you I should have gone solo ages ago,' she had said bitterly.

Mandy laughed at such an idea.

'Don't be such an ass, Jane – anyway, you can imagine old Timber caring what anyone looks like! He only cares about what one can *do*. Personal attraction does not count.'

'He's a man, isn't he?' Jane grumbled. 'A girl in the canteen told me yesterday she only got through her Harvard check because she was prepared to play the way her instructor wanted it.'

Susan flushed deeply. This type of backstair insinuation had always annoyed her.

'That is just vicious scandal,' she said. 'And what's more, I don't believe a word of it.'

'Well, wait and see – Miss Know all! You have only been in this racket three weeks.' And there the subject had closed.

This morning Jane was evidently in an equally sour mood. Susan approached her diplomatically.

'You can't fly on an empty tummy, Jane. Come on and have some breakfast. Dried egg won't kill you!'

'It may not, but you two beauties will if you don't shut-up!' and so saying she dived under the bedclothes again.

Susan and Mandy looked at each other.

'Well, I suppose it's your stomach, not mine!' said Mandy good naturedly, and went off to wash.

On the way up to the canteen John overtook them in his red roadster, his RAF cap set at a tremendous angle. He slowed down and saluted the girls showily.

'Anyone want a lift?'

'No, thanks, John,' Susan answered. 'It's only a few hundred yards, and I shall need an appetite to attack those sausages again.'

'OK, Toots! By the way, I shall be through with those flivvers at Barton in a couple of days, so I hope they don't prang all the Harts before I arrive – I'll show you a thing or three on those babies!' He let in the clutch and roared off up the street.

Mandy shook her head slowly, with all the wisdom of her nineteen years. 'He's very young,' she said sadly.

Susan had guessed the weather correctly when she got up that morning for the general weather report, which was telephoned from Thame and pinned up on the Barton notice-board every morning, predicted good visibility, a light south-westerly wind and a cloud base of two thousand five hundred feet. There was also mention of a warm front approaching from the west, but, as it was not to affect that district until nightfall, Susan paid it little attention. She was to learn, that day, that occasionally even the best of meteorological forecasters may be wrong.

Before lunch her instructor was busy with another pupil, and told Susan to go up and do some solo.

'Practise turning on to course again. Do some steep turns, and then some bad weather circuits. Those landings of yours are not too good yet. They are safe enough, but they need lot of polishing.' He clutched an imaginary stick to his chest. 'And don't forget to ease her onto the ground. Don't pull the stick right back until she is about to stall.'

'No, sir. How long shall I stay up?'

'Not more than an hour. I want you to do a cross-country this afternoon.'

Susan was certain that her heart skipped a beat.

'Solo?' she asked.

'Yes. Do you feel quite happy about it?'

'What a stupid question!' thought Susan to herself, for she was certain it must be obvious to anyone that she was simply bursting with happiness. 'Yes, sir,' she assured him, and hoped that she did not sound over-confident.

The hour in the morning went well, and Susan practised setting off on course in several directions. She flew a few miles away from Barton south to Luton, to have a look at the old airfield, and then north towards the Cardington balloons.

The air was not so calm as it had been in the last few days, and Susan realized that she would have to work out her drift carefully in the afternoon. By the time she finally landed the wind-sock was standing out quite stiffly in the breeze, and when she taxied over to the bowser to refuel her 'Maggie' she had some difficulty in keeping her nose from swinging into the wind.

Her instructor was standing at the door when she came into the locker-room.

'Well, how did it go, Mrs Sandyman?' he enquired.

'OK, sir, and I like that machine.'

'Well, you can keep it for your cross-country this afternoon. Now give me your Sheet Eight, and I will show you the route.'

When the map was spread on the table he smoothed out some of the creases.

'Now, I want you to go up to the Bletchley chimneys there – then west to Bicester airfield, down to Thame and back here. It should take just over an hour. Thompson will have Number Six in again by two thirty, and you can go as soon as it is refuelled.'

Susan was almost speechless. At last she was to fly off alone over that enchanting countryside – alone – alone—

'Thank you, sir,' she murmured.

Sharp at two-thirty she was waiting outside, trying her best to appear calm. It was half an hour since she had collected her parachute and signed out with Dick, who was timekeeper as well as parachute checker.

As each Magister touched down the landing was criticized mercilessly by the other pupils, although each knew that he or she could probably do no better themselves. There was an intense, though friendly, rivalry amongst the pilots at this stage, a rivalry which Susan was to find firmly stamped out in the next stages of training, for in ferrying each pilot must fly according to his own capabilities, known only to himself, and not in competition with others. The attitude 'If you can I can' only leads to disaster in the air.

At last there was Number Six taxiing towards the bowser, and immediately Susan jumped up and left the chattering group.

By the time she was sitting crosswind, running through her cockpit check before take-off, it was three o'clock, and although she did not realize it, the cloud-base was considerably lower than had been forecast.

She waited for one more machine to land, then turned into wind, opened the throttle smoothly but firmly, and in a few seconds was climbing round the dark and secret-looking wood on the hill.

She decided to fly at fifteen hundred feet as she had done with her instructor, but soon found that even at twelve hundred tiny wisps of cloud occasionally flicked disconcertingly over her wing-tips. However, she had such blind faith in Flight Lieutenant Adamson that it never crossed her mind that he would let her go up if the weather was in any way doubtful, and she was not to know that, out on a cross-country with another pupil, he was at that very moment casting an anxious eye to the west and hoping she would not take off. She was also not to know that the 'warm front', whose arrival had been forecast in this area for late in the evening, had doubled its speed and was rapidly approaching. In fact, being very honest with herself, it was only the day before that Susan had admitted to Mandy that she was rather vague as to what a warm or cold front really was.

In her usual happy-go-lucky way Mandy had said: 'Oh, I expect we shall recognize one when we meet it. I can't remember much about those lectures either.'

And they had left it at that.

Now Susan merely came down to a thousand feet and, as the

visibility was still good, she did not give the weather another thought and set northwards on the first leg of her flight.

She thought suddenly of Frank and wished most desperately that he could be with her. How he would love this flying! Somehow it did not seem fair that she should be up there, free and happy, when there was so much misery in the world below, so many thousands cooped up in prison camps and so many more yet to suffer. A sensation of unreality passed over her as if she were not sitting up there in Magister Number Six at all, but as if she were outside her body and watching herself from a great distance.

It was the compass needle which brought Susan's mind back with an unpleasant jolt to the cockpit, for in the few seconds her thoughts had been on other matters it had swung almost twenty degrees off course.

Her stomach felt suddenly hollow beneath the Sutton harness, and she looked anxiously from the ground to her map to discover if she was far off track. In spite of the wind her cheeks were burning with the effort of concentration, and it was with great relief that a few moments later she picked up a river and railway, running parallel, which she recognized.

To her joy she also saw that this railway ran on past the big factory chimneys at Bletchley, which was her first turning-point, and feeling very guilty she gave way to a spot of 'Bradshawing'.

A train puffed down the line in a friendly manner which Susan found rather reassuring, and she was surprised to find that she could see cars and people on the roads extraordinarily clearly. She glanced at the altimeter and the feeling of emptiness returned swiftly, not only to her stomach but also to her knees, for instead of flying at one thousand feet she was now down to five hundred, and the factory chimneys should appear at any minute. She climbed sharply, but, at eight hundred feet, again white shreds of clouds wound themselves hungrily round her wing-tips.

'Like sheets back from the laundry,' she was thinking rather foolishly when the chimneys were suddenly there, none too far beneath her.

It was then that she realized that the visibility had deteriorated considerably. Susan's mouth suddenly went quite dry, and though she was determined to remain calm her thoughts were curiously confused. Should she turn back, or was she fussing about nothing, and would her instructor think she had put up a very poor show?

While she was trying to decide she circled round and round the chimneys until the turns became rather too steep, and her thoughts more and more confused. At that moment she would have given anything to have Frank there to make up her mind for her.

Fortunately the north and south-running railway crossed an east and west line at this point, and Susan decided she would turn west on her course, keeping the railway well in sight, so that, in case the weather thickened still more, she could find her way back.

In a very short while it *did* thicken up considerably, and fine rain blotted out all forward vision. Susan stuck grimly to her course for another ten minutes, and then made up her mind to turn back the way she had come. Soon she wished she had done so before!

She turned to starboard so as not to lose sight of the railway, but half-way round she found she was gaining height and was nearly in the clouds again. Over her shoulder she also saw that the weather had closed in behind her and was equally bad now to the east, and finally, while she was busy keeping her turn below the clouds, the worst happened.

The railway line vanished!

Susan felt trapped. These soft, scudding clouds were gradually smothering her and pushing her nearer and nearer to the ground. Rain had misted up her goggles slightly; her map was a crumpled ball, and, whichever way she looked at it, it was upside down.

Beneath her there was a sudden roar, and Susan was afterwards certain that had she not been firmly strapped in she would have shot out of the cockpit with fright. As it was, she thought that the engine was dropping out of the 'Maggie'. But, strangely, the engine seemed to continue behaving in much the same way as before, and then the cause of her fright flashed into view. Another aircraft, which appeared huge to Susan in the murk, had passed close beneath her and seemed now to be making straight for the ground.

She held her breath and waited for the explosion. For the moment she forgot that she herself had no idea where she was, and that the visibility was down to about six hundred yards. To her surprise there was no explosion, and the other machine glided down through the mist and vanished. At the same moment a greenlight shot up in the air, and Susan realized with untold relief that she must have been over an airfield, and that someone was signalling to her by Verey pistol the position of the landing-run.

She banked cautiously in the direction from which it had come, losing height at the same time, but it was not until she was down to four hundred feet that she could distinguish the runways. As far as she could see there were no hangars or buildings, and a thick wood seemed to lie all along one side of the perimeter.

With partly lowered flaps Susan crept along as slowly as she dared, trying to find the signals area, and thereby on which runway she must land. She was glad that in Australia she had learnt to fly on an airfield with runways, for now she knew what to expect.

Another green light was fired from the ground, and this time Susan saw the black and white chequered Control Car, known to all pilots as the 'ice-cream box', at the end of the runway in use. It was not far ahead, so that, in order to land without doing another circuit, she had to make a very steep turn, which, with the already partially lowered flaps, was far from pleasant.

It was gusty near the ground, and before Susan touched down she ballooned up into the air again in such an alarming manner that she was quite certain in a few seconds there would be a horrible scrunch as the whole undercart collapsed. She waited transfixed, unable to do anything about it, while the machine just sank – sank – sank...

For some reason, for ever unknown to Susan, it finally settled quite softly, and there she was sitting, rather dazed and bewildered, not fifty yards from the ice-cream box, the 'Maggie' and herself still in one piece, the engine still turning.

With a dreamlike feeling clinging to her Susan taxied over to the Control Tower, which squatted in a corner of the field next to the wood.

'What a crazy place to put a Control Tower!' she thought. 'No wonder I could not see the signals area!' She was angry now as a result of having scared herself.

By the time she reached the tower the other aircraft, which had roared underneath the Magister on its approach, had just parked and switched off its four huge engines. Looking up at it now, from her tiny cockpit, Susan shivered. She felt like a sightseer before the Sphinx. It was a Stirling, and Susan knew that if it had touched her, or caught the Magister in its slipstream, she would have 'had it'. At this moment a girl in WAAF uniform, with two yellow bats, came out to meet her, waved her into a parking position, and then signalled her to switch off. Susan unstrapped herself, and looked on, feeling rather foolish, whilst the airwoman put chocks in front of her wheels. She did not want to admit to a 'WAAF' that she was lost; on the other hand she hated the thought of facing a crowd of strange officers in the Control Tower and asking where she was. Somehow she felt it would be letting down her sex, for she knew exactly what they would think. 'Just like a woman!'

Looking up at the cockpit of the Stirling she saw the pilot busy pulling off his helmet and goggles, and an idea came to her. 'Can you tell me the course back to Barton-in-the-Clay?' she shouted up to him, casually.

He leant out of the window.

'Certainly, if you can tell me where I am,' he laughed.

Susan stared. Was it? Could it be? Her mouth was open as she gazed upwards, and she was oblivious of the crick in her neck. It was. She was certain, now that his helmet and goggles were really off.

'Mark!' she shouted. 'Mark Cordner!'

Without recognition he stared down at her, then she, too, pulled off her helmet so that the fair curls fell round her face. At once his eyes lit up and an incredulous grin spread across his sunburnt face.

'Well, I'll be blowed!' he burst out. 'If it's not Susan Sandyman! What on earth are you doing here?'

'Come down from your perch and I'll tell you,' Susan called back happily.

Immediately he disappeared from the window and a few seconds later jumped out of a cavity in the fuselage of the Stirling, followed by the other members of his crew.

'Gosh, but it's good to see you!' he said, taking both her hands.

'Now, what in the name of Mike are you doing here?'

'Carrying on the good work you started, Mark. I have joined the ATA.'

He looked at her, admiration in his eyes. 'Well – well – you girls certainly do get around! Let's see – it must be four years ago I taught you to fly in Sydney, then you went off to Malaya, and now I have to come all the way to England to see you again. And what about that handsome husband of yours?' he asked. 'Can he keep up with you?'

Susan ignored his question; she was still too worked up from her flight to trust herself to speak of Frank.

'And what about you?' she countered. 'Squadron Leader, I see. That all looks very grand,' she said, touching the pale blue rings on his shoulder epaulettes.

He brushed her words aside modestly. 'As a matter of fact I have only been over here a few weeks. Took me two years to wangle my way out of instructing in the Empire Training Scheme, but I wore them down in the end, and now I am an OTU before joining a squadron.

'Where are you stationed?'

'Ah ha!' he teased her. 'Careless talk! Come on up to the Control Tower before you get any wetter, and find out where you are yourself first!'

Susan's pleasure at seeing Mark again was suddenly damped by his words.

'Isn't it frightful, Mark – I have put up the most awful black,' she said miserably. 'I have just lost myself on my first cross-country.'

'A very bad reflection on my instruction, Mrs Sandyman!' he said with mock severity.

'Don't worry. I'll fix it. I ought to know how to fool instructors if ever anyone did.'

Susan felt suddenly calmer. Here, she knew, was a man she could rely on completely. A man who, she sensed instinctively, would never let anyone down. With Mark's hand on her shoulder they climbed upstairs to the Control Room, his crew trailing in the background.

Contrary to the picture which Susan had conjured up for herself there was only one very young Flying Officer in charge, a corporal sat quietly at a table with earphones on his head, while two WAAFs somewhere in the background were busily brewing tea. Quite a homely scene.

'Hope you don't need refuelling, sir,' the Control Officer began promptly, 'because we are only just in the process of moving in here, and I don't think the bowsers have arrived yet.'

'No, no – just checking on the weather,' Mark said casually. 'Have you got a Met Office?'

'No, we haven't, sir, but I can ring Bicester for you; they could give you the gen there. Where do you want to get to; sir?'

'Downham Market.' Mark's eyes were laughing across at Susan's much as to say, 'So *now* you know.'

'And this ATA pupil wants to ring her station.' He turned to her. 'Where is it, Susan?'

'Barton. Barton-in-the-Clay – near Luton. I have the 'phone number here if that helps.'

While they were waiting for the call to come through Mark told her what to say, and what line to take. He also told her that from a notice he had spotted on the wall, he gathered they were at an airfield called Finmere.

The corporal interrupted. 'Through now, miss.'

Her heart pounding, Susan picked up the receiver, for in spite of Mark's reassurances she was quite certain that her flying days in ATA were numbered.

'Hullo, Barton? Is Flight Lieutenant Adamson there? This is Mrs Sandyman.'

'Yes,' croaked Dick's scarcely broken voice, 'I'll fetch him.' Susan turned her back on Mark and gazed over the rain-sodden airfield.

'Hullo, Mrs Sandyman. Where are you?'

'At Finmere, sir,' she answered, praying that her voice sounded calm. 'I landed here because of the weather; it seemed to me well below the ATA limit of eight hundred feet and two thousand yards.'

'Quite right,' came an approving voice at the other end. 'That warm front arrived sooner than expected – caught Met on the hop.

You'd better hang on there for an hour or so, and I will come over and fetch you.'

'Thank you, sir.' Susan put down the receiver with a sigh of relief.

She had got away with it this time, and no one but Mark would ever know that she had been hopelessly lost and not a little frightened.

SEVEN

IN THE EXCITEMENT of meeting her old instructor again Susan did not, at first, notice how the last four years had changed Mark Cordner. It was only after they had been sitting for some time in the Control Tower over a welcome cup of tea that she saw the grey flecks among the thick black hair, and the network of tiny wrinkles round his eyes.

She knew his age to be about thirty. She remembered that he was younger than Frank, whose thirty-first birthday had only just passed; but, looking at him now, she thought he seemed mature beyond his years.

Their tea finished, he brought out his cigarette case. 'Cigarette?' he asked, and as he struck a match for her their eyes met across the flame in a flash of unspoken understanding.

'Your husband is missing, isn't he?' Mark's words were spoken without preliminary.

'Yes.' Susan's answer came simply and directly. 'He was posted missing soon after I got home, but I *know* he is dead. I knew the night Felicity died. We had a daughter, you know: she died on the way home.'

'I am terribly sorry, my dear. He was a marvellous chap.'

The sympathy expressed by Mark's voice and eyes was almost too much for Susan, and Mark sensed it. Quickly, to distract her, he asked about her flying, and the training she was undergoing, in such a way that she knew he really wanted to know. After that it was easy to tell him how nearly she had come to grief that afternoon.

'You will find navigation difficult in this country after Australia,' he said. 'I do myself. That is why I am here this afternoon. I hadn't a clue either as to where I was! Our radio died on us. But knowledge will come if you work at it.' He smiled. 'Don't worry too much; we all boob sometimes.'

So much more encouraging, Susan thought, than John, who was always telling her that flying a machine like a Magister was child's play and all this ATA training and special cockpit drill really rather ridiculous. It was also a wonderful relief to be again with someone who had known Frank; to be able to reminisce and to talk of mutual acquaintances and places known and loved before the war. Almost every sentence began, 'Do you remember?' or 'Do you know what has happened to so-and-so?' and Susan was surprised when the Control Officer came over and said there was another Magister in the circuit.

'Heavens! How time has flown, and there is still so much I want to ask you, Mark.'

He looked at her very directly, his grey eyes searching hers. 'May I fly over and see you at Barton?' he asked. 'I can always find an excuse to land.'

A doubtful little frown gathered on Susan's wide forehead.

'You could never get a Stirling into Barton, Mark. It's only a corney little grass airfield, and to tell you the truth I don't quite know the form about visitors. I believe they are rather frowned on at this stage. But I tell you what. If you can give me a fortnight to get through these cross-countries I should love you to come and see me at Thame – I know they don't mind there.'

Mark's eyes lit up.

'That's a date, then, and I shall give you a ring before I come to make certain that it is OK. I think we had better be off now, too,' he said, looking out at the rapidly improving visibility. He turned to his crew who were lounging at the other end of the Control Room.

'Come on, chaps, we are off.'

He took Susan's hand.

'*Au revoir*. That is the first warm front that I have ever blessed! Take care of yourself, and don't forget that you can kill yourself just as easily in a "Maggie" as you can in Stirling!'

A tight little feeling came into Susan's throat as she watched them climb into the huge bomber. What a day it had been! Happiness, excitement, fear, and then – Mark! Somehow the past had caught right up to the present with a most unexpected jolt, and Susan felt she needed both time and peace in which to readjust herself.

The opportunity, however, did not arise that evening, for when Susan went down to Hopefield House to wash before supper she found the place in a state of upheaval. As she walked into the hall two girls came out of the box-room under the stairs dragging trunks behind them, their eyes swollen, faces as black as thunder, while upstairs she found Jane Pritchard lying prostrate on her bed in a paroxysm of sobbing, with Mandy vainly trying to comfort her.

Susan gathered it had been a black day all round, for Mandy told her that not only had these three girls failed to make the grade, but also two of the men in Hart flight, one of them a pilot with several hundred hours' experience.

'Some purge!' commented Mandy. 'Can't think how I escaped it.'

Walking up to the canteen later Susan told Mandy of her own day and how nearly she must have come to being chucked out herself!

'Shaky do,' was Mandy's brief comment. 'I, for one, shall be amazed if I ever get as far as a Wings check myself!' She sighed wistfully, and for a moment a silent gloom fell on them both.

However, depression could never settle very heavily on Mandy, and by the time they reached the canteen she had completely forgotten all the hazards that lay between her and the coveted golden wings.

It was not long before John Cherry joined them at their table. This was very usual. John Cherry and several other pupil pilots often forgathered in the canteen for supper, and then, by mutual, unspoken consent, wandered off either to the 'Crown' or the 'Rose and Thistle', a tiny timbered beer-house near the church. The same seven or eight were usually to be found together, or, if some were missing, the chances were that one of the others would know where they were.

Susan never fathomed the link in that loose-knit, but none the less definite, friendship, for eight more varied characters would have been hard to find. Now they discussed the happenings of the day, the merits and moods of their instructors, the vices and peculiarities of the machines they were flying at the moment, the bad luck of the pilots who had failed that day, and where they were going the next weekend.

As casual and happy-go-lucky a crowd as you could meet, Susan sometimes thought. There was fat Robin with his thick horn-rimmed glasses, who, from what one could gather, had been more or less a spoilt playboy before the war, while Max, the White Russian sitting opposite him, never had a penny to his name and had fiddled his way round the world for a living. Then there was little Russ, the Canadian – Susan never knew her proper name – who barely complied with the five-foot-two-inch regulation, and, always in close attendance, Robert, whose mother had been a princess. Given the chance Robert would talk for hours on end about an eccentric figure called 'Squirrel', who Susan only discovered weeks later was his wife. She always had a lurking suspicion that Robert was crazy, but he failed on navigation in the end, and so she never had a chance to make sure.

Gavin Reid, the schoolmaster from the Hebrides, whose bad eyesight barred him from the forces, and Nina, a Polish countess who had escaped after the invasion of her country, made the number up to six, while Mandy and Susan herself completed the eightsome.

That was how it had been so far, but, by the next evening, the circle was broken for the first time.

Susan came back from Barton tired but happy, having succeeded in completing a cross-country without losing herself. It was still too early for supper, so she wandered into the 'Crown', more to find some of the others than because she wanted a drink.

Then she found Max alone, sitting up on one of the well-worn stools at the bar, his chin resting on his fists, a large whiskey between his elbows. Apart from the obvious gloom which hung over him, Susan knew immediately that there was something wrong, for Max had never been known to drink anything but beer, and here he was with a large whiskey in front of him, and an air about him as if this were not by any means the first.

She walked up to the bar and quietly slipped on to the stool at his side.

'What's the trouble, Max?' she asked. 'Surely they have not dispensed with your valuable services, too?'

Max continued to stare straight ahead, misery in every line of his fine, expressive face. After a few seconds' silence he picked up his glass and knocked back the whiskey in one.

'Same again, please,' he said to the barmaid, then turned to Susan at last. 'Gavin bought it this morning,' he said. Then, before she had time to speak: 'I saw it all... I was in the circuit. Saw him burn up under my eyes... bloody fire-engine too damn' shlow.' He was beginning to slur his words badly now, and when he put his hand out for his new drink he missed the glass altogether.

'Shorry,' he said gently to Susan. ''Fraid I'm shtinking! You better go home... Gavin won't be coming,' he added emphatically.

Realizing that there was very little she could do for Max in his present condition, and feeling rather sick and dazed by his news, Susan left the 'Crown' and walked across the little square to a lane which twisted its way round the back of the village, eventually reappearing opposite the church.

The evening air was hot and sultry; thunder rumbled distantly along the hills, while in the heavy foliage of the ancient oaks beyond the churchyard not a leaf stirred.

'This,' thought Susan, 'is what novelists call a pregnant silence. I wonder when the storm will break?'

She was not left wondering long, for at that moment an ominous sigh ran through the trees and an eddy of white dust was stirred up viciously at her feet. Looking at the sky Susan knew she would not have time to walk back to the canteen before the rain came, and, in any case, she was not particularly hungry. On the other hand she could pop into the 'Rose and Thistle', which was only a few yards away, and have a sandwich supper, or she could go straight back to Hopefield House.

However, neither alternative appealed to her just then; she wanted to be undisturbed and alone. The first drop of rain splashed on her cheek, and Susan looked for nearer shelter. The church! She could shelter in the porch if it happened to be closed. She walked through the ancient lych-gate and hurried up the path, to find the heavy old door unlocked.

A clap of thunder crashed overhead and the sound reverberated the length of the vaulted Saxon chancel like the notes of a mighty cathedral organ. Susan sat down in a pew near the back of the church, a pew whose seat had been well polished by the worshippers of six centuries. She slipped to her knees.

'Dear God,' she prayed almost violently, 'help men to stop hating and killing. Help us to banish fear and misery from this beautiful world.'

At intervals lightning flashed through the stained-glass windows, illuminating the crucifix on the altar with swift, startling brilliance, then leaving it again as suddenly in an unnatural darkness. Normally no one would have said that Susan had an emotional nature, but could they have seen her now they might have thought differently; might also have realized that her normally calm exterior was a shell, deliberately cultivated to hide a more than usually sensitive nature.

The soft curls falling round her sunburned forehead were quite damp; the veins on her temples showed blue; her knuckles almost pushed through the tightly drawn skin where her fists gripped the back of the next pew. Her whole body was taughtened to snapping point. The stabbing sorrows of the last year, which she had so far kept under control, seemed now to well up inside her in one overpowering wave, and suddenly she let go. Her body crumpled, her head sank forward on to her arms, and she gave herself up to her grief.

How long Susan wept she had no idea, but when at last she raised her head and brushed away her tears the summer storm had also ceased, and slowly the peace of this simple village church began to seep into her troubled heart.

And strangely, with this peace, came thoughts of Mark Cordner and his quiet understanding.

'God keep him safe,' she murmured as she closed the ponderous, nail-studded door behind her and slipped into the sweet, rain-washed dusk.

EIGHT

THE STORM HAD cleared the air and was followed by almost a week of brilliant, cloudless days, and the Magisters at Barton were in the air from dawn to dusk.

Sometimes Susan did two cross-countries in one day; occasionally her instructor went with her to see how her navigation was progressing, but more often she flew solo. Since her experience at Finmere she took greater trouble over her navigation, and slowly confidence returned, but she was well aware that the present weather conditions were no real test.

One feature of the training which appealed to her, perhaps more than any other, was low flying. This was only officially permitted over certain areas, and then only with an instructor. However, it would be idle to pretend that this was actually the case, for most pupils only waited until they were out of sight of the airfield before they put in a little solo practice on this exercise, and Susan was no exception.

In fact, had she but known it, she was one of the worst offenders, for there was an irresistible fascination, for her, in skimming field of waving corn, swooping low over a sweet-smelling bean or clover field, or hopping the green hedges of Buckingham and Bedfordshire. Apart from the sensation of speed, Susan loved the exhilaration of having to co-ordinate mind, eye and hand with perfect precision, and she would return from these flights with eyes bright and cheeks unnaturally flushed.

Had she known how many people on the ground would, and often did, report pilots for this offence, she would undoubtedly not have risked it, but it was not until some weeks later that she was to learn this by another's misfortune. In the meantime it added to the untold joys of flying!

Since John Cherry had been checked out and was now in the Hart Flight at Thame, Susan found she had more time to read and study the theory of flight and navigation than before, which, in spite of his ridicule, she felt must be of some use to her.

Although she was unaware of it, as were most of the other pupils, the instructors did notice what each pilot did when he, or she, was not actually flying, and if the same pupils were continually to be found playing ping-pong, or lying idly in the sun, judgments were passed which were bound to influence chances of later success. Not that Susan was by any means always to be found with her nose in an aeronautical textbook. Far from it, as in any case her friendly nature would have made that impossible.

There was something about her that made others want to confide in her, and frequently she found herself sitting outside the pilots' hut, in the sun, listening to the past lives and experiences of other pupils as if they had known her for years, instead of a few weeks. Sometimes she would have really intimate confessions and worries poured out to her, and it was brought home to her more and more forcibly that her own misfortunes were, perhaps, preferable to some of the sordid and vicious tangles into which many other lives seemed to be woven.

At other times the conversation would be purely of flying, and then Susan often found there was something to be learned even from another pupil, a new angle on one of her own difficulties or a small crumb of knowledge to be stowed away until the right occasion should demand it again.

Unconsciously to herself, Susan's horizon was broadening. In spite of the fact that she had travelled more than most, she was coming in contact now, in ATA, with a wider cross-section of humanity than ever before. Her mind was fully occupied, her interest vitally aroused; and she came fully to realize that if she were going to be of real use in this ferrying service, and acquit herself well in the months ahead, she must learn not only to fly, but to work happily alongside all manner of men and women.

By the end of the week Susan was flying the Tiger Moth, and after an hour's dual, which included some elementary aerobatics, Flight Lieutenant Adamson sent her off to put in a couple of hours' solo.

'I should like to get your check in with Captain Twigg tomorrow,' he said. 'Then, all being well, you can start at Thame on Monday.'

'Yes, sir,' said Susan, inwardly quaking at the thought of another check.

The next morning, however, Captain Twigg was busy testing some new pupils before their first solo flights, and Flight Lieutenant Adamson told her to take a Magister over to Thame to fetch the post.

'Give you a bit more cross-country, anyway,' he said. 'Do you know where to go for the mail?' Susan shook her head, for although a pupil or instructor flew over to Thame daily for this purpose, it had as yet never fallen to her lot.

'You will find it already sorted in the General Office at Flying Control, and it should easily fit into the locker at the back; but if there are any large parcels see that they are well tied down in the front cockpit and cannot foul the controls.'

Susan was glad that she would have one more flight before her check, one more hour in which to practise her navigation, for the memory of her first cross-country was still in the forefront of her mind and she had a horror of losing herself with Captain Twigg on board.

As she went out to fetch her 'Maggie' she looked at the sky and suddenly realized that she had not seen the Met report that morning. For a second she hesitated, but it was such a perfect day there seemed no need to bother, and by the time she reached her machine the matter was forgotten.

The air was like a very dry wine, with that slightly bitter tang of early autumn which made Susan glad of the rough sheepskin jacket which Frank had bought for her during one of their holidays up in the hills, and which she had sent home. A feeling of wild exhilaration overcame her as she climbed into the cockpit, and she felt she could do anything from a loop to a barrel roll.

At a thousand feet she trimmed the little aircraft out perfectly, turned on to course, leaving the hill with its heavily wooded crown to port and headed westwards, singing at the top of her voice. Not that she could hear much, but just that her happiness was so intense it had to overflow somehow.

By the time Leighton Buzzard came under the starboard wing Susan noticed long fingers of morning mist were still hanging over the low-lying water meadows, and with every mile she flew further west the white blanket spread and grew in depth. But Susan did not worry unduly. From her Met lectures she knew that this mist was formed by the action of the cold air of the early autumn nights on the high temperature of the days, and as time progressed she knew that the sun would disperse it completely.

Time to worry lay five minutes ahead, when the strands of mist joined up to form solid white curtain hanging across the valley from the Chilterns in the south, and northward as far as she could see.

Hovering on the edge of this drop-curtain, Susan muttered to herself very uncomplimentary opinions on the English weather, but as she was herself flying out in the sunlight in fine calm air she was in no way perturbed. In fact the mist soon appeared to her as a definite challenge; something against which she could pit her wits and airmanship, as one would against an opponent in a game.

As a preliminary Susan poked her nose into the mist at a thousand feet and found she could see nothing, neither the ground below nor the blue sky above, but just a golden glow from the direction of the sun.

Out she came again, dived down to four hundred feet and tried again. At this height she found she could see the ground vaguely, but that all the outlines were blurred, and under these conditions she knew that although she was only six or seven miles from Thame she might easily fly over it without ever recognizing it as an airfield.

The game became more intriguing! Susan did not intend to be beaten, and her normally strong chin took on a very determined line. Then, suddenly, a shaft of sunlight striking one of the steel tracks of the railway line gave her an idea.

Banking away from the mist, she flew back a mile or more down the line, losing height as she went, and it was not until the altimeter showed two hundred feet that she turned and flew along the track towards the soft white curtain.

'How smug it looks, hanging there!' Susan thought to herself, and she smiled a very determined little smile.

Down went a portion of the flaps, down came the speed to eighty miles an hour, and down dropped the mist, hungrily hugging and pawing the intruder. At two hundred feet Susan found she could quite easily follow the railway, and as her eyes became accustomed to the gloom she climbed another hundred feet for safety.

A few minutes' flying and she saw the chimneys of Aylesbury below her, as she had expected. Her plan now was simply to follow the line a few miles south to Princes Risborough, and turn sharp right up the Bicester line which would eventually lead her right into Haddenham village, and so past the airfield.

That this was not the correct way to navigate Susan was well aware, but she was also perfectly sure that it was the only way she would ever find the airfield in such a mist, and, after all, surely that was the purpose of her journey? With the knowledge that, if she wanted, she could always turn back and fly due east until she came out of the murk into clear sunlight a few miles away, she had no fears, and crept happily on up the line.

When she landed on Thame airfield most of the pupils and instructors must have been in the snack bar drinking coffee, for having parked her 'Maggie' in the visitor's bay opposite the lecture-room, Susan went into the pilots' rest-room and found it deserted.

After pulling off her helmet she was about to go to the cloakroom and have a brush-up before reporting herself in and collecting the mail when a voice spoke so loudly from the tannoy, just above her head, that she caught her breath.

'Attention, please. Will the pilot of the Magister which has just landed report to Flying Control immediately.'

The amplifier clicked sharply, only to reopen almost at once. 'Attention, please!' came the impersonal voice and the request was repeated.

It was only after this repetition that Susan realized it was addressed to herself. She was the wanted pilot. Still glowing with the satisfaction of having beaten the weather, and secretly hoping that now she was to be congratulated on her performance, Susan walked confidently across to the hut, which housed not only Flying Control Officers, but also the School CO Adjutant, Chief Instructor and General Office Staff.

As she came in, the glass hatch of the Control Room snapped open and a large officer with large horn-rimmed spectacles glared at her.

'I am the pilot of the Magister,' she announced, smiling.

There was a silence that seemed an eternity, and before any more words were spoken Susan knew that something was wrong.

At last the Control Officer spoke.

'Commander MacKenzie would like to see you, Mrs Sandyman,' he said coldly. 'Will you wait there until he is ready for you?'

The hatch snapped down again and Susan was left in the passageway, her balloon completely deflated; all joy and pride in her flight vanished. However, she had not time to think of what her misdeed might be before a door opened behind her, a voice said, 'Come in, please, Mrs Sandyman,' and in a few seconds she found herself seated opposite the Commanding Officer of the entire Training School.

He was a tall, thin man this side of forty, and he looked across his desk at Susan with serious eyes.

'You were on the last Ground Course here, I believe, Mrs Sandyman,' he began. 'What did you learn there about weather limits in ATA?'

So that was it! She had disobeyed the weather regulations.

'Two thousand yards and eight hundred feet,' Susan answered automatically, and wished those steely eyes opposite were not quite so penetrating.

'And what would you consider the visibility to be now?' he asked.

The colour rushed to her cheeks and Susan wished the earth would open and swallow her up.

'About fifteen hundred yards, I should think,' she lied valiantly.

'Your judgment seems a little at fault today.' His voice was quiet but very hard now, and for the second time Susan thought her flying days were over.

'Actually the visibility is six hundred yards at the moment,' he told her. 'And you did your circuit at a maximum of three hundred feet.' He paused, his eyes never leaving her face.

'Now I don't know why you did it, and I am not going to ask you, but I must remind you that at this time the country cannot afford foolhardy ferry pilots; it wants every machine that can be produced, and it wants it delivered undamaged. That is your job. Remember,' he said, speaking slowly and emphasizing each word, 'you are not paid to be brave – you are paid to be *safe*!'

'This is the end,' Susan thought. 'I wish he would hurry up and get it over.'

Suddenly the suspense was broken by the telephone ringing busily on the desk between them.

The Commander picked up the receiver.

'Hullo! Commander MacKenzie here,' he said, and Susan heard a woman's voice at the other end.

'Sorry to disturb you, darling,' came the faint though distinct voice. 'But I thought I had better remind you to fetch the fish, because there's not a thing in the house for tonight, and the Marshes have just rung up and invited themselves to dinner. Isn't it hell?'

The stern face had softened. 'Don't worry, my dear. I'll remember—' and after a few more words he rang off.

The spell was broken. For Susan the great man had suddenly become human, quite normal – if not positively humdrum. He had to collect the fish!

A faint smile on his lips, the Commander's eyes came back to Susan's face, but now they had lost their hardness.

'I have already telephoned to Captain Twigg, and he says you have the makings of quite a useful pilot – this time I shall take no further action, but make certain it does not happen again.'

A feeling of such utter relief swept over Susan that she was almost speechless and only just managed a faint, 'Thank you, sir.' The Commander walked over to the window and, screwing up his eyes, peered out into the rapidly lifting mist.

'I gather you came for the Barton post,' he said. 'You will find it in the General Office next door. This mist will have cleared in an hour or so and you can go back.'

Susan slipped thankfully from the room and went straight over to the snack bar for a much needed cup of coffee.

But she would have been surprised if she could have heard the Commander talking to his Chief Instructor later that morning.

'The girl who brought that "Maggie" over has certainly got guts. Old Timber says she is going to be good, so keep an eye out for her when she comes over here. She's due next week, I think.'

Flight Captain Shillingford grinned. 'I suppose you tore her off a hell of a strip all the same!'

'Yes,' he answered, 'and she took it very well. I've had rather too many of the tearful type lately. I think I need a book on "How to tell a girl she's had it; in two easy lessons".'

In the meantime Susan found John Cherry in the snack bar.

'Pansy landing, Sue!' he congratulated her. 'I heard them call you on the blower; what had their Lordships got to say?'

'They were not exactly pleased,' she said with a wry smile. 'In fact I received an Imperial rocket from the Lord High Executioner in person.'

John raised his eyebrows in mock alarm.

'Dear me,' he said severely. 'Naughty, naughty!'

'None of these pilots,' Susan thought, 'will ever admit to each other any respect for authority; they will always be flippant about their misdeeds; treat rules and regulations as a joke'; and she realized that she, too, had reacted in exactly the same way. She would never let John know how small and scared she had felt just now in the Commander's office.

She caught sight of herself in a mirror hanging on the wall.

'Heavens! What a mess!' she said, running her fingers through her hair. 'You might have told me, John.'

'But I think you look lovely, Sue. I like you all windswept! Have another cup of dishwater?'

'No, thanks. I must go and get the Barton post from the General Office. I ought to be able to go soon.'

'OK. I'll walk up with you,' John said.

When they were outside he took her arm. 'What about that weekend you promised to come and stay at the cottage with George and me?'

George was his brother, a confirmed bachelor ten years John's senior, and a barrister of great promise. Too old for the armed forces – a state of affairs he felt very deeply – George ran the village Home

Guard with enormous energy, and at weekends John really saw very little of him. However, he did not mention this to Susan, nor did he think it necessary to tell her that George frequently spent the night at the Home Guard hut.

'I promised nothing, John,' she answered, 'and my weekend is already planned. Anyway, I am having a check with Timber this afternoon so, with any luck, I shall be over here on Monday. We can talk about it then.'

She had to admit to herself that John was very kind, very good natured and undeniably handsome. 'If only he did not know it!' she reflected.

They fetched the post together and then sat on the wooden bench outside the School rest-room to wait for the weather to clear. Already the sun was piercing the mist, and it was extraordinarily warm and pleasant outside.

Idly Susan flicked through the pile of Barton letters, and, to her great surprise, found that there was envelope addressed to herself. She did not recognize the somewhat spidery and essentially male handwriting, but opened it and turned straight to the signature.

Yours very sincerely, Mark Cordner, she read.

John was watching her intently, and on seeing the colour warm in her cheeks his interest was promptly aroused.

'Long-lost boyfriend?' he asked, apparently casually.

'No,' Susan answered. 'Long-lost instructor!'

'Snake!' John commented. 'They always are. Anyway, what's he doing at Newmarket?'

Immediately Susan raised the notepaper so that he could read no further, and if she had not been so interested in what Mark had to say she would have stopped to tell John that she was not used to people reading her letters over her shoulder.

As it was he had merely seen the printed address *Officers' Mess, RAF Station, Newmarket*.

My very dear Susan [Mark began].

It is now almost a month since we met at Finmere, and you must be thinking me very rude not to have contacted you sooner, but quite honestly what with being posted here, and my first few ops., my time has been rather full. Please forgive me.

There is a station party laid on here for next Saturday, 14th, and I am wondering if you would care to come? Should be quite amusing. I could pick you up in a Proctor about five o'clock and have hopefully booked a room for you at the Rutland Hotel.

At present very few of my activities can be committed to paper, so all news when I see you – please try and make it!

Goodluck with your flying.

Yours very sincerely,
Mark Cordner.

PS. Will you be at Thame by then?

'What's he got to say that's so interesting?' John asked as Susan proceeded to reread the letter. 'Shooting you the hell of a line, I suppose.'

'Um?' Susan murmured vaguely. 'Nothing.'

'Well, stop reading it, then, and promise you'll come and stay the weekend after this,' John persisted impatiently.

Ignoring this Susan rose and remarked: 'Time to be off. It's as clear as a bell now. See you on Monday – Timber willing.'

John walked over to her Magister with her and helped her stow the mail safely, then stood by and watched while a mechanic swung her prop. and she warmed the engine up.

'What a Popsy!' was his thought. 'Pity she's so obstinate.'

Susan, however, did not give him another thought, and most of the time on her way back to Barton she was wondering if her mother would mind very much if she accepted Mark's invitation. It would be fun and it was so many, many months since she had danced.

As the hills at Barton came into sight Susan was debating what she would wear – her old and much-loved midnight-blue crepe or the new and utterly ruinous chiffon creation which Grannie had insisted she buy herself, and, although she did not realize it, this was the first time since she had dined with Robert Jamieson that she had given a moment's serious thought to her clothes.

With even greater care than usual she did her circuit.

Subconsciously her determination to pass her final check out of Barton was strengthened, for then she would be able to tell Mark that she had mastered navigation and had progressed to the next stage of her training. Her conscious mind said, 'You must make a good landing because Timber, or your instructor, may be watching, and you've put up enough blacks for one day.'

Perhaps it was because Susan was concentrating so hard on her approach that she failed to see another Magister just beneath her, also preparing to land, and taking exactly the same line as herself.

She throttled back and, as her speed dropped to seventy-five miles an hour, she slipped down the last few degrees of flap.

Suddenly a red light rocketed into the air in front of her, and in the same moment she saw the other machine a few feet in front and below her. For a split second she hesitated, then automatically banged open the throttle.

The little craft responded valiantly, staggering through the air as if dragged by sheer will-power.

With nerves strung fiddle-tight Susan went round the circuit again. 'You BF,' she told herself. 'That's cooked your goose properly!'

However, to her surprise and intense relief, the incident had apparently passed unnoticed, except by the Duty Pilot who had fired the Verey pistol, and when after lunch Flight Lieutenant Adamson questioned her about her unfortunate performance at Thame that morning, he made no mention of it.

'Sooner or later you will kill yourself, Mrs Sandyman,' he said seriously, 'unless you learn to respect the English climate. More pilots are killed by weather in a month than by engine failure in a year, and unless you remember that you might as well stay on the ground.' Then seeing that his words had gone home, and that a cloud of depression was rapidly descending on his pupil, he changed the subject. 'Captain Twigg will take you on your "check" sometime this afternoon. Fly as you have been doing lately and you'll be all right.'

He turned to speak to another instructor who was passing and Susan slipped gratefully away.

In the rest-room she found Mandy sprawled in an arm-chair, a book open on her lap, her eyes focused somewhere in the middle distance. Susan flopped down beside her.

'Grizzly morning,' she said gloomily.

'What's the trouble? Gosh, it's hot!'

'Just plain finger trouble – firmly cemented in today. Two blacks already, and still a "check" to get through.'

Mandy's interest livened, and temporarily the heat became of secondary importance.

'Deep blacks or pale greys?' she asked.

'Deepish.' Susan sighed, and told her of her morning's dice to Thame.

'By the way, there were two letters for you. Did you get them?'

'Umm – from Mummy. Nothing but "jam-making – that impossible Major – and those noisy machines at night".' Mandy mimicked her mother to perfection. 'Mummy's really a scream,' she continued affectionately. 'Even with a house full of soldiers the war's still a myth to her. You know, she was far more worried about Cook getting off with a sergeant than she was about Dunkirk! And a hundred times more upset about Richard's uniform being torn than that he had had to bale out!'

Susan laughed. 'Perhaps it's a good thing,' she said tolerantly. 'What she doesn't know about she can't flap about.'

'S'pose so.' Mandy yawned. 'I've decided to blow some coupons on a new dinner dress,' she added inconsequently.

Susan raised her eyebrows. 'The other letter?' she teased immediately.

There was growing between the two that certain understanding, amounting almost to telepathy, which is inevitable if two minds live receptively alongside each other in the same environment, doing the same work. If one mind shot off at a tangent the other could jump with it, whereas to a third person the conversation would seem disjointed and meaningless.

'Could be.' Mandy's voice was studiedly casual. 'Think I shall try Fortnum. I've got an account. Daddy's a darling, but the Home Guard have been difficult lately.'

Susan needed no explanation; she had heard Sir Francis on the subject of his daughter's banking account.

'What colour do you—'

'Mrs Sandyman?' Susan had her back to the Instructor's Room door and had not seen Captain Twigg come in. She jumped up. 'Yes, sir.'

'Fetch Number Twelve, will you, and bring your Sheet Eight?'

'Yes, sir.'

As the square shoulders of the CO disappeared through the door again, Mandy prodded Susan with her toe. 'Now for goodness' sake don't make a nonsense of it, because I think I'm having him later, and I shall need a very sweet-tempered Timber to see me through.'

'OK. Here's hoping!' and Susan went off to get her flying kit.

As Mandy had said, it certainly was hot, and while Susan sat outside in Number Twelve, waiting for Captain Twigg, she could feel the heat throbbing right through her.

It would be good to get in the air!

However, as soon as the CO climbed into the forward cockpit Susan was unaware of the heat – unaware of everything except her instruments, the map on her knee and the voice coming to her down the rubber ear-tubes. It was impersonal and slightly gruff.

'Can you see a village called Nettlebed on your map, Mrs Sandyman? Not far from Benson.'

Susan had flown over Benson airfield once on one of her cross-country flights, and now she saw with relief that she had already drawn a direct line to it on her map. That would make things much easier! Nettlebed, she found, was up on the Chilterns, a few degrees south-east of Benson.

'Yes, sir,' she said into the mouthpiece. 'I see it.'

'Fly me to Nettlebed church, then,' came the voice.

'Yes, sir.'

Susan went through her cockpit check with more than usual care, repeating it aloud, as she did to her own instructor. Her take-off was good and she set off accurately on course along the line of hills to the south-west.

All went well, and very little was said until the reservoirs near Halton lay just to starboard, then Susan felt the throttle pulled right back by a hand in the front cockpit.

'Your engine has cut,' the voice announced dispassionately.

Susan had often practised forced landings, both with Flight Lieutenant Adamson and by herself, but never had the throttle been cut on her over such an awkward piece of country. To the left of her were the hills with the wind coming off them, to the right of her the two reservoirs, and in the only two fields she could see ahead there were men cutting corn. There was only one hope. She saw a narrow field, almost a gully, running up towards the steeper slope of the hills. It would be dead into wind, and, although from a thousand feet it did not look as if the Magister could possibly fit in, she determined to try it.

She trimmed the machine to its gliding speed and side-slipped off a little height.

'Don't lose so much height.' The voice seemed steel-hard to Susan. 'You'll need it.'

Commander Twigg was right, for when the hedge was still fifty yards ahead Susan found she only had a few feet to play with.

'I've got her.' This time Susan heard the voice with relief and she was able to relax slightly while Captain Twigg opened the throttle and swung swiftly away from the hills.

'You've got her,' he said, when he had climbed to a thousand feet again. 'All right, take me on to Nettlebed.'

On the way he asked her the name of a town down the railway to starboard.

'Princes Risborough,' she answered.

'Sure?'

A moment's ghastly uncertainty. 'Yes, sir.'

'Right.' Susan doggedly checked every road, every wood on her track, for she was determined not to get lost. There seemed to be a mass of woods and a network of lanes, and she was concentrating so hard that she almost flew right over Nettlebed without registering it as her destination. Then she saw the main Oxford road, and knew she was there.

'This is Nettlebed, sir.'

'Right. Climb to two thousand feet.'

Up she went in a climbing turn.

'I want a steep turn to the left and straight into a steep turn to the right.'

By the time Susan had repeated this exercise several times her sense of direction was slightly confused, and when Captain Twigg said, 'Fly me to Thame,' for a few moments she was at a loss. She looked at her watch. Four o'clock. Then at the sun. That must be getting on for west. Luckily Thame lay almost due north, and she re-set her compass with a certain amount of confidence. It was not long before Susan saw the hangars in the distance, for the visibility was good and her eyesight perfect.

Once in the circuit Captain Twigg said: 'Good. Take me back to Barton.'

This was a track Susan had flown over several times, and her course was dead accurate. Twice on the way Timber cut the throttle, and both times Susan made passable forced landings, so that the rest of the 'check' was uneventful, which is surely the most satisfactory state of affairs for which a pilot could wish. Before the CO called her into his office Susan felt she had made the grade, but her surprise was great when, looking her very straight in her eye, he said:

'If you continue to work as well at Thame as you have here, you will finish in the first flight. But, Mrs Sandyman,' he added, 'never forget the weather! Good luck!' and he shook her firmly by the hand.

NINE

SO EAGER WAS Susan to begin the second stage of her training that she awakened unusually early on that first morning, and before Mandy's clock had given its shrill warning she was up and dressed. Then, waiting only to see that Mandy was really awake, she hastened to get her bicycle and rode up to the airfield and round the perimeter track, just for the joy of it.

It was a lovely morning, and although Thame airfield was not over big it always seemed spacious. There were few people about so early, and Susan had the track and road almost to herself. She breathed deeply and joyously, and returned flushed and happy to breakfast in the canteen, possessed of a feeling that she belonged. Only to Grannie could she have explained her sensations. That precious sense of being blessed and happy and in communion with those who had gone and whose work she was helping to continue.

And so it was that Susan settled down to the new pattern of her life; a pattern that was no pattern; a routine that was no routine, because of the constant change of scene and faces, and the unknown and unpredictable possibilities which each day held.

The strict discipline of the School did not irk her as it did some of her fellow pupils. She saw it as necessary and inevitable, while others saw it as something to be despised and resisted. Saw it as the conventional border of a priceless rug; a frame to the intricate design woven a matter within, and she knew that if all went well with her it was only of time before she threw off the constrictions of this frame. Meanwhile she was perfectly content to rest within its limits and have decisions made for her and her daily life directed, while at the same time she was vividly conscious of a deep satisfaction that her feet were at last on the right path; that she was doing the thing she should be doing, and with it building life anew. She had loved every minute at Barton, and she brought her love and enthusiasm to Thame, where the mastery of the famous Hawker Harts and Hinds lay before her.

Powered by a Kestrel X engine, the Hart, though rather an old-fashioned looking biplane, was a beautiful machine to fly, but it had to be *flown*, and few liberties could be taken with it.

At the time of Susan's and Mandy's arrival in Hart Flight there were ugly rumours going round the School about these machines. 'Clapped out' was the general verdict, and John Cherry, who by this time had almost finished the course, told Susan one night at the 'Crown' that his opinion it was criminal to keep such 'crates' in a flying school.

'Some Wingless Wonder in the Air Ministry having an economy campaign, I expect,' he grumbled. 'I should just like to take him upstairs in one of those Harts for an hour, then perhaps we should have a few new kites sent along.'

As usual John aired his grievances at the top of his voice, and Susan saw his words register on her new instructor, who had just come into the bar. She tried to calm John down, for she knew that his tirade was by no means at an end.

'I think a lot of talk about the Harts is imagination,' she said soothingly, 'and not to be taken too seriously.'

But John was not to be pacified so easily.

'It wasn't imagination that killed Gavin, was it?' he persisted.

'Nor was it a Hart,' chipped in First Officer Marshall, who was now standing at the bar beside them. Susan, sitting between the two men, felt the temperature rising, for John's temper was quick and he was certain that he had forgotten more about flying than any instructor in ATA had ever learnt, and to Susan it was a miracle that he had survived over two months in the School without having first-class row with one of them.

She was thankful that the conversation was now interrupted by the entrance of Max Roskoff and Mandy, both hot and laughing, tennis rackets in their hands.

'Couldn't hit a ball!' Mandy announced. 'Nor could Max, so we gave it up. My turn, Max. What's yours?'

'OK. "Old", please. Next round on me, then!'

While Mandy ordered the beer the conversation became general, and, temporarily at least, the Harts were forgotten.

However, in spite of her words to John, Susan was glad of the seven hours' dual she flew that week before her instructor sent her off solo on the Friday morning, for with the Hart came Susan's first taste of power, a power which, if she did not completely control, she knew would master her. Although she was never again to experience the same degree of mental strain as before her first solo, yet each new type to which she progressed brought a certain tautening of nerve and muscle, stimulating but more exhausting than she realized. For the first time she was flying a fighter, which, although now obsolete and relegated to training purposes, had nevertheless been designed for action and not for pleasure. The cockpit was bare of comfort and accessories; there were no floorboards, and Susan found herself surrounded by wires, cables, rods, levers, wheels and dials. There was just a bucket seat for herself and her parachute, and the rudder bars for her feet, otherwise, both beneath her legs and on every side was just a maze of machinery.

At first she found this rather disturbing, but as the days went by she came to take it for granted, and the rods and wires sorted themselves out in her mind without conscious effort on her part. By the time she flew solo she felt as much at home in the Hart as she had after two months in the little Magister. In fact, Susan possessed one of the most important attributes of a successful ferry pilot – adaptability.

However, her first solo circuit was far from good, for she began by swinging on take-off, thus upsetting herself from the start, and as a result she finished by dropping the machine about five feet on landing.

Luckily, no damage was done. Susan was neither frightened, rattled nor even confused. She was angry and, as she taxied back, perhaps a little too fast, to the take-off position, her chin took on a very determined line.

On her second circuit she flew that Hart as if she were riding an unruly horse which had just thrown her. Completely concentrated, her blue eyes hard with something between temper and determination, every muscle controlled and tense, Susan opened the throttle. Straight as a die she shot across the field, holding the machine down longer than usual, then lifted it very firmly as the hedge rushed up towards her.

She did not relax for a second the whole way round and, when she landed, she seemed almost to *put* the old Hart on the ground by sheer will-power, rather than by flying skill.

Such high tension could not be kept up for long, and on her third circuit Susan relaxed slightly, and in consequence flew far better and with greater ease. She made several more good landings that morning: her confidence returned, and from then on she did not look back.

By the afternoon post came a short note from Mark reminding her that tomorrow was Saturday, August 14th, and that he would be landing about five o'clock to pick her up in a Proctor, and it was only then that Susan realized that today was Friday – the 13th! She was thankful that this fact had previously escaped her for, from childhood, she had been unreasonably superstitious, and would spend a miserable day, fraught with foreboding, whenever a Friday happened to fall on the thirteenth. She knew it to be ridiculous, but could not help it, so now, when her instructor told her that she was finished for the day, she heaved a sigh of relief. It would be misery to fly now she was aware of the date.

Susan did not smoke very much but, as she settled herself in a wicker chair in a corner of the pilots' rest-room with Mark's letter and the *Daily Express* in her lap, she lit a cigarette and was glad of it.

Rereading Mark's letter Susan noticed that this time he began, *My dearest Sue*, and anyone watching her closely would have seen the little frown, which at this moment puckered her normally smooth brow, suddenly clear.

The party promises to be quite a good show [Mark ran on], as the Bar has been quietly hoarding for several weeks and we are having the Blue Rockets Band.

As for flying, we have paid one or two visits to Fritz lately, but nothing much of note has occurred except one night, when a friendly type shot up my rear-gunner on the way home.

Susan thought: 'He   is   just   like   Richard. A   master   of understatement. One short sentence to describe what was probably an extremely "shaky do".' She folded the letter and put it in her pocket, then, picking up the paper, glanced at the headlines.

As usual they were chiefly concerned with death and destruction; less food and more bombs; atrocities and reprisals. What a crazy world! And while Susan was idly wondering if it would ever regain its sanity, Sandra Cushing flopped into the chair beside her.

'Hiya, kid. What's noo?' she greeted Susan.

'Nothing much,' answered Susan. 'I have soloed the Hart.'

'You look kinda high, so I thought maybe something good was cooking.' Sandra took the paper from Susan's knee and looked briefly through it.

'Boy, this little old world sure is screwy!' she sighed. 'I only hope it's all over before Elmer gets here. He's a cute kid.' Sandra beamed with maternal pride. 'You'd love Elmer. He's back home still, training for rear-gunner.'

With Sandra's words came memories of Felicity, and Susan was amazed to find that, suddenly, she could conjure up no regrets. What sort of a world was this for children – as it was nowadays? Full of hate, cruelty and uncertainty.

Sandra folded the paper and jumped up. She rarely sat down for more than three minutes at a time, and her forty years had utterly failed to curb her apparently endless store of New World energy and vitality.

'Well, I think I'll pop right over and have a cup of tea. I'm not flying again until half four. Coming?'

'No, thanks. I've finished for today, and there's a pile of washing waiting for me down at Hopefield, so I think I had better be off.'

'OK. Good scrubbing, kid!' and Sandra strolled out of the room.

For some minutes Susan sat staring into space, oblivious of the noisy game of ping-pong in progress at the other end of the room or of the radio, which played continually from nine in the morning until the last pupil left in the evening. Except for the news no one ever listened to the programmes, but it served as a background, of which one only became conscious when it stopped. As she sat her thoughts, for perhaps the first time in months, were busy with the future; the war and the horror must end some day, and what then? She could not imagine a quiet settling down with her mother at Hazeley. She was enjoying this life and its companionship. The keenness, the vigour, the constant exchange of opinions, the variety of outlook. It all added zest. But how would one feel afterwards? Would there be openings for girls as civil airline pilots? Or would the old prejudices arise once again? The thought that she might marry again, should Frank's death be confirmed, or the probability that she might lose her life, or her mother be killed, or that they both might be, never once entered her head. Somewhere, she decided, as she rose to her feet and gave herself a mental shake, she must find a life full of new scenes and interests, sufficient to occupy all her energies, both mental and physical. An essential job, and do it well. But where – and what? The one thing she must not do was give herself time to brood on what was past.

Today a flat tyre to her bicycle had necessitated her walking, so, with the idea of a little exercise before she settled to an evening of domesticity, Susan turned towards the airfield gate, instead of the shorter cinder path. Her mind still occupied, she walked unseeingly, until the repeated sound of a motor-horn aroused her, and looking up she saw John Cherry and his sports car awaiting her.

Under her breath Susan said a quiet 'Bother!' and she felt suddenly irritated. She was so tired of John's persistency about that stupid weekend, and he would try, as usual, to monopolize her evening, and she must do her washing and press out the new chiffon dress, unworn as yet, but which she meant to wear for Mark's party.

However, there was no way of escape at this moment, and John was already backing his car towards her. He looked rather grim and Susan sensed at once that something was wrong.

His first words confirmed it.

'Well, that's that!' he said bitterly. 'I'm out.'

Susan gasped. 'What do you mean, John! *Out?*'

Surely John, who had more hours in his log book than most pupils, had not failed? For if that were so what hope for someone like herself?

'Just what I say. They've chucked me out for low flying. Some swine of a ground type in the Observer Corps got my number and reported me – at least two of them did. The first one must have plotted my course and handed me onto the next one. My first trip in cross-country flight, too!'

He pushed his cap jauntily up on to the back of his head, as if dismissing the whole affair from his mind.

'Anyhow, I couldn't care less – this ferrying racket is pretty ropey anyway, and I shall be glad to get back to the RAF, and be left in peace.' He leant across and opened the car door. 'Hop in. Come and console me. I feel like a blind tonight.'

Susan knew that this was an exhibition of sheer bravado: that he really minded very much; for, with a bad report from ATA on top of his previous record, his chances of getting back on flying in the RAF were pretty remote. She also knew that in all probability he would act up to his words and get blind drunk that evening, a session at which she had no wish to be present.

'Sorry, John,' she said. 'I've got a domestic date at Hopefield which can't be broken.' 'Meaning you've some smalls to wash, I suppose. Damn them! Come on. They can wait. Don't forget I shan't be here next week.' Susan felt mean at refusing. John was obviously in very low spirits. After a second's thought she compromised.

'All right. I tell you what, you run me down to Hopefield now, and I'll meet you in the "Rose and Thistle" for a quickie before supper. How's that?'

John frowned. 'OK. I suppose that's better than nothing. Come on.'

Susan got in the car and the policeman on duty opened the gate.

'Well, you haven't said you are sorry!' John gloomed.

'You've hardly given me a chance. Besides, you know I am – very sorry.' In her heart Susan knew she was lying for, although she was desperately sorry for any pilot who was failed, yet lately John's public possessiveness had been more than irritating.

'Why don't you tell him just where he gets off?' Mandy had suggested one evening, when John had blatantly tacked on to them for dinner in the 'Spread Eagle', at Thame. 'The man's becoming a positive leech!'

Susan had tried, but John made it very difficult, and she couldn't be rude to anyone, so her efforts met with little success. Wherever she went, there was John. Once, even, when she had been flying quietly round the circuit, another machine had suddenly formated on her, its wing-tips almost touching her own, and behind the disguising goggles Susan immediately recognized John. Now she could not help but feel a certain amount of relief that such state of affairs had come to an end.

John turned sharply to the right down the lane, which ran round the back of the village and formed a short cut to Hopefield House. A few thatched cottages were scattered along one side, on the other lay the open country, and apart from a small urchin grubbing in the ditch there was not a soul in sight.

Suddenly John pulled into a field gateway and switched off the engine. In one movement he tipped his cap into the back of the car and flung his arms round Susan before she had time to protest.

His breath was hot on her cheek, the heavy scent of hair-oil stifled her, and he held her so close that she could not struggle.

'Susan, darling,' he whispered, 'will you marry me?'

'John! Don't be such an ass! Let me go!'

His grip only tightened. 'I'm not an ass, and I adore you.'

Then Susan used the weapon which rarely fails. She laughed! Immediately John sat back, his eyes hard with hurt pride.

'So now I'm funny, am I? And may I ask what is so hilarious about my proposal?'

Susan did not want to be brutal. She knew his pride had already taken one hard knock that day.

'So very unexpected, John. That's all. I never think of you as the marrying kind – neither have I ever thought of myself as free to marry again, and well – well, if I did, I should never feel that way about you. And you must admit that I have never given you any cause to think I did.'

'No. You've been a blasted iceberg. I suppose it's never entered your head that when a chap comes off Ops. he wants a little feminine warmth and sympathy – at least he doesn't expect to be treated like a pariah! It wasn't exactly the proverbial piece of cake, you know.'

Aware of John's operational history, and that after two sweeps he had been grounded for what, reading between the lines, obviously amounted to 'lack of moral fibre', Susan felt suddenly that she had had enough. She looked him straight in the eye.

'Surely, John, that's not a line that 64 Squadron usually needs to shoot? And now I think I had better be off.'

John's face fell, but before he had time even to ask her how she knew he had been in 64 Squadron Susan had opened the door and was standing out in the road.

'Goodbye, John,' she said quietly, 'and good luck.'

A few seconds and she was hidden by a bend in the lane, and the last Susan ever heard of John Cherry was the roar of an engine and the furious grinding of gears.

At Hopefield, Susan found Mandy in a fever of excitement. She too had been released early, and was now standing in the middle of their bedroom wearing an extremely worried expression and a pair of the briefest panties.

'What's the trouble?' asked Susan.

'Nothing to wear. Absolutely *nothing*!'

'When? Now?' Susan laughed. 'You look like it!'

'No. Tomorrow night. Who do you think just rang me? Michael Dundas. Wants me to go to a party at Hornchurch, and now, of course, all my frotties are at home, and I shan't have time to get down to Falcombe and collect one. Hell!'

'Why didn't he ask you sooner?'

'Said he had suddenly decided not to go on leave till Sunday. Talk about a woman's prerogative!' Mandy collapsed on her bed. 'And the silly part is I said I would go. I must be nutty! But I *should* like to see Richard!'

Susan's eye fell on the beautiful chiffon creation hanging on the back of the door – then she looked at Mandy's copper head.

'Of course you must go! Tell you what! *You* can have my green chiffon, and I'll wear my blue dinner dress. I'd really decided to wear it anyway,' she lied, 'because it fits me better, and, after all, Mark has never seen either.'

Mandy sat up, her violet eyes wide. 'Oh, I couldn't do *that*, Sue – it's brand new!'

'So what? It's about time it was christened.'

'But suppose I drop something on it? I'd be sure to!'

'I'll risk that.' Susan laughed. 'Try it on. It's so long it will be all right.'

'Oh, Sue, you are an angel! But are you quite, quite sure?'

'Certain sure. Go on.'

When Susan saw Mandy standing there in the beautiful and simply draped dress, for all the world like a young Greek goddess, she did not regret her somewhat hasty generosity. After all, she had seen Michael fall hopelessly in love with Mandy at Falcombe, and she had liked Michael.

Apart from what Susan had seen of him herself, she realized that he possessed a character not usually connected with a fighter pilot. At twenty he had come down from Cambridge with a first in Greats; he played neither cricket nor football, and although he had every opportunity on his father's estates in Scotland, he did not shoot or hunt. His chief joy, Susan learnt, was bird-watching, and he would go off for long days, even nights at a time, completely alone and carrying nothing but a pair of powerful binoculars and a camera.

'Michael really is a priceless type,' Mandy had said after her last weekend's leave. 'I met him in town on Saturday afternoon, and what do you think we did? Went to the Royal Academy, and ended up at the Zoo! Sounds boring, doesn't it, but somehow with Michael one can't be bored.'

'Have you any idea what he is going to do after the war?' Susan's thoughts, still running on the same lines, made her ask this question as she helped Mandy out of the dress.

'Well, apparently, when he came down from Cambridge, he decided to be an archaeologist and went off with some expedition to the Middle East for a couple of years, digging. But, somehow, when the war started, he was in India – I don't really know how he got there, or why. I expect he just got tired of digging; anyway, I don't think he is going on with it after the war.' Mandy gazed at the dress in her hands. 'Sue, it really is a honey, and it's sweet of you to lend it.'

'Are you in love with him, Mandy?'

'Oh, Sue! Think again! Can you see me falling in love with someone who takes one to the *Zoo*?'

'Oh, I just wondered.' Susan laughed.

'Somehow I don't think I fall in love easily,' Mandy continued meditatively, 'because here I am, nearly twenty, and as far as I know I've never been in love in my life – not counting the normal school-girl crushes, of course, which don't mean a thing. I'm not sure that I *believe* in falling in love, any more than I am quite certain that I believe in God. I'm a Christian only because I was: brought up to be one, and I take it for granted that one day I shall fall in love because everyone does, and I'm no different to anyone else. But that's as far as it goes. Besides, since the war everyone I know seems to be busily getting *un*married, which doesn't exactly add to the rosy picture of married bliss, does it?'

Susan was standing by the open window, her back to Mandy, a light breeze just stirring the soft curls at her temples.

'I think at nineteen one is apt only to notice the unhappy marriages and overlook the happy ones. Really, it's wonderful, Mandy. You'll see.'

'OK, Grannie!' In front of her mirror Mandy was pulling a comb through her hair, and at Susan's words she smiled a sceptical little smile at her own reflection. 'That's another thing,' she said, 'and I'm not referring to you, but I've noticed that as soon as any woman gets married – at least after about six months – she immediately tries to badger her unmarried girl friends into matrimony. "You ought to get married, darling!" "It's just too marvellous!" or "You don't know what you are missing!" and so they ramble on – which makes one think there must be a large snag somewhere!'

'You little cynic!' Susan swung round to face Mandy. 'You don't deserve a husband!'

'Sounds quite horrid, I know, but Richard agrees with me.' Mandy grinned. 'Let's put it down to the queer mentality of twins. I account for most things that way, and, anyhow, I would much rather go to a party with Richard than any other man I know – we always have so much more fun.'

Susan had to laugh. Mandy was so honest, and although in most ways she was essentially feminine, yet at times a strangely male streak would show itself; factual, dispassionate, almost the mentality of an embryonic surgeon.

And yet Mandy was far from unromantic. She would often see beauty where others would not, a legacy from her upbringing of which, as yet, she was quite unaware, but which was now to stand her in good stead, for therein lay the secret of her flair for visual navigation. Few of even the most insignificant landmarks of England passed beneath Mandy's wings unobserved, for the majority of them held some claim to beauty and for that reason caught her eye. At first this had amazed Susan, because she had then not known Mandy's background, but now it was clear to her, and fitted into the jigsaw of a character which earlier struck her as a mass of contradictions.

So that when, the following afternoon, Mandy suddenly stopped as they walked back together from tea at the snack bar towards the School buildings and pointing apparently at nothing said: 'Look! Listen! Isn't that heaven?' Susan was not surprised.

She had neither seen nor heard anything out of the ordinary herself, which was really not to be wondered at, for she was thinking of Mark at that moment and hoping that nothing would crop up to stop his coming to fetch her in just over an hour's time.

'What?' she asked rather blankly.

Mandy was still pointing towards the middle of the airfield.

'Can't you see? A hare!... That lark!'

Then Susan realized that for once there were no aircraft in the air, no one taking-off, no one landing. It was unusually quiet, and all she could hear was the song of Mandy's lark as it soared joyfully higher and higher. She followed the direction of Mandy's finger, and there, sitting up on its haunches in a tuft of grass, she saw a big hare, its ears pricked, its body rigid except for the twitching of its sensitive nose.

'Somehow they look slightly out of place, don't they?' Susan remarked.

'Oh, I don't know – after all, they were here first. One of the engineers told me he found a sparrow nesting in a Harvard in the hangar the other day, which *did* strike me as being rather a poor building site!'

They laughed and walked on, each immediately lost again in her own thoughts, for they had now long passed the stage in their friendship where conversation was necessary.

If the airfield seemed quiet now, it was even quieter an hour and a half later. Instructors and pupils alike were keen to get away at weekends in time to catch the London train from Aylesbury, and organized their day's work accordingly, so that by five-thirty Susan found herself alone in the School buildings.

Restlessly she walked up and down the long empty rooms. She flicked open the pages of some of the magazines on the rest-room table, but they failed to hold her attention and soon she went outside,

She had changed from the slacks and shirt she had worn that day whilst flying, and wore a stone-coloured corded suit and a spotless, white, open-necked silk shirt. The evening was clear and cloudless, but it was not hot, and the faintest tang of autumn, already sharpening the air, made Susan glad she had brought her cherry Kashmir scarf.

In the distance she could hear the faint drone of a small engine, and eagerly she scanned the sky to the east. However, in a few moments her hopes were dashed, for it only proved to be one of the Ferry Pool taxi-craft returning to base. Glad of any distraction she watched it land, but soon it had taxied away to the Pool dispersal, and, after a final burst, its engine was switched off and all was quiet again.

Too quiet – it was getting on Susan's nerves. She thought of going up to the Flying Control Room, where there was still an officer on duty, and signing Mark in and out, in order to save time when he arrived, but finally she decided against this, for she was afraid he might not come at all and did not want to appear foolish.

However, she need not have worried, for within five minutes a Proctor entered the circuit, waggled its wings in greeting, and almost before Susan had time to powder her nose – which did not need powdering – Mark had touched down and was taxiing towards Flying Control.

Susan ran out on to the perimeter track and waved to him;

dropped her suitcase, and went into the Control Room to tell the officer who Mark was, from where he had come and to where he was going. The number of the machine he had noted through his binoculars.

'Newmarket! Well! Well! So the merry widow is off on a merry weekend, eh?' – and the fat officer gave her such a suggestive look that Susan could have happily slapped his fat face, but as he was a First Officer and she herself a mere pupil, she had to be content with slamming the glass hatch down rather harder than usual.

'What cheek!' she thought angrily, and when she stepped into the machine beside Mark her cheeks were almost as brilliantly coloured as her scarf.

'Sorry I'm late, Susan,' he apologized, 'but the OC kept me nattering in his office, and I couldn't get away.'

'I thought something like that must have happened,' she smiled, as they swung round and taxied out towards the Control Car, 'so I wasn't worrying.'

But it was only then she realized just how anxious she had been.

'Got your strap fixed?' Mark asked, as a green light flashed from the black and white chequered car and he turned into wind.

Susan fastened the safety harness round her waist. 'OK,' she said happily, and without more ado Mark opened the throttle.

Mark Cordner was a polished pilot, for he had been instructing for at least five years before the war and had flown many types of aircraft. Susan's knowledge by contrast was very small, and to-day she once again felt herself to be his pupil, and immediately was reborn that same sense of perfect trust and confidence she had always experienced when flying with him in Sydney.

Conversation was difficult against the noise of the engine and they hardly spoke during the next forty-five minutes. Their course took them over Barton, which Susan pointed out to Mark, and once he dived down to tree level to show her an old castle which had caught his eye on the way over to Thame; otherwise they were silent.

By the time Cambridge came into sight the shadows were lengthening and only the spires and highest college buildings caught the glow of the setting sun. Mark turned to Susan and smiled, but they did not speak.

Susan was happy, but did not know why, nor did she stop to analyse her feelings. She was just content to let her thoughts wing smoothly along the calm air of the moment as the Proctor did, completely at her ease with Mark and strangely at peace.

Then they had landed on the long grass strip, once the famous Rowley Mile, and as Mark had finally parked and switched off he turned to her, a questioning look in his dark grey eyes.

'Happy?' he asked quietly.

She smiled, then quickly she turned away and stepped out.

After giving instructions to a mechanic, Mark left Susan for a few minutes while he checked in at the Control Room, and she had time to look about her.

On every side of the airfield, looming unnaturally large in the half-light of dusk, were dispersed the great Stirling bombers, like the hungry monsters of a nightmare. Round the Control Tower clustered a maze of huts and sheds, while on the eastern side of the field lay the massive, camouflaged hangars. Incongruously the old grandstand, with its Royal Box and tiers of seats, still stood in the centre of the camp, and, although it was now put to a far different use, it still held an atmosphere of grandeur.

The Officers' Mess, as Mark had told Susan, was a large house, once the property of a millionaire, at the other end of the town. It was well over a mile from the airfield and quite close to the Rutland Hotel, where he had booked her a room.

To the Rutland they now drove in Mark's ancient Ford coupé, down the hill into the town and up the old High Street.

'Ever been here before?' he asked. 'No, never. I just flew over it once. It's attractive, isn't it? How do you like being stationed here?'

'Well, so far I don't seem to have had much time to look around, but everyone seems most friendly – even the racing community, who might be expected to resent us.'

'What do you do in the evenings when you aren't flying?'

'Usually take the car to Cambridge – it's a change from the Mess and the inevitable beer sessions. They have pretty good concerts there most weeks.'

Susan looked at him with raised eyebrows. 'I didn't know you were musical, Mark! Do you play, yourself?'

'Oh, I strum a bit on the piano,' he answered casually, but it was not until half-way through the party that evening that Susan discovered just how much Mark had belittled his talent by that remark.

Susan was enjoying herself. She was a beautiful dancer and the 'Blue Rockets' was a first-rate band.

This was the first time she had been in the Mess of a RAF operational squadron, and she was immediately aware of the unique atmosphere. Most of the pilots, she noticed, were New Zealanders, but there was also a faint sprinkling of British and Australians. The CO, Wing Commander 'Blacker' Hay, so called because of the 'Blacks' he was continually putting up with higher authority, was English, as were also the Padre and the Medical Officer.

Yet all difference of nationality, of upbringing, of class, and even of age, were submerged by the one thing common to them all: they were an aircrew – a team – a squadron, and their pride in that squadron overrode all else.

The fact that one officer brought the barmaid from the 'Half Moon' as his guest, while the wife of another was a peeress mattered not at all; neither did any of the guests evince the slightest degree of disgust at the statues which, left behind by the owner of the house, were now somewhat crudely and gaudily embellished by the new inhabitants. Susan herself could not repress a smile when she caught sight of a bust of Caesar, in the corner of the ante-room, with an RAF cap set jauntily on its head, one eye well blacked, and well-rouged lips.

Just at first, during the earlier hours, the presence of an Air Vice Marshal made for a certain amount of restraint, but after eleven, when the band knocked off for supper and this very senior officer and his staff departed, the party really got going.

Susan was in the bar talking to Mark and the 'Doc' when an extremely youthful flight lieutenant came up to them and seized Mark by the arm.

'Come on, Ropey,' he said firmly. 'The music-men are having a breather – now it's your turn.'

Susan had been highly amused to discover Mark's nickname, which was, of course, derived from his surname of 'Cordner'.

Mark hesitated, and asked the barman for another whiskey.

'Come on, Ropey, you know you love it!' the young Flight Lieutenant persisted, then, turning to Susan: 'Did you know? Our infant prodigy!'

Finally it was Susan who persuaded Mark to sit down at the big Bechstein, and although he did not know it, it was for herself that Mark played, his heart in his hands. 'I knew Ropey was good, but I didn't know he was that good!' a blond New Zealand navigator told her. 'Now he's swinging it, let's dance!' And so Susan danced with Shorty, the Squadron's six foot, six crack navigator.

She danced with many other members of Mark's squadron, too, that night, for they swooped on her immediately Mark left her side, and it was while she was executing a most unorthodox rhumba with a red-haired pilot called 'Blackie' that two rear-gunners came roaring into the room on bicycles.

They were tremendously happy and far from sober. One ran his machine smartly on to the sofa while the other tried to ride his backwards. The dancers scattered and cheered him on with shouts of 'Keep your flying speed!' and 'Look out! You're stalling!' until 'Blacker' Hay yelled 'Bale out!', and the rider immediately fell off in a heap on the floor, his bicycle on top of him.

And from there the party gathered speed. It was a revelation to Susan. Towards one o'clock she noticed that several of the girls had already gone, and when Mark suggested that, as things looked like becoming rather rowdy, perhaps it would be as well if he took her to her hotel, Susan willingly agreed. She was very tired.

It was raining, and while she waited for Mark and his car at the front door Susan heard what at first she took to be the strains of 'Greenland's Icy Mountains'. It was bellowed from the ante-room, but soon she realized it was only the tune which the boys had borrowed, for she managed to catch the two lines:

'And when we drop our cargoes, we do not give a damn.

The eggs may miss the good's yard, but they muck up poor old Hamm.'

What a crazy gang they were! Or was it only this surface of craziness which made it possible for them to cover their real feelings? Susan knew that only the night before two crews had failed to return – boys they knew well, and worked with and played with, yet here they were, apparently full of the joy of life – the fate of their friends forgotten.

When Susan remarked on this to Mark a few moments later, he said:

'It's the only way – otherwise you'd go nutty. It's the same with fear. Anyone with imagination is scared stiff, but they don't say so – or else they say so so loudly that they know no one will believe them.' He turned into the cobbled yard. of the old hotel, and stopped. 'Enjoyed yourself?'

'Enormously. I'm sorry it's over.'

'Come again, Sue. Any time you like, tho' I can't promise there will always be a party.'

He passed his hand across his forehead with an unconscious gesture of weariness. 'I expect you'll want a long lie in. I'll ring you about twelve and, if I can get away, what about lunch together?' he suggested.

'Lovely. Is there a piano in the hotel? I want to hear you play again. It was beautiful.' 'I don't think the inmates of the "Rutland" would appreciate it much on a Sunday afternoon, do you?' He laughed.

Suddenly he leant across and kissed Susan very gently on her cheek. 'Goodnight,' he said, softly. 'God bless you – and – and thank you for coming.'

TEN

MANDY'S PARTY IN the Fighter Mess at Hornchurch had apparently been as great a success as Susan's at Newmarket, for when Susan met her struggling into her flying overalls in the locker-room early on Monday morning she could, obviously, hardly keep her eyes open.

'Had a wonderful time,' she yawned. 'The only trouble is I have hardly been to bed at all, and had to get up directly I got there to get *here*,' and she yawned again. 'Just can't think how I'm going to get through today. Old Spink would make me go up first!'

'You'll be OK once you are up,' Susan encouraged her. 'Blow all the cobwebs away! By the way, how was the dress?'

'Heaven! Richard said it was the prettiest frock he has ever seen me in. Thanks again, a million.' Mandy sighed as she pulled on her helmet. 'Oh well, I suppose I *must* make the effort! Tell you all about it later – if I live to tell the tale!'

It was not, however, until they were going to bed that night that Susan had a chance to hear about Mandy's weekend, for they were both kept hard at it all day.

Susan had done an hour's circuits and bumps in the morning, an hour's dual after lunch, and then some forced-landing practice, so that by nine o'clock she was quite ready for bed.

'How was Michael?' she asked as Mandy unpacked the chiffon dress. 'Oh, in great form. He has got another bar to his DFC, *and*, strange to relate,' she added irrelevantly, 'he dances beautifully!'

'Why strange?'

Mandy laughed, and before answering she tipped her suitcase upside down on the bed, so that the entire contents spilled out in a heap.

'Well, somehow dancing doesn't quite seem to go with archaeology and bird-watching, does it?' she mused. 'But then, Michael really is incredibly unexpected at times. You know how it rained and blew yesterday? Well, they released most of the pilots after lunch, and Michael drove me up to town – said he must dance with me again –

so we went to the Officers' Sunday Club at Grosvenor House, which as far as he knew was the only spot one can dance on a Sunday afternoon in London. Then after one dance he said he couldn't stand it – wouldn't explain why – and we went to a flick instead. And then, after the flick, we went to a dive in Soho with wonderful food, which could only have been black market, a wizard band, and we danced well into the early hours. I only hope he didn't have to fly too early today.'

Mandy scooped everything off her bed on to a chair, and curled up between the coarse sheets. 'He said he would ring me tonight, but he hasn't – expect he's forgotten – the so-and-so!'

But Wing Commander Dundas had not forgotten to ring Mandy; he just could not bring himself to speak to her, for he did not want to be the one to break the news that Richard had been shot down in flames, that day, over the Channel.

It was not until the following afternoon that a telegram from her father reached Mandy, and then she told no one, not even Susan. She just left the ominous slip of paper on Susan's dressing table, and added underneath, *Gone for a walk. Don't worry. Be back later.*

But Susan did worry. She knew that Mandy loved Richard with a very real and great love – loved him more than anyone else in the world, and she also knew what strange effects such a shock can have on even the strongest of characters.

By ten o'clock there was no sign of Mandy, and when by eleven Susan had slowly undressed, had her bath, and still no Mandy, she began wondering if she ought to go out and look for her.

She tried to read but, having looked at the same page for half an hour, gave it up, switched off the light and just lay in the darkness, thinking.

The illuminated hands of her travelling clock moved slowly on past midnight, and they were crawling down to the half hour when Susan heard the heavy front door click to in the hall below. Should she say anything to Mandy, or feign sleep? Before Susan had time to decide the door opened very softly, and a slim, lonely figure slipped across the dim light of the windows.

Susan did not speak, but in a few moments she was aware by the way Mandy moved about the room that she knew she was awake. Finally Mandy got into bed, but did not lie down; she sat bolt upright in the darkness, and at last she spoke.

'Sue!' It was a very small voice, husky and little more than a whisper.

'Yes, Mandy? I'm awake. I couldn't sleep—'

But Mandy was not listening, she only repeated 'Sue—' and Susan waited.

'I didn't know – didn't know it could be like this – I feel cut in half. It's – physical pain –I can't think how you bore it! Don't tell anyone, please. I couldn't bear it. Goodnight,' and Mandy humped down under the bedclothes.

'Of course not. Don't worry. I won't even talk about it to you, unless you wish. Goodnight.'

For some time Susan lay wide awake, her heart aching for Mandy, but whether Mandy was awake or not she could not tell; there was neither sound nor movement from the second bed and luckily, as yet, there was no one in the third bed, since Jane had failed to solo.

Susan's thoughts followed a circle. Was it never to end – this sacrifice of the best? She thought of all the men she had known directly and indirectly. Began with Richard and came back to Richard. But the mental storm of the night Gavin was killed had done its work. It was not that she had come to think dispassionately, but the whole thing had been lifted to a higher plane. That night had left her with a firm belief that their sacrifice was not in vain. They were free of their shackles. Some deeper sense, of which Susan was hardly aware, comforted her. Each one had left something. It was difficult to define exactly what. And there would be more. She herself, perhaps? Perhaps Mandy? Only God knew. ATA had its sacrifices. That disastrous Sunday, last year, of which she had heard. Six pilots in one day! Suddenly it all reached a dimension with which Susan's tired mind and body could not cope. Very gently the god of sleep descended.

Susan fully intended to stick to her promise, and for the next two days Richard was not mentioned. That Mandy was desperately unhappy was obvious to her, but not to others. Outwardly she appeared gayer and more light-hearted, but Susan understood. Mandy was making an almost superhuman effort to behave as Richard would have wished.

On Thursday evening, after a pretty stiff day and an early supper, about eight o'clock, they had just reached their room when Susan heard the sound of a car entering the gateway and coming to a stop just under the windows. For a moment she took no notice and was startled when Mandy, who had dropped full length on her bed, suddenly raised her head and exclaimed, agonizingly:

'Sue! That's Michael! I know that hooter! I can't – *can't* see tum. Oh – *do go*. Stop him – send him away. I never want to see him again.'

Susan glanced out of the window. Mandy was right. It was Michael. He was just getting out of his car.

'Yes. It is Michael. All right. I'll go down—' and anxious to stop him before he could ask anyone for Mandy, she ran and was on the doorstep, a little breathless, as Michael, having immobilized his car, turned about.

'Susan!'

'Michael!' Their names were their only greeting. Michael was pale and hollow-eyed. He looked as if he badly needed sleep.

He gripped Susan's hands in both his own.

'How is she? Where is she?'

'Upstairs. She heard the car and begged me to come down. Michael' – and Susan's eyes grew troubled as she looked into his – 'I'm so sorry – but I'm afraid she won't see you—'

'She *must*.' Michael's tone brooked of no contradiction and his face was very grave. 'I have something to tell her and something to give her – from Richard. How is she?'

'Steeling herself to bear it and carry on as usual. Will have no one told.'

'But they will know. Sir Francis – I have just come from Falcombe

– is putting it in all tomorrow's papers. Can I go to her *now*?'

Susan shook her head.

'No. No. I'll fetch her. There's no privacy here. Just wait.'

'All right.' Michael leaned wearily against the doorpost and Susan returned to Mandy.

Mandy was still lying on her bed face downwards, very still.

'Mandy!' Susan put a hand on her shoulder. 'Mandy, listen.'

'Is he going?' Mandy's voice came muffled.

'No. He *must* see you. It is a message – from Richard I think, and he has something to give you.'

'I can't. I can't.'

'Yes, you *can*, and you *must*. Michael looks worn out. He has just come from Falcombe. I expect he has taken Richard's things home.' Susan felt a little brutal as she delivered this piece of probable news. Mandy gave a little moan and Susan gently shook her by the shoulder.

'Come along. You *must*. It would be cruel not to,' and to her amazement, and without another word, Mandy half rolled off her bed, shook back her hair, and without one glance in the mirror, and dishevelled as she was, left the room.

From the window, Susan saw Michael open the door of his car and Mandy enter it. The next moment they had disappeared.

Once again Susan lay awake and waited. It was not so late tonight, not yet midnight, when she heard the hall door open and, almost soundlessly, close again, but she did not move when Mandy entered the room. This time Mandy came straight to Susan's bed and fell on her knees beside it.

'Sue! Oh, Sue!' and Susan's outstretched arms found her, and for a few moments they clung closely together and their tears mingled. At last Mandy sat back on her heels, and, in the darkness, Susan could see her eyes, unusually bright.

'Oh, Sue. Michael was wonderful. They had talked and Ric *knew*. He gave Michael his watch just before they took off – to give to me – if – and inside there was a tiny note. Just two words – 'Courage

– Sis'. We had talked of courage – that last night, at home – I don't know – I can't think yet – but I feel Richard isn't very far away. Are they near us? Can they be – do you think?'

Susan half smiled in the darkness. Suddenly she felt as old as Grannie.

'I know they are. Frank is – but we mustn't cling too much. We might hold them back – perhaps they go on – to other things. Now, darling, get to bed. We *must* sleep. They will all be ashamed of us if we fail to make the grade, *now*.'

There was no need for further concern over Mandy. She was stiffened. No need to doubt either but that she would make the grade all right. She did not refer again, and neither did Susan, to Michael's visit, but quietly accepted the proffered sympathy of her other colleagues when the facts became known. Robin's spluttered remarks were the only ones Susan overheard.

'You must be proud to belong to a family where the men have died enviable deaths,' and Susan found herself wondering about Robin and his curiously expressed thought. Perhaps Robin was envious? His physical capability was so limited. Neither conceit nor pride were his. Good-hearted and clean. Perhaps Robin desired above all things to prove his manhood by the supreme sacrifice.

Susan wondered, too, about Michael; and watched Mandy for any sign. She noticed that letters bearing the Hornchurch postmark arrived frequently. It would be a wonderful thing if Mandy could, at this juncture, fall in love with Michael. Susan thought much about them both, and so the days passed and, in her concern that all should go well for Michael and Mandy, Susan hardly noticed their passing, and the advent of her 'Wings Check' at the end of her course in Hart Flight came upon her almost as a surprise.

The excitement of that September morning made another happening that Susan was to remember all her life, for it suddenly dawned on her that, if all went well, within a few hours she would be a Cadet Ferry Pilot, entitled to wear the gold-embroidered wings on the navy-blue uniform and a narrow gold stripe on her shoulders. Not that the idea of a uniform impressed her; she was too intelligent for that, but she felt that at last she would be out of the kindergarten, and would be spreading her newly won wings far and wide, and also be a little nearer to becoming a useful member of an essential service.

First Officer Marshall told Susan that Flight Captain Shillingford, the Chief Instructor on Harts, would be ready for her at eleven-thirty, and as the time drew nearer Susan felt more and more as if she were waiting for a major operation, or at least a prolonged session with the dentist. But perhaps she would not have worried so much had she known of the conversation some weeks before between Commander MacKenzie and his Chief Instructor, or had she even known that, ever since she arrived in Hart Flight, Flight Captain Shillingford had picked her out as the best of a fair bunch of promising pupils.

In fact he was already so certain that she was going to be good that now he merely took her for a flip over to White Waltham, where he had some business to do at HQ, gave her some forced landings on the way and on arrival made her do a bad weather circuit at three hundred feet.

On the way back he made Susan fly him to a tiny emergency landing-field near Farringdon of which he was particularly fond, and which went by the same name as himself, Shillingford.

At first, although Susan knew she must be within half a mile of it, she could not pick out this field, and she circled the area for about ten minutes in vain. It was only when these circles had shrunk almost to tight turns and a gust of wind blew up the fat white body of the windsock in a field to starboard that she spotted her goal.

Immediately Flight Captain Shillingford realized this he cut the throttle, and his pupil managed to pull off a very pretty glide approach and landing. This satisfied him that she was ready to be launched into Cross Country Flight, and from there into the Ferry Pool as soon as possible, so that, the next afternoon, Susan found herself on the London train, armed with a chit signed by the School Adjutant, permitting her to order from Messrs. Austin Reed two navy-blue uniforms, consisting of skirt, slacks and jacket, plus one greatcoat, raincoat and cap. Also that day she had been issued with an official Flight Authorization Card, which allowed her to authorize her own flights irrespective of what the RAF might advise; an identity card from the Air Ministry which would carry her past the guard of any airfield, or aircraft factory, in the United Kingdom, and last, but not least, the Bible of all ferry pilots, the small blue book entitled *Ferry Pilots' Notes*, from which Susan was rarely again to find herself parted.

To her great disappointment she was told that her first uniform could not possibly be ready inside three weeks, and she realized that, in spite of the fact that she had already bought her pale blue shirts, black ties and shoes, she would have to complete most of her cross-countries in civilian clothes. And this, as she had discovered from other pupils, was somewhat trying, for during this time one would often be 'stuck out' and have to overnight at RAF stations, an ordeal made infinitely easier if one were in uniform oneself.

Not that the RAF were particularly averse to a civilian in their midst, but just that it was awkward and rather shy-making to be suddenly thrown into a Service Mess with no explanatory uniform, or even insignia of rank. As far as the girl pilots were concerned there was yet another snag in this, namely that in autumn and winter there is undoubtedly only one garment in which to fly an open machine, and that is trousers; on the other hand, corduroy slacks as an evening garment are not smiled upon by senior officers in an RAF Mess, which meant that, while awaiting their uniforms, female cadets were forced to take a change of clothes with them each day in case of necessity.

Also neither a Magister, nor any single-engine machine which from now on Susan might have to fly, had been constructed with much of an eye for luggage space, and the ferry pilots' overnight bag had been designed accordingly, so that after maps, *Ferry Pilots' Notes*, sponge bag, pyjamas, slippers, an extra sweater and a change of underwear had been stuffed in, there was little room for a skirt or dress.

'All very tiresome,' thought Susan as she left the shop, and she stood on the pavement to count her few remaining clothing coupons and wonder about the possible purchase of a ready-made pair of navy slacks, and wish she had not been quite so impulsive in parting with all her Red Cross uniform. The coat, minus its badges, could have been pressed into service. But coupons were scarce, and it would mean Grannie's again, or her mother's – so Susan sighed a little sigh and gave it up, deciding to manage somehow.

'But *we* are all right' was Mandy's surprising answer when Susan bewailed these facts that same evening.

'All right?' echoed Susan questioningly. 'What do you mean?'

'Just that. You forget my year with Ferry Control. Now you can wear one of my uniforms. They are just the same, jacket and slacks.'

'Oh, Mandy! Will you? But why haven't you been wearing them yourself?'

'Too jolly hot to wear a collar and tie when one doesn't have to. Besides, they'd only have got filthy in the School, and I'd get tired of explaining. People would keep asking how I'd got my uniform so soon. They'd think I was shooting an imperial line,' and Mandy laughed and stooped to open the lower drawer of her dressing chest. 'Here we are! I left them with Nanny. She had them cleaned and pressed, and she has mended and so we are as good as new.' She flung the parcel on to her bed.

Susan began to protest. 'I really shouldn't.'

'Rot! Who lent me her new frock before she had worn it herself? One good turn deserves another, etc. – *ad lib*,' and Mandy laughed as she unfolded and, unnoticed by Susan, picked out the better of her two tunics. 'Come along. Try it on. Should be perfect, judging by the way your frock fitted me.'

Susan needed no more persuading. A moment later Mandy was patting her shoulders and saying: 'Couldn't be better. Fits like a glove. Now try the slacks. I'm a bit of a longshanks, but they'll tuck into your boots, or take an extra turn-up.'

It was true. Mandy's legs were abnormally long, but the serge of the uniform was not over thick, and a double turn did the trick. Satisfied with her appearance, Susan pirouetted in front of the mirror, pressing the gold wings and ATA badge in place on the left breast of her jacket.

'You know, Mandy, I'm beginning to like myself and, I don't care what anyone says, I do think *dressing* for the part, helps.'

'Of course it does. Why, no one would recognize an angel without its wings – let alone a pilot!'

ELEVEN

ALMOST A WEEK elapsed before Mandy passed her Wings Check and joined Susan in Cross-country Flight, for although her navigation was brilliant, her flying lacked the steadiness and constant watchfulness so essential to a ferry pilot.

One evening her instructor, returning from a cross-country with another pupil, had seen a lone Hart practising loops some eight thousand feet above the Chilterns and, recognizing it for a School machine, climbed up on it unawares and took the number. This he immediately saw was the very machine he had allotted to Mandy in which to put in an hour's solid 'circuit and bump' practice, and here she was not only not doing as she had been told, but busily practising aerobatics, a sport much frowned upon in elementary flying schools.

Although on this occasion Mandy's instructor did not report her to the CFI, he did, in Mandy's language, 'tear her off a colossal strip' himself, and he made her wait yet another two days for her Wings Check.

In the meanwhile, however, an autumn gale blew up from the southwest, bringing in its wake driving rain and low cloud, which made it impossible for the little Magisters of Cross-country Flight to take off at all, so that, finally, Susan and Mandy started this course on the same day.

The Flight was designed to give cadets experience in ferrying conditions, to teach them to look after themselves and make their own decisions in every emergency, so that they should not be posted straight into a Ferry Pool, to fly strange types of aircraft over unknown country and under completely different conditions from those they were used to in the School.

In this it most certainly succeeded.

In all there were twenty-five different routes, varying in length and not necessarily to be completed in strict rotation, so that whereas Susan found her first chit was made out for Route Two, taking her to Aston Down, Lyneham, Odiham and back to Thame, Mandy's was Route Sixteen, and led her from Andover to Colerne, and so back.

During the third night the storm blew itself out completely and next morning the sky was cloudless, the trees barely stirred, and the day showed every promise of perfection.

By ten o'clock Susan was airborne in Magister Number twenty-three and, circling the airfield before turning on to course, she could see a black speck disappearing to the south-west which she knew to be Mandy, while beneath her several more Magisters were ticking over impatiently by the Control Car, waiting their turns to take off.

The last hour Susan had found trying in the extreme, for she had not realized how much preparation was needed to set off on a trip in Cross-country Flight, and the brilliant weather only added to her impatience. To begin with she had gone to Flying Control to collect the chit, telling her which route she was to fly and the number of her machine, and at the same time had been presented with two more chits. The first to be signed by the officers of Flying Control at two of the airfields where she was ordered to land, to prove that she had actually completed the course, and the second, more mundane, was for a threepenny bar of chocolate, in fact an iron ration, as in all probability she would miss her lunch. This had to be presented to the General Office across the passage from Flying Control and the chocolate duly collected.

Then there was Met and the Maps and Signals Office to be visited, which meant walking some four hundred yards round the perimeter track to the Pool buildings, where the offices were situated. Even this had not been too simple, for the cadets from the School were not the only ones anxious to check up on the weather. When Susan arrived there were at least a dozen pilots from the Pool apparently all asking questions at the same time, talking to each other, or exchanging views on the 'jobs' they had been allotted that day.

'This is the third damned Whitley I've had this week!' one tiny dark girl was complaining to the bearded officer at her side.

'Wait till you have three on the same day!' he grinned, waving a sheaf of Ferry chits under her nose. 'Then you really *will* have something to bind about!'

'What's it like over the Irish Sea?' a grey-haired man with a limp asked the WAAF Met Officer.

'Any fronts lurking about?' enquired a very fat man with a very bright complexion.

'Llandow? Let me see – nothing to worry you there. Three-tenths at three thousand visibility fifteen miles.'

'What about Silloth?' chipped in a red-haired Third Officer, with an incredible pair of green eyes.

The Met Officer bent over some charts and shook her head.

'No good! You could probably creep into Hawarden, but not a mile further north. There's a warm front moving in and it won't be much good before late this afternoon.'

Ginger looked upset.

'That cooks it!' he said to another Third Officer beside him; who also had a chit for the north. 'We are sure to be stuck out because I'm going on leave tonight!'

Laughing, they went out together, and at last Susan had a chance to ask about the weather on her own route, for she did not as yet trust her own ability to read the weather charts correctly for herself. Having discovered that there was no chance of meeting bad weather on her own particular route, back she went to the School, conscientiously marked her track on her maps, worked out her course, put on a thick sweater under her jacket, a scarf round her neck, and temporarily stuffed her helmet, goggles and gauntlets into her already bulging overnight bag.

Finally she drew a parachute, and then, feeling more like a barrage balloon than a pilot, went out to Flying Control to sign out. This was always the last thing for cadets to do before getting the Field Car to drive them round to the far side of the 'drome where the Magisters were parked, and Susan was greatly relieved when she heaved her parachute and bag aboard, and flopped into the seat beside the driver.

Before the week was out, however, she had the whole performance down to a fine art, and no longer found it so exhausting. She realized that, within limits, nobody minded how long she took over a route, whether she were stuck out or not, and she learnt that far more kudos was given to the pupil who took no risks with the weather than to the one who pressed on, regardless of safety, even though he might arrive back at Thame unscathed.

Slowly at first, and not without occasionally losing herself and frequently frightening herself silly, Susan was finding her way about England. As the larger contours took shape in her mind and before her eyes, so they fell into their rightful positions as if they were pieces of a gigantic jigsaw puzzle and, as the whole picture became clearer, so Susan's confidence grew.

Day by day her store of knowledge was enlarged, not only of the more important factors, such as weather wisdom and her actual flying technique, but also of the details which go to make the life of a ferry pilot easier, and considerably less hazardous than it otherwise would be. She began to know where she could refuel quickly; which airfields always had 73 octane petrol on the spot and which took an hour or more to fetch it in two gallon cans from a store some miles away.

Soon, too, she realized the importance of keeping on the right side of the ground crews, so that even if she arrived outside some strange Flying Control Tower so cold that she could hardly move her hands or feet, she still managed a smile and a pleasant word for the men who were to refuel or service her machine.

Luckily Susan had a good memory, for she felt certain that otherwise she would never have remembered the characteristics of each airfield at which she landed, details which do not matter much in good weather when the signals area can easily be seen, but which in bad weather, or an emergency, can spell the difference between safety and disaster.

For instance by 1943 most airfields had runways, but quite a number were still grass; a few had right-hand circuits instead of the usual left; at some one could taxi over the grass between the runways in safety: at others one could not, for there were hidden obstructions, which could very easily tip an aircraft up on to its nose.

Even the positions of airfields at which she did not land Susan tried to fix in her memory, for, later on, any one of them might prove a useful haven in time of need. In some parts of England this was almost unnecessary, as the countryside seemed positively littered with airfields and Susan thought she must always be in sight of at least two.

Such a district was East Anglia, with its clusters of bomber stations and its eastern fringe of fighter airfields, and yet it was during Route Fourteen, the first leg of which had taken her out to Bircham Newton, an airfield near the coast of Norfolk, that Susan nearly came to grief.

Her next port of call was Little Rissington, a large aerodrome on the hills between Oxford and Cheltenham, and her course took her right across the centre of the Fens, over miles and miles of rich black cultivated soil, a land void of hedges and trees, its vast fields separated and drained by innumerable canals.

This course should have taken Susan directly over Ely, and when after three-quarters of an hour there was still no sign of the cathedral spire, she began to get worried. Had her compass packed up, and was she, perhaps, flying in a completely different direction? Up into the Lincolnshire Fenland, maybe? Anxiously she checked her course and then re-checked it, both by compass, sun and watch, but each time she arrived at the same conclusion: she should have passed over Ely at least ten minutes ago, yet here she was, with ten miles visibility, and not a sign of it. Fifteen hundred feet below her lay nothing but hundreds of acres of black mud, a few windmills scattered here and there, one or two isolated farms, and these endless canals, which Susan felt by now had been specially made to upset her navigation.

Where had all the airfields gone that she had seen – surely only a few miles further east – on the way up to Bircham Newton? They couldn't just vanish into thin air! Susan decided that the only thing to do was to fly due east and find them; maybe she would recognize something she had passed over earlier in the day, and so be able to pin-point her position.

But what Susan had not noticed was that the sails of the windmills were whirling crazily and that the few stunted trees clutching wildly on to the canal banks were more than usually bent; or that the game little Magister was making less headway than was its wont – in fact she had been far too worried about her navigation to realize that in the last hour the strength of the wind had increased by about thirty miles an hour and that she was now heading right into the teeth of yet another south-westerly gale. It was only after she had been flying east for some minutes that she realized what a colossal amount of drift she had on, and found some difficulty in holding the machine straight and level.

Ahead she soon saw, with some relief, a huge area of woodland, and her map told her that it could be only one thing – the forest round Brandon, and in that case she knew she must be over Feltwell Fens and within a few miles of Feltwell airfield.

Almost as the thought crossed her mind hangars came into sight, the great runways and the dispersed bombers. In order to give herself time to think Susan circled the airfield several times, and she saw that the wind-sock was being blown above the ninety degree position, at times almost pointing vertically upwards. She felt certain she ought to land, but here the wind was across the runway in use, and she had no desire to practise a cross-wind landing at the moment.

She glanced at the petrol gauge and then at the map. Eight gallons left, approximately an hour's safe flying, and some twenty miles to the south-west lay Newmarket – and Mark!

It was roughly on her track, no one could deny that and, after all, being a grass airfield she would be able to land into wind, while Lakenheath and Mildenhall, although she would reach them sooner, both had runways. Of course there was Snailwell and that was grass, and it was a few miles nearer than Newmarket, but well – after all – so what? Susan had already made up her mind to land at Newmarket.

Away she flew into the wind again, eyes bright and blood tingling. High above her several squadrons of Fortresses lumbered towards the North Sea, the sunlight burnishing them in spite of their camouflage, the wind swallowing the roar of their engines.

When Susan landed the airfield had a very deserted look, and glancing at her watch she supposed everyone to be at lunch, and suddenly felt that she could do with a square meal herself.

As she taxied towards the Control Tower an airman appeared, waved her to a parking place and signed her to switch off.

'Refuel, miss?' he asked.

Susan pulled off her helmet. 'Please,' she said. 'Seventy-three octane.'

'Have you got the Seven Hundred?'

Susan opened her locker in the fuselage and gave him the thin, buff book, which is part of the equipment of every machine and is known as the form Seven Hundred. The importance of this document had already been firmly drummed into her during her ground course, together with the fact that she must never take off, in any machine, without first insuring that the Seven Hundred was up to date, the last daily inspection completed, and signed for, not more than thirty-six hours previously, and any defects, reported by the last pilot, corrected.

Now the quantity of petrol and oil put in would be entered, along with the date, the name of the airfield and finally the signature of the corporal, or sergeant, in charge of the Duty Crew.

Susan left her Magister, completely confident that it would be serviced correctly, and walked towards the door of the Control Tower. As she passed under the platform which surrounded the Control Room, some thirty feet above her head, she heard a man chuckle and speak to someone in the room behind him.

'Looks like Ropey's Popsie's dropped in! What's that boy got that I haven't?'

Susan did not hear the answer, for at this moment the door in front of her opened and out ran Blackie, the red-haired New Zealander whom she had met at the party.

'Why! Hullo!' he greeted her with a wide, welcoming grin.

'What brings you here?'

'The wind, *and* hunger! Any chance of lunch, Blackie?'

'Sure! I'm just going to the Mess myself. I've got the car: I'll wait for you.'

'OK. I won't be a sec.,' and so saying, Susan ran upstairs to sign it.

'What's the wind strength?' she asked the Control Officer. He consulted a slip of paper on his desk.

'Well, at thirteen hundred hours it was forty miles an hour, but judging by the wind-sock I should say it might have increased a bit since then.' He raised his eyebrows. 'Bit strong for your little flivver, isn't it?'

Susan agreed with him. 'What is the forecast?' she asked.

'I'm not sure, but I don't imagine this will drop much before dusk. Would you like to go downstairs and have a chat with Met yourself?'

'Well, I've just got a lift to the Mess for lunch, but I'll be back soon after two o'clock, and visit Met then.'

'Right! Where are you heading for?' he asked as Susan turned to go.

'Little Rissington.'

The Control Officer grinned. 'That's bad' he said, 'you don't want to get stuck there for the night – awful dump!'

Susan laughed. 'So I gather, but with any luck I shall make Thame by last landing-time. It's not till five twenty-five this evening.'

However, Susan did not have any luck, or maybe she had a great deal, depending on how one looks at it, because the wind continued to blow a small gale all afternoon and when she rang Thame, to let them know where she was, they told her to stay on the ground unless the wind force dropped considerably.

But by last landing-time the wind-sock was still horizontal, and Mark Cordner, who had appeared fresh from sleep and a bath about four o'clock, was cursing the fact that he was going on Ops. that night and so would not be able to spend the evening with Susan.

Another three trips and he would have finished his tour! Mark was looking forward to that; already planning his leave, and he wondered if it would be tempting fate too strongly if he dated Susan now for some of those precious days. He knew she could get up to town in the evening from Thame, and as the days grew shorter she would finish flying earlier.

He was about to ask her as they walked from the Control Tower to his car, but, at that moment, Section Officer Grant overtook them on her bicycle and dismounted to tell Susan that she had organized a room for her in the WAAF Officers' quarter for the night.

Susan thanked her, and the highly efficient WAAF pedalled purposefully on her way, but somehow to Mark the moment was lost and he could not bring himself to mention his leave again.

'I'm afraid the Mess will be rather dull for you tonight. I'm sorry it's happened so. I imagine there is quite a big "do" on – fifteen kites are going from here.'

'I suppose,' Susan asked hopefully, 'I wouldn't be allowed to come up to the Control Tower and see you all take off?'

Mark thought for a moment.

'Don't see why not. I'll ask the CO. But we shall have to get a move on,' he added, looking at his watch, 'because briefing is at six-thirty.'

He changed down rapidly as they approached the roundabout at the top of the town, and somehow his hand slipped from the gear to Susan's knee.

'Sue,' he said quietly, 'I want to take something of yours with me tonight. Could you part with that scarf – temporarily, of course?' he added hurriedly.

'I'm not a very lucky type, you know, Mark!' Susan's eyes were wistful. 'But if you want it, of course you can have it – and keep it. There you are!' and she took off the navy blue silk scarf with its monogram 'F.S' embroidered in white in one corner. It had been Frank's, but somehow Susan did not feel disloyal in giving it to Mark. Frank would like him to have it, and would not have grudged it to anyone setting off through the hazardous night skies with a few tons of high explosives in the bomb-bays beneath him.

'It *could* be cleaner,' she apologized, 'but it's very warm.'

Mark put it to his cheek. 'And very soft, and it smells heavenly! Thank you, Sue – darling…,' he added, almost to himself.

Susan said nothing. There were things she would have liked to have said, but for some reason decided, as Mark had earlier, that this was not the moment. In fact she was quite glad that, as they had by this time reached the Officers' Mess, intimate conversation was impossible during the remaining half-hour.

'Blacker' Hay, the Wing Commander, gave his permission for Susan to watch the take-off, and the Control Officer, who was just going on duty, offered to take her down with him.

Soon after six o'clock Mark went down to the briefing-room with the rest of the aircrew, together with the CO, the Intelligence

Officer and the Met man. Although he laughed and joked with the rest, Susan thought that he looked unusually strained and wondered why. Perhaps an extra risky 'do'? He was wearing her scarf when he nodded to her and went out to the waiting car, and in answer to the look he gave her, Susan found herself wishing they had a moment alone; she would have liked to have adjusted Frank's scarf.

'Do you know how many more trips Squadron Leader Cordner has to do?' she asked the Control Officer as they drove down the airfield.

'About half a dozen I should think,' he answered, 'but I'm not dead certain – maybe one or two more or less.' He turned to Susan in the darkness of the car. 'You're not worrying yourself on Ropey's account, I hope? He's easily our best pilot and his crew is first class. Looks a good night, too,' he added cheerfully. 'Bags of cloud about.'

With the coming of the darkness the wind had dropped as suddenly as it had risen earlier in the day, but now the sky was heaped high with long, rolling banks of cloud.

'Is cloud such a good thing?' Susan asked. 'Why? I should have thought it made the location of the target more difficult?'

'Oh no. It makes for cover, you see. Jerry night-fighters can't spot them so easily in cloud.'

At the Guardroom gate they halted, were recognized and passed on.

'Got a tremendous cheek these Jerries, you know,' continued the Control Officer. 'They come right in here sometimes and shoot the boys up as they take off, which means we have to maintain complete radio silence from the moment of take-off – no last-minute chats in the circuit!'

'Good heavens!' ejaculated Susan, and she looked up and swiftly scanned the sky. 'Does it happen often?'

'No, not often, but the trouble is you don't always know when. They slip over the coast unobserved occasionally.'

Susan uttered a heartfelt prayer that none would molest the Stirlings tonight, and she remembered to give thanks when, later, she knew her prayer had been answered.

The take-off of the fifteen Stirlings was perfectly timed and accurate to the second.

Susan stood on the wooden balcony surrounding the Control Room, muffled from ears to ankles in the RAF greatcoat which the Control Officer had lent her, for the early October night held a definite hint of frost.

She seemed to be quite alone, poised in space, almost part of the darkness, for behind her the long windows of the Control Room were completely blacked out, while in front of her lay the airfield in restless and noisy blackness.

One by one the four great engines of each bomber coughed into life, and only occasionally Susan could pick out the position of a machine by the flash from an exhaust, until finally the whole night pulsed with power.

To Susan's right a door opened and three shadowy figures stepped out on to the balcony beside her. Their voices were unfamiliar, it was too dark to see their faces, and not until one of them struck a match to light a cigarette did Susan realize that the CO of the Group, Air Vice Marshal Maitland, was one of them.

He was speaking now, and his voice was gruff.

'Bright moonlight the other side, so Met says – bound to be a pretty hot night.'

In spite of the greatcoat Susan shivered.

Suddenly the lights of the flarepath were turned on and the night lost some of its sinister cruelty. The Control Car at the extreme eastern end of the flarepath was now easily discernible, and Susan could also see the black bulk of the first Stirling taxiing slowly towards it.

'Here they come, sir!' a voice beside her announced – rather obviously, Susan thought. 'It'll be tricky taking-off tonight – maximum load and a slight cross wind.'

'Too slight to matter,' the Air Marshal commented, and Susan could hear the confidence of experience in his voice, which made it quite unnecessary for her to see him to know he wore wings to his chest.

The bomber had stopped, and the pilot was clearing his engines. Vividly Susan could imagine the scene inside the belly of that monster.

The straining young faces in the almost complete darkness; the taut nerves; the light-hearted cracks over the inter-com; the last verbal check-up by each member of the crew in turn, and then the captain's final word of command.

Slowly the Stirling rolled forwards, lumbered down the flarepath and – Susan held her breath – would it ever clear the dyke? At last the wheels unstuck and with great skill the pilot lifted his machine gently over the thirty-foot fortification, a relic of wars waged by the Early Britons.

Almost immediately the roar of the first machine was drowned by the noise of the second, which by this time had moved forward to the take-off position, and Susan noticed that as each one drew level with the Control Car a light was flashed on the letter and number painted on its fuselage. She could see this quite clearly from where she stood, and yet when the shaft of light picked out the letter 'C' on the side of a Stirling it was as if she were seeing it for the first time. She could not quite believe that Mark was sitting up there in the cockpit, the pilot and captain of 'C' for 'Charlie'. Surely no one she knew, no mere man of flesh and blood, could survive these endless nights of cold and danger in the enemy-haunted darkness!

Susan dug her hands deeper into her pockets and tried to watch 'C' for 'Charlie' as dispassionately as she had watched others. But it was no good pretending to herself that she was not anxious for Mark, because she was, and as his machine disappeared into the night a small, hard lump rose involuntarily in her throat, and again she prayed: 'Keep him safe, oh God – keep him safe.'

It was almost a relief when the last Stirling had taken off. The flarepath lights went out, the door of the Control Room was opened and a buzz of conversation came to Susan's ears. Emotionally she was exhausted, and although it was not long after eight o'clock she had a great desire to sleep.

However, the Air Vice Marshal saw her when she came into the Control Room and immediately drew her into the conversation, and she gratefully accepted his offer of a lift back to the Mess when she discovered that it did not mean taking him out of his way.

'Marvellous, you ATA people,' he complimented her in his deep,

224

gruff voice. 'Don't know how you do it – no radio, all weathers, any old machine, all alone – very good show!'

Modestly Susan protested, but he would not listen, and when he dropped her outside the WAAF. Officers' quarters he wished her goodnight and saluted her as an equal.

The bedroom which Susan found she had been given was, like the other WAAF rooms, above the stables surrounding an old cobbled yard, but it was as bare of furnishings as her room in Hopefield House and this emanated a certain friendliness, born of familiarity.

Just down the passage Susan could hear a buzz of voices, and guessed correctly it must be from the WAAF Officers' sitting-room. She hesitated. Ought she to go in for a few minutes or could she, without being rude, go straight to bed?

The decision, however, was made for her by Section Officer Grant, who had followed her up the stairs.

'Hullo! So you've found your room all right?' she beamed. 'You must be tired – I must say I am, and I haven't been flying. Sorry you can't have a bath; the boiler has died on us.'

'Oh, that's all right. Thank you so much for fixing me up. Yes, I think I am for bed.'

After exchanging a few more words and arranging what time Susan should be called in the morning, they said goodnight, and half an hour later Susan was asleep.

It was shortly after two o'clock when she was awakened by the drone of engines overhead and went to the window to watch the returning bombers. They had their navigation lights on now, and she tried to count the machines, but it was no good, for some of them had already passed over the house, and it was not until some hours later that she knew that three of the gallant Stirlings had failed to return, and that one of them was 'C' for 'Charlie'.

TWELVE

THE WEATHER HAD cleared, but, that morning, Susan flew back to Thame like an automaton. Mark missing! 'C' for 'Charlie' failed to return. Over and over in her mind the words repeated themselves. Every throb of the engine of the little Magister, even the vibration, seemed to emphasize them. The clouds were high. She looked at them reproachfully, light, fleecy clouds, and thought: 'You weren't thick enough. You didn't protect "C" for "Charlie" after all.'

Before she left Newmarket, Wing Commander 'Blacker' Hay had tried to comfort her. 'Missing doesn't mean *lost*. Probably baled out. May be in the ditch and will be picked up before the day is out. We expect him back. May take some time if he baled out over Holland.

Ropey is an Australian. Don't for get that. He has slept out and found his way by the stars before today,' and Susan had thanked him, accepted his sympathy, but had said little. Indeed, she had only asked if she might 'phone in the evening for possible news.

But she was not comforted. Mark was her dearest friend. He had known Frank, and been a part of their short, happy married life. That was the bond between them. As she flew back to Thame, Susan felt she was fated. 'I am just one of those,' she told herself, 'fated either to be killed myself, or to have no one left when it is all over – except, of course, Mother and Grannie.' Mark was falling in love with her. Of that she was sure. That was something women always knew. And she knew, too, that this fact was giving comfort to her soul. But wasn't that being very unfair to Mark – because of course there never could be anyone but Frank. And Mark was the last person in the world that she would wish to trifle with – or hurt, because Mark was like Frank – she knew this instinctively – his love would be real and lasting. Of course – that was the reason that the knowledge of his love did so comfort her. It was only when one had possessed this precious thing that one felt the bitter loss of it – and that look in Mark's eyes when he had taken her scarf and laid it to his cheek had been as balm to unhealed wounds. The truth was, the happier that strong, unfailing love had made one, the more one ached for it. Still – that wasn't fair – unless one returned it. She gave herself a mental shake, forced herself to think of Mandy and her courage, and abruptly discovered that her thoughts had gone round and round all the way from Newmarket to Thame, that she was landing and had no recollection of doing those things she ought to have done! She was actually parking the Magister! Everything was right. She had made the circuit and come in exactly as she should. But how? Every action had been mechanical. A soft breeze fanned her cheek – a little breeze from nowhere. Susan climbed out of the 'plane.

Again it was not until evening that Susan and Mandy were alone. Susan's cross-country had taken her south that day while Mandy's had been north. It was three days since they had seen each other and Susan had not noticed Mandy's occasional puzzled glance while they were in the canteen or scarcely heard Mandy's 'I'll come along, too, and have an early to bed,' when she herself declined to join the crowd at either the 'Crown' or the 'Rose and Thistle'.

'Something is up,' thought Mandy – but being Mandy she cycled alongside and talked gaily of her own night out.

Hopefield House was silent.

'No one in as yet, thank goodness,' said Mandy, and without preamble she added, 'What's up, Sue? You look – distrait.'

'Mark!' said Susan.

'Not—? Oh, Sue!' Mandy's voice said more than her words.

Susan quickly shook her head. 'No. No. Not as far as I know. I watched fifteen 'planes take off – only twelve came back. "C" for "Charlie"—' Her voice broke.

'Oh, Sue!' Mandy sagged down on one side of her bed, but before she had time to think Susan spoke again:

'Mandy! Come down to the phone. Keep guard – as if you are waiting next turn. I'm going to ring up Mark's Wing Co. There may be news.'

But no one came. The house remained silent and Susan's call came through quickly. Mandy watched her and knew by the way she replaced the receiver that there was no news.

'He says,' said Susan, 'not to bother to ring. If they hear anything they will contact me. Mark has no relations, he knows, in England.'

Side by side, with Mandy's arm linked in Susan's, they reascended the stairs, and Mandy was thinking, 'Oh, Hell! That's put an end to it. I did hope Mark was the solution of her future.'

Both went quietly to bed. There was nothing to say.

Mandy, who always fell quickly asleep, was apparently soon asleep, but Susan lay awake long after the other inhabitants of the house had returned. They came in twos and threes, calling goodnights to their companions. She heard the bath water running it seemed for hours; heard the drone of bombers passing over and with hands clenched prayed fervently. Then, without realizing what she was saying and with her face buried in her pillow, found herself saying over and over, 'Take care of Mark wherever he is. Keep him safe. Bring him back.'

It was a mid-October afternoon when Susan parked a school 'Magister' for the last time. A few minutes earlier she had landed after completing her twenty-fifth cross-country flight, a route which had taken her the length of England, across the border into Scotland and as far north as Prestwick.

She had been away for four days. The weather had closed in – 'absolutely foul' was her expression – and she had been 'stuck out' at Cark, an airfield on the desolate west coast of Cumberland, for three nights. Time had been long; she had taken only one clean shirt and collar, and by some mischance, or fit of mental aberration, had forgotten both her soap and face powder, so had been obliged to borrow from the only WAAF officer on the station, one whose knowledge of cosmetics apparently went no further than talcum and carbolic. Apart from these minor irritations the weather on this particular day above a thousand feet had been little short of arctic, so that Susan had sat blue and numb hour after hour, until she was almost past caring what happened, when, at last, Thame airfield hove into sight.

Never had any airfield appeared more beautiful or desirous. Susan's one thought at that moment was of hot tea.

Yet, in spite of cold and discomfort, Susan was sorry to come to the end of her cross-country flights. The next morning would bring her final 'check', and if all was well she would then be posted into Number Five Training Pool. She would be finished with the 'school'. Life would be different. She would have more opportunity of meeting experienced pilots. She wanted, and wanted badly, to start real work, but she couldn't help a little regret. 'Cross-countries' had been a carefree period to a certain extent. She had been responsible to no one but herself and for nothing except one Magister. If only she had not been so worried about Mark! It was now over a month and nothing had been heard of the crew of 'C' for 'Charlie'. It would all have been such fun. She had loved her freedom, when at last she had evaded the critical prying eyes of instructors, and winged her way untrammelled across the length and breadth of England. It had all been so wonderful. Herself and the Magister – which grew to be alive and friendly. She felt a veritable explorer and thought she must have experienced many of the same sensations that Columbus did when he discovered his New World. She had certainly discovered hers. 'England,' she told Grannie, 'is too beautiful. The glowing tints of autumn and the stubble still golden in the cornfields. It changes every day and stubble looks like a thick golden carpet from the air, and it is all cornfields or airfields or woods – and I love the deep valleys of Wales and having a peep at the sea on three different coasts, and sometimes I follow a seagull for a bit, or a river, and then I come back like a homing bird to the Chilterns and the Chiltern country is lovely.'

It was all true. Susan's geography of England had been sketchy. Now it was complete. At first she had never been quite certain what she would find, nor what country would pass beneath her wings each day. Cities, rivers, hills, great country houses, dozens of them, which up to now had been mere names, became solid realities. Susan felt she knew England, and agreed when Mandy said:

'What I can't get over is the doing of anything so lovely and getting paid for doing it'; and it was Mandy who discovered so much. A cross-country was always more interesting if Mandy had been over it first.

Then there had been the novelty and excitement of staying

when 'stuck out', or visiting for odd meals, in the Officers' Mess at several different RAF Stations. She had met so many new people with such varying characters. She had talked with pilots from many different squadrons; heard stories of such hair-breadth escapes that her heart was cheered. Mark might be lucky. And she had loved the young boys, embryonic pilots, in Elementary or Operational Training Units. They were so young. Such hero-worshippers. Had such enthusiasms and were so shy about them. They reminded her of her brothers and, knowing what pleasure it would give her mother she tried, unsuccessfully, to find a pilot who had trained with Claude in Canada. Reluctantly she ceased to ask; she decided it was too long ago.

Last, but by no means least – Time. In Cross-country Flight time, to a certain extent, had been no object. But from now on, as Susan discovered when she joined the Training Pool two days later, it was to be the most important factor in her life. Second only to safety.

This most serious fact was impressed upon her by her Flight Leader, First Officer Bartlett, who called her into the Flight Leader's room and delivered his usual 'pep talk' always given to cadets on their first posting into the 'Pool' – plus a few wise observations of his own, which were not to be found in Standing Orders or Daily Routine Orders, but which in their way were to prove as useful as either. Amongst other thing he warned her again about low flying, and 'beat-ups' – otherwise stunt flying at low level – as well as the inadvisability of getting 'stuck out' too often at the same station and putting up 'blacks' generally.

'I was once a cadet myself,' he grinned. 'I know the temptations, but don't forget that what you can get away with as a first officer earns you the sack as a cadet!'

After a few more words of wisdom, First Officer Bartlett suggested that, as there was still an hour or more before last landing time, he 'should take Susan up for a few circuits and bumps in a Fairchild', the four-seater, high wing monoplane that all ATA Pools used as taxi machines, and which she was to come to know so well in the next few months.

To begin with Susan found it strange, for it was the first cabin machine she had flown and she experienced a very slight sensation of claustrophobia. It was odd, too, not to be wearing a parachute, to find the throttle on the instrument panel in front of her and the trimmer in the most unexpected of positions – in the roof! However, Susan's third landing was smooth enough. It was comforting to be assured that she was safe, and that, as she would have plenty of practice on Fairchilds in the near future, her Flight Leader thought that enough.

'Very satisfactory,' he said. 'You will probably be flying it far better than I can in a few weeks,' and he added as they taxied towards the Pool dispersal, 'Not passengers for a while yet, but remember, when you do have them, be sure to see they have their parachutes stowed correctly. A Fairchild is a very sweet little job, but it does need even loading, and four "bods", three parachutes and maybe some extra luggage is a hefty load for a machine this size' – advice which Susan was to see practically demonstrated the very next day when she was sent over to Hullavington to pick up three pilots, one of whom, returning from leave, carried a suitcase as well as his parachute, and neither exactly a light-weight. Moreover the wind was almost non-existent.

One of the three was a flight captain, and, as senior pilot, he took over from Susan, it being a rule that a cadet could not fly passengers, and neither were two cadets allowed to fly together. He now asked Susan if she would mind stowing his parachute under her feet on the floor.

'With those "two-ton Tonies" behind we shall need little ballast in front,' he said with a glance over his shoulder at the two occupants of the rear seat as he trimmed the little craft considerably more nose heavy than was usual for take-off.

One friendly grunt of resentment at such rudery came from the back seat, and Susan turned to see that the pilot just back from leave was nodding drowsily and far beyond caring what personal remarks were passed about him. By the time they had taxied round to the Control Car he was fast asleep.

Although the runway in use was one of the longest Susan had

seen it took the Fairchild, so excessive was the load on board, three-quarters of its length to unstick, and she noticed that the Flight Captain held it down until far more than the usual climbing speed had been reached.

This was the first of many taxi flights for Susan, and each time she learned more about the Fairchild, although to begin with she had thought there could be nothing more to know. She learnt the best way to land it cross-wind, and in thick weather, and by the end of a fortnight she felt as confident in it as she had done in a Magister.

Certainly a cabin machine, in an English winter, had many advantages. Instead of landing blue and frozen with fingers too numb even to comb her hair, Susan enjoyed the comfort of warmth, and appreciated not having constantly to wear a helmet and several layers of extra clothes.

There *were* one or two occasions, however, when she did have to don a Sidcot suit again, plus all the paraphernalia necessary to an open machine, for during these early weeks in the Training Pool Susan was given her first few machines to ferry and the majority of these were Tiger Moths.

Her very first ferry job Susan was never to forget because, although it in no way differed from hundreds of other flights she was to make in the future, yet the very fact that it was the first stamped it indelibly on her memory.

With six other cadets, including Sandra Cushing, Robin, Nina and Mandy, who by now had also been posted to the Training Pool, Susan set out one extremely fresh October morning in a Tiger Moth for Llandow, an airfield on the coast of South Wales.

It was weeks since she had flown a Tiger in the school at Barton, and when the spotless new machine was wheeled out of the factory hangar at Cowley it looked so different from what she expected that Susan knew a moment's panic. The factory airfield looked even smaller than Barton, and what made it far more formidable was the fact that it was encircled on three sides by houses and factory buildings, while on the fourth rose a steep railway embankment along the top of which she was quite certain a train would roar just as she flew over it. The log books having been duly collected from the man at the Aeronautical Inspection Depot, or AID man as he was called, chits handed over, signatures signed here, there and everywhere, Susan tottered out to the tarmac feeling that she must have taken over at least a squadron of Tiger Moths and signed away a round million.

'Have you any idea what we signed for on all these forms?' she asked Mandy.

'No, not a clue, but I don't think it matters much. I can't pay for it if I do break the machine, so if that's what they meant someone may be unlucky!' Mandy laughed lightly, dismissing the matter, and looked round for her Tiger.

'Ah! There it is! NM 118. See you at Llandow... I *hope*!' she added over her shoulder as a mechanic took possession of her parachute.

'Probably see you most of the way as well. I could hardly lose sight of you on a daylike this!' Susan answered as she looked up at the few high mares' tails which streaked an otherwise clear sky.

But Susan was wrong, for although there was every foot of twenty miles' visibility, after ten minutes' flying she could see only one of the other six Tiger Moths, and half an hour later she seemed to have the whole sky to herself, while stranger still was the fact that, some two hours later, all seven little Moths landed at Llandow within a few minutes of each other.

Until now Susan had not realized the vastness of the sky, nor how difficult it is to spot another aircraft flying below one and which is therefore camouflaged against the mottled colouring of the countryside. She was the fourth to land, and as soon as she touched down she wished she had taken more notice of the plan of Llandow airfield which the officer in the Maps and Signals Room had shown her before she set out that morning. Her ferry chit told her that 38 Maintenance Unit Llandow was her ultimate destination, but just where the MU was to be found, and in what sort of building, was quite another story.

A very fresh, stiff breeze was blowing in from the sea, which was less than a mile away from the edge of the airfield. Susan was aware of this fact, but what she had not considered was that she would have to taxi any distance cross-wind in the Tiger Moth. Unlike any other machine she had flown the Tiger Moth had no brakes, and for directional control the pilot must rely entirely on his rudder and throttle, so that when the wind is above a certain strength he is more or less at its mercy.

Susan knew that she must turn off the runway on which she had landed immediately, for she had been in the circuit with at least three other machines, each now awaiting its turn to land, but the question was which way should she turn? For a second she hesitated; the airfield was enormous, there were hangars and huts tucked away in almost every corner, and any one of them might house 38 Maintenance Unit. In cross-country days it had been simple enough as one always made for the Control Tower, which could easily be seen and recognized from any point on the runway. 'What a prize idiot!' she was thinking, when suddenly there was a tremendous roar above her, and, as she instinctively ducked, Susan saw two great wheels and a huge fuselage sweep by within a few feet of her head.

Slowly the four-engined giant lumbered round the circuit again, leaving Susan blushing for shame that her slowness had caused this. Could she have heard the language with which she was most colourfully described by the pilot of the Liberator, she would undoubtedly have blushed an even deeper hue.

Now it was without caring where 38 MU might or might not be that Susan turned off the runway down a left-hand intersection, hoping against hope that she was aiming in the right direction, and it was only at this point that she realized how difficult it is to taxi a Tiger cross-wind. Continually the little machine tried to weather-cock into the wind, and Susan found herself careering round and round in circles, zigzagging across the runway and bumping up and down on to the grass. Just as she had decided there was nothing for it but to switch off and fetch someone to help her, she spotted two figures, in the familiar RAF blue, emerge from a long hut a few hundred yards away and make towards her across the grass, but because they were both wearing battle-dress it was not until they were quite close to her that Susan saw they were officers, and noticed also that they were both roaring with laughter.

'Wish I could change places with them for a few minutes – that would teach them!' Susan thought irritably, for by now she was not only angry with herself but with the machine, which had behaved as if at least half a dozen evil-minded gremlins were squatting on its tail. On top of all this Susan was very cold; the possibility of ever finding 38 MU seemed remote; she had had nothing to eat since a rather nauseating sausage and a wishy-washy cup of coffee in the canteen at eight o'clock that morning, and, above all, she would have given a great deal at that moment to be magically transported to some well-equipped and well-heated cloakroom! 'You bloody fool! What on ear—' one of the officers shouted when still some ten yards away, but he suddenly stopped short, realizing that the pilot of the Tiger had not exactly the air of the raw RAF pupil pilot he had expected. His expression was puzzled and Susan could see that he was completely baffled.

His companion, however, was considerably quicker in the uptake, and without hesitation walked straight up to the cockpit, still wearing a broad grin on his face. He was good-looking in a flamboyant way, and, quite obviously, was aware of the fact. Immediately he reminded Susan of John Cherry.

'Ah-ha! A damsel in distress!' he shouted cheerily above the noise of the little gipsy engine. 'What luck! Where are you making for?

'Thirty-Eight MU,' Susan bellowed back.

'OK. We'll give you a hand and hang on to the wings. The MU is right on the other side of the airfield. By the way, little gal, are you staying the night here?'

This sort of remark no longer worried Susan. During her cross-country days she had heard them so often and now knew exactly how to cope. At first she had not realized that there is a certain type of male, found among officers as well as in the ranks, who once he dons a uniform thinks it an open sesame to the adoration of the opposite sex, and immediately imagines himself to be 'the hell of a fellow' and something of a rake. In the ranks he whistles at any female from fifteen to forty whom he may see on the road; his tent, in all probability, is festooned with semi-nude pin-up girls, and he always wears his forage cap, or beret, at the most tremendous angle when he is not on duty. His counterpart in the Officers' Mess, whilst possessing the same taste in mural decorations, refrains from whistling at girls in the street, and is usually slightly, though not much, more subtle in making their acquaintance. Instead he may offer them a lift in his car, or 'a drink on me, m'dear' at the bar, or open with the type of remark such as had just been addressed to Susan.

'I hope not,' she replied, looking straight at him. 'It seems an awful dump!' Then, because he was fingering his carefully groomed moustache a trifle *too* lovingly, a very wicked gremlin whispered in her ear that it might be a good thing to open the throttle just a fraction further.

Which was exactly what Susan did, so that by the time his hand had moved from the beautiful moustache to grab its owner's cap the latter was lying some yards away on the muddy grass.

Most ungrateful one might think, but under the circumstances wonderfully efficacious.

'Come on, Gorgeous, grab a wing – the lady wants thirty-eight MU, not a game of Romeo and Juliet!' and the second officer grinned his approval at Susan.

Nothing daunted by losing his cap, or by Susan's action – for it did not cross his mind that it had been purposely done – 'Gorgeous' now caught hold of the port wing tip and with his companion on the – other side they set slowly forth round the perimeter track.

Even so it was not easy taxiing, for the wind was becoming stronger all the time, and once or twice the two men had to hang grimly on, and dig their heels into the ground to prevent the Tiger weathercocking into the wind. Half-way to the Maintenance Unit Susan's helpers handed over to two airmen who seemed to have nothing in particular to do, and waving to her set off back towards their own hutments. Susan raised a gauntleted hand in thanks, but at the same time swore to herself that, in future, she would always find out exactly where, on any airfield, was situated the particular unit to which she was actually delivering the machine. Another valuable lesson learnt with no damage done – a lesson which could later prove vitally important, for a half-hour's unnecessary dallying on a strange airfield, with a *Priority One* machine, might make a vast amount of difference to an operational squadron in urgent need of a replacement.

By the time Susan's new escort reached the Maintenance Unit hut they were panting and blowing, in spite of the cold sweat pouring from their foreheads. As they approached the hut a little old man in civilian clothes hopped out, and waved Susan to park the Moth on the grass opposite, but it was only when she had switched off the engine that she was able to hear his shouted instructions. Even then she could make very little sense of them, because from long habit he went on shouting, and spoke with a broad Welsh accent, accompanied by a strange sing-song intonation. However, he helped her with her parachute and fetched her overnight bag and the log books of the machine from the locker in the rear fuselage, and he had such a worn-out, wizened look that she had not the heart to make him repeat what he had been saying.

38 Maintenance Unit! Susan almost gasped when she saw where it was housed. Absolutely unlike anything she had pictured was the small wooden hut with its extremely crooked and roughly-painted notice above the door announcing the fact that this was indeed 38 Maintenance Unit, and had it not been for the presence of this notice, and also that of Flight Captain Shanks, the pilot who had brought the taxi Anson to pick up the cadets, lounging in the doorway, and who, judging by his expression of extreme boredom, had already been waiting some time, Susan would have been inclined to think that there must be some mistake.

Inside was even less like Susan's picture than was the outside. It was dark, all the windows were tightly shut and a strong smell of stale tobacco hung on the air. At the crudely-made wooden desks sat two or three collarless men, while on the corner of an upturned sugar-box perched a girl whose blue dungarees vied for greasiness with her lank hair.

For a moment Susan stared, her eyes not yet focusing after the glare of the bright day outside, her mind unwilling to accept the unglamorous and unexpected picture within. Was this typical of all the Maintenance Units she had heard about, or was it merely an improvisation until better quarters should be ready?

No one took any particular notice of her and the man whom she supposed to be in charge, by virtue of the fact that he wore both collar and tie, continued to pore over a much-thumbed and grimy news-sheet.

Susan dropped her overnight bag and waited while the paper was slowly lowered and a pair of shrewd green eyes peered at her over the top.

'Log book's 'ere, miss, *and* Seven 'Undred!' he shot at her without preliminary, and proceeded to check them over with the speed of long experience. He also signed her delivery chit; took her signal to confirm her arrival at twelve forty-seven hours, and lastly her snag sheet, which she signed to the effect that to the best of her knowledge nothing was wrong with the machine.

The girl, who had been sitting on the edge of the soap-box swinging her legs and staring vacantly into space, now pushed a chair towards Susan.

''Ave a pew,' she suggested kindly.''Stoo darned cold out there.'

Susan would have accepted this offer gladly, for she had a sudden and overwhelming desire to relax and light up a cigarette, but a sudden warning shout from outside made her walk quickly over to the door.

The shout had apparently come from Flight Captain Shanks, the warning only too clearly was meant for Mandy! There she was some fifty yards away, approaching the hut along a pathway which was not only slightly downhill but at the moment also down wind, and from her own recent experience Susan could see that Mandy was quite unable to stop. Mandy herself had only just realized this, and although she immediately switched off the engine she still rolled forward in a beeline towards the hut, and seemed helpless to do anything to prevent the inevitable collision.

One and all the onlookers stood as if petrified, motionless, eyes wide, mouths open. They might just as well have been a cinema audience watching some improbable drama unfold before them on the screen, themselves completely incapable of altering the sequence of events.

The Tiger Moth trundled slowly on, by now its propeller only flicking over lazily every few seconds.

Inside the cockpit, however, things were far from inactive. There was a whirl of arms, straps flew out over the side slapping hard against the canvas of the fuselage, and were swiftly followed by Mandy's long legs. In spite of the cumbersome flying-boots and bulky Sidcot flying-suit Mandy climbed out of the cockpit as if she were in a gymnasium, and before Susan realized what she intended doing, she had wrapped her arms round the rear end of the fuselage, had dug in her heels, and, half walking, but soon sliding on her backside, she hung on for dear life.

The whole thing had happened so quickly that even now no one went to her assistance, and it was only when the nose of the machine was some ten feet from the window of the hut and still moving very slowly forwards, that Flight Captain Shanks and Nina rushed to Mandy's help and flung their combined weight against the leading edge of the lower wing.

A few inches from the glass panes the machine came to rest, Nina and Captain Shanks with their feet braced against the wooden walls of the hut, Mandy by now lying flat on her back with her arms still clinging to this her first delivery, her face scarlet and giggling weakly with sheer relief.

'Not exactly the correct way for a ferry pilot to arrive!' Flight Captain Shanks remarked dryly as he offered a hand to help Mandy to her feet. 'Try not to approach buildings downhill and downwind next time you fly a Tiger – it doesn't pay!'

Mandy looked up at him. 'No – it doesn't – on trousers!' She giggled again as she took his hand, pulled herself up and immediately looked over her shoulder in an endeavour to view the extent of the damage. 'I'm a little afraid of the perpendicular! Am I torn to bits?'

There was a general shout of laughter and Susan and Nina both stooped to look.

'You are all of the soil, but no holes,' announced Nina.

Susan was quick to grasp her opportunity. 'Let's find a cloakroom and brush it off,' she suggested.

That it was the merest fluke she had not made the same mistake herself Susan was well aware. She was also quite certain that she would not have shown such presence of mind in switching off the engine and jumping out to drag the machine to a standstill. But then that was Mandy all over; she could always be relied upon to pull something out of the bag in an emergency, and one could be equally sure that it would be something completely unorthodox.

Still laughing, Susan complimented her on the way back in the Anson. 'I only wish the designer of the Tiger could have seen you. It might give him a few new ideas!'

Mandy shrugged. 'Couldn't think of anything else! Anyway it's damn silly not having brakes. Oh, look!' Suddenly she swung round and pointed excitedly down the Bristol Channel, above whose centre the Anson now flew.

Out of the corner of her eye she had seen the Cardiff barrage balloons rising like big-bosomed, full-skirted nannies into the smoke haze which hung above the city.

All eyes turned to starboard where some miles away, across the water, lay the dirty heaps of houses, factory chimneys and smoke stacks that was Cardiff.

'Must be some Jerries about!' Fat Robin blinked and scanned the sky short sightedly. 'Hope we see the fun!'

To the relief of Flight Captain Shanks, Robin was doomed to disappointment. He had no desire to be a sitting target in a cloudless sky over the Bristol Channel with a cargo of cadets on board.

From her seat just behind him Susan was amazed to see that he did not refer to his map once the whole way back to Thame; in fact it remained unfolded and tucked down the inside of the leg of one of his flying-boots. She could not imagine that the time would ever come when she would both pilot and navigate a machine like this, nearly two hundred miles, with such certainty and nonchalance. It was uncanny... this man must be the possessor of the same instincts as guide the homing pigeons, or the migratory birds! Fascinated, she followed his course on her own maps and found that he was indeed flying in a dead straight line towards his destination. She turned to remark on this to Mandy, but found that, in spite of the noise, she had fallen asleep, her head pillowed like a child's against Robin's broad shoulder, her copper hair flopping across her face, nor did she wake up until the Anson touched down at Thame.

'Two o'clock!' she yawned as she opened her eyes and glanced down at Richard's watch. 'Too late for lunch, and I'm starving! Hell!'

'Come and have coffee and sandwiches at the snack bar?' Susan suggested.

'OK – but I must thaw first,' and taking off her gauntlets Mandy blew on her hands.

'I'll rub them for you.' Robin took Mandy's hands between his own. 'It's far the best way.'

Susan thought, 'There'll always be someone to help Mandy – all her life; and it's not just her beauty – it's – well – it's—' and without any sort of jealousy Susan continued to analyse this compelling quality that Mandy possessed as they trudged towards the Pool buildings, across the perimeter track from where the Anson had decanted them, but she came to no conclusion.

After this, her first ferry delivery flight, Susan was more tired than she would have cared to admit for, apart from the concentration of the actual flying, there had been a fair amount of hanging around and waiting, which can be very exhausting to those who do not know how to wait. She had humped her heavy parachute about and, apart from a three-ounce bar of chocolate, she had not eaten since breakfast-time.

However, the day's work was not yet over, for it was to Susan that the Fairchild taxi sheet was given when she handed in her ferry delivery chit to the officer in the Operations Room a few moments later.

'Captain Hart won't be at Bicester before three-thirty, so you have plenty of time to get something to eat,' the Ops Officer told her. 'He's bringing in a Beau, and you'll find him in the Control Tower; I expect.'

But Susan did not find Captain Hart at Bicester, although she waited an hour and a half, and then, just when she was really beginning to worry, for there was only twenty minutes left before last landing time, the Ops Officer at Thame rang through to say that he would not be coming after all as one engine of the Beaufighter had failed and Captain Hart had made a successful emergency landing at Pershore.

Unashamedly Susan flew back down the railway line to Thame. She had had enough excitement and variety for her first day as a ferry pilot and did not feel that she could concentrate another minute on navigation – anyway, the railway seemed to be as short a route as any.

Away to starboard the Chilterns were dusking up, fat fingers of shadow splodged blue and purple in the hollow of their rounded flanks, and Susan wondered if Mark were hiding somewhere in just such a landscape on the other side of the channel... or was he really dead?

BOOK THREE

ONE

WITH HER ENTRY into the Ferry Pool at Thame Susan once again felt herself settling down to yet another pattern of her life. A kaleidoscopic, ever-changing pattern, full of what within herself she termed 'the expected unexpected'. Only time passed too quickly – even during those first days, when she felt she could contentedly have spent weeks as a 'stooge' taxi-pilot, flying the Fairchilds and other light aircraft, because all the time she would be gleaning a volume of valuable and varied knowledge of 'planes, and people, and places. It was glorious, she told herself, to have a job one could be so keen about, one that sometimes both thrilled and scared her to the very marrow of her bones, The days at Hazlewood House, in retrospection, looked so dull; but she had loved that old van.

Twice during her cross-countries she had kept her promise and circled the hospital, but on neither occasion had there been anyone visible on the roof. Also now that King's Lane House was let and her mother in London, the little notes from one and another of the VADs dropped off, and it was only rarely Susan thought of the gay little crowd of unsophisticated girls – so different from her present associates – except Mandy – and Mandy also was different.

The late autumn weather was treacherous and no two consecutive days dawned alike. Either the country lay enshrouded in fog and mist, or southerly gales made the trees bow their leafless crowns, or soft blinding rain just blotted out the entire landscape. Only very occasionally there would dawn a freak day, warm, soft, clear as spring, a day that was in fact as Mandy put it, 'the perfect answer to a young ferry pilot's prayer'.

There were days when all flying was impossible and the orders piled up, but whenever cloud base and visibility fulfilled ATA regulations, the pilots were busy and with the rest of the cadets Susan determinedly groped her way round the sky – and although more than once, during that first fortnight, she was really scared and her heart was in her mouth, she always reached terra firma, valiantly telling herself she would rather be frightened than bored any day; and all the time she was, consciously and unconsciously, hearing, seeing and experiencing something new. Sometimes it seemed more knowledge came her way than she could possibly assimilate, but always she tried to tuck it away, in some not too deep recess of her brain, ready to be called upon if wanted, only regretting that so many new ideas came at such impossible speed.

A fortnight passed and just as Susan was beginning to think that she really had got the hang of things, a notice appeared, with what seemed almost cruel abruptness, in Daily Routine Orders, known as DROs, with a list of 'Pilots – Postings and Secondments', at the bottom of which Susan saw her own name. Cadet Susan Sandyman was ordered to report at Number 12 Ferry Pool, Cosford, on the third of November, for one month's secondment as a Class One Pilot. With a sensation somewhat akin to panic Susan realized that today was the first of November. The day after tomorrow! Hastily she scanned the rest of the list.

Mandy and Nina were to go to Hamble; Robin – to his huge delight – to Prestwick, and Fang and Sandra Cushing to Ratcliffe. Only Susan was for Cosford. And she had never even landed at Cosford. Somehow, too, she had gleaned the fact that Cosford wasn't exactly the most popular of Ferry Pools. Now she began to wonder why?

Of course, she told herself, it was in a horrible part of the country. One of those places where 'industrial haze' ruled more or less all the time. Near Wolverhampton. Near slag heaps and coalmines, on the edge of the Birmingham industrial area.

Well, she must make the best of it, and that was all there was to it.

And so it was that, two mornings later, having watched the gay departure of Mandy and Nina and their innumerable suitcases, Susan boarded one of the Anson taxis going to pick up a bunch of Thame pilots at Shawbury, and it seemed a very short time before she was dropped out in front of the Control Tower at Cosford, complete with her two suitcases and parachute.

The pilot of the Anson looked down at her as she strained to lift her belongings out of the slipstream. 'Sign me in and out, will you?' he shouted. 'Granville's the name, and I'm going to Shawbury.'

'OK,' Susan yelled back. 'Thanks for the lift,' and she watched him taxi away to his take-off position. She felt in no hurry to report.

From Evesham onwards the haze had been so dense that the fields and roads directly beneath them had only just been visible, yet the pilot, a new acquaintance to Susan, had sat apparently unconcerned and completely confident of his navigation. Susan had watched him enviously and wondered once again if she would ever achieve this assuredness and nonchalance. Now she watched him take off and disappear into the murk again before she humped her parachute over her shoulder and, with a suitcase in either hand, made her way slowly across the perimeter track to the Control Tower.

Perhaps it was a pity that Susan had heard Cosford described as 'unpopular'. She called herself an ass. Told herself she must not to be biased, and that one could not always believe what other people said – but the hard fact was that the next half-hour did nothing to convince her that the general opinion was wrong.

No one seemed at all concerned about her arrival. The MT driver who fetched her and her baggage could not have evinced less interest had she tried. What Susan had expected she hardly knew. She supposed she would have had to report to her Commander, but on her arrival in the Pool she found this was not expected. No one took any notice. Comforting herself, Susan reminded herself this was no party; she wasn't a guest; she had come to work.

The building itself was pleasant enough. Compact, bright and well designed, although, like most ATA Stations which Susan had seen, it merely consisted of several wooden huts strung together and partitioned off to form various rooms and offices.

At this time Cosford was a sub-pool, belonging to Ratcliffe, near Leicester. It was one of the two pools reserved for women pilots only, Hamble being the other, and it was undeniably efficient.

Susan found herself billeted in a WAAF officer's room in a

separate house, near the RAF mess. It was very cold and cheerless, and there were no fires. However, that was more or less what she had expected and did not matter. Also, a month was not for ever. Bit by bit she took stock of her surroundings.

The Mess itself was huge, but everyone in it seemed to be grumbling because the beer was always running out. She discovered, to her amusement, that it was rationed. No one was allowed more than three pints in one evening. The habitués were almost all 'wingless wonders', except the glider pilots, and the pilots of the Whitleys which tow them. That was interesting. The glider school. But somehow, with the shortening days and little fear of being intrusive, Susan found she was not able to discover overmuch about it all. Then there were some Fleet Air Arm officers on a course, the RAF hospital personnel, doctors and dentists, and the MU Spitfire personnel, plus their test pilots. Susan liked the look of some of them, and from an occasional smile and greeting she came to the conclusion that there were some who would have liked to know her, but it remained a very lonely month. Everyone, it seemed, wanted to be elsewhere; and, except for the camp cinema, where the programmes changed twice weekly, there was nothing to do in the evenings. In a letter to Mandy Susan found herself writing, *We sit around and stare at each other, and most people go off early to bed. Wolverhampton is six miles away, but so deadly and dirty, drab and dreary in the blackout that one is not attracted. Factories all the way, slag heaps, smoke stacks, etc., ad lib. There is no point in going there.*

At this time also Susan's correspondents were few. A weekly exchange of letters with her mother and grandmother was all it amounted to – so when, at the end of the first week, a bulky letter arrived from Mandy, she fell on it as on manna. Mandy was enthusiastic over Hamble.

Dearest Sandybags (Susan read),
Just a note (Susan's eyes smiled as the closely-written sheets in her hand fluttered) *to ask if there is any chance of your being able to get down here on the 25th? The Pool is having a most gi'normous party and we can each invite three guests. Michael has a 'forty-eight'*

that weekend and is coming down, and I could easily find a partner for you. No lack of men. The village swarms with them. Navy and all sorts. Do try – it promises to be good value.

Sue – you'll love this place. I do. The people, the flying, the country, in fact everything about it. I ask for nothing better, altho' I've seen little of the other pools, and only hope I am lucky enough to be posted here, if I survive Class Two.

The CO, Com. Gore, is a honey – most understanding – and all the pilots extremely friendly. None of that new girl feeling we experienced at Thame to begin with, and even after a week I seem to 'belong', as you always put it.

The billeting question is definitely tricky as the village, which isn't over-big and nestles right down on the Hamble river, is chock full already, and such big houses as there are have been requisitioned by the Army and Navy, and what with several big aircraft factories and ship repair yards up the river and just round the corner on the Solent, most of the more modest houses positively bulge with strain. As a result most of the pilots have cars, or share them, and billet a few miles away, the most popular spot, I gather, being a village called Old Bursledon, just a little bit further up the river. Several of them have rented cottages there and I went along to tea with one of them the other day – Ann – can't remember her surname – when we were scrubbed early. It was a darling little cottage. I longed for one like it myself. Wouldn't it be too marvellous if we were both posted here and managed to find something of the sort ourselves? A distant day-dream!

Some pilots have to billet as far away as Southampton. Rather depressing, I think. It's been so badly bombed. Great chunks of the High Street seem to be missing. Most of the week I have been Fairchilding, but I have also ferried a Swordfish and a Reliant. The latter very like a Fairchild. At the moment I have a chit in my pocket for an Auster from Aston Down to Tangmere, which should be fun, only, as usual, I am inwardly flapping as much as if I had been told to fly a Fortress. Nina has one too and is trying to calm my shattered nerves with endless cups of coffee and tales of turning Austers round haystacks and landing them in back gardens. She is in the seventh *heaven here as there is another Polish girl, one Anna, with 'whom she can natter away in her native tongue, and reminisce to her heart's content. A heavy sea mist is rolling over the coast at present and the vis. is down to nil, so I don't expect we shall be flying for an hour or two, and, as you see, what started with every intention of being 'just a line' is fast becoming a young novel, and I'm being chivvied to make up a bridge four. So shall finish this in news flashes.*

(1) Had a letter from the Babe yesterday, already in a panic over School Cert. next summer! He sends you his love.

(2) Your Diana! I've met her. She is just as sweet as you said. Let me fly her back from Colerne in a Fairchild. We detoured a few inches to get a good look at Lacock – it was that one lovely afternoon. Was thrilled to hear you'd made it and looks forward to seeing you.

(3) A husband of one of the pilots here has just turned up after being missing for six months. He escaped with the help of the Dutch underground. So – cheer up! You never know!

(4) You'll be amused at the sick bay here. It's just an old caravan with a nurse in charge. She says there is going to be a hospital sometime.

(5) Oh! The blackout curtains! Most original. The black is cheered up with the signatures of each pilot – written large in yellow paint. I have added mine already. Took a lot of paint!

The bridge will wait no longer – so 'bye for now, Sandybags. Write me your news one day and do your d'est for the 25th.

(6) By the way, you'll be interested to know that the airfield here was AST. (Air Services Training) before the war and besides ATA there is a large Spit factory on the field.

And so Mandy's letter ended, the signature being merely a twist of hieroglyphics that might be anything. Susan dropped her hands and the letter on her lap. So Michael would be at the party! Just what did that mean? For a few moments, as utterly absorbed as she had been while reading, Susan continued to think of Michael and Mandy, until a tremendous noise, that sounded like guns close at hand, forced her to take notice.

It was a morning of weather too thick for flying. There was

nothing to do but sit about and wait. Susan glanced round the room at the close-cropped heads, while the clatter outside continued. On a similar morning at Thame there would have been at least one bridge four in progress, and a game of ping-pong, played in gay and friendly rivalry in the outer rest-room, as well as some spirited discussions and arguments, mostly on flying subjects, to be heard in an atmosphere charged with aviation. Here it was utterly different. The scratching of pens, one hacking cough and only a very occasional murmur of desultory conversation.

Susan half turned and her chair creaked. The pilot nearest, deep in *The Times*, glanced up and their eyes met. Susan seized her opportunity and asked:

'What's the ghastly racket?'

'Spit guns. Testing.' The answer was laconic and the speaker's eyes returned to her *Times*.

'Thank you.' Susan rose to her feet and went outside. Perhaps there was something to see which might make her letter to Mandy more interesting, A look-see, a visit to the Met and a scribble to Mandy could be made to fill up the morning, and she had little, so far, to write about except the routine duties of a stooge pilot to murky Midland airfields.

But, once outside, although the very ground vibrated under her feet, she was thrilled. The noise was terrific, and no wonder. The Armoury Unit were busy and the testing site for the guns was just outside. The Spitfire, with its tail lashed down and blocks under each wing, to which the wings were tied, looked somewhat curious and helpless, rather like a hampered hen, thought Susan. Inside the bare head of a man was just visible. The propellers were motionless, and as the firing started again Susan covered her ears and tried to focus on the bullets as they spat into the huge sandbank some yards ahead. She had previously noticed this and the concrete wall ahead of it, and had wondered vaguely as to its purpose.

From a passing groundsman, whom she stopped to question, she now learned that this was a constant occurrence, taking place intermittently throughout the day. For some minutes she watched and wondered how she had previously missed it. Of course she had been busy. But the thought uppermost as she listened and watched was – 'One could die as fast as those invisible bullets sped. Amazing!'

Half an hour later the haze lifted sufficiently for the day's work to begin, and Susan's first chit was for Hawarden. She began to feel things cheering up. When she arrived it was to find that the haze had held up her passengers, so she lunched at Number Three Ferry Pool for the first time, and felt the gods were kind. If this happened frequently, she thought, life would be more bearable. She was much entertained by a junior of the ground staff who told her of Hawarden's beginnings, and pointed out the semi-detached cottage, beside the railway line, which had been the first headquarters, and told stories of an ATA hero, whom he called 'Wally'.

But time was short, and very soon she was on her way back to Cosford, and no sooner back than off again, to Ringway this time, and by the time she returned flying was over for that day.

Next morning was clear, and Susan hoped she would be sent to Hawarden again, but it was not to be. In fact that one lunch at Hawarden remained the high spot of the month and as, at Cosford, Class One Ferry Pilots do only the shorter journeys they are never 'stuck out', the whole month passed without any change for Susan.

However, there were moments of interest. One, when flying north, over the Wrekin, and being told how on the top a red light winks throughout the night for the benefit of the many Operational Training Units in the area, who are out on night flying practice, and others at the many airfields she visited when she practised recognition of the different types of aircraft she saw, and longed for the day when she herself would fly some of them. She grew to know the airfields served by Cosford very well indeed. High Ercall, Shawbury, Pershore, Tern-hill, Hawarden, Lichfield, Aston Wheaton, Halfpenny Green, Wolverhampton and others. She spent one 'wash out' day when all flying was impossible in Lichfield, and loved the little city and its cathedral, the smallest in England she was told, and felt she would always love Lichfield because, reading her way by canals, coalmines and slag heaps, it was actually the first airfield to which she flew directly without consulting her map.

But the end of the month brought another thrill when she got her first Swordfish, commonly called a 'string-bag'. Her chit showed it to be a P1/G machine, and she was to fly it from High Ercall to Worthy Down near Winchester. Susan's mind worked at top speed for a few seconds. She wasn't afraid of the Swordfish; knew it to be rather like the Hart to look at, only it was slower and heavier to fly, and even heavier now because P1/G aircraft meant some secret device aboard which would necessitate an RAF, or even police, guard should she be obliged to make an emergency landing. She guessed the 'secret' to be some sort of heavy radar set, making a bulge under the tummy of the machine. With luck she should reach Worthy Down about lunchtime and it was her long weekend before reporting to Thame. If luck held someone might be flying from Worthy Down to Odiham, and in that case it was possible to get to Grannie's in time for tea.

So, at 10 am, her month of secondment finished and, without any reluctance, Susan left Cosford as unceremoniously as she had arrived and flew as a passenger in a Fairchild to High Ercall to collect her Swordfish. For once she did not look at the scenery in passing. Instead she studied her 'handling notes'. This was her first Swordfish and she meant that nothing should go wrong if she could avoid it. She was going to be very careful.

All went well. She took delivery, inspected her papers, found there was plenty of room for her luggage in the back seat, had a very thorough 'look-see' at everything, and prepared to set off, but as she settled herself in the pilot's seat a thought came to her. She had only seen one ship-launching in her life, but the phrase she had heard uttered then suddenly came back to memory. She had watched the bottle of champagne swing on its blue ribbon and had distinctly heard the voice give the ship its name, and had been impressed by the added words, 'May God bless all who sail in her'. Now here was a new machine! Never flown before except on her test flights! Under her breath Susan said, 'A Swordfish. May God bless all who fly in her,' and, at the same moment, was born a resolve. Perhaps in the next few months, or years, she would deliver many new machines. Never, *never* would she take over a new machine without uttering those same words.

It made the finishing touch, and as Susan passed the Vale of Evesham that morning and flew on to the Cotswolds a wonderful sense of freedom took possession. South again! Out of the Midland murk into the sunshine; and gleams of pale, wintry, late November sunshine did light up her way. With half an eye on the country and half on her map and one on her gauges Susan flew on, singing to herself. Suddenly her oil temperature began to soar, and Susan stopped singing. The nearest airfield? Where was it? She had been flying for three-quarters of an hour. Her eyes fell to her map. Brize Norton near Oxford – that was it!

The oil temperature continued to rise. Susan circled the airfield. Luckily she was given a green and could land immediately. Once down she taxied very carefully to the Control Tower, parked outside and reported to the Control Officer exactly as she had been taught. Then, after seeing the guard take charge and the duty crew busy, she went to the mess for lunch.

There was no one to talk to and Susan did not want to linger, but later she wished she had. A dirty oil filter was found to be the cause of the trouble, and she was told that repairs would take some time, so she spent the greater part of the afternoon wandering in and out, waiting and trying to interest herself in out-of-date magazines, until at last, at four o'clock, the Swordfish was ready.

Susan thanked the crew and heaved a sigh of relief as she clambered in. It would have been sunset already if it were not for double summertime. As it was she would do it comfortably, but her cherished dream of a possible flight back to Odiham would have to be abandoned. Only heaven knew what time she would eventually get to Hazeley. One couldn't hitch-hike with two suitcases and a parachute.

The Swordfish lumbered on. The landmarks were well-known ones now, and one by one Susan recognized them as they passed beneath her wings. Obeying a sudden impulse she deviated from her straight course. If the oil wasn't all right and she had to come down again it might as well be at Odiham. At least she'd be sure of a comfortable bed. Her new course took her straight over Hazlewood

House and Susan smiled to herself as she thought of her cross-country flights when she had come this way. There had been no one on the roof then and certainly there would be no one now, nor probably a gleam of light. She was right. It was difficult even to locate the house so buried was it among its surrounding trees, and Susan thought of the many times she had walked round to inspect the blackout. Now there was the long ribbon of the road down which she had bicycled so many times; 'And,' she thought, 'if I veer to the left I'll go clean over Grannie's garden. What a pity I can't tip out my luggage.' Now King's Lane – and there was the mushroom field, the house and the church tower: then Odiham, and Susan looked at her oil temperature. OK now. And there was Hackwood. She had taken patients there more than once. How the buildings sprawled! It looked as if that Canadian hospital grew ever bigger. No 1 Neurological. How well she remembered! All head injuries went there. Mostly motorbike accidents. Very few flying ones. One of the sisters had taken her all round – but what a pity she had wasted that year! Yes – oil still all right. She'd be at Worthy Down very soon. Perhaps the year was worth it – to Mother and Grannie. But she might have been a First Officer and flying big bombers by now. Did they really feel as nonchalant as they appeared? Would anything ever excite or thrill them ever again? Not far now, and she would be well ahead of last landing time, and Hamble wasn't so far from Worthy Down. She'd put a 'phone call through to Mandy and ask her about the party and Michael. It seemed ages since she had seen Mandy. Odd – next week they would be back at Thame together and then, surely, Mandy would tell her – if there was anything to tell. Was she in love with Michael? With all her heart Susan hoped so. That would soothe away that ache she had for Richard as nothing else could.

Now the sunset was beginning to glow. How lovely it was, and – 'Oh!' – Susan caught her breath. The merest thread of a new moon hung low in the sky. Of course a new moon was due! What luck she had seen it! Now she must wish.

Mark – but no words formed themselves in her mind. Only a prayer for him – beyond words, born of that curious, almost mystical feeling, the prerogative of airmen and mountaineers, which is born of a great loneliness of spirit and an extraordinary sense of mental peace.

'How lovely!' she thought again. 'That solid square tower brooding over the ancient city. The sunset and the new moon—'

Susan made her wish as she circled the airfield and saw the whole city of Winchester spread below, a dark pool against the glow of the sky, with that mothering tower keeping guard and girded by a white ribbon of road that was the by-pass. It should be for Mandy and Michael, of course.

'May they be as happy as we were!'

TWO

AN HOUR LATER, in darkness, Susan dropped off the RN lorry outside Winchester station whence she had been driven from Worthy Down.

Worthy Down was the first Fleet Air Arm Station at which she had landed, and it had held many surprises for her from the moment she had seen the warning of an uphill landing written quite plainly in a great square of white-washed stones, reminiscent of a coast-guard station. Instead of aircraftsmen, commonly called 'erks', sailors in bell-bottom trousers, with only a difference of badges to distinguish them from their fellows at sea, were on duty, and everywhere around the airfield were parked aircraft of the FAA. Other Swordfish, Barracudas, Reliants, Fulmars, Hell Cats, Wild Cats, Avengers. All new and strange types to her, and she was glad that sufficient daylight lingered and she could see and ask questions. There were WRNS instead of WAAFs in the Watch Office, otherwise the Control Tower, and all talking Naval jargon and not averse to giving information. One had said she was 'going ashore' shortly, which she explained meant 'out of camp', and when Susan asked 'How?' answered with a laugh, 'In the Admiral's pinnace, of course!'

They had been a jolly crowd, and Susan had soon discovered the 'pinnace' to be, on this occasion, nothing more than a RN lorry, so, before she did anything else, she had begged a lift. Then there had been things to do. First and foremost her delivery chit to be signed and posted back to Cosford: then 'phone calls to Mandy and Grannie – Grannie must not be kept waiting for dinner. She had been lucky in catching Mandy, who was just leaving for the weekend, to what destination she would not say. Even when Susan pressed the point by asking if it were home, she had answered with her usual 'Could be,' and with a gay 'OK. See you on Tuesday,' had rung off.

And now, disembarked from the Admiral's pinnace, complete with her two suitcases and her parachute, Susan groped her way to the dimly lighted ticket office, and wished with all her heart she could have bribed the driver of the lorry to take her all the way to Hazeley.

After procuring her ticket, she managed to find a seat on the unlit platform, and deposited her impedimenta round her, so that she could collect it easily, for it took time nowadays to find a seat in overcrowded trains, when one was forced to open the door and peer into the dim-out of the carriage before one could see if there were room or not.

Other figures emerged from the ticket office and the seat began to fill up. Susan edged herself close against the hard, iron arm-rest. Finally a very fat man deposited himself beside and half on top of her, and with irritation she rose and stood beside her luggage.

'How I *hate* travelling by train!' she thought. 'All these pushing, shoving people! And a little more than an hour ago, in the glory of the sunset and her own solitude, the world had been transfigured! Her conscience pricked her. Probably these poor creatures round her struggled daily in this way to and from their work. It was pretty mean to feel impatient at their very existence, which they could no more help than she could her own. But wasn't that always the reaction after being on 'an high mountain – apart'? There everything 'did shine as the sun' and was 'white as the light'. It was 'good to be there', but for the present generation the admonition to 'tell the vision to no man' was unnecessary.

But the 'much people' – the sordid rabble and the fuss – when one came to earth! Frank would have understood her mood. There was something that he was fond of quoting – something by Blake – what was it? The words evaded her, but she knew they epitomized the thought. The sound of the train approaching diverted her musings, and the welcome glow from the engine fires gleamed in the night.

Susan deemed herself fortunate to find a seat, even though the space was restricted, and other bodies pressed her on either side. Under the dim blue lights the faces of the other occupants looked drawn and weary. Most of them sat with closed eyes. Susan closed hers too. 'Men and mountains' – that was it! Now she remembered! She sat up and opened her eyes.

Great things are done when men and mountains meet;

This is not done by jostling in the street.

By seven-thirty Susan was seated on her favourite seat on the end of the fender stool, close to her grandmother.

'And so, my dear, now you really are a ferry pilot!'

'Yes, Grannie,'

'How does it feel?'

'Rather satisfactory, I think.' The last two words came slowly and after a second's hesitation Susan continued: 'The truth is, that I am much regretting that year at Hazlewood. I do wish I'd begun earlier.'

Old Mrs Ledgard shook her head.

'No. No, my darling,' and she spoke emphatically, 'that year was *very* necessary. It steadied and restored you.'

'Did it? I wonder! Perhaps you're right. I might have been over enthusiastic and over-shot myself. I'd have died if I had failed!'

'And that, my dear, is an exaggeration.'

Susan laughed. 'I know. May I have some more sherry, please?'

'Of course.'

It was several weeks since Susan had paid her grandmother a visit, and then she was still in the School and wearing Mandy's uniform, about which she had been almost over-conscientious, changing directly she was off duty, so this was the first occasion on which old Mrs Ledgard had seen her in uniform. She had, so far, made no comment. But when Susan drew in her legs and with one athletic movement rose to her feet, preparatory to fetching more sherry, the old lady's eyes watched her, and followed her, amusedly. Decidedly becoming, she thought.

Susan turned about with the decanter in her hand. 'Some more for you?' she questioned, and at the same time caught her grandmother's glance and added, 'What is it?'

'The masculine garb! It is very becoming. You have the right figure for it.'

'Thank you.' Susan gave a slight bow and laughed. 'Now you *must* have some more sherry and drink that I never, never disgrace it!'

'Well, only a spot, darling.'

Susan carried two glasses carefully across the room. Her own brimming, the other half full.

'There!' she exclaimed. 'Hold it carefully while I do "tops and bottoms".'

Susan clinked her glass above and below her grandmother's and then drank and sat down again.

'It's lovely to be here, Grannie! D'you mind if I don't change? I'll just wash downstairs, if I may. I think if I saw my bed I'd have to drop into it. It's so lovely to have Rose to unpack.'

'Have a long morning in bed tomorrow,' said Mrs Ledgard.

'If Jason will let me! Wonderful, isn't he, Grannie? Never makes a mistake, no matter what one is wearing.'

'He has sat with his nose glued to the window ever since I told him you were coming, and barked almost before the taxi stopped.'

'Good old Jason!' Susan stopped to pat the dog lying at her feet, and asked 'Does he still go up to King's Lane?'

'Every day,' answered old Mrs Ledgard. 'Now, my dear, run and wash, and tell Rose. We are keeping them all waiting.'

* * *

'Isn't Mother coming? I thought she might be this weekend,' asked Susan, as they took their places round the candle-lit dining table.

'No. She telephoned this morning. Some unexpected change of plans. She was down last weekend. Didn't she tell you?'

'No. I haven't had a letter this week. I told her to write to Thame.'

'Then you haven't heard her news?'

'No. What? Anything special?'

Susan held her soup spoon poised as she spoke.

'I suppose it is, in a way. Your Mandy took her young man to the flat, and they've made a great friendship.'

'Oh! The lousy little wretch! Blast her! She didn't tell me—'

'Susan!' Old Mrs Ledgard's eyes registered horror, and in the background Susan heard Rose gasp.

'That's nothing, Grannie. It doesn't mean a thing. I 'phoned Mandy, and she was as non-committal as an egg. She was just rushing off. I'll bet that's where they are – I'll 'phone presently. Honestly, Grannie, isn't it odd how young men fall for Mother? Let me see the party at Ramble was on Thursday, and Michael had a forty-eight. So – he's probably due back tonight, or tomorrow. That's it!' Susan laughed as she finished speaking, and not for a moment did she realize that her grandmother's mind had gone back eighteen months, and again she saw Susan as she was when she arrived from Singapore, frightened – although she would never have owned to it – tired and grief-stricken, and she had watched the slow metamorphosis, of which Susan was unconscious.

But strangely, at that moment, Susan was also thinking of much the same thing.

'I'm sorry, Grannie,' she apologized. 'I shouldn't shock you, and I agree that "lousy" is a foul word really, and Frank used to hate it. Sometimes I think I must suffer from schizophrenia, because at times I am myself – as I used to be – and then, almost directly, I find myself using all the swear words and slang I know, like everyone else in ATA.' Susan hesitated, and her grandmother waited whilst Rose removed the soup plates before Susan continued. 'I said as much to Mandy in a letter, and she answered that it all comes of buttoning one's coat the wrong way.'

'The wrong way?' Mrs Ledgard looked puzzled.

'Yes – look! We button like a man.' Susan looked down at her tunic, and her grandmother smiled, and Rose put a plate in front of her and offered her a dish.

'Pheasant! Oh, Grannie! This is the first I've had. What a lovely dinner! And, you know' – and with the words Susan's eyes looked across the table – 'it is such a treat to see your table after eating in canteens and messes. There aren't any social amenities. One grabs for oneself; and one constantly gets a spoon or fork that tastes of onions, or fish, to eat one's sweet.' Susan's eyes left the gleaming silver and glass and came to rest on the fork in her hand. 'It is only here that things look the same as they used.' And then the pattern and the crest on the fork arrested her attention. It was identical with the silver presented by Grannie when she married – she gave a slight shiver. For a fleeting moment she saw herself and Frank, frantically digging, burying what they could. For a moment Susan sat motionless, her eyes on the crest, until old Mrs Ledgard asked: 'What is it, my dear? Don't let your dinner get cold,' and with a sudden catch of her breath Susan came back to the present. She looked from the fork to her grandmother.

'It's part of the same service you gave us, isn't it? I was just remembering how Frank and buried it.'

Some half-an hour later, back by the drawing-room fire, Susan was about to re-establish herself on the fender stool when old Mrs Ledgard intervened.

'Susan, push the fender stool aside, and bring that chair nearer the fire. It's a very comfortable one. Then, if you're not too tired, I would like you to explain some of the terms you use. I am so often puzzled. For instance, what exactly do you mean by a "pool"?'

Susan pulled up the chair, sat down and laughed.

'No, I am not tired now. I'll answer anything you like. Actually a "Pool" is a ferrying unit. Just the place and the people. It may consist of ten, or may be sixty, pilots. But their 'Pool' is really their Headquarters. There are fourteen "Pools" up and down the country, and they are – must be – in industrial centres. They are all over England, and it's just incredible the number of airfields there are. The fourteen "Pools" are, five Northern – as far as Lossiemouth – four Southern, and five Midland. You see, wherever aircraft factories have sprung up you will find a "Ferry Pool" in the middle of them. Actually the duty of the ATA is to empty the factories of new aircraft, and get them delivered where they are wanted, as speedily as possible. And we don't ferry only new aircraft. We collect and deliver for repair and breaking up the old, or damaged, or worn out – as ropey as they can be some of them – labelled on the chit NEA, which means "Not Essentially Airworthy". Is that clear?'

'Yes, my dear. But what does "ropey" mean? That is a new one to me.'

Susan gave a half-laugh. The word, Mark's misnomer of a nick-name, was one she avoided as a rule.

'Ropey?' she repeated. 'Oh – just that NEA People apply it to clumsy landings, and things damaged – sort of beyond hope.' She paused, staring into the fire, and for some moments there was silence in the room. Old Mrs Ledgard waited. She saw, by her expression that Susan's thoughts were far away, and fearing lest for some reason they had drifted back to the days when she flew with Frank, she said:

'Thank you, my dear. That is quite clear,' and then reopened the conversation with a gentle question: 'But you haven't told me anything about your senior officers yet!'

Susan's eyes left the fire and she turned her head quickly. The word 'ropey' and the sentence she had used, 'sort of beyond hope', had for a second linked themselves together in her mind and filled her with dread. 'If – if—' she questioned herself' inwardly. 'Oh – it couldn't be – it would be *too* much!' God grant the words did *not* apply to Mark! It was with an effort she came back to the present; and the picture of cold, shadowy moonlight and a parachute drifting slowly down, buffeted by the wind, that had come unbidden, vanished from her mind. Only a few seconds had passed, but, to Susan, Grannie's drawing-room looked strange, and she blinked as she answered:

'I hardly know them. In the School they are our instructors and one really hasn't time to get to know anyone else. You'd hardly believe it, but, so far, I've not set eyes on the Station Commander at Thame.'

'You mean the Pool Commander?'

'No – no. The Station Commander is senior to the Pool Commander and the School Commander. It's a "station" where ATA are the sole, or principal, occupiers. At Cosford there is a factory, and the RAF, so that ATA are a "lodger" unit there.'

'But you had a commanding officer?'

'Oh yes. She spoke to me once only. To reprove me about my hair.' Susan rubbed her fingers through her hair as she spoke, and looked ruefully at her grandmother. 'Said it was too much on my collar. I didn't like Cosford over-much, but don't know why. They are all wonderful pilots, and some of the girls awfully nice.'

'Is that why you are wearing your hair shorter?' queried Mrs Ledgard.

'Yes. I snipped off bits as best I could, and pushed it up. I didn't want a black mark, even about my hair! No one bothered in the Pool at Thame, but they're mostly men, and Susan Slade, who looks after any of the girls who need it – she is a flight captain – is a dear, only beams on us. Somehow she reminds me of Robert Jamieson. Perhaps it's because she wears spectacles, but I like her smile. And Mandy loves her OC at Hamble. Says she's a honey! Oh! I haven't rung Mandy yet. May I?' Susan glanced at the clock and jumped up and exclaimed : 'Heavens! It's nearly ten, and I've made you miss the news!'

'It doesn't matter, child. I listened at six.'

'Was there anything fresh?'

'Only about the bombings. There can be little of Berlin left.'

Susan returned in a few minutes.

'Wasn't that lucky? I got through at once. Mandy is there, but she'd gone to see Michael off, and Mother will be down in time for lunch tomorrow.'

Susan and her grandmother talked for another hour. There was more slang to explain. Susan laughed aloud at the question, 'And what, my dear, is a "wingless wonder"?' and then she found herself telling of the night on which she saw Mark take off. Also there was much to tell of her visits to other operational aerodromes. 'Sometimes,' she explained, 'I have to wait a bit, and then I try to see all I can. It's marvellous always; just to watch the various 'planes coming in and out, and landings controlled by radio in bad weather. But what I'm longing for is to get to White Waltham. That is Number One Ferry Pool, where some of the most important people are. I want to meet the people who are, as yet, only names.'

'When will that be?'

'Not until after Christmas, I'm afraid. Next week, at Thame, we shall be back on Fairchilding and small ferrying. Then, I expect, we shall get three days' leave at Christmas, and after that, a little bird told me, both Mandy and I will be seconded to White Waltham.'

As far as Susan was concerned it was a very quiet weekend. She felt she needed it, and the warmth and softness of her comfortable mattress and linen sheets made bed the most delectable place. The news of the Eighth Army pushing on in Italy, and of the repeated bombings on Berlin and Stuttgart, left little to discuss. Her mother, when she arrived, brought John Pitts' latest letter, with news of his engagement to a Canadian girl, 'with blue-grey eyes like Susan's', and so, after an afternoon visit to the tenants of King's Lane, and a rummage for extra linen that Mrs Ledgard said she must have, Susan settled down to write and congratulate John Pitts in the quiet of her bedroom, overlooking the old-fashioned garden.

Her thoughts wandered as her eyes strayed to the window, through which she could see the leaves from an ancient beech tree fluttering silently to the ground in the still, moist, November air. How mixed one's feelings could be! One revelled in the beauty of the golden shower, the many-hued carpet they formed around the smooth-skinned grey trunk, and at the same time regretted their passing. One rejoiced at hearing that one's friends were going to be married and at the same time experienced a sense of loss. Of late she had been hoping so much that Mandy would find a restitution of real happiness again by returning Michael's love for her, and yet she knew she would feel a little pang at the thought of a companionship that would never be quite the same again. Yes – and there was something more she would feel – not jealousy, but the accentuated realization of the loneliness of the years to be – the dread of a life emptied of purpose when the struggle of war was over; when she no longer was one of a carefree band, sustained by good fellowship and life filled with changes and chances and a sufficiency of danger – which makes one realize its value.

When the storm was over – when it was once more peaceful and quiet – like this room and this autumn afternoon – then – if what she hoped came to pass – Mandy would find with Michael what she had found with Frank, and if she did – if she could – it would be more than restitution. Whereas for herself...

But to think like this was all wrong. She pulled herself together with a jerk. She had gained a friend in Michael, and so had her mother. Mother was different. She had found her restitution in other mothers' sons. John Pitts was not her only correspondent, and

Michael not the only one who was bidden to take possession of her second tiny spare room whenever convenient. Susan dipped her pen in the ink.

There is nothing in the world, she wrote, that gives one such thrill as to hear that any of one's friends have found real happiness.

'And that would apply most of all to Mandy,' she added, half aloud, to herself.

THREE

SUSAN AND MANDY MET, as pre-arranged, in London and travelled back to Haddenham together in the late afternoon of Tuesday. Both regretted their departure could not be put off until the morning, but with uncertain weather, probably a dark morning, and difficulties over taxis and luggage, to accomplish the journey and report at nine o'clock seemed almost an impossibility.

Susan had looked forward to the journey as an opportunity to compare notes and perhaps hear the latest news of Michael, but in this she felt she was being deliberately foiled. Mandy was in high spirits, and talked at length about Hamble and the party, which had been, it appeared, a very gay one, but of Michael hardly a word before they fell to comparing notes about people and pilots, and places and Pools generally, and once back at Haddenham, and again in Hopefield House, intimate conversation became impossible. To their disappointment what they called their 'own' room had other inhabitants, and now they found themselves sharing a room of four beds with Nina and Sandra, both of whom had already arrived.

Nina had loved Hamble as had Mandy, and was just as enthusiastic, while Sandra Cushing had occasionally to be forcibly stopped when she began to enumerate the advantages of Ratcliffe, which, she said, was just like 'a lil' civilian flying club'.

Susan knew Ratcliffe, high up on the Fosse Way, north of Leicester, and she knew it to be the peace-time private aerodrome of the Leicester Flying Club, founded by Sir Lindsey Everard, and that some of the senior pilots lived at his home, Ratcliffe Hall. Also that it was entirely ATA and retained the warm friendliness of its former status. She had landed there once only, and as on that occasion her passengers had been ready waiting for her, practically all she had done was to climb from the pilot's seat of the Fairchild to the back seat, and so had seen little. The surroundings and Charnwood Forest she remembered from her cross-country flights.

Now while she unpacked she listened to Sandra's monologue.

'I've gotten to know it and the country round pretty well. But – say – you've got to live in it to know it! And that Hall! Why, it's right out of an English story book – butler and all! My – if you watched that man closely you could almost see him move! If only I'd been billeted right there! – Say, Honey, I dropped right into Cosford one day and asked for you.'

'Did you? No one told me.'

Sandra shook her head. 'Seemed they hadn't even heard of you. Just plain dumb I thought them.'

Susan laughed and Sandra continued her eulogies of Ratcliffe.

'It's just the cutest lil' place. My – it'll be grand in summer! There's a swimming-pool – and that old, old Roman Road! It gets me. To think of all those Roman doughboys footslogging along it after they'd made it all those centuries ago! And they've some lovely dogs at Ratcliffe! They keep them in little wood way over the airfield – their runs and their kennels are right in it. Great alsatians. I'd be scared stiff to meet one in the dark, but my – are they trained! I just had to sit right down and tell Elmer all about it, and how the alsatians guard the airfields all over England all the long night. Elmer's just crazy about dogs.'

'But what about Fang? Did he like it?' broke in Mandy.

'Fang? Why he's just as tickled to death with the place as I am. Say, I almost thought I saw an expression on his face one day! He called Leicester "the rose-red city of England"—'

'Well, it is – from the air,' broke in Susan. 'It's the acres of red brick.'

'But it's not "half as old as time",' interrupted Mandy – 'but this bed *is*! Sandra, if you don't stop talking I'll suffocate you with this pillow. It's filled with wood-shavings.'

The next morning Susan found herself feeling very much at home and very happy to be back at Thame where everyone greeted her with a smile.

Back on Fairchilding and small ferrying the next few weeks passed very quickly, and as the days closed in and flying hours grew shorter and the weather deteriorated, sometimes very little work was possible. More than once, when everything was 'scrubbed', Susan betook herself to London, and on these occasions Mandy usually accompanied her.

One evening, towards the middle of the month, Susan returned rather later than usual to find a telephone message awaiting her from Mark's CO, 'Blacker' Hay. She opened the scrap of paper with trembling fingers and read:

News for you. Please ring after twenty-two hours.

With a beating heart, and almost breathless, Susan ran to the telephone, only to find that she had to wait while one of the new pupils concluded what seemed to be a flippant, long-drawn-out conversation. But at last, with several 'OKs' and 'so longs', it ended, and with a still wildly beating heart Susan picked up the receiver, moist and warm from the other's hands.

It took but a few minutes to get through to Newmarket, but Susan waited in a fever of anxiety while someone went to look for Wing Commander Hay. It seemed ages until she heard his voice.

'Mrs Sandyman! Ah! Good evening.'

'Yes. It's Susan Sandyman. Good evening. I've been in town, and only just got your message – is it – Mark?'

'No – not Mark. But there's a chance he may be all right in Holland. His rear gunner's just got back. They came down in Holland. Mark ordered them all out. As far as I can gather it was somewhere over the North East polder. D'you know where I mean?'

'Yes – yes – I know,' said Susan, who had studied the map of Holland more times than she would have cared to own.

'Mark was ready to jump after Sergeant Martin. I can't tell you more over the 'phone. Can you get over?'

'I'll do my best, and thank you so much,' answered Susan. 'I'll tell them in Ops, and perhaps they can fix a job your way, but I don't know when.'

'Chance it whenever you can, and if I'm not about ask for Sergeant Martin. He maybe here.'

But a few days later, when Susan eventually got to Newmarket, there was little more to learn. Mark had dropped his bombs and had been caught by the flak, and the Stirling was much damaged. The sergeant, a very silent man, seemed to find great difficulty in talking, and said he was under promise to mention neither places nor names of the people who had assisted him to escape. He had apparently been rescued by a Dutch farmer, and, with two Dutch boys in a fishing-boat, had been picked up far out on the North Sea in bitter weather.

'I just had luck—' was all he would say.

But Susan felt he was holding something back. Half afraid, but with an urgency that would not be silenced, she pressed him further.

'But if you met with friendly help, wouldn't he, too?'

The sergeant fidgeted with his feet and looked uncomfortable.

'Well – we were trying to get home or to the sea.'

'But I don't understand,' she persisted, 'you said you were all baling out, in turn.'

'We'd left it a bit late, you see.' The words came slowly and unwillingly. Susan's eyes searched the sergeant's face, while the inescapable truth stabbed her consciousness. His expression had conveyed more than his stumbling words, 'a bit late' – 'we were trying to get to the sea'. Mark's turn would come last. . . 'a bit late'.

After a few words of thanks she turned away. She felt numb. The sergeant stared after her and shook his head and muttered, 'I couldn't tell a lady like her about that blaze. Couldn't have been more than five miles away – perhaps seven.'

* * *

Only to Mandy did Susan speak of Mark, but Mandy remained undaunted, and, for Mandy, was vehement.

'You mustn't get downhearted, Sue. You are only where you were. No – in fact I think there's more hope. Mark must have jumped within a few moments of Sergeant Martin, and it wasn't by any means his first jump; but, when people are working in secret, dropping even a few miles away probably gets one into a completely different set. So don't worry. I feel *sure* he's all right, and so does Michael.'

'Have you seen Michael recently then?' asked Susan.

'No. He just happened to ring up and I told him.'

Susan asked no further questions but she felt much comforted. Mandy seemed so sure it gave her confidence, and for the next few days work pressed. A short spell of fine days kept all the pilots very busy. The weather was cold with a biting wind, and often all Susan's thoughts were occupied with the not so simple problem of how to keep warm.

During the next week or two Mandy kept a very close eye upon Susan, and tried to give her no time to brood. Susan was rather a good needlewoman. Mandy was not, and a partly made nightdress of apricot ninon had fallen in and out of Mandy's so-called 'workbag' ever since June. Everyone knew it and at times rescued it. One evening Mandy spread it out on her bed, and with a wistful:

'Sue – Honey! I know you've no sewing on hand. Couldn't you finish it for me? I *do* need it!'

She also produced a couple of evening scarves of ivory silk that had been Richard's, and showed Susan what she had seen several of the girls at Hamble doing.

'I told you about the blackout curtains? How we painted our names? This is practically the same idea. Get all the celebrities and your little pals to sign your scarf, and then embroider over the signatures in coloured silks. Every and any colour under the sun. They are most effective! Nina has started hers.'

Susan was caught by the idea, and the scarves became very much in evidence during the hours of waiting in the rest-room; but the conversation remained – aviation.

It would have been difficult to find four more eager cadets than were these four, Susan and Mandy, Nina and Sandra. The very fact of having begun together, and made the grade more or less together, cemented a bond that would have held them; but, apart from that, they really liked each other, and there was so much to learn from each other. Their varying and varied experiences of life gave topics for much entertaining and enlightening conversation. Nina, a Pole by birth but the daughter of parents both born in Warsaw when Warsaw was Russian, was equally at home anywhere in eastern

Europe. She was full of stories of a childhood spent partly in the Crimea and partly in Warsaw, with occasional visits to grandparents in Moscow. Sandra's experiences of life had carried her from New York to Los Angeles, and from Boston to Florida, and she had much to say of 'God's own country and the great open spaces'. Susan's travels, too, had been pretty extensive, and only Mandy deplored the fact that except for holidays she had hardly been out of England.

'But you aren't grown up yet,' comforted Nina, while Susan added, 'Neither had I at your age,' and Sandra said, 'Now – let me tell you something. I am forty-three, and Nina is, I guess, about ten years younger, and Sue is about twenty-six, isn't it?' Susan nodded. 'Well, you must wait and see where you get in the next twenty years. Elmer and I will sure make you welcome should you ever visit the States.'

Bantering conversation, half serious, half fun, intermixed with technicalities about aero engines and all other problems of the ferry pilots, made for happy hours, spent evening after evening in the cosy bar-parlour of the 'Crown'. The room grew crowded and the atmosphere thick with tobacco smoke, and the benign 'Bert' smiled on all and drew pint after pint of beer. Closing time always came as a shock. Susan loved it, and often reflected that there were few evenings when she did not add some small item to her store of knowledge. Fat Robin and Fang always joined them, and seniors of the ground staff and pilots of experience always came and went. From everyone there was something to learn.

Susan was popular. 'No side, quiet and sensible, and very determined. It's refreshing when the limelight has spoiled not a few.' The words were those of a flight captain of the ground staff. Susan did not hear them, but they were very applicable.

Sometimes the 'Rose and Thistle' saw them instead of the 'Crown', and it was strange how the six survivors of that original loose-knit eight hung together. The Polish flight lieutenant had gone. It transpired that his ATA service had been a temporary thing – a way of doing useful work while recovering his nerve and awaiting his reappointment to his own squadron.

Quite suddenly, one evening, he had insisted on standing extra drinks all round to 'celebrate', after which ATA saw him no more.

It was during one of these evenings that the new little handbook, *ATA Pilot's Reminder Book*, which had recently been issued to all ferry pilots, came under discussion.

There was nothing but admiration for it, and the amazing amount of technical information it contained. Fang had just said: 'It deserves the appreciation the CO gives it. I shall keep it all my life,' when Mandy, who had been drawing Sandra's attention to some particular paragraph, suddenly laughed and exclaimed, 'Oh, Sue!'

'Yes?' queried Susan.

'D'you remember what Commander MacKenzie said to you that day you went over for the post?'

'Yes – couldn't forget! I felt such a worm!'

'Well – here you are – in black and white,' and Mandy read aloud, '"You are paid to be safe, not brave. Use your head; don't lose it."'

Immediately a babel of conversation broke out. Some had read unnoticing, and some had read and inwardly digested. Susan had already quickly read right through the little book, as was her way, and now was diligently plodding and memorizing so that she would know exactly where to look for any hurriedly desired information.

Now she had to re-tell the story of her adventure through the mist to pick up the post, and as she told it the memory of another day came back, when she had sat outside the rest-room at Barton, in the sun, talking with the adjutant, Flight Captain Ellis. Their conversation, which had gone back to Dunkirk, had left an indelible impression. So vivid was the memory that even through the haze of tobacco smoke she seemed to visualize the clear atmosphere, and even feel the hot August sun upon her, and to see again the lovely outline of that last spur of the Chilterns, crowned with its mysterious wood: the bantering voices around her dissolved themselves into the familiar sound of engines ticking over on the ground, and the droning of those in the sky. The adjutant's words had been:

'Heroes! England breeds heroes at four a penny. We have courage to spare. It's vision and common sense and guidance we need, and shall need for many a long day to come.' The same thought really, only in different words.

'Well, boys and girls' – and Sandra's voice broke in and disturbed Susan's reverie, and she smiled as she listened – 'that reminder to be safe, not brave, is OK by me! It's a wisecrack.'

'Right!' It was Fang who spoke. '"Wise" it is, and a "crack" to let in the wisdom. In America you have clever words; they epitomize much, and one remembers.'

Someone, whom Susan could not see, clapped Fang on the back and exclaimed, 'Good for you, Fang!' and once again, amid a general laugh, the conversation veered to other subjects.

But in their room that evening, alone for once as the others were in the bathrooms, Mandy suddenly said:

'You did a bit of good spade work this evening, Sue.'

'Me? What?' Susan, already in bed, lifted her head in surprise.

'That story. You told it so well, and, you know, no one will forget it.'

'Well, I haven't forgotten it,' said Susan. 'It made a great impression on me. It's the way the older men say things. They sound so experienced, and – well – fatherly, and honestly I like their pi talks. Especially Timber's, and the casual remarks dropped by Sister and old Ellis at Barton. Then here – Commander Mackenzie and Captain Sloper – they're all so keen to help one and make one do one's best. It isn't only that they make one feel machines are precious, but they make one feel that one also is precious.'

'Glory be to the fathers, and to the sons, and to—' Mandy began chanting in a clerical voice, but a well-directed pillow brought the blasphemous sentence to an end.

'The collection will now be taken up during the singing of the hymn "Hark! A thrilling voice is sounding!"' Mandy retrieved the pillow and placed it squarely on Susan's face. 'I never heard such bosh,' she continued. 'You know perfectly well we are always having it rubbed in that the 'planes are precious but pilots are two a penny!'

But Susan remained unruffled, and a moment later said:

'You know, Mandy, before I came into this I thought ATA was a government service.'

'So do most people,' answered Mandy. 'It's industrial – the

country's service, if you like that better.'

'Industrial!' repeated Susan. 'That is such an unattractive word!'

But Mandy was still in a flippant mood. 'Makes me think of bees! "How doth" et cetera—'

'Well,' Susan laughed again, 'BOAC,' she said, with emphasis on the 'B'. I was so surprised when I found myself being paid by the British Overseas Airways Corporation. Sometimes I wonder what is the ultimate future of ATA when the war is over.'

'Dunno,' said Mandy, as she stepped into bed. 'Time we went to sleep, Sue. Michael says it's a better training for civil flying than the RAF.'

Susan pricked up her ears at the mention of Michael's name, but did not interrupt.

'Any craft – any where,' quoted Mandy. 'A Class Six Ferry Pilot may find any one, or half a dozen, out of a hundred and thirtyfour on his chit.' A door banged along the corridor. 'That's Sandra! I'm foxing sleep. Goodnight, Sue.'

Mandy pulled up her bedclothes, and Susan turned her back to the room before Sandra entered.

Since they had returned to Thame, Susan had noticed the increasing frequency of those letters with the Hornchurch post-mark addressed to Mandy. But Mandy maintained an irritating silence on the subject of Michael, so it came about that one morning in the rest-room, about a week before Christmas, Susan opened a letter in what was, to her, a strange handwriting, all unsuspectingly. To her amazement it was an invitation from Sir Francis and Lady Dalrymple-Ducane 'to the marriage of their daughter, Amanda Althea Isobel, to Wing Commander Michael Dundas'. Susan gave a gasp, and stared for a moment before she looked across the room to see Mandy lounging in a chair watching her. Mandy's cheeks were unusually flushed, and her eyes unusually bright. She raised a hand and put a finger casually across her lips, and after a moment drew in her long legs, got up and strolled, just as casually, in the direction of the cloakroom. Susan waited a moment and then followed. For once they had the room to themselves.

'Mandy!'

Mandy's smile had vanished and her eyes held the glint of tears as she put an arm across Susan's shoulders and said:

'Forgive me, Sue. It's a hell of a surprise to spring. You could wear that green frock and be my bridesmaid, or my matron of honour, couldn't you?'

'Mandy! You villain! Why on earth didn't you tell me you were engaged to Michael?'

'Because I'm not. I wouldn't be. I'd be in flap that what happened to Richard might happen again. I only said I wouldn't be engaged, but I'd marry him when he came off "Ops". He's going to Stanmore, so – we thought Christmas Eve would be a good day to get married, and we're going to honeymoon at your mother's flat. She is going to Hazeley.'

Susan laughed. 'Well – you have it all cut and dried!'

'Your mother suggested it,' said Mandy. 'And she's going to leave us Jane!'

'And I suppose Jane knows all about it?' said Susan.

'M-m,' said Mandy. 'I told her.'

'What about clothes?' asked Susan. 'Not bothering. Mother's wedding dress. It's really quite lovely, and doesn't look a bit out of date – and great-grandmother's veil. But you haven't answered my question. You will be my bridesmaid, won't you?'

'Not in the green dress,' Susan replied. 'You can have that to eke out your trousseau. After all, I've never worn it.'

'Oh, but I couldn't!'

'Yes, you can, and you shall. You wore it the first time you danced with Michael. Call it a wedding present if you like, only tell me what you really want for a real one—'

'Nothing,' interrupted Mandy. 'And that is the truth. Michael has too many worldly goods already. But, Sue – what can you wear?'

Susan shook her head. 'Don't know, and I've no coupons!'

'Nor I. Oh! But – I know! We don't want them! I've got it!' and Mandy began to giggle, whilst Susan waited for what might come.

'Uniform! Trousers and all! It will be unique.'

'Oh – but – trousers?' Susan's voice was hesitant.

'They aren't allowed, for funerals—'

'But this isn't a funeral – it's a wedding – idiot!'

'I was going to say perhaps that means they are taboo for all church functions.'

'Let's go and ask Susie Slade,' said Mandy. 'I know what you're driving at. You wouldn't feel respectable.'

'Exactly!' said Susan. 'Well, come along before the weather clears. I must talk to Susie. We really need to get home early on the twenty-third. I wonder if it's 'poss. That'll be grand. A uniform wedding—'

'Except the bride,' interrupted Susan. 'And Mummie. One couldn't see Mummie in uniform,' said Mandy.

It was a very beautiful bride that Susan followed up the aisle of Falcombe Church on Christmas Eve. Radiant and beautiful. Lady Dalrymple-Ducane's wedding dress had been made, Nanny explained when showing it to Susan the previous evening, in 'Princess' fashion, as a background for lovely family lace. The heavy satin gleamed softly through it, and Mandy's hair shone like burnished gold through her great-grandmother's wedding veil. The only concession to the present-day fashion had been supplied when Lady Dalrymple-Ducane, with a handful of lace and a few small safety-pins, had arranged cascades of lace on Mandy's shoulders at the last moment.

Although she had seen her dressed and ready, Susan was hardly prepared for the vision of loveliness Mandy presented as she entered the grey porch of the ancient little church, and, as she stooped to help the Rector's small son lift and hold Mandy's train correctly, she was aware of the gasps of admiration from the close-pressing crowd of villagers and others, and of old Mrs Botting's repeated up-and-down curtseyings. It was a moment of personal triumph, exactly as she had anticipated it; but so much sooner than she had thought possible.

Then the strains of 'Praise my soul the King of Heaven' floated out to meet them and Susan caught her breath. That hymn! Why hadn't she thought it possible? She had a momentary struggle to swallow down the lump that suddenly tightened her throat, and, as she followed the straight back of Sir Francis in his Home Guard uniform – for Mandy had been insistent about uniform – up the aisle, the strong male voices of the Canadian Unit swelled round her almost drowning the strains of the organ, and the difference of a wartime wedding was forced upon her. The little church was crowded, and mostly by men in khaki. The colour of dresses and flowers, with their scents and perfumes, associated in her mind with weddings, were absent. Instead there was a smell of leather and tobacco and men's hair-oil, the time-honoured decorations of honesty and holly, and the legends on the window-sills: 'Unto us a Son is born' – 'Unto us a Child is given' – in rather battered gold lettering, as incongruous, she thought, at this moment, as were her own black shoes and stockings under her short uniform skirt, and her flying cap. Thoughts flashed even as she listened, and yet did not listen, to the voices around her. A war wedding! But, even so, the comradeship. These men from the far corners of the earth, gathered in their thousands to share the dangers and the hope for triumphs and entering into the spirit of this joyous occasion.

As they reached the chancel rails Susan looked to where she knew Michael would be waiting. One look, and she glanced away and fixed her eyes on the tall lilies on the altar. Michael saw no one but Mandy. Just so had Frank looked. Once again that lump and tightness roused by the hymn was in her throat. After a moment she bent down to free the lace the little page clutched too tightly. Then the service began, and word for word Susan remembered and re-lived it all, until the Rector reached the prayer for the blessing of the ring. This was new to her and she listened intently.

'Bless, O Lord, this ring which we bless in Thy Name, that he who gives it and she who wears it may abide in Thy peace, continue in Thy favour, live and grow old in Thy love; through Jesus Christ Our Lord. Amen.'

Although the Rector's voice was quiet, every word penetrated clearly through the intense silence of the little church, but during the psalm that followed the roar of 'planes overhead drowned the music. The noise died away as the address began, and then, a little later, when Susan was bracing herself for the expected strains of 'O Perfect Love', instead came a hymn she had known since childhood, and her one thought was 'How like Mandy!'

'Father hear the prayer we offer;
Not for ease that prayer shall be,
But for strength that we may ever
Live our lives courageously.

'Not for ever in green pastures
Do we ask our way to be;
But the steep and rugged pathway
May we tread rejoicingly.

'Not for ever by still waters
Would we idly rest and stay;
But would smite the living fountains
From the rock along our way.

'Be our strength in hours of weakness,
In our wanderings be our guide;
Through endeavour, failure, danger,
Father, be Thou at our side.'

Once again Susan struggled with that tightness in her throat. Then came the blessing and the service was over. Michael and Mandy were married. The organ and choir began again softly:

'God be in my head,
And in my understanding.'

Would that be Mandy's choice, or Michael's? Susan wondered. A little later, in the vestry, as Mandy stooped to sign her maiden name for the last time, she suddenly stopped and, pen in hand, said:
'Listen! That is Richard's – I promised.'
And while the registers were signed the music and words of 'St Patrick's Breastplate' rang out triumphantly, gloriously.

Gaiety, food, champagne, speeches – the afternoon fled. The Babe, who, from the moment of her arrival, had attached himself to Susan, even while playing his part as the only brother present, never deserted her. His high spirits were infectious.

A chance remark 'I say, I think the fog's coming down' sent Mandy scuttling off to change into travelling clothes, and amid much joking and cheering from the many uniformed men gathered about the old oak door of Falcombe, the bridal pair drove off in their car. Surprisingly quickly the guests melted away, some to hurry off on their Christmas leave, and those of the Canadians who remained to attend to some last-minute arrangements for the party they were giving, partly on account of Christmas Eve, but also as the final celebration of Mandy's wedding and as a gesture to the owners of the house. Sir Francis disappeared for a spell of Home Guard duty; Lady Dalrymple just drifted away and disappeared. The Babe appropriated Susan to himself, and made her come to view his treasures in his bedroom, where they had perforce been stored when his own 'den' had had to be annexed as a bedroom.

'Beastly bore,' explained the Babe, displaying with pride a heterogeneous collection of butterflies, stamp albums, fishing tackle, a stuffed pike, a shabby-looking owl, which he announced he had 'taxidermized' himself, and which looked as if it must have been moulting at the time.

'Nanny's a foul nuisance – she will dust them,' he said – a remark which, privately, Susan thought a sad perversion of the truth from Nanny's point of view.

Then, later, all the household, and many visitors from outside Canadian camps, met for an early cocktail party, and the evening grew more and more hilarious as it developed into a dance, complete with a supper such as only an overseas unit could have provided, and which made even the Babe feel that, for once, he had had more food than was necessary for his existence.

Just after twelve o'clock the party broke up, and after many 'Happy Christmases' and 'Goodnights' Susan found herself walking down the long corridor towards her bedroom with her hostess at her side.

Lady Dalrymple-Ducane was the one member of the family with whom Susan still felt not completely at her ease, and by way of making polite conversation she said, 'I wonder how Mandy and Michael have spent this evening.'

'I'm so thankful for Mandy.' Lady Dalrymple's eyes seemed far removed – just as her remark sounded.

But just as Susan was feeling a little nonplussed at the apparent inattention of her hostess, she found two forget-me-not-blue eyes looking straight into hers, coupled with an ineffably sweet smile and the explanation. 'You see I'm so thankful because Richard was here last Christmas, and this Christmas she has Michael, and she's never been alone – not even before she was born.'

Quite suddenly Susan felt drawn to the elder woman. She was conscious that it was not only to her daughter that she was extending love and sympathy, but to herself. As if those thoughts, which she had entertained in that quiet little bedroom at her grandmother's on that still November afternoon, were as known and understood as if she had uttered them aloud.

'And, my dear,' she continued as they reached the door of Susan's bedroom and paused, 'don't be lonely in life. Don't miss what life may offer you again until you find it's too late.' She laid a long, slim-fingered hand gently on Susan's shoulder. 'I know you have a very loyal nature, but remember that those we have loved and temporarily lost are above our ideas of loyalty.'

Susan looked uncomprehendingly into those two kindly eyes, and Lady Dalrymple continued, almost patiently:

'What I mean is that they have arrived at something we have not – we have not even a word for it in our western languages – we can be unconscious or conscious, but I feel they have – direct cognition. Goodnight, my dear.' And unhurriedly, but without further pause, she continued her way along the corridor towards her own room.

For a second Susan stood quite still before pushing open her door. She felt strangely soothed. Something – some almost unacknowledged doubt in the back of her mind – had been removed. That short conversation which had so surprised her, and which she had not fully understood, seemed to have touched something within her as an electric switch turns on the current. She felt she could sense wider horizons – 'more like I feel when I'm flying alone' she thought. The ache of pain, which had not quite left her since those disturbing memories had been revived in the little church – in spite of her outward appearance of joining in the high-spirited celebrations of the Canadians – was stilled. Thoughts of people and personalities crowded in on her, giving her a feeling of being hedged about with friendship and with love. Frank – Mark – who Mandy could not believe was gone – Mandy herself – her husband – all her family – newly made friends these, but now she knew that they would not be just passing friends of wartime.

How wonderful complete sympathy and understanding was! Until a few moments ago she had felt alone in the midst of many people – now she no longer felt solitary although she was alone.

She had thought Lady Dalrymple a little vague – rather aloof. How unaware one could be! Susan smiled to herself. The fact was that it was Mandy's mother who held all the clues.

FOUR

SUSAN AND MANDY were both due to report at White Waltham airfield at 9 am on December 29th, but on the principle that perhaps the early-comer get the best billet, Susan left London soon after lunch on the twenty-eighth. She had two reasons: one, that she hated being rushed, and the other, that if she 'spied out the land' Mandy could more comfortably stay an extra night with Michael. Also they had taken the trouble, before leaving Thame, to verify the rumoured fact that an ATA bus did meet a certain train from London every morning at Maidenhead station, and, finding it true, planned accordingly.

Susan was much looking forward to this, her second, secondment. She knew it was to be for six weeks, and that it would be spent taxiing and ferrying small aircraft. Taxiing was always exciting. One never knew where one was going, nor whom one would be sent to pick up, and Susan, at heart a hero-worshipper, looked forward to meeting some of the pilots and personalities famous in the annals of ATA. White Waltham was Number One Ferry Pool, and it was Headquarters; and, at some time or other, pilots from all the other Pools came in. Actually, that cold December afternoon Susan felt she wanted to get back. It had been lovely at Falcombe. She had a real affection for parents and the Babe, and it was sweet of Lady Dalrymple to want her to stay over Christmas, but she was still restless, uprooted, lonely and chaffing to get on; to fly bigger and faster 'planes and to have the list of her deliveries pile up. Then, perhaps, she would feel satisfied that at last she was doing something worthwhile.

So Susan came to Number One Ferry Pool full of enthusiasm. From the first moment she felt she belonged. The policeman on guard at the gate was the one who had befriended her before. That somehow made a good beginning. He recognized her and said, 'Nice to see you again, miss.' It was to Susan, a welcome. She left her suitcases with him and proceeded to find the billeting officer, and thought about some tea. Here again she was greeted warmly, and found herself the first of the cadets to arrive. There was even a slight choice of billets.

'Surprising,' she was told, because 'the billeting problem is a perpetual headache.' She and Mandy were to be at Cookham. For a moment Susan thought of the distance. Half a dozen miles at least to cover by 9 am! But Captain Trimnell was speaking again.

'The bus leaves the village street at eight-thirty every morning, and takes you back after last flying time every evening. You will be the only two in that house, and they are kindly people. What did you say Miss Ducane's married name was?'

'Dundas.'

In a few minutes all was settled, and Susan found herself with forty or so minutes to spare before the bus left for Cookham. She vaguely knew the plan of White Waltham buildings from her former brief visits; but they had been brief. Only an occasional picking up and putting down. This, she thought, was a good opportunity to explore a little, but tea first. She made her way to the pilots' snack bar. Here luck was with her. As she pushed the door to go in, someone, on the other side, pulled it to come out. A tall, fair girl. She smiled, and Susan immediately recognized the first officer whom she had seen, and who had talked winter sports at her preliminary interview. Nowadays she knew her to be Audrey Sale-Barker of England's ski team. She was apparently hurried, but paused to answer Susan's greeting, and added, 'How is it going?'

A little later, as she collected her tea, Susan still felt a glow of satisfaction. It was childish, perhaps, but it was nice to be remembered and asked how she was getting on.

There were few people in the snack bar and no one she recognized, so Susan carried her tea across the room, established herself beside a radiator and wondered, with Mark in her mind, if it were worthwhile to look for possible letters. One or two more pilots came in and she watched them join the little group about the buffet. Voices and laughter rang out and she felt, momentarily, out of things. Then someone, not over-tall, waved a hand in greeting and detached himself from the group. It was the doctor from Thame whom she had already met. He brought his cup and sat down beside her, and, not knowing of her secondment, offered a lift back to Thame. He was, he said, just leaving and anxious to get back before dark, but he seemed in no hurry, and in the end it was Susan who moved first and said she must go if she was to have her walk round and get her bearings.

'Come and see my new car first,' he suggested.

So Susan went and duly admired the second- or third-hand scarlet painted MG, a replica of the one her brother had owned, now stored in Grannie's garage, and of which she had said, 'Don't let it go. I may want it,' when her mother had suggested selling.

The bus was already filling up when Susan entered it, but again, although a few faces were familiar – people and pilots she had previously seen – there was no one she actually knew and most of those left the bus at Maidenhead. Some smiled and said 'goodnight', but the rattling of the bus had prevented overhearing of anything but the usual shouted, and sometimes ribald, remarks.

It was growing dark and a cold mist was rising when the driver of the bus dropped Susan and her suitcases at her billet. She shivered and touched the doorbell. This, she thought, was the real Thames valley. She knew exactly where she was, on the low-lying Berkshire shore, with the cliffs and woods of Cliveden gently rising their two hundred feet on the opposite, Buckinghamshire, shore. One of England's beauty spots. Lovely in summer – but, in winter! She shivered again as the door opened, and a few minutes later she felt rewarded. The early cadet certainly caught the best billet. Susan found herself far more comfortably housed than she had been either at Thame or Cosford. She and Mandy were the only guests in a quiet private house and in what probably had been the best spare bedroom.

As soon as she was alone Susan switched off the light and drew aside the curtains. Momentarily she had lost her bearings, and she was one of those people who liked to know what could be seen from her window.

For a moment, a curtain in either hand, she stood and stared. A new moon! Was it possible? Just a little more of a thread than she had seen at Worthy Down. Of course – it *was* a month ago!

Susan laughed softly to herself, hastily bowed, and under her breath said, 'Thank you, Moon. Michael and Mandy have found their happiness.' Then, with a heart full of thankfulness, and the points of the compass and prospective view completely forgotten, she stood and gazed upwards for some moments. Above the river mist the sky was a Holbein blue, except where, low down, the faintest trace of the afterglow of the sunset was still visible with the moon just disappearing into it. It must be a good omen! And she must wish again – her dearest wish. Susan thought and watched as the golden crescent of the moon sank lower.

'Please,' she whispered, 'bring Mark safely back.'

A moment later she drew the curtains closely and switched on the light and once again surveyed the room. It looked comfortable, so did the beds – and possessed a gas fire with a meter. That was luck!

Work in real earnest began next morning, and before the day was over Mandy's wedding, Christmas and Falcombe had taken on as vague an aspect as a dream. Mandy arrived according to plan, but there was no time to talk; the morning was clear, and both had their first jobs right away.

But, between her jobs, even on that first day, Susan began to get a far clearer idea of how the whole service worked; of the intricacies of the interchanging and dovetailing of routes and pilots, which avoided delays, and she began to appreciate much more than formerly the efficiency which resulted in such speedy delivery of the 'planes. In a way, too, it was a bewildering day. She had no deliveries and flew Fairchild taxis only, fetching and carrying pilots from Radlet and Hatfield. Other things also happened. She met her own Senior Commander, Miss Pauline Gower, and someone pointed out the creator of ATA, Commodore d'Erlanger, whom she had expected to see looking much older. At mid-day she found Mandy in the Pilots' Mess, talking to a girl pilot from Hamble, whom she introduced as 'Joy', and while they lunched together more personalities were pointed out. Douglas Fairweather was one, of whom Joy said, 'He flies through anything in any weather,' and then she spoke of

Joan Hughes, 'tiny, pretty, and full of achievement', but the tannoy interrupted, calling 'Cadet Sandyman', and Susan fled.

Her so-called passenger proved to be a senior pilot. He greeted her with 'Hullo! You're new!' and indicated that she should fly the machine. For a moment Susan looked askance, then said, 'D'you really mean it?'

'Of course. Why not? Get all the flying hours you can.'

And so Susan flew him to Hatfield, and when she returned the weather was closing down and flying over for the day.

It was an experience that was to be repeated many times. The senior pilots at White Waltham allowed the cadets to do far more flying while taxiing and Susan looked upon this privilege as added 'dual' and found that she picked up many items of useful knowledge.

Perhaps they were let down lightly for their first day, and Susan said as much to Mandy when at last, having got rid of Nina and Sandra, who were also billeted in Cookham, they found themselves alone for the night.

'Don't think so,' said Mandy. 'I expect it's only a momentary aftermath of Christmas. The factories must have let up a little.' But Mandy's thoughts were not on aircraft at that moment; with hardly a change of tone she continued, 'Your Mama is a brick, Sue. We've had a wonderful time – and – look – what Mummie did!' She stooped as she spoke and pulled one or two garments from her still unpacked suitcase. 'I hadn't bothered about trousseau, only one or two things and the nightdress you finished – that's why I wanted it. When we got to your mama's flat Jane gave me a parcel, and *this* was in it!' and Mandy shook out a nightdress of white satin and lace. 'I was so surprised. Didn't think such a thing would enter Mummie's head!'

'I think,' said Susan, 'your mother is more practical than you think.'

'And yours' – Mandy suddenly laughed – 'more *romantic*! You know Michael has been trying to rent a flat. He will be at least three months on rest at Fighter Command at Stanmore, and while the days are short and weather bad, if we had a flat in town we thought we could spend lot of time together – but – flats!' Mandy broke off with an expressive gesture. 'The agents haven't a thing – it's just hellish.

But your mama – she said "Give it up! It isn't worth the struggle for three months, and have my spare room instead." It's lovely for Michael. Jane adores him. Spoils him to death – puts all the tit-bits on his plate as if he were six. He will be hopeless.'

Susan laughed. She knew old Jane and her ways, but Mandy continued:

'D'you mind? Seems awfully possessive.'

'Me! Mind? Of course not! I think it's a very good plan, and lovely for Mother. As it is I often as not sleep in the little room when I am there.'

In spite of bad weather, snow, sleet, rain and the special brand of fog peculiar to the Thames Valley, it was amazing how those weeks at White Waltham fled. Often, it might be for two or three days together, flying was impossible, but whenever 'Met' promised even a few clear hours the ferry pilots were in the air. Susan and Mandy grew familiar with all the London area and home counties' fighter stations. With the Norwegian Squadron at North Weald and with Hornchurch, Castle Camp, Rochester, Biggin Hill, Northolt, Redhill, Gatwick – names famous in the Battle of Britain, names that brought a thrill.

One day, when, as is the way of English weather, the sun shone from sunrise to sunset, Susan landed on ten different airfields in a Fairchild, for, at these times, when the weather allowed, there was no question of the hours worked. The work went on as long as there was work and the light lasted. The factories had to be kept clear, the aircraft had to be delivered, bomber fighter stations needed them and ATA saw to it that the job was done and well done.

There were dreary days too, with endless hours of waiting for the weather to clear; when all one could do was to sit around the restaurant or rest-room and knit or sew, or read or talk with one's fellow pilots.

The School at White Waltham was closed for the winter, but Susan did not miss it, although she was told again and again, 'You ought to be here next summer on Class Three.' There were really instructors in plenty. No one was loth to pass on information and the conversation when any group of pilots came together was almost always shop. And there were sad days too, although little was said. A faulty machine, a risk taken, unforeseen weather difficulties and once again the ranks of the ferry pilots closed, and an obituary notice in *The Times* would tell of yet another life lost 'while ferrying His Majesty's aircraft'. Occasionally *The Times* was one's only informant, and Susan would think of John Potts and his 'very silent service'.

It was on one of these occasions, from a remark overheard by chance, that Susan first became aware that ATA had its own Benevolent Fund. 'Poor chap! I know he hadn't a bean, and he leaves a widow and three children – one's about a week old.' All that day she could not get it out of her mind, and at the first opportunity she made enquiries, and learned that the pilots, apart from an insurance that amounted to £1,500, depended on this fund, made of their own and voluntary contribution. Three children – the wage-earner gone – and fifteen hundred pounds! These men risked more than their lives. After all in the Services there were pensions. She wished she were rich. Being practical she made her own contribution, and decided to speak to her mother and arrange that, if her fifteen hundred were ever due, it should be given to the Benevolent Fund. She passed on it enthusiastically, adding the suggestion to Mandy, who greeted thoughtfully:

'You know, Sue, from ATA's point of view it's a wizard idea, because if they are deprived of our invaluable services from our demise – or is it demises? – they'll get the fifteen hundred for the Benevolent Fund. In other words what they lose on the swings they'll gain on the roundabouts!'

During those six weeks more often than not Susan and Mandy spent the nights in town. It was such an easy journey and the evenings were long. They were a very 'happy family' that gathered in Mrs Ledgard's flat, or went forth for a gay evening. Sometimes, if Mrs Ledgard happened to be away, and she frequently went to Hazeley, Susan would stay behind so that Michael and Mandy could be alone, but it often happened that Michael could not get away. His job 'on rest' was an office one with uncertain hours. He hated it as he hated any indoor job and despised what he called pen-pushing, and longed for the time when he could be back in the air. Mandy, however, was content. She confided to Susan that she liked things as they were, and added: 'I'll be sorry when Michael's three months are up. Got the feeling they are all being nursed for something, and often find myself wondering what, when and where? Invasion time *must* come.'

Then, very suddenly it seemed, their secondment, followed by a month in the Training Pool again, was over, and both felt back at their beginnings. Mid-March found them back at Thame, back at Hopefield House, back in their original room, and back in the School for Class Two Ground Course, two weeks of it and no flying!

Four disgruntled girl cadets, because Sandra and Nina, of whom they had seen surprisingly little at White Waltham, had also returned to Thame, as had Fang and Max and Fat Robin, to do the same course. It was amazing how they had kept together. Quite where and when the rest of the class had joined ATA none of them knew, or troubled to enquire. They were doing the same job, and as keen as the rest to get on, and that's all there was to it.

It was gruelling. Susan caught a cold and felt depressed. Some days she felt certain she would never take it all in, but she mopped her streaming eyes and stuck to it, and dreamed of supercharged engines and retractable undercarriages, and all the other subjects, boost, variable pitch airscrews, different brakeing systems and cooling systems, of which the lectures and lessons consisted. Mandy called it 'absolute hell'.

But Susan's cold departed and her head cleared, and by the time the fortnight was over and the day arrived for both oral and written examinations on these subjects she felt that, with luck, she might satisfy her examiners.

She did, and so did the others, and the next move, still in the School, was Class Two Flying on Harvards.

Although the Harvards with their strong frames and wide undercarriages seemed solid enough to Susan, and comparatively difficult to break, that fortnight's Class Two conversion course was not without its quota of what Susan overheard a mechanic classify as 'unfortunate incidents'!

Max Roskoff set the ball rolling. The first time he flew the Harvard solo he contrived to ground loop on landing, and although the undercarriage did not actually collapse, it was badly strained.

Perhaps less excusable was Mandy's effort.

While carrying out her preliminary cockpit check, before even starting up the still parked Harvard, she inadvertently selected the UP position with the undercarriage lever, a few seconds later pressing the power knob. With a long-drawn hissing sigh the Harvard sank, as in an ever deepening curtsey, to the ground, leaving Mandy as one transfixed with horror, helpless in the cockpit.

'Never felt such a fool in my life!' she told Susan that evening. 'Thank goodness old Mac doesn't seem to have taken as black a view as I expected. I just can't imagine how I *could* have been so dim!'

Susan laughed. 'Well, perhaps it was rather clottish! Only hope I don't prang the Spit. Something tells me I'm for it tomorrow or Thursday.'

After some twenty hours of dual and solo on Harvards, and before being posted to Number Five Ferry Pool as Third Officers and a Class Two pilot, each pupil had to put in two hours' flying on one of the Spitfire Mark Vs in the School.

This, as every pilot before Susan had discovered, was an ordeal far worse in anticipation than in actual fact. It was not unknown for a pupil to sit in the cockpit of a Spitfire for three or four hours, technical notes in hand, learning the positions of each control and each instrument until he or she could find them blindfold. Susan herself spent well over an hour.

Finally she knew that she was merely procrastinating and forced herself to go in and fetch her flying kit, collect her parachute and sign out with Flying Control.

Unlike any machine that Susan had yet flown, the Spitfire could not be allowed to tick over indefinitely, so that from the time she ran up and checked the engine until she had taxied out to the Control Car only a few moments elapsed.

Already the gauges showed the Merlin engine was heating up, and Susan knew it would only be a matter of seconds before it would become too hot to take off in safety.

Being really honest with herself she admitted in retrospect that it was more the thought of what others would say if she had switched off at that moment than from a desire to take off in the Spitfire which made her turn into wind, release the brakes and slowly – slowly – open the throttle.

The sudden surge of power was overwhelming and wholly unexpected. Susan never quite knew how she lived through the next few seconds. She just felt a punch in the back, the breath left her body, the great nose in front of her dipped slightly and she felt herself rocketing away from the earth. As in a dream she lifted the undercarriage lever, went through all the other motions which the past weeks of training had so firmly instilled in her brain, and suddenly found she had already climbed two thousand feet.

With the return of breath and full consciousness came also a swift surge of fear. She was up there now, but would she ever get down again?

For the next half-hour Susan roared round the sky, alternately more exhilarated and more frightened than she had ever been in her life. The slightest pressure on the stick and the machine answered like a live thing. It was uncanny. Slowly, however, her confidence grew, and with it the determination that she would master and not be mastered. 'I shall now make a circuit and land,' she bravely told herself.

She did, and that first landing was the best of the four she made during those first nerve-racking two hours in a Spitfire. But finally, when she had switched off, unstrapped her Sutton harness and parachute, and climbed once more on to terra firma, she found that her legs were trembling and felt her shirt clinging limply to her body.

It was over – she had won – it could never be the *first* time again!

FIVE

THE NEXT DAY brought its reward. Susan and Mandy, running neck and neck this time, were no longer cadets. After a final check on a Harvard with Captain Shillingford, they were promoted to Third Officers.

As always they compared notes on their experiences, Mandy's in the Spitfire having been much the same as Susan's, but Mandy, as always, was philosophical, and remarked, 'Well, after all, one can't jump from a speed of a hundred and forty miles to two hundred and fifteen miles an hour without getting a bit agitated!'

With the changing to the wider shoulder-stripe, worn by third officers, Susan began to feel more sure of herself. She sewed on her own and she sewed on Mandy's stripes, with a deep sense of gratification. Sprawled on her bed, Mandy looked at her and remarked:

'You're grinning like a Cheshire cat, Sue! What is it?'

Susan looked up and retorted: 'Any rudery from you, my child, and I'll sew yours on crooked. There! That's three done! Where's your other tunic?'

Mandy laughed and stretched out her arm to pick her tunic from the chair beside her and fling it across.

'You couldn't if you tried! You're too precise. But, Sue, promotion is much slower than it used to be.'

'Yes,' said Susan.

It was true, but Susan felt that did not matter. The smaller aircraft were equally as important as the big ones, and now that she would fly Spitfires she felt her feet were firmly on the ladder that leads to success, and the rest was up to herself.

For the last fortnight of April they were, all four, posted over to the Thame Training Pool again, and Susan found that she was given almost continual ferrying and very little taxi work. By now, too, the Pool was full of familiar faces. From Commander Hale, the Pool Commander, down, she knew all her senior officers; and she also knew by sight many of the pilots from other Pools who came and went, and she loved the general atmosphere of camaraderie. The

Station Commander, Commander Hills, she met for the first time at a concert given for the benefit of the Benevolent Fund, of which he was the leading spirit. There was, however, very little time for talking to anyone. The weather rarely held one up and flying hours were long. One was too tired to do anything but get to bed as fast as possible.

Bed and flying made up the routine, but it was with satisfaction that Susan saw the list of her deliveries pile up. Her first was a Master, from Miles factory at Reading, to be delivered to Wroughton near Swindon, an uneventful flight. Then, almost daily, there were Hurricanes to be delivered from Hawkers factory at Langley to Silloth, or to Sherburn-in-Elmet.

This latter flight came to be rather a favourite of Susan's. She loved the heading due north, right up almost the centre of England, and the swift return due south, and the picking up at various airfields. Also, Hawker's factory, at this time, was very interesting as it was just beginning to change over from Hurricanes, which were becoming obsolete, to Typhoons, and Susan had several opportunities of seeing the 'Tiffies' in the factory while under construction. But she never got used to landing at Langley. It was always terrifying. The encircling barrage balloons, although one always had one's directions beforehand as to which would be hauled down, loomed so large, and the little grass airfield looked so small. Susan was only comforted when she discovered that even senior pilots found the experience just as alarming.

The outstanding event of the fortnight as far as Susan was concerned occurred the day she ferried a Mustang from Kidlington, near Oxford, to St Athans in South Wales.

It was the first Mustang she had ever flown, an old Mark I, with an Alison engine, and although no onlooker would have guessed it if they had watched her climb into the cockpit, Susan was suffering from a violent attack of what Mandy described as 'butterflies in her tummy'!

For over a quarter of an hour she just sat there with both her ferry pilot's notes and handling notes in her lap, learning the exact position of all the controls and instruments and making herself familiar with the general layout.

It all seemed so unnecessarily bewildering to Susan, and so much more complicated than a Spit. The air speed indicator read in kilometers instead of the usual miles per hour; the boost gauge in inches of mercury instead of pounds per square inch, and then as a final complication she found that the hood would not slide open or shut over her head, but that it had to be firmly clamped down and had only two small perspex panels, one on each side, which could be opened for ventilation. There was, of course, the lever for releasing the whole hood in the event of an emergency, but Susan did not think much of this and a slight sensation of claustrophobia overcame her.

'At this rate I shall never take off,' she told herself severely, and with a mental shake stuffed her ferry pilot's notes and handling notes down the sides of her flying-boots, open at the right pages in case of need.

The run-up was entirely satisfactory and as Susan opened the throttle her qualms vanished as quickly as the runway behind her – until suddenly... The ASI! The needle... it had not moved! The hedge was coming up fast now – too late to stop – the wheels unstuck and Susan was airborne with no air speed indicator. Now it is only to a pilot that the full meaning of this will come home, and only on a pilot with some imagination will the full horror dawn, for he must remember that it is the first time he has ever sat in the cockpit of a Mustang – the first time an ASI has died on him – and the first time that he has taken off or landed on this particular airfield. In fact, at this point, if he were dreaming – he would wake up in a cold sweat!

As it was Susan never quite knew how she lived through the next few minutes, although she distinctly remembered saying aloud to herself as she made her final approach, 'Better too fast than too slow. Keep your speed up. It should be a hundred – make it a hundred and twenty for safety!'

In actual fact she must have come belting in at well over a hundred and thirty, because although the hedge whistled by a few inches beneath her wheels, the far hedge rushed up to meet her with alarming rapidity. Luckily the ground was none too firm and her brakes good, so that she just managed to pull up with a few feet to spare.

Although she felt like slapping his face when a complacent rigger came up and asked, 'Anything the matter, miss?', Susan refrained, swallowed hard and switched off before answering:

'Yes,' she replied calmly. 'The ASL is US. The needle doesn't budge!' In a few moments a mechanic had the pitot head to pieces, and there, curled up asleep and blissfully ignorant of the disaster it had almost caused, was a fat, green caterpillar!

Everyone laughed, including Susan, although thinking about it later that day, on her way back from St Athans in a taxi Anson, she was well aware that the whole thing had been due to the idleness of someone who had failed to see that the Mustang's pitot head was kept covered when it was not in the air; and there and then Susan made up her mind that, in future, she would always make a mechanic blow down the pitot head before she started up. Anyway it was another lesson well and truly learned, the hard way. Certainly hours and knowledge and flying wisdom piled up together.

The end of the month came and with it their new orders. Three days' posting leave and then Susan and Mandy to Number Fifteen Ferry Pool at Hamble, and Nina and Sandra – much to the latter's delight – to Number Six Pool at Ratcliffe.

'Say, girls, Mother's come to say goodbye!' The door of Susan's and Mandy's bedroom opened as if by a strong blast of wind, as they were hurriedly packing their bags to go on leave, and Sandra's head appeared round it.

'I just hate leaving you two,' she continued as she kissed Susan in her warm-hearted American way, 'but right now I'm making plans to track down the owner of that old, old English house and his old, old butler, and just make all three of them mine! My! Wouldn't Elmer be proud of his mother? Goodbye, Mandy, my pet' – she began to embrace her with equal heartiness. 'Say – when will we three meet again?'

'When the hurly-burly's done. When the battle's lost or won!'

said Mandy.

'Why – that's Shakespeare, isn't it? My, that man just had something cute to say about everything,' said Sandra enthusiastically. 'So long, girls. I'll be inviting you up to stay at the Hall when my battle's won!' She slammed the door and was gone.

SIX

WITH TWO EXCEPTIONS Susan found Ramble very much as Mandy had described it to her, and far from a feeling of strangeness, which one might well expect on being posted to a completely new Ferry Pool, she found such a strong sensation of familiarity about the place that it was as if she had been there before – not once but many times.

On the morning after her arrival, when told to report to the CO's office, Susan was not greeted with the usual 'pep' talk, which she fully expected, but merely found herself engaged in an informal and friendly chat about ferrying in general, and her own flying in particular.

Commander Gore was one of those few women blessed with the art of asserting authority without appearing to do so. An experienced pilot herself, having flown most types from a Tiger Moth to a Fortress, she never forgot the time when she herself had been a junior pilot, so that without their realizing it she saw to it that every new pilot was nursed, rather than kicked, along. No Ramble pilot was ever pushed on to a more advanced aircraft before she was ready to cope with it, and as a result a deep confidence in the CO's opinion had grown up. Yet in no way was she remote or aloof from the common herd, and in the ante-room she mixed with even the most junior pilots, taking a lively part in any discussion that might crop up, no matter whether it were lingerie or politics. As Mandy had prophesied, Susan liked and trusted her immediately, and her first impression never altered.

The fact that Mandy had been seconded to Ramble during the previous winter helped enormously, for she already knew most of the pilots and so was able not only to tell Susan most of their names but to introduce her generally.

By the end of a week Susan could fit a name – although in some cases only a christian name – to most of the thirty-odd pilots, whilst after a fortnight she could also name most of the MT drivers, the Adjutant and Assistant Adjutant, the Operations Officers and even some of the typists in the General Office.

Since joining ATA – almost a year ago by now – Susan found her memory, especially for names and faces, had become doubly retentive; her mind, in every way, sharpened. Nowadays she was aware of a new vitality coursing through her, not only physical, but mental, and in this, she felt, lay the secret of the exceptions in Mandy's otherwise accurate description, a description which in some ways had proved to be such an understatement.

Of course, she told herself, she must not forget that Mandy had written from Hamble in November and that now it was full spring – almost summer. Now there was a throbbing and pulsing in the very earth and air, which made one see everything a hundred times more vividly, and which compelled one to feel a fundamental gaiety of spirit unknown in winter.

But Mandy had never told her how close the Isle of Wight lay across the blue, restless waters of the Solent, how green it looked in the sunlight, nor how blue and secret in the dusk. In November the island had, most probably, appeared as a dark grey mass looming out of a steel-grey sea and Mandy had not thought it worth mentioning.

There were other things, things that filled one with joy, like the great chestnut tree by the church with its myriad salmon-coloured candles – but again it had been winter. Probably all Mandy saw was gaunt branches and skeleton fingers against the sky. It reminded her of the great white one in Shottesbrooke Park, adjoining the airfield at White Waltham, the blooms of which had been fading on the day she made her test flight. It would be lovely now, and most probably within the next few days she would see it, traffic between Hamble and White Waltham being frequent. Susan also loved the way the narrow lane twisted steeply down between ancient cottages to the perhaps more ancient hard, where it widened into a square, with the Yacht Club on one side and the half-timbered Bugle Inn on the other.

One evening, about ten days after their arrival, as the two girls walked back through the village to the Yacht Club, where they were temporarily billeted, Susan taxed Mandy with these omissions and understatements. For a moment Mandy did not answer. She waited until they rounded the last bend in the lane and before them there lay the Hamble river, a bar of liquid gold in the sunset. Then she stopped and stood quite still, and said simply:

'There is the answer. It's alive now – the river, I mean – it's all quite, quite different.'

She walked slowly on, swinging her overnight bag thoughtfully, until her ear caught the buzz of voices coming from the 'Bugle'. It was almost eight o'clock. They had both been flying right up to last landing time, so, by now, the two bars of the inn were overflowing and a crowd of soldiers and sailors had brought their mugs of beer out onto the small terrace overlooking the river.

'And that's another thing.' Mandy nodded in their direction. 'The village is alive now, too. Take the "Bugle" – full to bursting every evening, and they are all so painfully self-conscious about "Careless Talk" that it's obvious there is something big in the wind: besides, look at the ships – new ones every day, and now those barges. I couldn't possibly have told you about all this last winter because it just wasn't there.'

Mandy was right of course. Last November the second invasion of the Continent, which wiser brains were planning, had been to the ordinary person a matter of conjecture and dreams; now here, today, was the result of that planning.

Sitting on the wall outside the Yacht Club after dinner that evening, with the tide rising rapidly beneath their dangling feet, Susan became even more aware of this and something of the tenseness and expectancy so clearly mirrored in the eyes of many of the soldiers she had seen in the village entered into her own heart.

It was dark long before the girls went indoors and for the last ten minutes neither of them had spoken. Susan's thoughts were conjecture. Perhaps the coming invasion would aid Mark's escape – if he still lived. Mandy's thoughts were of her husband. She wondered where he was tonight, who with and what doing. It was over a week now since the Mosquito Squadron had left Marham, and the only news she had received of him was quite by chance – a word overheard in the Mess at Tangmere – 'Good lord! You're weeks behind the times, old boy!' one pilot had been saying to another as they left the room together and paused just behind Mandy's chair. 'I'm on Mossies now – sixteens – Groupy Dundas is our CO, you know.'

As this information registered Mandy jumped up and followed them out, but she was too late. They had disappeared, probably into their cloakroom, and she had not seen their faces sufficiently well to recognize either of them again.

True, Michael had spoken to her on the 'phone, from where he could not say, and had told her not to worry if she did not hear from him for some days, but when one has been married only five months and spent little enough of that together, a week might just as well be a year. Not that Mandy really feared for Michael; he was such a superb pilot, and besides, now that he was a Group Captain, she knew he would not be allowed to go on most Operations, a fact which continually irked him. But one could never be sure nowadays – life was so uncertain, so insecure – so – so unlike Falcombe...

Her thoughts jumped to her home and family, but at this moment Susan stood up and began industriously banging the brick-dust from the seat of her trousers.

'Backside getting cold,' she announced briefly. 'Think I shall go to bed.' They went in together, pausing only in the hall for a word with the retired Admiral who was secretary of the Club, and then went straight on up to the big double bedroom which they were, temporarily they hoped, sharing.

For a long while Susan lay awake in the darkness listening to the voices which, though subdued, came clearly to her across the water. Once or twice a naval launch swept up the river, its powerful engines turning so sweetly as to be almost silent, its passage marked only by the swish of water in its wake. From the old wooden quays a few hundred yards up the river Susan could hear the hollow tramp of heavy boots on boards; small ships had been loading there all day and judging by the sounds their crews were still bard at it. Occasionally she could hear a muffled word of command, but although its owner could lower his voice he could not expel the note of urgency from it.

And as the days went by Susan could feel the tempo of life on the river speeding up like some great irresistible engine, so that by the end of May the suspense had become almost intolerable.

The huge military camps in the area were sealed; no one, neither officer nor ranker, was allowed outside camp bounds and the penalty for breaking out was rumoured to be death.

When Susan thought that no more ships could possibly crowd into the river she would wake in the morning to see that there had been many new arrivals during the night, now all skilfully moored and tucked away.

Once she thought the moment had really come, for she and Mandy were awakened simultaneously by the sound of many voices and great activity on the river, but the morning only brought anticlimax and weather more suitable for January than the first week in June.

'Perhaps some of the barges broke loose,' Mandy suggested, and they left it at that, but next day the old salts shook their heads knowingly, sucked their pipes longer than usual in the 'Bugle' bar, and said, 'It warn't no weather for no 'vasion yet.'

The weather, however, did not hinder the swift war machines of the air and there was more than enough ferrying to be done.

Susan saw the hours in her log book rising rapidly, and strange new names appeared in its pages. Barracuda, Hellcat, Fulmer, Avenger, an old Defiant and a black-painted Lysander. When she delivered this last machine to a squadron at an airfield of which she had previously never even heard the name, she naturally asked why the 'Lizzie' was painted black, and why it had a little ladder running up one side of the fuselage; but the Control Officer, whom she had asked, skilfully evaded answering and it was only later that she learned that these machines were flown over, and landed at night, in occupied territory on the Continent, in order to drop and pick up the allied agents and their priceless information.

However, in spite of all the new types Susan flew, the Spitfire remained her first love and she never changed her mind. It was like riding a racehorse after a hired hack! There was such a grace and simplicity about it – no vices – no complications, none of the snags that so far Susan had found in every other machine she had flown. For instance, the cockpit of a Barracuda she felt must have been designed to fit a giant, for in order to reach many of the controls she had to undo her safety harness and reach right forward, while to get into the cockpit at all she had first to climb up on to the big tyre and then clamber several feet higher up the fuselage – not so easy as it sounds with a parachute over one shoulder, and perhaps a Mae West as well.

Then once, in a Fleet Air Arm machine, the deck arrester hook came adrift, through no fault of Susan's, and although she was blissfully unaware of it herself, she was told on landing that it narrowly missed catching some telegraph wires which ran dangerously near the end of the runway.

Again in some types one had to worry about ballast being in place and secure, in lieu of a passenger or equipment; in others unless certain bolts and locks were in the correct position the wings would fold up in mid-air. Yet again, in Fleet Air Arm machines the speed would be measured in knots instead of miles per hour, or, in American machines, in kilometres; while the Boost might be measured in inches or centimetres of mercury instead of the familiar pounds per square inch. All small and simple differences to the experienced ferry pilot maybe, but apt to be confusing to a new pilot flying a fresh type of machine for the first time. Not so the 'Spittie'. In spite of new Marks, more weight and higher speeds, it always remained the same, and, in Susan's eyes at least, perfection itself.

During these first few days of June the weather remained blustery and overcast, and it was not until the afternoon of the fifth that there was even a hint of a break. By seven o'clock the wind had died away, the sun was quite hot and it was only then, back at the Yacht Club, and sprawling flat on her bed, that Susan realized just how long and exhausting the day had been.

On the ante-room table that morning she had found three Ferry chits waiting for Third Officer Sandyman, each for a different type of aircraft. Since then she had been up over the mountains of the Lake District in a lumbering Barracuda which she had handed over to Number Sixteen Ferry Pool at Kirkbride for on-ferrying: she had then taken a Dauntless, a new type to her, over the border to the great Scottish airfield at Prestwick and finally had winged her way swiftly south again in a Mustang to Farnborough.

Apart from a cup of tea and a sandwich at Kirkbride, and her chocolate ration which she had sucked on the way to Prestick, she had not eaten since breakfast – somehow she had not felt like it and even now she was not really hungry. She just lay on her back, her arms behind her head and her eyes closed.

It was good to relax after so much concentration and to be still after the ceaseless motion of the day.

'Hullo, Sue – you lazy hound! Why didn't you come swimming?'. Susan raised herself on an elbow as Mandy came into the room.

'Doesn't look to me as if you have done much swimming yourself!' Susan countered, noticing that Mandy was carrying a bone-dry swimming-suit.

'Right! I didn't go in – the river is too oily,' she admitted. 'Those LCPs and MT8s make the water foul. Gosh – I'm tired!' She yawned. 'After four hours in a Fairchild I had to wait nearly another two hours at Odiham for Veronica who was US at Prestwick.'

'Yes, I saw her there,' answered Susan. 'As far as I could make out she was waiting for a Mosquito to be built!'

For some minutes they carried on a desultory conversation until finally both fell silent.

The air was so still that from the tennis-court in a garden some hundred yards up the river Susan could hear the tink-tonk of ball against hard-strung racket, and man's voice calling the score as clearly as if he were standing beside her. From the radio, which had just been switched on in the lounge below, came the haunting strains of 'As time goes by', and every now and then a seagull would drift lazily across her field of vision. Everything at that moment seemed to Susan painfully romantic, the war infinitely remote, yet she knew she had but to lift her head to see the armada waiting on the river.

So they lay for some minutes, each lost in her own thoughts, until a noisy little Fairchild fussed overhead to disturb them.

'That's Anna,' Susan announced without opening her eyes. 'She had to take the CO up to White Waltham for a conference. Wonder what it was about this time?'

'Winter woolies for ferry pilots, perhaps,' Mandy suggested, with her usual lack of respect for authority. 'Or a Comfort's Fund for Commanders, maybe!'

'I heard a rumour that it was to discuss ferrying to the Continent later on,' Susan said. 'Hope so, anyway.'

'Where did you get that from?' Mandy asked suspiciously. 'Honestly, I've never met such a place for rumours! Do you know an ATC cadet told me quite solemnly that old Frizzy had gone for a Burton in his first Lib. at Aston Down, and while I was waiting at Odiham just now who should step out of a Mossie but the Frizz in person – incidentally in a furious temper because he had been posted up at Lossiemouth.'

Susan laughed.

'Well, something always does seem to happen to Frizz. I can quite understand rumour trying to bump him off. Actually my news came from PK today, so it's red-hot. Jerry told me. He said their CO had gone down to White Waltham for the same conference.'

Suddenly Mandy sat up, her head on one side, listening.

'That's the phone. Wonder if it's Michael? I think I'll go and see; no one seems to be answering it.'

A few moments later Susan heard her rushing upstairs again.

'Quite wrong!' she announced, her eyes bright with excitement. 'It was Alison ringing from Ops – more work for us, Sue. Two Pl Spits.'

'No fooling?' Susan was disbelieving although she was already on her feet. 'If this is a leg-pull, Mandy, I'll push you in that oily river!'

'No, honestly. It's a squadron job – Colerne to Hawkinge – Nines. And Alison says we must get weaving or we shan't make it by on the way down to fetch us and Anna is waiting last landing. A car is with the Fairchild. I gather that 41 Group are flapping like mad!'

Shirts and socks, shoes and panties were scattered all over the room, for both had partially changed, but within ten minutes they were in the big ATA Humber, speeding towards the airfield.

'What a stroke of luck we are in!' said Mandy, gazing up at the June sky. 'And what an evening for a Spit!'

Susan made no comment. As they approached the main gate the driver slipped into third gear and sounded the horn. Immediately the policeman on guard recognized them, and opening the gate let the car pass.

In the Operations Room the ferry chits were waiting for them, their parachutes were already stowed in the Fairchild, which was ticking over outside, and within half an hour from the time the telephone rang at the Yacht Club Susan saw the host of ships in Southampton.

She looked at her watch. Ten minutes to eight! It was going to be a near thing and she had no wish to land a Spitfire in the dark; besides, she remembered, Hawkinge is a saucer-shaped airfield and none too large for mistakes. She turned to Mandy who was sitting in the back sorting her maps.

'What's the course?' she asked. Mandy told her, and then, peering out of the window at the ground, announced: 'No drift at all. Isn't it amazing after such a day?'

What a difference, Susan thought, from the old days at Barton when one had measured each course with such care, and meticulously ruled a line on a map along which to fly. Now, although she always had her maps folded correctly and at hand in case of need, it was usually only in bad weather that she referred to them. England, especially the southern half of it, was as familiar to her as the human body to a surgeon, and sometimes she thought that ferry pilots must eventually acquire some of the instincts of the homing pigeon.

There was a sign-post for her now in the shape of every wood and hill, a landmark in even the flattest and most monotonous stretches of the country, and each town and village had its own particular message for her. It was only under snow that the land became strange and faintly hostile, and then Susan felt that the furrows of each ploughed field were frowning at her, each factory chimney a pointing, black, disapproving finger.

Now the whole countryside seemed warm and friendly; the slanting rays of the sun burnished the meandering waters of the Test; they gleamed in the small panes of cottage windows and gave even the barren acres of Salisbury Plain a certain radiance.

Soon the Wiltshire Downs dropped to starboard, and by eight-thirty the Fairchild touched down on the east-west runway at Colerne.

Quickly Anna taxied round to the hut belonging to 39 MU. She asked Susan to signal her in and out with Flying Control, and by the time Mandy and Susan had collected their log books they heard the little taxicraft overhead and homeward bound.

Two of the ground crew came up to carry the girls' parachutes over to the Spitfires, which were dispersed some way from the hut. Mandy had already donned her helmet. She turned to Susan and said, 'If I'm up first I'll wait in the circuit for you. Might as well fly together.'

'OK,' answered Susan, and she delved into her overnight bag for her gauntlets. 'Plus four and twenty-four, or we shan't make it!'

'Right! See you at Hawkinge.' Mandy went off in one direction, while Susan was led round a blister hangar to where her machine was parked, and, busy polishing her goggles, she did not notice, until she was within a few yards and a voice called out to her, that an RAF officer was sitting in the cockpit.

'Hullo! I've been waiting for you, and amusing myself giving your Spittie a final check for luck. Don't you remember me?' Susan looked up, puzzled for a moment. He was capless, and suddenly she remembered. There was no forgetting that hair!

'Why – of course! Blackie!' It was the red-haired pilot with whom she had danced at Mark's party at Newmarket. 'But how did you know I was coming?'

'Oh, chased you round a few Ferry Pools, until someone in your Ops Room told me.' He climbed out of the cockpit as he spoke, and standing beside Susan he dropped his voice. 'It's a bit of news…' but he broke off as he saw the anxiety in the questioning look of her eyes, and her lips framing the one word 'Mark?'

'No. No. It's not Ropey,' he continued hurriedly. 'It's his navigator though. Just got back. Thought you'd like to know.'

'Oh, Blackie, how kind of you! Did Blacker Hay ask you to contact me?'

'No…' The weather-beaten face flushed a little under its tan. 'Sort of thought you'd like to know. Luck, your coming here tonight.'

In the distance Susan heard a Merlin roar into life and knew that in a few minutes Mandy would be taxiing out.

'I wish I could stop, Blackie, but Hawkinge is flapping for these two Nines for Ops early tomorrow. Quick! Tell me what you know.'

'Precious little,' answered Blackie. 'This navigator chap seems to have sneaked his way half across Europe, Free France, North Africa and finally Italy. God only knows how he did it. One of our chaps 'phoned me about something else and just happened to mention it.'

'Thank you – thank you more than much, Blackie. You're a brick.' She turned to climb into the cockpit. 'And thanks for checking the Spittie.'

He followed her and stood on the wing root, bending over to help her strap herself in. Just as he was about to step down he paused a second and said haltingly, 'You see – they can come back after a deuce of a time – even when no one's heard anything.'

Susan shot him a grateful glance. 'Goodbye, Blackie, and thanks again,' and immediately she slid to the perspex hood. She was disturbed. Too deeply disturbed for this moment when she must apply all her concentration on her job. She would have liked to question further, but there was no time.

It was with a definite effort that she started up and forced herself through the cockpit check. As she signalled to the mechanic to remove the chocks she half-turned to look at Blackie. He stood with his hands deep in his pockets, and with the wind from her slipstream ruffling his very red hair and making it stand on end; but out of the corner of her eye she saw the coolant temperature gauge already reading eighty-five, so that automatically she released the brake and gently opened the throttle.

Blackie gave her Mr Churchill's 'Victory' sign, but when she had taxied away he did not move. He just stood and, oblivious of the curious glances of the mechanic, waited until he heard the Spitfire take off from the far end of the airfield. Then he lifted his head and watched it climb swiftly to join the other Spitfire in the circuit. He watched until both were out of sight, and as he strode away he sighed to himself, and under his breath said: 'Not for you, old man. She's Ropey's popsie.'

Beyond thinking how kind, Susan gave Blackie no further thought, but he had given her new hope. If two escaped, why not three? Six months! It was a long time. Most people said that there wasn't much hope after six months. Then other things claimed her attention. A new Spitfire! And if all signs were true it was destined for D-day. So, this evening, her prayer for a blessing on the new machine was more intense. 'A new Spitfire! God bless, more than ever, all who fly in her.' For a second she hesitated before she added, 'And me, too, please.' Then deliberately she put Mark out of her mind.

It was a perfect evening, almost freakish after the blustering day, but very soon Susan saw that the shadows on the grass were already longer than the height of the trees, and by the time the Wiltshire Downs, the Hampshire woodlands and the Surrey hills had rolled beneath her wings she had climbed another thousand feet so that she could still see the sun, which by now must be quite invisible from the ground.

Mandy was flying a mile or more to starboard at a much lower level, for she always said that above two thousand feet she felt lonely. But then everything about Mandy's flying was extremely feminine, if not unorthodox! Outstanding landmarks for her were ancient and lovely houses, or unusually shaped woods, whereas factory chimneys, wireless masts and railways remained for ever unnoticed, and she would remember the exact position of a beautiful garden in much the same way as she might take in the detail of another woman's hat.

On the other hand, although she too loved low flying, Susan sometimes chose to fly really high.

Then she would feel completely detached from her own personality. Temporarily all earthbound worries would be erased from her mind as if they had never been, and she would feel herself to be on the verge of a final understanding.

It was into such a mood that she fell this evening as the Weald of Kent spread out beneath her. Occasionally she glanced at the instrument panel as a perfectly trained automaton might, but the machine so sweetly that was so perfectly trimmed and the great engine running it required very little attention.

At five thousand feet she felt, not as John Cherry had once

remarked, 'Like God in a greenhouse', but as if she were one with the sky and the sunset – bodyless and timeless.

With a certain amount of surprise she looked down and realized that the hand on the stick belonged to her. Glancing at the petrol gauge she noticed that the figures were beginning to show luminously, and she knew that there was not much daylight left.

Some miles ahead Susan could just make out the dim line of the coast, and in a few minutes Folkestone showed up as a purple smudge.

The airfield lay on top of the line of hills behind the town, a grass field with sides sloping gently inwards to form a shallow basin.

She circled twice, for the boundaries were already slightly blurred, and she wanted to make certain of the best line of approach. A green light shone up at her from the control box and at the same moment she saw Mandy enter the circuit.

Susan throttled back. Wheels down – a few seconds and two green lights shone reassuringly on the panel before her to tell her they were locked. Flaps down. There was a high-pitched whine as she went into fine pitch – ninety miles an hour – and the hedge swept by a few feet below.

If during the last hour Susan had temporarily forgotten the war and given her thoughts to other things, now she was brought back to reality with a jolt. Normally at this time in the evening she had noticed that most of the personnel of a day Fighter Station were to be found either in the Mess, in the local cinema or in the bar-parlours of various pubs in the neighbourhood – anywhere, in fact, but on the airfield! There were the inevitable exceptions to this, such as the Control Officer, Duty Crew and Crash Crew, but never the hive of humanity Susan now found humming with activity at Hawkinge.

It was at once apparent that this was no ordinary evening! To start with, the enthusiasm with which the last-minute arrival of the two Spitfires and their pilots were greeted held unusual significance, as also did the sight of the ground crews still feverishly servicing the several squadrons of Spitfires and Typhoons dispersed round the field, refuelling, re-arming and giving the hundred and one other finishing touches to an extensive toilet!

If this struck Susan and Mandy as abnormal, the atmosphere they found in the Mess struck them even more forcibly.

'Maybe it's the house itself,' Susan thought, as she and Mandy ate the excellent cold supper which had been especially laid on for them in the dining-room of the huge mansion which had long since been taken over as an RAF Headquarters and Officers' Mess. This dining-room, for instance, was certainly unusual! Never before had Susan seen lapis lazuli walls in an Officers' Mess, or for that matter in a private house, nor could she remember having been in a room with bronze doors.

'Obviously something brewing!' Mandy remarked as they finished their meal. 'It's the big day tomorrow for a cert!'

In the ante-room they found the same undercurrent of excitement as on the airfield, and by the time they went to bed there was little doubt left in either of their minds as to what, as Mandy put it, 'was brewing'.

By midnight surmise became certainty, for a continual stream of heavy bombers swarmed across the coast droning relentlessly on towards France, and when Susan finally fell asleep it was with the rumble of distant explosions in her ears.

The roar which wakened her early next morning had a more familiar note – the thunder of engines being warmed up, Merlins and Sabres – she could hear the difference distinctly. It was still quite dark, although the darkness now had the changing quality which heralded the dawn. For a moment the room was unfamiliar and Susan had to concentrate to remember where she was. Then it all came back to her; she was in the WAAF Officers' cottage in the grounds of the Hawkinge Mess – she and Mandy had arrived in Spits – Nines – and today – *today must be D-day*! She dozed off again.

Although it was not long after eight o'clock when she and Mandy walked down through the garden with its loggias and terraces to the Mess for breakfast, they found the dining-room deserted, except for an elderly-looking Education Officer and a Flight Lieutenant Dental Officer, but within a few minutes they, too, gulped down the last of their coffee and, nodding to the girls, left the room.

'I feel rather out of things today,' sighed Mandy. 'Rather useless, too!'

'Don't forget the Spits we brought last night were probably over France before you were awake,' Susan reminded her. 'You can hardly call *them* useless!'

Impatiently, Mandy pushed back her chair.

'Anyway, I hope they fetch us early: I want to see some of the fun. I wonder how they got on up the Hamble river?'

But Mandy was in for a little more frustration that morning, for on arriving in the Control Room she was told that Hamble had already rung through to say that they were too busy to fetch Third Officers Sandyman and Dundas, and would they come back by train as soon as possible.

'Hell!' Mandy exploded. 'That'll take all day!' Her voice trailed unexpectedly away as her eyes caught an entry in the Visitors' Book, an arrival even later than their own the previous evening. 'Group Captain Banks. Oxford PP 474, from Portsmouth.'

'Is this Oxford still here?' she asked the harassed Control Officer without lifting her eyes from the book.

'Yes,' he answered abstractedly, at the same time focusing a pair of binoculars on a Typhoon which was circling the airfield. 'He's going back to Portsmouth this morning and that Tiffy's in trouble!'

The Typhoon certainly was in trouble, and a few seconds later made a very rough belly-landing, finishing right up in the centre of the airfield. The ambulance and crash-wagon drew up to it almost before it came to a shuddering standstill, and orders were flying about to have the mobile crane remove it immediately as other aircraft were expected every moment, most likely with a minimum of fuel on board and in no condition to wait around in the circuit.

So enthralled had Susan been watching this scene that she had not noticed a thickset, grey-haired Group Captain come into the Control Room, nor had she seen Mandy approach him, so that when Mandy nudged her arm and said quietly, 'All OK. I've cadged a lift to Portsmouth; we are taking off now before the rest of the squadron get back,' she was somewhat surprised.

'Mandy! How wizard! Talk about quick work!' she gasped. 'Anyway, thank goodness!'

The grey-haired Group Captain proved to be rather a silent soul. He wore a trio of medals, chief among them that of the Distinguished Flying Cross, the sight of which intrigued Susan. She would have liked to know the details of its award, but he wasn't the kind of person one could ask, even had there been the opportunity.

As they entered the aircraft, and perhaps as an introduction to conversation, Mandy remarked on the extraordinary change in the weather.

'Temporary only, I fear,' he answered. 'Met predict a return of the high winds this evening.' He paused a moment before he added: 'I'm afraid you two are going to be disappointed. I think we had better keep behind the downs or we might get in the way of the boys going out.'

'Oh, damn!' said Mandy. 'I did want a squint at the Channel.'

There was no answer. The Group Captain was already in the pilot's seat and concentrating on his take-off, but Mandy continued after a moment.

'There's something wizard in this weather, Sue.'

'Yes – what?' answered Susan, whose eyes were busy taking in the details of the Airspeed Oxford, the first she had seen, and watching the ground fall away below as they became airborne.

'You weren't in England at the time of Dunkirk,' Mandy continued. 'That was wizard, too. A dead calm sea for all the little boats, and now, look at this! The sea must be as rough as rough, and last evening was lovely. I almost feel that God had done it on purpose to fox the enemy!'

Susan laughed softly, before she answered, 'Perhaps the wind's being tempered to the shorn lamb!'

'Damn it all – we're a lion – not a lamb!' said Mandy. 'If they did tweak our tail before Dunkirk!'

The Group Captain did not speak again, but Susan watched him, and understood exactly on what he was concentrating. The cloud base, she reckoned, must be about fifteen hundred feet and it was broken; at any moment something might fly out of one or another of those cloud banks. They reached Portsmouth with only a momentary glimpse of Chichester Harbour, and although both craned their necks there was little to see.

An hour later, having 'phoned and got transport, they were back at Hamble, and the first thing Susan saw on the ante-room notice-board was an order for herself, Mandy, Nina and Sandra to report to White Waltham on June 14th, 1944, before sixteen hundred hours, for the next Class Three Conversion Course. 'That's a good omen!' was her thought. The Class Three trainer *was* the Airspeed Oxford, and this morning had given her her introduction.

Ferrying chits were awaiting them both, and it was last landing time before Susan and Mandy met again. Both were anxious to hear the news, because the one topic of conversation everywhere they had been that day was 'D-day at last!'.

Susan was ready and waiting when Mandy appeared, and greeted her with 'Hurry up! Everyone's going down for a drink at the Yacht Club, and I'm dying to see what happened on the river.'

'Me too,' said Mandy, as she disappeared into the cloakroom, and a few moments later she rejoined Susan, and together they hurried down the long roadway to the guard gate, swinging along through the village until they almost broke into a run as they rounded the last corner leading to the hard, so anxious were they to reach their destination.

The moment the river was in full view both stopped abruptly. The river was half empty.

SEVEN

SUSAN FOUND HERSELF regretting that her posting to White Waltham had come quite so soon, and felt, for the first time since she had started her training, a little torn between two desires. She badly wanted to get on to her Class Three Course, but somehow, at this moment, she just as badly wanted to stay at Hamble. With the invasion of Europe an actual fact she felt more in the swim of things on the coast than she would either at White Waltham or Thame. However, she had no choice, and so found herself back at White Waltham on the appointed day, battling for her old billet at Cookham. She was lucky. She and Mandy were housed just as before, and they immediately began to make plans for doing the same things, only Mandy would have to do them without Michael. She still did not know bis whereabouts.

Those first days between D-day and their departure from Hamble bad been full of interest. Work had been heavy and the weather still rough, but the very air seemed full of news. Whispers of the artificial anchorages and harbours, the 'Gooseberries' and the 'Mulberries', made in secret and towed across the Channel, despite the roughest June for twenty years, were getting about; and, day by day, the fact that the beaches were held, and that several of the girl pilots at Hamble had husbands, brothers and fiancés in one or other of the Services, made the longing for news intense. The first question on anyone's lips after any flight was 'Any fresh news?' and the radio was turned on at every possible opportunity.

To leave an atmosphere of such excitement for one of intensive study was difficult; but Susan had another reason for regret. She had not met Diana Barnard. Diana had been *hors de combat* after a crash and had spent her convalescence in getting married. She was due back the very day Susan and Mandy and their compeers left.

But White Waltham was also seething with excitement. The prevailing topic of conversation among the pilots concerned the possibility of ferrying, or delivering supplies, to the armies on the Continent. Everyone hoped for this and everyone felt expectant, and more than ever Susan, despite what Grannie had said, wished she had the seniority that extra year would have given her. She might have been a first officer by now – but – well – there were other things – Mark, Mandy and Michael – so once again Susan pushed what she called 'silly' thoughts out of her mind.

The next day she heard another rumour, and later realized that the morning of June 13th, 1944, was stamped indelibly on her memory, not so much because it marked her promotion to flying twin-engine machines, but because it was on that day that she first heard vague whispers of the mysterious, pilotless 'plane, later to be known as the 'doodle-bug', or 'buzz-bomb'.

During the spring of 1944 the German bombing attacks on London had been very spasmodic and Susan had not worried unduly about her mother and Jane. People were living safely enough in London.

Susan first heard the rumour in the snack bar. As she collected her coffee she heard a flight captain ask, 'Is it, d'you think, old Hitler's long-vaunted secret weapon at last?' and the answer, 'Press flapping again, I expect. Just something new for the Fleet Street boys to blurb about,' and during the few moments at her disposal she searched her newspaper, but, except for the fact that a German aircraft had been brought down on the outskirts of London, found nothing. For the next few days the general attitude seemed casual. No one, at least of those that Susan happened to meet, took the rumour very seriously. But she had few opportunities for chatting, because with the eleven other pupils on the Class Three Course she spent the entire day, with the exception of one hour for lunch, in the big bare lecture-rooms far across on the east side of the airfield. From nine in the morning until six in the evening she struggled to assimilate the theory of twin-engine technique, of safety speeds and flying on one engine, of fuel and emergency hydraulic systems, all very new and strange, while all the time there was the distracting sound of aircraft flying overhead. Two days of very real concentrated effort. But it was soon over and on the second evening they were released exactly on time.

It took quite a while to catch the field car which ran round the perimeter to the main buildings, and after happily congratulating each other on the fact that the worst was over and that on the morrow they would be flying again, both Mandy and Susan fell silent, a silence that lasted until they reached the locker-room.

Mandy flung her books impatiently into her locker and, straightening up, said, 'Thank goodness that's over! Come on, Sue. Let's go to town and blow it off our chests!'

Susan, whose mind was still on the lecture, and was at that moment making the books in her locker into a neat pile, looked up with surprise.

'But what about the telephone?' she asked.

'No good hanging about,' answered Mandy despondently. 'I'm sure Mike's in France. Your mama won't mind being taken on the hop, will she? There's no time to 'phone.'

'You ought to know the answer to that by now,' Susan replied. 'Come on. The station bus goes in three minutes. If we catch the six thirty-eight we'll have time for a bath before we take Mother out for dinner.'

'M-mm,' said Mandy. 'Seven-forty-five when we get there? She'll be having dinner.' 'We'll chance it,' said Susan.

They ran and caught the bus, and when, some five minutes later, the tannoy blared, 'Telephone call for Third Officer Mrs Dundas', they were half-way down Cherry Garden Lane.

Mandy was right. It was precisely 7.45 when they ran up the steps leading to the flat. Susan slipped her key into the lock, threw open the door, stopped short and ejaculated:

'Mummy!'

And Mandy, pressing close behind, ejaculated, 'Michael! and a second later was in her husband's arms.

Mrs Ledgard, in a black lace semi-evening dress and her fur cloak, was dressed ready to go out, and apparently she and Michael were just setting forth on some expedition.

Susan, turning her back on Michael and Mandy, smiled at her mother with surprise.

'Mummy, you look lovely! Turn round – let me see your hair.'

Mrs Ledgard's hair was beautifully dressed, and although Susan ignored it, she was perfectly aware of her mother's skilful make-up. It was years since she had seen her mother look like this – not since – could it have been – of course – not since her wedding-day. But her thoughts were interrupted by Michael's voice.

'Trust one's wife to come butting in when one's taking the other woman out!'

Mandy, with a lapel of Michael's coat in either hand, was making energetic if futile efforts at shaking him. 'You villain!' she said. 'Why didn't you telephone?'

'Pretty obvious reason, I should think!' laughed Michael. He waved a hand towards Mrs Ledgard. 'Look at us! All dressed up, off to enjoy ourselves at the Mirabelle – and then you come along and spoil it all!'

'Don't believe a word he says, Mandy!' Mrs Ledgard broke in. 'He's been 'phoning half over England to find you – on my telephone. He's taking me out to dinner to pay off the bill.'

She began taking off her gloves. 'Now, of course, you must go.'

'No "of course" about it,' answered Michael. 'We'll all go. I'm not going to be done out of going out with my best girl because my wife's turned up!' He put an arm affectionately round Mrs Ledgard's shoulders as he spoke and Susan looked on incredulously. In her experience it was only Claude to whom her mother responded in this way. Apparently Mrs Ledgard was quite eager for the outing, for she waved them away, saying: 'Hurry up, my dears. We don't want to be too late. All these places close at half-past ten.'

'As if we didn't know that!' laughed Susan, as she and Mandy ran to the bathroom. 'Mummie's gone all gay tonight.'

The Mirabelle was full to overflowing, and it was gay. The lights and the glitter of plate and glass and the music made it look and feel very festive. Michael was in his most extravagant mood and Mandy in her gayest. The champagne on which he insisted was, he declared, totally inadequate to balance the bill he had run up in his telephonic pursuit of his errant wife, to which Mandy retorted that he could not put that old story over her. 'It's just the usual sop to Cerberus provided by errant husbands!'

Susan looked across the table at Mandy and thought how young she looked. The respite to her anxiety about Michael, the thrill of the unexpected meeting, had added brilliance to her eyes and flushed her cheeks a deeper rose. There was no doubt of her happiness.

Susan also saw a boyish-looking naval officer at the next table deliberately eye both their wedding-rings, and she could see him wondering which of them was Michael's wife as plainly as if he had asked the question.

An hour passed swiftly. Their conversation amounted to very little; it was merely light-hearted jokes and merry banter, to which Ledgard added her quota. Once or twice Susan looked at her mother in amazement.

It was Mandy who first heard the buzz-buzz of the flying bomb above the music and the laughter, and with her glass poised half-way to her lips she exclaimed:

'Listen! What's that?'

As she spoke the band finished playing 'Where and When', and as of some sort of de-synchronized engine suddenly the curious sound could be heard overhead. An almost perceptible lull fell on the room. For a split second spoons, forks and glasses poised 'twixt table and lip even as Mandy's, and for that split second time stood still. Then, immediately, a wave of chatter broke bravely on the shore of suspense. China and silver clicked and clattered; everyone assumed the air of vacant unconcern, and the band broke into a rollicking dance tune – but Susan still listened.

She heard the buzz-buzz suddenly stop as if the engine had cut out, and at the same moment she heard her mother calmly answer Mandy.

'It's just another of these new bombs. It's amazing how used one gets to things nowadays.'

'Have there been many?' Susan heard Mandy's question, but no one answered, because at that moment came the sound of the explosion, and not so very far away. She felt the slight tremor of the walls around her, and then heard the young naval officer's voice, as he said, 'Baker Street, or Regent's Park way, I should think,' and he seemed to be speaking to Michael. Then Susan's mind registered one fact. The naval officer and Michael had looked directly at each other, and their eyes had held each other's during that fraction of a pause. She looked round the room. Uniforms were everywhere. Were they all as braced? All as ready? She shivered. Supposing that bomb hadn't got quite so far – and *supposing*—? It would have been the Café de Paris over again! She switched her thoughts, and once again listened to the banter between Michael and Mandy.

They lingered, and when closing time came were almost the last to leave. It was not yet dark and the street was full of people vainly demanding taxis. Michael turned to Mrs Ledgard.

'How are you shod? Shall we walk to the tube?'

'Of course. I came prepared,' and before Susan realized it Mandy had slipped her arm through Mrs Ledgard's and said: 'Come along. We'll lead the way,' and a moment later she herself was walking side by side with Michael.

For a few yards, until they were clear of the crowd before the restaurant door, they walked in silence. Then Susan found hers: if saying suddenly, as she had once said to John Pitts, 'What have you done to my mother?'

Michael looked down on her with surprise.

'Done? Nothing. Why?'

'She's quite different. She's so gay. So much more – getatable.'

But Michael was not listening; he was thinking, and after a moment he took her arm and said gravely: 'Sue, I want to talk to you about your mother. Can't you get her away from London?'

'Why?' asked Susan, a little startled. 'She wouldn't go.'

'Did you realize what that buzz-buzz was?'

'One of the new bombs, wasn't it?'

'Hitler's long-vaunted secret weapon,' said Michael. 'We've been expecting it for months. For the last year we have heavily bombed their experimental stations and launching-stations in Northern France, and from what I gather there is worse to follow. Haven't you read your newspaper this week?'

'Hardly,' she replied. 'This week's been hectic. So much to cram in that one just hasn't had time. But, Michael, Mother would never consent to leave London, and after all she's been here a year now.'

'I know, but these new things worry me. When's your leave due?'

'The end of the month.'

'Have you made any plans?'

'No. I thought I'd stay half the time with Mother and half the time with Grannie, and they've asked me to Falcombe for a weekend.'

'No,' said Michael. 'Get right away, and persuade your mother to go with you.'

'But I don't quite know where. We used to go to Strathpeffer, but that's a forbidden area now.'

'What about Cornwall, or Wales?' suggested Michael. 'As far away from London as you can get.'

'But I don't think I could induce her to come, Michael. You know I've no influence over Mother. I've never understood her.'

Michael laughed. 'And she says she's never understood you!' He gripped Susan's arm little tighter. 'Now listen to me. I got to know your mother pretty well during that three months I lived at the flat, and she told me quite a bit about herself. She'd all brothers and no sister, and she just doesn't understand women in the way she understands men.'

'I'm sure you're right, Michael, because men understand her. Father adored her, and he was twenty years older, and Claude could twiddle her round his little finger.'

'She thinks the world of you really – I didn't know about your baby until she told me. And I *know* that if you say you badly want her for company – and you can't get anyone else – she'll be as pleased as punch. Then perhaps while you're away you could persuade her not to come back to London for a bit.' He was silent a moment before he added: 'I love your mother, Sue, and I want her out of London. If she were my mother, and I had any authority, I'd insist.'

By this time they had reached the tube station and Mandy and Mrs Ledgard had turned round to wait for them.

It was almost midnight before Susan went to her mother's room. She had had what she called a brainwave. She tapped gently on her mother's door.

'May I come in, Mummie?'

Mrs Ledgard was already in bed.

'Of course, dear. Did you want anything?'

'No, only to ask you something. D'you mind if I sit on your bed?' Susan seated herself on the end of the bed and pulled the eiderdown over her legs. She was dressed only in her pyjamas. 'Mummie, have you ever been to Anglesey?'

'No, dear. Why?'

'My leave is due in a fortnight's time, and I'm longing for a real holiday, and I want to get right away. I can't go to Scotland because the places I want to go to are in the forbidden area, and I've flown over every speck of England, and I want you to come with me.'

'But, darling, I really can't leave London just now. Our mobile canteens are busier than ever, and we are very short of drivers.'

'But, mummie' – and Susan deliberately made her voice sound pathetic – 'I've *no one* to go with.'

Mrs Ledgard began to raise objections.

'But where should we stay? All the hotels would be full! In Wales particularly, because a great many people have gone off there in the last few days a good spot to be safe from buzz-bombs.'

Susan's expression registered innocent surprise as she continued, 'D'you remember that little VAD with the sweeping eyelashes who I brought to tea one afternoon, and who amused you so?'

'Yes,' said Mrs Ledgard. 'The girl who was so enthusiastic about her home.'

'Well, they have a property in Wales, and their big house is being used as a hospital, but they've turned their smaller one into a guest house. We could go there. I think there would be fishing, and in any case there's the sea, and you always loved swimming, and all I want is to sunbathe and swim and let the days slip by. It would be rather fun, wouldn't it, Mummie?'

Mrs Ledgard looked at Susan and relented. She must be lonely, and she had been very courageous, and she must miss Mandy now that she was married. It went very much against the grain to leave her canteen at this moment – all those nice boys – but after all it was only for a fortnight and it was something to be wanted by one's daughter.

Her voice was tender as she answered:

'All right, darling. I'll see what I can do.'

Susan was too wise to say anything but: 'Thank you, Mummie. It will be lovely,' and after kissing her mother goodnight, she retreated to her own room with the feeling of a triumphant diplomat.

Next morning, after their usual scramble to catch the train, a scramble necessitated by the fact that they had to leave the flat at 7.30, Mandy suddenly awoke from her torpor in the corner of the railway carriage with a subdued chuckle. Susan opened an eye to enquire the cause.

'What now?'

'Leave,' said Mandy.

'Got it settled?' enquired Susan.

'Rather! We're going to Ireland. Mike's grandmother wants a sight of the bride.' 'Didn't know he had one. Where does she live?'

'Somewhere in southern Ireland.'

'But you can't get there,' said Susan. 'There are all kinds of restrictions.'

'Masses,' said Mandy. 'They don't mean a thing once you're in the country. John Robertson told me. He and Bob Latter have just come back. You ferry a machine for the ATA Pool at Belfast, change out of uniform there and proceed down to Dublin on the train.'

'Sounds a piece of cake,' said Susan. 'But what about getting back?'

'Just as easy,' announced Mandy, with a yawn. 'You ferry a machine or cadge a lift. It seems Number Eight Ferry Pool takes Stirlings directly over to East Anglia almost every day, and anyway their taxis are always at Hawarden. I'm wangling my trip, and Mike's wangling his, and we meet in Belfast.'

'Marvellous! said Susan. 'Here we are at Maidenhead.'

As Susan walked into the Headquarters Building that morning she heard her name reverberating the length of 'the long, high passages, and a voice ordering her to report to the Instructors' Room immediately, and she smiled to herself as she thought how agitated she would have been a few months ago. Nowadays, in Mandy's language, she did not bat an eyelid, nor did she hurry herself unduly, but stopped on the way to leave her cap and overnight bag in her locker.

When she reported she found her new instructor was to be First Officer Howland, a small dark man with exceptionally blue eyes, whom Susan rightly guessed was very little older than herself. She noticed that he wore a DFC ribbon on his ATA uniform, and discovered later that he had started the war in the RAF, in a Blenheim Squadron, but that a chest wound had barred him from further operational flying. He had joined ATA rather than accept a ground job in the RAF.

As soon as she took off on her first hour dual with him, Susan realized that she had a first-class instructor; and her heart warmed to him when he pointed out a small, white cottage, down by the river at Cookham, and, beaming with pride, told her: 'That's where I live. My wife is down there. She's expecting our first baby next week. P'raps I should say 'babies', because the doctor has threatened us with twins!'

Daily, after this, Susan enquired for Mrs Howland, with the result that she found herself on a much more human footing with her Class Three instructor than she had ever been with his predecessors, and she grew very friendly during the crucial twenty-four hours when she shared his anxieties. In fact, she felt quite annoyed with Mandy when Mandy implied that this friendliness was not entirely due to the babies, but to the fact that, in an Oxford, pupil and instructor sit side by side and can talk with ease to each other. One's instructor was a person and not a voice down a rubbertube. 'And I must say,' continued Mandy, 'that ever since Michael told me of one type he had in his EFTS, I like to know what my instructor is up to. That one lit a cigarette in the rear cockpit, and blew smoke down the speaking tube, so that it came out in the pupil's ears – just to see if he was the panicky sort!'

Susan laughed. 'What a wizard idea out on the spot. I'm sure I should have baled on the spot.'

In spite of this friendly footing Susan found First Officer Howland quite as strict and exacting a master as the rest. After two hours and forty-five minutes' dual he sent her off solo, but not before he was completely satisfied that she was able to cope with any emergency which might arise, such as failure of one engine, swinging on take-off, or failure of the normal system of lowering the undercarriage and flaps.

This first solo in a twin-engined aircraft Susan found far less nerve-racking than expected. Perhaps it was because speed was so much less than in the single-engined fighters which she had been ferrying lately, or perhaps it was that confidence in her own ability had naturally increased with the hours in her log book, but whichever it was she now felt completely at ease and in control; there was no question of the Oxford flying Susan – Susan flew the Oxford.

In all Susan only had just over nine hours' dual and ten hours' solo during this Class Three course, but the School was full and instructors busy. June had given place to July and Susan was impatient to get away on her leave, for the V1s were falling on London with greater frequency, both by day and night. Susan began to hear stories of the death of friends, or even from people to whom she talked relations. The disaster to the Guard's Chapel had its repercussions among the personnel of ATA. One bomb had fallen in the woods close to Falcombe. Susan began to worry on her mother's account.

At last, in the early morning of the third of July, Susan passed her final Check Flight with the Chief Flight Instructor of the White Waltham School, and by the afternoon she was on her way to London.

At an unpleasantly early hour, the following morning found Susan and her mother at Euston Station awaiting the Holyhead express, en route for Anglesey. Such had been their anxiety as to whether or not they would be able to find a taxi that, after securing two corner seats, they now found themselves with half an hour to spare. For the first time Susan relaxed. All their plans were complete. Now there was nothing to think about for the next fortnight – except perhaps that formidable task, suggested by Michael, of persuading her mother to stay away from London.

'Why – there is one of those nice boys who come to the canteen!'

Mrs Ledgard was looking out of the window as two or three young-looking soldiers passed. 'He's called Charlie.'

'Charlie! A thought flashed through Susan's mind. 'C' for 'Charlie'! Suppose – just suppose that news came through of Mark – it wasn't likely of course after so long – but – if it did – if he turned up like the navigator that Blackie had told her about – they would not have her Anglesey address. And Mark would be so disappointed. She looked at her watch. There was still time to send a wire to 'Blacker' Hay. She rose hurriedly.

'Mother,' said Susan. 'I shan't be long, but I've just remembered something. I must send a telegram.'

Left alone in the carriage her mother watched Susan's retreating form hurrying down the platform. 'Now, I wonder,' mused Mrs Ledgard. 'It's something very important to her. I could see that. If only it were someone – someone who means a great deal to her – I wish it were!'

EIGHT

THE TRAIN JOURNEY as far as Chester seemed tedious to Susan. There was no restaurant car, and nothing to break the monotony but the very infrequent stops. The rushing off to send the telegram had disturbed her. She felt Mark to be uppermost in her mind. She tried to read, but soon her book dropped to her lap and for the first time in months she gave herself up wholly to her thoughts. She felt poised between two phases of her life, sensing the past and the future as two entirely separate epochs. What she had had was finished; her present work was, as it were, the corridor between that and the future, which, when she allowed herself to think of it, brought Mark's face vividly back to memory. He couldn't be dead – there was none of that feeling of remoteness which she felt when she thought about Frank. Frank was remote, inaccessible and yet ever present, whilst Mark, against all reasoning, was vivid. Surely she would see him again – how she longed to – her one remaining link with the happiest time of her life. Involuntarily a slight sigh escaped her. It was more a catching of her breath. And suddenly she was aware that her mother, whom she had thought to be asleep, was looking at her with a new expression in her eyes, which, as Susan looked up, changed to an indulgent smile. Susan smiled back.

There were other people in the carriage so talking was impossible, but Susan understood. Without being intrusive her mother was wondering of what, or whom, she was thinking, and Susan was instantly aware that her own future was a very deep concern of her mother's.

The train ran into Chester. Susan said 'Chester!' One or two people crowded to leave the train, and a few more pressed to get in, and, as soon as she could, Susan scanned the platform and remarked:

'Never know who one will see in Chester.'

'Do you come here often?' asked Mrs Ledgard.

'Fairly. It's quite a good place to be stuck out.' The train gave a jolt and rumbled on, and Susan sank back in her seat and added: 'Now we shall soon see the sea!'

'That will be nice,' answered Mrs Ledgard. 'I haven't seen the sea since that summer of 'thirty-eight.'

'Oh, Mummie, haven't you? I hadn't thought of it. How different—' and Susan wanted to add, '—and I see it practically every day, and have seen it from every coast,' but the restraint of those innumerable posters cautioning silence was too strong.

It was hot in the crowded railway carriage. No one talked. The arm-rests between the seats had been pushed up and each seat held an extra two people. Passengers standing in the corridor excluded any possibilities of fresh air, and a Rear Admiral snored off and on in his corner. Paper rustled as sandwiches were eaten, and Susan, although not hungry, was glad of the iced drinks in Mrs Ledgard's thermos flasks. She felt very grateful to providence, as the train turned westwards to run along the north coast of Wales, that quite unwittingly they had chosen seats on the right side of the carriage, and wondered afresh if the Admiral was the VIP for whom the train was, today, stopping at Bangor, which was lucky for them.

The coast of Wales looked lovely that sunny afternoon and, wherever visible, the beaches were crowded.

'Such a safe place to bring children!' murmured Mrs Ledgard, and Susan fell to wondering once again if there was any hope of persuading her mother to stay.

Bangor at last! 'What hours!' thought Susan, and the contrast of arriving and feeling a mere speck on a large airfield after a flight of incredible swiftness to this – crowds of hot, jostling people – noise and confusion was forced home as, with a heavy suitcase in either hand weighing her down, she was borne along to the exit.

But once there her troubles were over. A voice called 'Sandy!' and she found herself literally pounced upon by the little VAD member, whom she had known at Hazeley, and who was absolutely clinging on to an ancient porter, while outside waited their host in a four-seater tourer.

A little later, as they approached the suspension bridge over the Menai Straits, and the car was slowed down while both father and daughter pointed out the training ship the *Conway* lying below, Susan felt her holiday had really begun; but even while she listened to her host's description of the ancient ship's adventurous voyage after the bombing of Liverpool, her eyes were on the many white-painted sea-planes lying at anchorage, and directly the story was finished she interrogated:

'But the sea-planes? I didn't know they had a base here.'

'Oh yes,' replied their host. 'They fly straight in here from America,' and the girl's voice from behind asked eagerly: 'Have you flown one yet, Sandy?'

'Heavens, no!' Susan replied gaily. 'But I know a few state secrets as to where they're parked on the other side of England.'

'How far have we to go?' Mrs Ledgard asked the question.

'About fifteen miles,' came the answer, and the car moved forward once again.

The drive through the languid, summer afternoon, leading as it did by highways and byways apparently undisturbed for a century, the picturesque cottages, the absence of any traffic, except for an occasional farm cart lumbering slowly along, all made for an air of indefinable peace. The war seemed very far away, until, as they entered the gateway of the drive, two figures in hospital blue waved as they passed on towards the mansion, while the car took the lower drive which led to the old farmhouse, built on and added to several times, now the family home. 'Even here one doesn't really get away from it,' thought Susan, but the thought was quickly dispelled as the car stopped and out of the open door, across a tiny courtyard and up two or three old stone steps, came a woman whom Susan afterwards described as having 'the face of an angel', their hostess, to bid them welcome. The friendliness, and the friendly atmosphere of a comfortable and beloved home; time-honoured furnishings and tea ready; nothing was lacking. There was no feeling of being a paying guest, but that of a very welcome and loved friend.

* * *

The fortnight passed only too swiftly. Petrol was scarce, so the opportunities of getting about the island were very rare, but they did do a certain amount of sightseeing in the immediate neighbourhood. Most of the days, however, when warm and sunny, were spent on the beach of Red Wharf Bay. Susan and her mother would lie side by side, sun-bathing and watching the clouds and the occasional 'planes pass overhead. The bag of newspapers and knitting was often neglected for hours, but the luncheon or tea basket always returned empty. Of their fellow guests they saw little, they being indefatigable walkers. Only a few weeks later Susan was to look back on this fortnight with thankfulness in her heart, and gratitude to Michael who had suggested it. During these few peaceful days she grew closer to her mother than she had during the nineteen years of her early life – although she had totally failed in her efforts to persuade her to stay away from London. At first she put it down to a change in her mother, but it slowly dawned on her that her own outlook and sympathies had broadened. It amazed her, too, to find, when they swam together, that her mother was by far the better swimmer, and when she commented on this all her mother said was, 'Well – I had three elder brothers.'

'I never knew I had *three* uncles,' said Susan.

'Yes, but two wars—'

Susan was silent.

One lovely hot day, almost the last of their holiday, soon after breakfast, only having awaited the arrival of the newspapers and the completion of the luncheon basket, they set off for the beach as usual. It was midday before, resting after their swim, Susan, lying at full length on her tummy in the sun, stretched out a lazy arm and dragged the bag with the newspapers towards her.

'Are you ready for your lunch?' asked Mrs Ledgard.

'Not yet, d'you think? Let's just see what the rest of the world is doing.' She spread out *The Times* as she spoke, and glanced at the births, marriages and deaths announcements.

Mrs Ledgard, busy with the luncheon basket, made some remark about the food, and, getting no answer from Susan, looked round.

Susan was lying in the same position, but the newspaper was cast aside and her head was buried in her arms. Her whole attitude was one of deep despondency. Mrs Ledgard glanced at the paper and back again at Susan, but forbore to speak. After a few minutes Susan rose to her feet, and, without turning her face to her mother, said, 'I'll be back in a few minutes.'

Mrs Ledgard watched her as she walked down to the edge of the sea and stood there, apparently gazing out over the water. Quickly, while Susan's back was turned, she leaned forward and picked up the newspaper. It was obvious – something in that paper. Only she herself knew how she looked down that column every morning, and how quickly her eye picked out 'His Majesty's aircraft' – yes – here it was – 'Slade' – a woman pilot. A Flight Captain. Mrs Ledgard's eye left the paper and looked at her daughter. Someone's daughter...

'You must be hungry, Mummie!' Susan remarked as she returned. 'Shall we have lunch?'

'Yes, dear. I have it all ready.'

Susan sat down and picked up a chicken pattie and began to eat abstractedly. Mrs Ledgard did not speak, and there was silence between them until Susan said, 'Oh, Mummie, I do wish you'd stay here, or go and live with Grannie until the war's over!'

For answer Mrs Ledgard picked up the newspaper.

'Look, my child!' she said gravely, and she put her finger upon the announcement. 'I always see these. There have been quite a number since you joined ATA, and the number given on that little balance sheet of the Benevolent Fund, which you showed me, gave the figures of the number of fatalities up-to-date as well over a hundred. I realize the dangers you face. That might have been Sandyman instead of Slade, and I should be feeling as desolate as that mother must feel, but I do not try to deter you from what you think your duty, so, darling, please do not try to deter me.'

The last day of Susan's holiday was the first of Mandy's, and Mandy's plans had so far fructified. Weather permitting she was to fly from White Waltham to Hawarden the next day, and from there on her journey was, she said, in the lap of the gods. So for one night she was in London, and Susan and her mother found her at the flat awaiting them when they returned.

'How did you manage it?' asked Susan, when she heard this.

'Honesty being the best policy, I asked for it, and got it.'

But Susan's first question when they were alone was, 'What happened to Susie?'

Mandy shrugged her shoulders. 'Mystery. A Wellington, on take-off – nobody knows why. There's been a gloom over everything ever since.'

'When's the funeral?' asked Susan.

'The day you go back. By the way, I've loaned Wendy your skirt.'

'Are you going to Falcombe at all?' asked Susan.

'Yes. These damned buzz-bombs are dropping all round the place. I'm going when I come back. I'm in a perfect funk lest the house gets hit and somebody's killed. The Babe is furious because he's being sent to Mike's mother for the holidays, and Mummie's as vague as ever; you'd think it was only a door slamming when a bomb falls.'

Susan smiled.

Back at Ramble Susan found herself to be the only one of the ferry pilots billeted at the Yacht Club, but not in the double room. Instead she was given a corner one, on the first floor, just above the bar. Susan liked it at once, chiefly because it had two windows. One looked south across the hard, and right down the Hamble river. She could see the Isle of Wight in the distance. The other looked east, across the river, to the green meadowlands, woods and trees beyond.

Susan had returned in the late afternoon, via Maidenhead and White Waltham, so had arrived on the airfield and bad seen several of her fellow pilots, heard all the news and, after arranging to meet again, after flying hours, for a drink in the bar at the Yacht Club, betook herself to her billet.

It was a somewhat subdued little party that met an hour or so later. The OC, Alison from Ops, Diana, Mary, Joy – one after another they drifted in and collected their drinks and joined the others crowded about the window. Conversation flagged. Mary's husband was missing in Normandy, and, although no one mentioned it, the funeral, to which an Anson had carried a full load, was perhaps uppermost in all their minds. Wendy arrived with Susan's skirt thrown over her arm, and returned it with thanks, remarking: 'Hope you didn't mind, Sue. Mine was filthy with oil and Mandy suggested it.'

'Of course not,' answered Susan.

Despite one, two, sometimes even three, drinks, conversation continued to flag and merely consisted of casual remarks concerning the weather and ferrying and the fighting in France, and a little later, one by one, they all drifted away and Susan was left to eat a solitary dinner. She missed Mandy and felt a little flat. After dinner she sat awhile on the sea-wall listening to the sounds from the 'Bugle' bar, and noting the progress of the work on the hard, where, for weeks past, American troops, with their bulldozers and cranes, had been busy enlarging it, for the convenience of repairs to the little ships. A lot had been done, and when at last Susan drifted bedwards she felt she had been away a long time.

In the hall-way she met the Admiral, who told her they had had some very disturbed nights, and expressed a hope for a peaceful one. More for the sake of conversation than anything else Susan asked:

'Did you have to get up? Where is your shelter?'

'Oh no—' answered the Admiral. 'There's nowhere to go. We haven't a shelter – nobody gets up.'

When she returned to her room she stood awhile at her open window before she closed her curtains. The hard was in shadow under the hill, but the long rays of the setting sun lingered on the roof-tops. The evening fell quietly after one of the loveliest days of the summer. But Susan found herself much overlooked by people still wandering about on the hard, so soon closed the curtains and prepared for bed.

Sleep was long in coming; unaccustomed sounds, which bad not disturbed her in the other room, kept her awake for some time, but, with complete darkness, silence fell and Susan slept.

It might have been about two in the morning when she was startled awake. She had been deeply asleep, and although her bed was vibrating she did not for a moment realize what had awakened her. Then it seemed as if every gun on the south coast of England was blazing away over her head. The noise was indescribable. Both her windows were wide open, and the curtains drawn back, and Susan sat bolt upright in bed and gazed, first out of one and then out of the other, while the guns fired again.

'Must be something about,' she thought, and wondered what she had best do, and for a moment glanced down at the narrow space between her bed and the wall. Would it be funking to lie down there and pull mattress and bedclothes on top of her? But before the question was really formulated in her mind a distant noise-a sort of chug-chug – caught her ear. She recognized it at once. A doodle-bug! She leaned forward in her bed, the better to out of the south window. The noise came from that direction. A moment later a black mass loomed up against the faint starlight of the moonless sky. Apparently it had come over the Island, and was coming straight up the river. Without a thought for her personal danger Susan watched, fascinated. It never occurred to her that if it deviated a matter of fifty yards or so it would hit the Club. She could not take her eyes from it. Chug-chug – it came steadily on, and she continued to watch until, still keeping to the centre of the river, it passed straight before her eyes on a level with the window. A black mass of which the extreme end was a wicked, lurid, orange glow. In an instant she was out of bed with her head out of the window, watching that receding glow, until the guns, blazing again, sent her swiftly back to bed with the thought, 'If they get it bits will fly in every direction.' She pulled the bedclothes well up, and a pillow over her head, and waited, while the guns continued to fire. After a while silence fell, and once again Susan slept.

The flying bombs were a worry. There was no getting away from that fact and during those days, when so many deliveries of replacements, Spitfires, Tempests, Typhoons and others, had to be made to the forward airfields of the south coast, in Hampshire, Sussex and Kent, Susan, being observant, noticed that her CO sometimes looked harassed. She was perfectly aware that no one better understood the strain of this added menace, and when, at the end of a long day, when perhaps twenty or thirty machines had been safely delivered, it was good to meet a welcoming smile, and know that the cloud had lifted, even temporarily.

They were very busy days, with long intervals of waiting for weather. On these occasions the rest-room became a mixture of writing and work-room, gymnasium and bridge parlour, with perhaps one or two bridge fours intent on their game. It was all so good-natured and good-humoured; the babel of voices intermixed with various sounds emanating from the radio which, someone told Susan, they had won in a raffle for ten shillings.

It was during these weeks that Susan got to know some of her fellow pilots very well indeed. She visited them and dined with them in their cottages and billets, and, in return, had one or two little parties for them in the Yacht Club. They had all had, it seemed, interesting and various careers. 'Chili' – nicknamed for her country – who had learnt her English while working as a ground engineer, and was now a first officer. 'Jackie' from South Africa, with her mop of dark hair, who had made her first parachute jump when little more than a child, who did her exercises and somersaults on the rest-room floor and could sleep peacefully on the rest-room sofa despite the noise. Then Diana was back again, and sat for hours darning small-size socks; she explained, 'You see, when they shrink and are too small for the boyfriend, I take them over.'

Susan was soon discovered to be a good bridge player, and she was also very handy with pair of scissors. Occasionally the medley of old letters, ink-pots, newspapers and magazines were pushed aside while a cutting-out session took place on the one large table. Or it might be on the floor. The rest-room was home to them all during those hours of waiting. Then, when the weather cleared and the tannoy blared and summoned 'All pilots to report to Operations Room for their chits', almost immediately the room would be empty and the scurry of departure would begin. Cards, jig-saw puzzles, sewing, half-darned socks and half-written letters lay just as their owners had dropped them. It was surprising how quickly it was done. Each individual was so independent. One's chit, received at a hatch-way or seized from the ante-room table, was quickly scanned and noted; one's helmet and maps collected from one's locker; the 'Met' visited for the day's weather in the district where one would fly; handling notes collected from the library – if the type of machine to be flown happened to be a new one; a visit to Maps and Signals, to get the latest information on balloon barrages and so forth, one's chocolate ration, overnight bag and parachute. It all became a matter of routine and minutes, while taxi pilots warmed up the Anson or Fairchild ready to carry the pilots to their destinations.

Susan loved it all, and lived every minute.

There were moments and happenings both alarming and amusing. Mary returned one evening with a story of an engine that had suddenly died on her, 'and just when I thought all was over,' she said, 'I looked ahead and there was the airfield coming up to meet me!', and all was well. And on another very hot evening, when the day's flying was really over, an urgent call from the adjoining RAF airfield necessitated a Spitfire being delivered to Eastleigh. Everyone had gone, but Jackie, dressed in a gay little sleeveless blouse and the briefest of shorts, had been playing tennis and for some reason had drifted back to the rest-room, and so into the Spitfire climbed Jackie. Later, when Susan heard the story, she wondered what impression Jackie, looking about sixteen at the most and so sketchily clad, made when climbing out! They were happy days. It was seldom Susan thought of either past, present or future. She had no leave during the two weeks Mandy was away, but a late delivery one evening took her to Odiham, and she spent the night at Hazeley with her grandmother.

Grannie she found just as usual and very glad to see her, and as Susan had not seen her since D-day, there was much to tell of Anglesey and her holiday, and her work.

Susan tried to avoid the subject of flying bombs, but that, she found, was the one thing Grannie really wanted to talk about, and in the end she had to give way.

'Yes, Grannie, you're right. They have been coming over in thousands; everything that can be done to stop them is being done. There are four lines of defence. Fighters out on the Channel, guns behind and fighters again, and then balloons. About forty per cent are being brought down, and Michael told me how the RAF have been bombing the launching sights ever since December. But the bombs are difficult targets...' Susan's voice trailed away – Grannie must not be alarmed – so she deftly changed the subject and talked of Port Lympne, the wonderful house at Hawkinge where she had stayed, and enlarged on the fact of it being the headquarters of an RAF Typhoon Squadron.

Next morning found Susan back at Hamble and Mandy returned from her holiday, having left Michael in London to return to Falcombe for the last day or two of his leave.

A few mornings later, when a mist hung over Southampton Water and the ferry pilots of Hamble were waiting for it to lift, Susan, one of a bridge four, was sitting contemplating her hand. She held a good one and was intently anticipating her partner's bid and awaiting her own moment.

With a fraction of hesitation Mary, sitting opposite, said:

'Four hearts.'

Susan flashed a smile and after an opponent 'No bid', said: 'Four spades.' With luck she and her partner would work this up to a little slam!

But Susan was destined not to play her hand, for at that moment the voice of Alison in Ops was heard over the loud-speaker.

'Will Third Officer Sandyman please report to Operations' – and Susan was not the only one of the girls who noticed the slight difference of Alison's tone. She spoke more gently than she was wont to do.

Susan looked up and called to Mandy, who was lounging in a chair dose by. 'Come on, Lazybones – carry on. It's too good to miss,' and as soon as she had passed over her hand to Mandy she walked out of the room.

Oddly they all turned to watch her, but Jackie was the only one who spoke. Sitting bolt upright in the middle of her exercises on the floor, she said, half under her breath, 'That's something personal.' But Mandy, endeavouring to make the best of Susan's hand, did not hear. Some minutes elapsed and Susan did not return, but even while seemingly absorbed in their various pursuits, the girls were listening. Finally, when the door opened and Alison came in, the hitherto unspoken question rose to several tongues.

'What's up, Alison?'

'Has anything happened?'

'Yes,' said Alison gravely, and she looked at Mandy as she spoke.

'Susan's mother – killed last night – a flying bomb.' Mandy, white to the lips, the cards scattered in every direction, was on her feet in a second.

'Mike! Was Michael there?'

'Oh, my dear…' said Alison, 'I'm sorry. No! *No*. It was he who 'phoned. He's just through again and is waiting to speak to you.'

Mandy fled, while sympathetic comments echoed round the room.

'Poor Susan!'

'Where is she? Is she going home?'

'She's gone. The weather is clearing. Anna's flying her to White Waltham.' Jackie, still sitting bolt upright, looked up and said: 'Now I don't believe she has one single relation in the world left but that old grandmother!'

NINE

MICHAEL MET SUSAN at Paddington. She had clung to her CO's hand at parting and had tried to thank her, and she had vaguely remembered that Anna had said, 'Group Captain Dundas will be there to meet you,' but at that moment words registered little, and questions as to how it had been arranged, or how it was that she had got so speedily to London, never entered her head.

Outwardly calm, but inwardly overwhelmed and stunned by this new blow of fate, both in the Fairchild and in the train, she had sat staring out of the window. For a moment or two, when as gently as possible the news had been broken to her, she had felt nothing, only a numbness; but, very soon, the pain of deep sorrow had gripped her – she knew it so well – it was physical as well as mental – it cut so deeply – and her mind questioned, 'Why – what have I done? Why can no one be left for me?' – and as the train drew into Paddington she struggled for self-control.

But one glimpse of Michael and his grave, sorrow-stricken face, and Susan literally fell into his arms, and her first words were a cry of pain.

'Michael! It can't be true! It can't.'

Michael kissed her as a brother and answered gravely, 'I've been there—' and twenty minutes later, after having passed the police cordon, Susan's mind realized there could be no further question. Where her mother's flat had been was now the very centre of a vast heap of closely-packed rubble. But her heart still hoped.

Jane's battered body had been found, but of Mrs Ledgard there was no trace. Half a dozen men were working and searching.

Susan turned to Michael. 'Michael! Are they *sure*? Sure Mother was in the flat?' and the agony of her voice tore his heart. He took her hand in his. 'Couldn't she be at Hazeley?'

'Sue, darling, I saw her – yesterday. She was here, and not going away. I didn't leave her till after six—' and he tried to lead Susan away. 'We can't do anything, Sue. Let me take you to Hazeley. They will let us know if anything is found.'

And it was only then it occurred to Susan it was strange that

Michael should have been at hand.

'But – can you? I thought—'

'I'm not due at Marham until tomorrow. Come. Let's go.'

But for a while Susan could not tear herself away. She stood silently watching the workmen, until Michael forcibly gripped her arm and said gently: 'Sue, what about your lawyer and the bank? There are formalities. Shouldn't we—?' He broke off with the question.

'I suppose there are.' And, at last, Susan allowed herself to be led away and her thoughts went to her grandmother.

'Does Grannie know yet?'

'Yes – the police let her know,' answered Michael, 'at the same time as they phoned me.'

''Phoned *you*?' Susan's tone was a question.

'Yes,' answered Michael. 'She – your mother – arranged that.'

It was strange that anyone so frail and old as Grannie could be such a tower of strength. With Jason lying with his head on her feet, Susan sobbed her heart out with her head on the old lady's lap, and found comfort.

'I feel,' she sobbed, 'I have lost her just when I had found her.'

The old lady's sentences dropped one by one as her hand caressed Susan's head.

'Mother half expected it, darling. She wanted to follow your father. They loved each other very dearly. She left a message for you. She said I was to tell you that the war is only an interlude in your life. That she knows that you will be happy again. You are not to fret, but to remember she now has her soul's desire.'

'I know. I know,' sobbed Susan, 'but – but to take them all—!'

Almost a week passed before Susan returned to Hamble. She had done everything she could. Jane's funeral, interviews with bank manager and lawyer had taken up most of the time. Both gentlemen received her with sympathy, and with that deference which seems the prerogative of those blessed with this world's goods. She found she was, if not exactly wealthy, very well to do. Except for an annuity to Jane and a legacy to Rose, Grannie's maid, 'for being so good to Jason', Mrs Ledgard had left everything to 'my beloved daughter Susan'. That 'beloved' wrung Susan's heart as nothing else could. Now she was indeed desolate, and the settling of business affairs wearied her and made her feel even more desolate. Not that there was much business to which to attend. Everything was in such perfect order, and Susan sole executor. A few papers to sign; a few practical questions.

'Had she any wishes about King's Lane House?' was one of the first. 'Will you live there?'

Susan passed a weary hand over her brow. What had she thought about King's Lane? The question rose in her mind. With a pang she remembered she had dreaded the possibility of settling down and living there after the war. But had Mummie wanted to either? What had she said? 'Shadows and memories in every corner. One must break away before they over come one.' And, now, more memories. Settle down and grow old – alone – there? Slowly she shook her head while Mr Scatliffe wondered, and then she was still again, thinking about King's Lane. Her father had built it to be a happy home for his children. It was essentially a house for children. A family home. No use to her. She looked up and found Mr Scatliffe looking at her.

'No. I shall never live there again. Don't disturb the present tenants. They have it for duration. Then sell it, Mr Scatliffe. Sell it, and try to find someone who has children – we were – happy children – there.'

Mr Scatliffe nodded. 'I understand, but houses in the country are at a premium. It should fetch a good price.'

'That,' answered Susan, 'is a secondary consideration. Send me the particulars of possible purchasers and I will decide.'

'Very well,' said Mr Scatliffe. 'And now, what about the furniture? You will keep some?' His tone was gentle.

Again for some seconds Susan was silent. Then for another second or two she closed her eyes, as if she would shut out all these things, and again Mr Scatliffe waited. He was wise enough not to hurry her, and his sympathy was deeply stirred. She looked so young – and was so courageous – was striving, he knew, to hold on to a semblance of self-control – but he could not see what Susan saw. The pile of old newspapers – the packing-cases – the plate chest, and her mother so busy, packing for store the treasures of more than one lifetime. Almost she heard her voice, so practical and so sane.

'This Worcester dinner service! It was my grandmother's. You have her name. If it survives the war you can have it.'

Other items of information about glass and silver and pictures. Sentences intermixed in memory with the rustle of newspapers and fingers black with printer's ink. Sorting and packing. Getting the house ready for letting; and the renewed heartache as she thought of Frank and their own treasures – Felicity's cot blazing; and she heard her own voice, as if from a long distance, answering Mr Scatliffe as the voice of a stranger:

'All the most valuable things are in store. They can stay there until the war is over. The insurance value will do for probate, won't it?'

'Yes,' Mr Scatliffe nodded and answered. 'I have a copy of the list. And the cars? Mrs Sandyman, believe me, I am sorry to be so insistent – but—'

'Yes. Yes, I know. These things must be done.' And for the first time in this interview Mr Scatliffe knew Susan's tears were not very far from the surface, and again he waited while Susan was thinking.

'The Rover? That can go. It has no association for me, but the boys' car – the drophead MG – I don't think I could part with it...' She was almost talking to herself now, thinking of the summer when Jack had taught her to drive, and of the many picnics and swimming parties – the dashing down to Lee-on-Solent on hot summer days – the point-to-points and the dances in the winter, all the gaieties of beautiful pre-war England.

'Will you sell the Rover, please, Mr Scatliffe? The MG I am going to keep. I shall want it. I am trying to get a billet some distance from the airfield. We are allowed petrol to a ten-mile limit.'

'Very well,' said Mr Scatliffe once more, but he had not finished. He made a few notes, coughed quietly, and then spoke again. 'And now, Mrs Sandyman, we come to the most important thing of all.' He hesitated and leaned forward a little, and Susan's eyes looked into his wonderingly. She was thinking, 'Is there no end to it?'

'Your will.'

'Oh—' a long-drawn 'Oh—', and Susan rose to her feet. 'No – no, Mr Scatliffe, I can't – not today. I haven't thought, and – and I don't know what to do.'

'Well, another day, but remember delays are dangerous,' said Mr Scatliffe soothingly, and, at last, Susan escaped and decided to return to Hamble the very next day. She was weary and heartsick, and knew the best panacea was hard work, and, as she journeyed once more back to Hazeley and Grannie, she fervently hoped that the weather would improve. Clear, calm, sunny days all over Britain – that was what she wanted. So that work would go on until she was too tired to do anything but drop into bed. Then the thought of the possible new billet, which she had mentioned to Mr Scatliffe, intruded, and she wondered if Mandy had succeeded in getting it.

It was a cottage in the middle of Old Bursledon, about two miles further up the river than Hamble. It looked deserted, and she and Mandy had had an eye upon it for some weeks past. They had never seen anyone enter or leave it, and although, by peeping between the cracks of the drawn curtains, they could see it was furnished, it looked as if the occupant had been away for some time. It was very old and half-timbered, and stood right on the village street, from which it was completely secluded by a high, mellow, brick wall. On making enquiries, they had been told that until after the last war it had been an inn, and, in bygone times, a favourite haunt of the Solent smugglers. Also that there was an underground passage which ran from its cellar down to the river some quarter of a mile away, but now all that remained of its disreputable past was its name, the 'Dolphin', and the old wrought-iron frame which had once supported the heavy wooden inn sign.

From the barmaid at the 'Swan' they learned that shortly after the last war it had been bought by a wealthy yachtsman, who had converted it from an inn into a private house, installing main water, electric light and two bathrooms, and since 1940 it had been let to a naval officer and his wife. Susan and Mandy had started negotiations with the local agent, and both hoped that, in time, something would come of it.

But Susan's thoughts soon left the cottage. Mandy was on the spot, and if the opportunity of acquiring it arose, she would not miss it – and went to her journey on the morrow. The weather did not look too promising, but she decided, if it should be a fine morning, she would 'phone her CO. A taxi-craft, Anson or Fairchild, might be coming to Odiham. That would make for a very easy journey. If, on the other hand, it should be cloudy and wet, she would get the local garage to take her to Basingstoke. Neither was that difficult. Not like having to get to White Waltham. And so Susan made her plans, only to awaken next morning to clouds and rain.

She left early. The weather might clear and there might be deliveries that afternoon. She wanted above everything to get into the air. She wanted to feel untrammelled. But, in the hired car, as the rain beat on the windows and almost obliterated the countryside, it recalled to memory another wet day, and, suddenly, Susan remembered. Those two – Dorothy and David Verner – months ago now – but no news had come. It was a curious meeting. Could it be a sort of destiny? It would be strange indeed if she eventually heard how Frank had died because of that meeting with them. Then a singular thought drifted through Susan's mind. 'DV' – their initials! Two 'DVs'! The abbreviation of 'Deo volente – God willing! Susan half smiled. The thought came – like a message – from outside. But one day, when the war, both in Europe and the East, was over, she would go back to Singapore. She would find out, if it were possible, for herself. Perhaps go right back and see the plantation – but they had reached the station, and the car stopped and interrupted Susan's thoughts.

Mechanically she took her ticket, and her thoughts kept her standing absolutely still, staring into space, seeing nothing, until the arrival of the train. Of what she thought she could hardly have told, or what she imagined. But once in the train, sitting in a corner, fortunately vacated by a man who had got out, and still hot from his body, and in an atmosphere thick with tobacco smoke, the clickety-clack of the train's wheels beat a rhythm to her thoughts, just as they had done on that seemingly long-ago afternoon when she had arrived from Singapore.

She had felt utterly desolate then – but she had expected to see father, mother and brothers – but now – there was no one left, only Grannie, and Grannie was old – she wouldn't have Grannie for long. Even Mark – the link with happiness…

Too sad for tears, too heart-sick, Susan sat quietly in her corner, one elbow on an arm-rest and her chin cupped in her hand. The noise of the train, the disturbance when it stopped and people got in or out, affected her not at all. Her thoughts slipped along until, after a while, they became constructive. They were gone. *All* of them. She could do nothing for any of them now; but she could justify them. She was left, and she had her work. Important, useful work – thank God! Susan drew a deep breath. 'Only me—' she whispered the words to herself. 'Only me left to fight for them all.' That was what she had said to Grannie months ago, only the fight was harder now. While her lips still trembled, Susan's jaw took a firmer line and tragedy died out of her eyes, and in its place there dawned the light of determination. The enemy should not take everything. They would not break her. 'Only be thou strong and very courageous.' That had been Jack's motto ever since he had been a little boy. It would be hers henceforth.

But, if Susan had only known it, comfort and joy were both on their way to her that day.

Mark was back.

And on that self-same morning, while Susan was contemplating the past, present and future, so was Mark, and also in a train.

His first impulse had been to telegraph or telephone to Susan.

During the long months of his captivity she had seldom been out of his thoughts – but there were possibilities. She might, in some odd way, have heard about Frank. After all – he might not be dead – equally he might be; and she had never given him any encouragement – nothing but the natural friendship of old acquaintance. Never a word that could be construed to mean anything beyond that – and she might have married again – but that fear was dismissed almost as soon as it arose – he was not so afraid that she had married again than that she never would. In any case this idea was immediately squashed by his first conversation with his Wing Commander on his arrival, who, after hearing a few particulars, said, 'Now – before I listen to another word I have a promise to keep,' and Mark had looked at him interrogatively.

'Yes,' 'Blacker' continued, 'Mrs Sandyman. She has kept in touch all the time. I have to let her know.'

Mark put out a hand to stay him. 'Hold hard, sir. Then – she still is – Mrs Sandyman?'

'Blacker' nodded.

'Well, then,' said Mark, 'I think if you will leave it I will go and see her. Where is she?'

'Blacker' raised sympathetic eyebrows.

'Like that, is it, old chap? I had an inkling. She's at Hamble. Go in and win!' and he dived into his pocket and produced a notebook. 'Here you are – telephone number and all.'

'Thanks, sir, but I must go and see that chap's mother first.'

Mark's story was not spectacular. It was presumed by the enemy that the crew of that particular Stirling had baled out over Germany, or had perished with their 'plane. A few surreptitiously-placed fragments of burnt uniform, a badly scorched button or two and even a few bits of bone, also well burnt to disguise their bovine origin, produced by the gang of Dutchmen employed to clear, by forced labour, the mass of twisted metal for transport to Germany, had given colour to the illusion, and so stayed a search that otherwise might have been made.

Mark had waited till the last possible moment before he jumped, and had deemed himself lucky to have escaped with his life. He had landed in the darkness that comes just before dawn, when the moon had set, on the edge of a deep dyke between two fields, and had got thoroughly soaked and dirty while burying his parachute deep down in the mud. He was absolutely unharmed and seemed to have floated down unnoticed, but for safety he crouched down while he made his plans and took his bearings by the luminous dial of his pocket compass. He calculated that he was somewhere on the edge of the North East Polder, with the width of the Issel Meer between him and escape. Things could have been much worse, he decided, and wondered where the rest of his crew were. Anyway it was no good walking westward. He'd probably only encounter open fields and water that way. North or south? Probably the same. Better go east and hope to strike a friendly farmer.

So he had set out, trudging through mud and several times getting wet again as he came upon unseen dykes, too wide to jump; but fortune had favoured him. Just before daylight he had reached what he took to be a stackyard, and creeping about he eventually found a stack up which it was possible to half climb and half shin himself. He fell exhausted on the top. He couldn't have walked more than a couple of miles, but it had been very heavy going. He knew that the aircraft had fallen probably three or four miles to the north-west, and he had seen the lurid glow illuminating the sky behind him, but he had not dared to stand erect, and now, as daylight came and he looked from his vantage-point, he could still see smoke rising against the dawn. So that was that. Mark wriggled himself deeply among the hay, the only dry bit of him was his head, and after pressing Susan's scarf to his lips he fell into a sound sleep.

He must have slept some hours. He awakened, wondering, from a dream of Susan, and it took him a full minute to remember what had befallen him and to open his eyes. For a moment he stared up into a sky of cloudless, translucent blue, and then became aware of bodily discomfort. His clothes were sticking to him, hot, moist and smelling, And, meaning to examine their condition, his eyes left the sky, but never got as far as his ruined clothes. Instead they encountered other bits of blue, as blue as that sky into which he had gazed, and he blinked before he realized that they were a pair of eyes, and that a little Dutch boy, wearing a little round cap, was half sitting, half lying beside him. He might have been nine or ten years old. He did not speak, but raised his finger to his lips before he crept closer. Mark uttered a voiceless 'Hullo' and the boy smiled and whispered, 'Engleesh Airman – not move – sister come dark – speak Engleesh—'

Mark smiled and nodded understandingly. So the kid had some English, and he had fallen into the hands of friendly people. So far so good, and Mark had heard of the escape routes and how the people of Holland risked their lives over and over again to get stranded airmen safely back to England. The message was clear. The boy was going to bring his sister, who spoke English, after dark.

But the boy was doing something with Susan's scarf. He had gathered the loose end in his hand and was solemnly shaking his head. Mark was puzzled. What did he mean? He didn't want it, did he? He couldn't let him have Susan's scarf. After all it was only borrowed! But apparently that was not it. The little boy was now rolling it up. One end was still round Mark's neck, and when he rolled the end which he held as closely as possible he pushed it under Mark to join it, and stopped shaking his head. If it had not been for the warning signal cautioning silence Mark would have spoken. His knowledge of Dutch was not very good, but he had spoken it in his childhood. He had been born in Australia, but his father had held for some time a post in the Dutch East Indies, and Mark's earliest years had been spent there. Also he had, since joining the RAF, studied German, and this had brought his almost forgotten knowledge of Dutch back to memory. Perhaps it was as well, he reflected, to keep his rudimentary knowledge of both languages secret until he discovered exactly where he was, and with what people.

But the little boy had moved, and now he had something in his hands, a parcel, wrapped in a piece of white rag. Very shyly he pushed it towards Mark, who discovered it to be a large slice of bread and cheese, and suddenly Mark realized he was starving.

The little boy did not stay. On his stomach he wriggled to the edge of the stack and looked carefully this way and that before he slipped down out of sight. Mark rolled over to a fresh patch of hay, a little way from where he had been lying, and, munching his bread and cheese as slowly as possible, longed for a pint of beer.

The hours passed slowly. Mark dozed and wakened and shifted his position. Luckily it was not a cold day. The sunshine that early October afternoon was warm, and the south-westerly gale of yesterday had died down. What wind there was had veered to the south. Mark wriggled out of his tunic and spread it to dry. Also, by burrowing deeper into the hay, he managed to remove his flying-boots and his socks without sitting up, and get the worst of the wet out of them, and several times he wondered how the little boy had found him and reflected that by the way the child had moved, a sitting position had its dangers, and as he wrapped Susan's scarf affectionately about his neck he wondered anew at the little boy's action, and what his objection to it had been.

Darkness had fallen some time before a stealthy movement warned him that someone was coming, but it was not until he heard a soft breathing close at hand and a whisper that he knew that the little boy had returned and that a girl followed. She crept close to Mark's side, and lying with her lips close to his ear, whispered, 'English Airman?'

'Yes,' answered Mark, also whispering.

'We must get you to the house before the moon rises.' Her English was good. 'Are you hurt?'

'No. I'm quite all right.'

'Now don't speak. Just come. Give me your hand. There is one place we can slip down easily.'

'How did you find me?' whispered Mark.

'Hush! Don't talk. My brother saw the end of your scarf fluttering.'

Quietly, stealthily, they all three slipped to the ground, and, only deeper shadows against the darkness, moved round the stack. The girl held Mark's hand; the little boy went ahead. Once they waited, crouching down, while heavy footsteps passed close at hand, and the girl cupped her free hand over Mark's ear and whispered:

'Han is very clever to see in the dark.'

But Mark's eyes were also becoming accustomed to the blackness of the night, and, after they had walked for perhaps a quarter of an hour, he saw the outline of buildings looming ahead, but not a solitary gleam of light. Then, for some yards, the way continued by a wall, and the strong aroma of a farmyard was all about them, until, guided through a doorway, Mark became aware, from the warm smells and sounds of cattle, that they were in a cowshed, and the girl whispered, 'Step carefully. The floor is broken.' Mark kept behind her with a hand on her shoulder until she said, 'Stoop. There is a door,' and he passed through a low doorway. Then, in absolute silence, he felt the girl's fingers press his lips, and he stood and listened, as apparently did the boy and girl.

After a few minutes a voice, crooning softly an old hymn tune, came to his ears, and the girl gave a little laugh, and Mark sensed the relief in her voice as she said: 'It is my mother. She sings to let us know the way is clear.'

A few minutes later, Mark was sitting with food before him in the farmhouse kitchen. Fried eggs and potatoes – how good they tasted! – washed down with what he would have despised twenty-four hours ago – deep draughts of new milk. The mother listened while the boy and girl talked, but Mark noticed how quietly they spoke, never raising their voices, and he found to his joy that he could follow most of their conversation. The boy was explaining again to his sister how he had discovered Mark. The fluttering end of Susan's scarf! He had thought it to be a bird. The girl apparently had only arrived from some journey that evening.

He laid down his fork and, speaking slowly in Dutch, he said: 'I can speak little of your language. I lived in the Dutch East Indies when I was a little boy.' The old woman clasped her hands and said, 'God *zij dank*!' and the girl looked at Mark with shining eyes.

'Then you are heaven-sent!' she said, and she pointed up to where, at the end of the kitchen and reached by a short, steep ladder, ran a sort of wide gallery. Mark knew it later to be known as the '*op-kamer*'. A wide shelf that was half the size of a room, and used as a sort of storeroom. 'Up there we have another airman hidden,' she continued. 'A month. He is very ill. His back is broken. The doctor says he will die. He speaks only English. No French, no German, no Dutch. I do what I can, but I am only here sometimes – like tonight – secretly.' And while the older woman climbed the ladder with some hot milk, talking quickly in English, she explained the position.

She was very young. Mark thought her to be about eighteen, later he knew her to be twenty. She was working for the underground movement, posing as a trained nurse, and she was, in fact, partly trained. In the strict sense of the word she was not pretty, but there was a steadfastness of purpose about her which Mark found attractive, and she looked so wholesome. She breathed courage. She was wearing a sort of uniform coat, and her fair hair, which Mark could see must be very long, was twisted about her head in plait, as if to keep it out of the way, but little loosened tendrils curled, caressingly, about her forehead and neck, and her eyes, as blue as her brother's, looked frankly into Mark's, like a boy's, as she said:

'Please do not tell me your name, or anything about yourself. If one is caught – and – and punished, one cannot tell things one does not know. We will call you Piet. I leave you again before it is light. It will be perhaps two weeks before I can get here again. We will pass you along to friends. But it all takes time, and there is—' and she broke off and again pointed upwards. 'We must burn your uniform tonight and dress you as a farmer's help. It is the only way. Then will you try to get the local accent? My mother and my brother will help you. Speak with a stammer – I think that is what you call it? – it will give you time to think how you speak, and if you will look after the sick one...?' and a questioning look came into her eyes.

'Of course,' said Mark. 'That goes without saying.'

'Thank you.' The words came quietly, and Mark saw the anxious expression in her eyes give way to one of gratitude and trust, and the look she gave him warmed him as she continued: 'That will help me very much. He must be kept very quiet. The doctor thinks be may live another month, more or less. He is paralysed from his waist down, but his mind is clear. There is nothing to do but to keep him clean and feed him, and talk to him. I will get back as soon as I can with forged papers. We must give you an identity. Until then you must hide. We are not disturbed here very much. Now and again the Germans make an inspection. We never know when they will come, and we have good hiding-places. We keep them well supplied with eggs and cheese and milk, and Han' – she looked at the little boy and smiled – 'is absolutely to be trusted. He keeps watch. You will be our cousin. Now I don't think we should waste any time. There is a lot to do before I leave.'

* * *

And so began two long, cold months, while Mark tended his fellow pilot, helpless and incontinent, as one would a baby, and learned farm work, and studied his new identity, and Dutch, with Han and his mother. He longed for his freedom and sometimes at night, when he heard the bombers flying over from England and back again, he chafed at present conditions. But the plight of his patient was in itself enough to make him thankful he was not in a like predicament. Hidden between the walls of a cowshed and '*op-kamer*', in an airless cavity, but open it seemed to every odour of cattle, with the air weighed down with the over-powering smell of sickness, Mark, lying close in the restricted space, found it at first difficult to sleep. But one becomes accustomed, and they were warm, although their bedding chiefly consisted of hay.

A week before Christmas Smith died, leaving Mark with his name, number, station and home address all carefully committed to memory. They buried him secretly in the small orchard, and then Mark impatiently awaited the girl, Ans', next visit, hoping to get on his way towards freedom.

He had seen very little of Ans, and the old woman and the boy seldom spoke of her. He knew that she bicycled for miles and that her supposed nurse's bag was often extraordinarily heavy, but he never saw her either arrive or depart. The winter nights were long, and she obviously came, as she went, after dark. The one service Mark was able to render her was the overhauling of her bicycle while she slept. It gave him pleasure and she was grateful.

Two days after Christmas she arrived; she had everything arranged, and as a stammering, slouching farm labourer, wearing wooden sabots, Mark made his way from village to village, and from friend to friend, until one bitter February morning he found himself in Groningen, searching for a house wherein he would find a man, who, somehow, would get him to the coast.

Despite the fact that his journey had taken him to the east, and so much nearer Germany, Mark was happy that morning; he felt escape imminent. For a moment he forgot he was supposed to be over age for forced labour. He squared his shoulders and walked more quickly. It was his undoing. On that particular day the Germans were making a house-to-house search in the endeavour to find men for forced labour.

Mark realized his peril too late, and, even as a house door across the street opened and a woman beckoned to him frantically, three German soldiers rounded a corner and he was seized. The result was that the evening of the day he had hoped he might be safely at sea saw him in a train en route for Germany and forced labour.

Six long weary months. At first Mark was put in a factory, but a cultivated, clumsy, fumbling stupidity soon proved him useless. Punishments were unavailing and in the end, with half a dozen others, he was literally kicked out to farm work. This was what he wanted. The conditions in the factory and the living conditions had been loathsome. At farm work, he thought, his chances of escape would be better, and at least he would have fresh air.

Mark had learned his lesson. Never once during the six months did he give away his identity. While inwardly seething at his frustrations and pondering plans for his escape, to outward seeming he was a phlegmatic, half-dumb Dutchman.

From the farmer who employed him, and who, Mark suspected, was at heart no Nazi, he learned that good behaviour gave privileges. The Germans still wished to placate the Dutch, so at the end of six months a week's leave was granted, and Mark lived for that week and his chance to escape. The six months seemed unending; the days passed so slowly, but he grew attached to the cattle he tended – and slept with.

When the time came Mark was given his ticket back to Groningen where, after making perfectly sure he was unnoticed and no one watched his movements, he made his way to the house of which he had been in search when arrested. To his astonishment, Ans herself opened the door and quickly drew him inside, and her first question, when she had ascertained from whence he had come, was, 'Are you quite sure you have not been followed?'

He reassured her, and briefly gave her an outline of his capture; told of his week's leave and his intention of using it for the purpose of escape, and all the time he watched the play of the changing expressions on her face as she listened. But her first words when he spoke of escape startled him.

'No! No! You mustn't do *that*. You would be caught! This week you must loaf about the city, show your papers whenever you are asked for them – so that they know you are here – then, when it comes to the day you should return, you go to the station and report yourself as going back – your name will then be on the list as having gone back – but you – you slip away. Come back here – I will be here with new papers.' She broke off with a question, 'The farmer you worked with – what was he like?'

'I think,' answered Mark, 'disposed to be sympathetic.'

She nodded understandingly. 'That is all to the good. He may not report you for perhaps a week. Anyway probably not for several days. It has happened so before. In three or four days we will have you in the south – perhaps over the Belgian frontier. It is easier now. The Germans are – what you call it? – slack. They do not watch so much. I think they lose heart. I will go with you, but I must have a week to arrange and to plan.'

'But,' Mark protested, 'I can't have you running risks for me.' She smiled and shook her head. 'I have run risks for four years. I am still here!'

Exactly as Ans had planned so it happened, but this time the journey took them south and Mark rode a bicycle without tyres. The going was heavy; when possible they avoided the main roads. But Ans, it seemed, knew from experience every inch of the way, and they spent their first night at a village near Zwolle. Everywhere they were greeted with joy and were met with stories of the advance of the allies in France. Everyone was anticipating liberation, and what Ans had said was true – the vigilance of the enemy was diminishing. In Normandy he was in full retreat.

Ans said little about plans, and Mark vaguely thought he would be passed on through Belgium until perhaps, in the end, he reached France and the advancing troops. Neither would Ans answer questions. To all she shook her head and said, 'Wait. We'll see'; but Mark was much alarmed when, one night, after they had arrived very late at an isolated farm somewhere near the Belgian frontier, she disappeared and was gone for some hours. Mark could not sleep; he sat and waited, and when she returned, pale with exhaustion, forbore to question and insisted that she must sleep.

The next morning, to his astonishment, she told him they were not pushing on that day but were to remain hidden until dusk. But even at dusk she lingered, until some mysterious messenger appeared, and left again. Then quite calmly she said, 'Now we will go,' and Mark once more found himself on his bicycle, wondering if they were making for Belgium, but was very surprised when they reached a wayside cottage, and Ans said: 'Now we walk. We leave the bicycles here.'

She was so serious that Mark was puzzled. He asked softly: 'Where are we going? Can't you tell me?' and she whispered back, 'It is a possibility of escape. As soon as it is quite dark we start.'

'But where – how?' Mark persisted.

She came closer and dropping her voice said:

'It may be a great disappointment, but we expect an aeroplane.'

The words left Mark gaping, but Ans would say nothing more.

A little later they left the cottage and walked across country for perhaps two miles, and every now and again Mark thought he heard a rustling of footsteps, and feared they were being followed. It was so eerie in the darkness, but Ans walked steadily on. She must have nerves of steel, he thought. His own were on edge.

Eventually she stopped and crouched down under a hedge. Ahead, Mark thought, was an open field, but Ans' whisper, 'Come closer – listen!' distracted his attention. 'Sh – don't speak! Take this', and she pressed something into his hand. 'It is your identity disc. You will want it. The aeroplane is due to pick up someone very important, and we are getting you on board. It was a lucky chance. If all goes well you will be in England before morning.'

Mark pressed her hand, and under his breath whispered back: 'Ans – I haven't words, I shall never be able to thank you.'

'Don't try. Keep quiet.'

A little 'Sh – sh—' from behind warned them they were overheard and together they crouched down on the warm, dark earth. It had been a lovely day and the night was breathless. Mark could hear the thumping of his own heart. He scanned the faintly starlit sky. It was so silent, and yet he had the feeling that there were unseen people all about him. Then, from afar, came the sound of an aircraft, coming nearer every minute, and round the hedge it seemed as if fireflies fluttered. Tiny points of light, and now Mark's heart thumped wildly as he gazed upwards. A Lysander! Landing secretly! What a risk – what a pilot! And these gallant Dutch people – what a risk they took! It was difficult to see even the outline of the machine. The night was too dark and there was little time; everything happened so breathlessly and so quickly. Tall figures, two of them, rose from the ground close beside them – he had not known they were there – and began running as the machine touched down. Ans squeezed Mark's hand and was on her feet in a second. 'Come,' was all she said, and she ran with him. A minute later he found himself with his hands on the ladder attached to the fuselage and climbed up close on the heels of the man ahead of him, and a second later he had dropped inside and a voice asked, 'Have you anything to show your identity?'

A speck of light, carefully shaded, glowed for a moment on the identity disc in Mark's palm, and the voice said 'OK', and Mark thought of Ans. She had thought of everything and he had hardly had time to bid her goodbye.

Before Mark had recovered his breath the engine was being revved up and the 'Lizzy' took off. For the next two hours he sat in darkness, without one glimpse of the faces of his fellow passengers, although in the restricted space he sat so close to them. They did not speak, not even in a whisper, but Mark knew perfectly well who they must be. Secret agents. He knew, too, that Lysanders were used for this purpose. They could land in such a small space, and rise like a lift. But over and over again the sensation that he was dreaming overcame Mark. Nothing he had imagined in all his conjured plans of escape equalled this. Several times he took a deep breath and sniffed gently, just to make sure he was awake and there was no smell of the cowstalls. All had happened like magic. Ans must be well known to have achieved this. He could never be sufficiently grateful, and after the war he would certainly look her up.

* * *

Just before dawn, while it was yet dark, the 'plane touched down, and the same voice that had spoken before, and which Mark now knew to be one of his fellow passengers, bade him wait a minute, and he stood aside until the two muffled figures climbed out and he was joined by the pilot. The next minute he had followed him out, and as his feet touched the runway Mark uttered a fervent 'Thank God!' He heard the pilot give a sympathetic half-laugh.

'That how you feel? Don't wonder. Where have you been? How long?'

In a few words Mark told him, and asked, 'Where are we?'

'Blackbushe. Come along. We've got to get you identified.'

* * *

It all took time. Three days elapsed before Mark was free to go to Susan, and meanwhile he was overjoyed to find his squadron still at Newmarket, although their time was short. He would get a leave and then go 'on rest' with them.

His first duty had been to report to the Air Ministry, where he had to answer endless questions and tell his story more than once. This he did in borrowed kit. The shabby black trousers and the coat of very ancient and doubtful cut in which he had arrived, and which were the best that Ans could manage, he deemed hardly suitable, and all the time he dreaded lest someone, something, from somewhere, should contact and tell Susan.

So it happened that on that same morning, when Susan returned to Hamble, Mark journeyed by train from Lincoln to Newmarket.

He had been to see Smith's mother, and had almost dropped asleep as he talked to her. He hardly knew how it came about that he had stayed overnight and slept in Smith's own bed. But this morning he felt as fit as a fiddle and 'Blacker' Hay had promised the loan of a Proctor. So, if the gods were kind, if his luck held, he would see Susan that evening. 'Hope to God she is not stuck out somewhere,' was his one thought. He felt he could wait no longer. He must see her. The impulse that had made him stop his Wing Commander and refrain from getting in touch with her himself had been an inspiration. He would know by her expression – if only he could take her by surprise – whether or not in the future there would be hope for him. His one fear was not that Frank was alive – that would be happiness for Susan – but that Susan's loyalty would dedicate her to his memory for the rest of her life.

TEN

IT WAS GOOD to get back. Susan 'phoned from the station for transport and so arrived directly on the airfield. The weather had cleared, the sun shone, the air was soft and all the Hamble ferry pilots were out. Susan went straight to the Ops room to report her return. Anna, her CO, and Alison were there, and she was warmed and comforted by the more than friendliness of their greeting. No reference was made to the tragedy of her mother's death, only the 'Hullo!', and 'It's nice to see you back', told her far more than any words of commiseration could have done. It was as if she had come home; and when she asked, rather wistfully, 'Is there any job for me this afternoon?' and was told that they had saved the Anson for her to collect some of the others at Colerne and gave her a chit, she was overjoyed.

'Have your lunch first. There's plenty of time,' said Alison.

A clear afternoon with the sun gleaming on rain-drenched country. Once in the air, Susan thought of the many times she had flown this way, and of the many Spitfires she had delivered since D-day.

At Colerne she found Mary, Joy, Diana and two others. Mandy had not turned up. But there was a message to say her machine was US, and that she would probably have to wait for it until the morning. Susan was disappointed. She longed to see Mandy. It was disappointing; it meant a lonely evening and there was much to talk about.

Diana took over the Anson, and throughout the journey back Susan was silent. She sat beside Mary. Behind her, in the back of the machine, the others played bridge.

Another chit awaited her, this time to Odiham, and again she flew off, only in the Fairchild, to pick up Chili and Ida, a Dutch girl, whom she did not know very well, but liked. It was not late when she finally landed at Hamble, but the day's work was finished and most of the girls had gone. Reluctant to return too soon to the Yacht Club, and still hoping that by some fluke Mandy would arrive. Susan hung about for a little, tidying her locker and enquiring if there had been any letters.

'Yes,' she was told, 'there were three or four, but Mandy took them down to your billet,' and Susan found herself vaguely wondering who could have written. 'Lady Dalrymple,' she thought, 'but who else?' Perhaps Nurse Robinson, or Matron, or another of the girls from Hazeley. There was no one else. Her maiden name wasn't known in ATA, even if anyone had noticed the newspaper announcement, three or four? If only – if only it could be Mark – but it was too long: he must have crashed with the Stirling – or perhaps the 'DV's'? – as in her mind she called the Verners – equally impossible.

Susan was the last to leave the ante-room that evening, and she almost wished she had asked Diana, or Mary, to come in and keep her company. But neither of them would mind if after dinner she drifted across to their billets and spent the evening with them.

With her overnight bag in her hand Susan wandered out on to the broad pathway between the two grass plots. She looked across at the landing-ground. Everything seemed strangely deserted, and then she was aware of a Proctor coming in from the north, and automatically she glanced up at the wind sock. It hung so limply that it hardly seemed to matter which way one landed, but whoever was piloting the Proctor had very definite ideas. For a second she hoped it was Mandy, but soon saw that the Proctor had only one occupant.

The pilot made a wide sweep over the Hamble river, and came in over the buildings about twenty yards from where she was standing. She saw the pilot lean over and look down at her. 'Well,' she thought, 'I must look curious, standing here like a solitary fool who has never watched an aircraft land before!' and she started to walk across to the road that led to the main gateway.

But something made her stop. The pilot of the Proctor had waggled his wings. Susan's heart gave a leap. Perhaps it was Michael – and Mandy was stuck out! Anyway she would wait and make sure. She walked back a few steps to where she could look across the airfield and watched the Proctor touch down not much more than a hundred yards away and taxi towards her.

It stopped, and immediately the pilot clambered out. It was not Michael and Susan's heart sank. But something was familiar – it couldn't be – but no one else walked just *like* that! For a moment she stared and then, as in a dream, took a few hesitating steps – then – all doubts vanished – she dropped her overnight bag and ran the remaining few yards, and fell, half sobbing, half laughing, into Mark's arms.

'Mark! Oh, Mark!' she repeated.

Mark had hoped for little. He had not thought that Susan's self-control would give way and, unaware of the recent tragedy, he was overwhelmed. He took her into his arms, kissed her gently several times, and murmured, 'My darling…' over and over again.

Susan recovered first and drew back. 'Oh, Mark! – it's so wonderful – forgive me – I'm behaving like a fool. When did you get back? Can you stay?'

'Yes, I'm staying the night.' He kissed her again and released her. 'I'll just report myself in and get the machine parked for the night. Wait – I won't be a minute.'

He dashed off, and Susan's knees gave way. She flopped down just where she was and sat until Mark returned, leaning her head forward. Everything was swimming, and all she could do was to tell herself she mustn't faint.

There was no one about but a couple of 'erks' – otherwise ground crew – who stood by the Proctor, apparently awaiting Mark's orders, and he was gone some minutes. It gave her time to recover. 'What on earth,' she asked herself, 'must he think of me? Chucking myself at him like that?'

But she was faint. He was beside her before she knew and she heard his question, 'Where are you billeted, can I get a bed?' as from a distance, and he held out a hand to help her to her feet. With an effort she looked up, and he exclaimed: 'Hullo. What's up? Have I given you a shock?'

Susan took his hand and got slowly to her feet before she answered: 'No – you are perhaps only the culminating shock, and I lost my head just now.' The colour began to return to her cheeks and Mark smiled, and Susan noticed the network of new lines about his eyes as she had already noticed his hardened palms and the broken fingernails of the hand he had held out.

'I liked you losing your head. Please do it often. Only it mustn't make you faint. Now – come along. Is it far? Can you manage? Can we get dinner?'

He carried his own overnight bag, and now he picked up Susan's, and when she protested 'Don't. I'll carry mine,' he answered: 'Not a bit of it. You don't know the muscles I've developed, or the things I've carried,' and with the two bags in one hand and with the other holding Susan's hand and with her arm well tucked through his own, he smiled down at her.

'All right now? Lean on me,' and Susan nodded, although her legs felt as if they did not quite belong to her.

They started, but the fifteen minutes' walk to the hard took them at least twice that time. Anyone watching would have seen them, every now and again, stop, standstill and face each other while one or the other talked. But in the end they finally got there, and Mark secured a room at the 'Bugle', and, after dinner, they sat for hours on the little terrace overlooking the river and talked. Mark heard the full story of Susan's troubles, and she heard, almost twice over, the story of his escape.

'I'm still bewildered,' commented Mark, 'and I'd like to know how Ans got wind of that machine. I didn't see either of those two chaps – I mean not to recognize them again, the car waiting for them was on its way before I was allowed out, and I thought the chap who spoke to me first was the pilot, but he couldn't have left his seat. The take-off was too quick.'

'What was it?' asked Susan.

'A "Lizzy". The only possible in that space. I got on in the dark and I got off in the dark. If they'd blindfolded me I couldn't have seen less. I hope that Ans doesn't get into trouble. But I'm sure it's a thing that couldn't have happened a while back. Even in Groningen it was very different to six months ago. The Jerries *know* they're beaten.'

'I wish Japan was!' said Susan. 'I'm going back, Mark, when it's all over. I feel I must – must find out if I can – what happened.'

Mark's hand closed over hers. 'When the time comes, I'm going with you,' he said. He heard Susan catch her breath. 'But, Mark...' she began, and hesitated. 'But – because I lost my head it doesn't mean anything.'

Mark lifted her hand and kissed it before he answered: 'I know, darling. I'm not asking anything.'

It was almost midnight when Susan reached her room. What a day! – and she had forgotten all about her promise to telephone to Grannie! but... She walked to the window and stood gazing out. It was silent on the hard and a hot still night. In the distance thunder growled and for a moment Susan wondered if a storm would break before morning. It was almost morning now, but she made no attempt to go to bed. Instead she pulled a chair forward and sat down and for a long time stared into the darkness and thought of all that had happened. Strange that Frank's scarf should have played such an important part in the rescue of Mark. There must be, she felt sure, some purpose behind such a chain of coincidence. Mark had not returned the scarf. Whimsically he said, 'It no longer smells of you, but of another lady,' and for a second she wondered if he meant Ans – but he continued, 'Her perfume is over-strong. She is a cow! I'll get it cleaned,' and she had answered: 'Let me have it. I'll wash it, in the soft water at Grannie's.'

She thought of it now, and then of Mark's leave. He would get two weeks' leave right away. What a pity they hadn't secured the cottage but had they? Mandy might have left a note, and she ought to go to bed. Reluctantly Susan drew her curtains and left the window, and only thought of her letters as she switched on her bedside lamp.

The little pile lay on her dressing-table. Nothing from Mandy, but a handwriting that she recognized as Lady Dalrymple's lay on top. Susan turned it over and then stood absolutely staring at the next one, the letter that lay beneath Lady Dalrymple's. Her mother's handwriting! Mummie's last letter! 'Oh—' Without conscious volition, Susan crossed the room and sat down on her bed close to the light, and for a long moment looked at it, hardly daring, and yet eager to anticipate the moment of opening it. When she did so it was with very tender fingers. The date it bore was that of the evening of the night she was killed, and the words 'very late' were written beside the date.

Susan looked at the post-mark – the next day? – then Mummie must have gone out and posted it – or perhaps Jane did? It must have lain in the post-box all that terrible night – if they hadn't she would never have got it – it would have been under all that rubble. But even while she thought this she was gazing at the beginning. It was different. My darling – that was unusual – her mother's usual beginning had been prosaic – just *My dear Susan* – no more, no less. Susan read on.

There is no news and it's very late, but I feel like writing, if only to round off a very successful day. Michael was here this evening to collect some clothes, but did not stay, and for some reason I'm glad to be alone. The great success of the day is that I found some very good toilet soap at Harrod's and the new comb you need so badly. It's horn and it's strong, and I paid 5s. for it – of course it would have been about 1s. 11d. in the old days! I'll send it on to you tomorrow.

And also I had a wonderful morning with the canteen. We go to wherever the flying bombs have fallen, and more I feel how wonderful are the people of England.

For a moment Susan's hands holding the letter fell to her lap. But there was very little more. Only a few lines:

Since Jane went to bed I've been looking through the boys' snapshot albums – picturing you all as you were. My memory has more pictures. They all feel very near tonight.

Suddenly Susan stood upright, and with a few sweeping movements shed her clothes and stepped into her pyjamas. She had not bathed, she had not washed, she had not even brushed her teeth, but she did not care. The next second she was in bed. Her mother's letter was under her pillow, and her cheek – only she did not realize it – rested on the hand that Mark had kissed. Her one prayer was: 'Let me sleep. Let me sleep.'

ELEVEN

MARK BREAKFASTED WITH Susan next morning, and together they walked up to the airfield. Susan told him of her mother's letter. Somehow it had suddenly become quite natural to talk to Mark of anything and everything. Susan gave it no thought. It just was. And she told him how her mother had always scanned the newspapers, and finished, 'She was far too aware of possible danger to me...' and after a momentary pause added: 'Now it can't hurt her any more. She was spared last week's crash.'

'Bad one?' asked Mark.

'Yes – rather.' And in staccato sentences Susan explained. 'We lost a senior woman pilot. Her sister, too, who was with her, another pilot, is badly hurt. There's a baby – four months' old, and the father – also an ATA captain – was lost in the spring. One of the nurses, too. They were going to fetch a patient from the north. April and thick fog. I feel so sorry for the baby, orphaned so soon.'

'Penniless?' asked Mark. 'They usually are.'

'In this case, mercifully, no. But so many are. I keep thinking about that baby. If it were penniless I'd like to adopt it! Felicity was four months when I left Singapore.' She broke off with a sigh.

They said goodbye on the corner of the airfield, and Mark's last words were: 'I'll 'phone this evening. What's the best time? I'll know then about my leave. Couldn't you get a spot soon?'

Susan shook her head. 'Impossible. I've had it. Leave your call lateish, Mark. About ten.'

'All right. But I'm coming back to stay at the 'Bugle'! Don't mind, do you?'

'No – of course not! Now I must run.'

They parted, and Mark went to collect his machine while Susan turned to the ATA building.

To her amazement, the first person Susan encountered as she entered the ante-room was Mandy. A wind-blown, excited Mandy, who looked as if she had just landed.

'Mandy!' she exclaimed.

'Sue! Oh, I've been *dying* to see you!'

'But how did you get here – so early?'

'Just flew. They couldn't get that machine going yesterday, so they gave me another – for Bognor. I got in just before last flying time, and a pilot I met last night was flying to Eastleigh this morning. He dropped me a few minutes ago.'

'Trust you to organize it!' said Susan with a laugh. But Mandy was not listening, and her tongue ran on as excitedly as a child's on Christmas morning.

'I signed the lease the day before yesterday – at least Ann did for me – because I'm under age and you weren't there. Oh, Sue, why must you always be away when something exciting happens—!' she broke off and clapped her hand over her mouth. 'I'm a beast! Forgive me—'

'But you were the one who was away when the most exciting thing happened,' said Susan quietly. She understood Mandy, and fully realized how Mandy had pulled every possible string to get her this distraction on her return.

'Me!' said Mandy.

'Yes. Mark. Last night. He's back.'

'Mark! Oh, Sue! I'm so glad. Where's he been all this time?'

'Doing forced labour in Germany. Got caught, as a Dutchman.'

'Oh – tell me some more.'

'I'll tell you all about it this evening. Tell me about the cottage.'

The cottage at that moment, in conjunction with the thought of Mark's leave, was the more important subject to Susan.

'I only hope it's OK by you,' Mandy ran on. 'Three guineas a week and it's beautifully furnished, and another thing I hope you don't mind is that we have two large Persian cats with it, as the naval doctor who lives there has been posted to—' This stream of information was halted by a voice from the tannoy announcing that all taxis were to take off by nine-twenty, and Susan had already seen a taxi sheet, with her name on the top line as pilot, lying on the table. She glanced at the clock and gave a gasp.

'Heavens! Ten minutes past!' she ejaculated and made a dash for the locker-room. 'What time will you be back this evening?'

she shouted to Mandy as she stuffed a handful of maps into her overnight bag.

'Not much before six!' Mandy called back. 'I've got two Spits and a Dominie, and I've got to go up to Prestwick. Wait for me here and we will get someone to give us a lift over to the cottage. I'm longing for you to see it. We can have dinner at the "Swan" – lobsters – walk back – 'bye.'

"Bye—' shouted Susan. 'All right. As long as we are back at ten. Mark's 'phoning.'

That day turned out to be one of the most exhausting Susan could remember, and the hottest. On the ground one would have said 'What a perfect day!' – calm, drowsy, hot. And one would not have noticed a thick heat haze bringing the visibility down to about three thousand yards, and causing any pilot to peer continuously about him and make his eyes ache with the glare.

Inside the Fairchild it was stifling and for the first three-quarters of an hour Susan had to fly a very senior officer, whose one phobia was draughts, so that not only was she wearing a greatcoat and a scarf and a cap, but also insisted on having all the windows and ventilators tightly shut. In her shirt sleeves alone Susan was absolutely dripping with heat, and it was a mystery to her why the captain beside her did not faint. However, having dropped this passenger at Lyneham and opened all the windows wide, Susan flew on to Colerne. Here she had to pick up three Hamble pilots, who had already delivered three Seafires and were now due to collect three Wellingtons from Kemble.

In all Susan landed at seven different airfields that day, refuelled twice and finally spent two hours waiting at Lasham for a pilot who failed to arrive, so that, when she finally dropped into Hamble just before last landing time, she found that Mandy had 'beaten her to it'.

By this time Susan was so tired and thirsty that her one desire was for a bath, followed by a long, long drink, and Mandy was wise enough to see that she was really tired and suffering from the strain of the past week, and found her easily persuaded not to attempt to see the cottage that evening.

But an hour and a half later, as Susan sat in the cool bar of the

Yacht Club, with a pint tankard of Pimms Number One in her hand and feeling much refreshed, her mind went back to the cottage.

'When do we move in?' she asked.

'Ours from tomorrow,' said Mandy. 'Let's pack up our things here tonight, Sue, and move in after work. It really is too late to go over for a look-see now, and get back by ten, so you will just have to curb your impatience until tomorrow, and hope that neither of us is stuck out.'

'I think we'll both have to curb ourselves until I get the car,' said Susan.

Mandy sighed with deep contentment and took a deep drink before she spoke again. 'That will make it perfect. Michael will adore it. It's exactly the sort of cottage we want ourselves.' And so, until Susan's telephone call came through, they sat and discussed plans, and Susan decided to ring the Hazeley garage and ask them to get the MG down off its chocks, and ready for the road as soon as possible, while Mandy gallantly said she would be responsible for the finding of a woman in the village to undertake the daily chores, and when, at last, they both went to bed, it was with the feeling that the 'Dolphin' was already well organized and well under control.

But 'the best laid schemes o' mice an' men' – as everyone knows – do 'gang aft agley'. It took only a day or two before they realized all the difficulties of wartime housekeeping, and quite three weeks passed before the cottage was running smoothly and without frequent crises.

To start with the two cats, Gin and Whiskey, proved to be the most accomplished thieves. On the very first Sunday they made away with the so-called 'joint' when Susan's back was turned. Susan was furious but philosophical.

'I expect the truth is that they have suffered while the house was shut up. Cats always thieve if they're hungry. They sleep when they're satisfied.'

Mandy laughed. 'Cat nature and human nature – it's all the same, Sue. "The way to a man's heart" we are told… Leave them to it, Sue. Let's see what they have at the "Swan"!'

Then, the very next evening, Mandy left the electric iron switched on while talking to Michael on the telephone, so that when she came back some twenty minutes later the room was filled with smoke from the charred and smouldering ironing-board.

Also there was the burning question of the 'Mrs Mop' whom Mandy had so gaily promised to produce, but who took about three weeks to materialize. And last, but far from least, the ever-urgent problem of rations.

It really was difficult. They had to be on duty at the airfield, over three miles away, by nine o'clock, and, on these long August days with their double summertime, they rarely finished before six, so there was little time left for either housework or buying rations; and anyway, after a hard day's work, neither of them was exactly in the mood for it. Luckily Susan could cook, and rather liked it, although she loathed the subsequent washing up. But Mandy knew nothing at all about it, and at first had even gone so far as to mistake the Frigidaire for the electric cooker.

On that first Saturday morning Mandy sat on the edge of the kitchen table and dangled a duster rather wistfully.

'Sue, you'll just have to tell me what to do. You see nobody ever has, and as a result I don't even know what to do with *this*' – and she flicked the duster at one of the cats. 'Tell me – how exactly does one '*do*' a room?'

Susan laughed, and vowed that when next she saw Michael she would warn him what was in store for him, and she ended up by sending Mandy down to the village shop with a large basket, a long list of groceries and the ration books, while she 'did' the sitting-room herself.

Mandy returned crestfallen and dumped the basket on the kitchen table. 'Not very successful, I'm afraid, Sue. Is everything on points? I couldn't even get a big tin of treacle – and look at this – it won't last five minutes!'

But it was Mark who in spirit of glorious fun came to the rescue. He arrived unheralded and booked a room at the 'Bugle'; but as events turned out he rarely slept there. He loved the cottage. To his Australian eyes, unaccustomed to any building over a century and a half in age, it seemed like something out of a fairy story – with Susan his princess of course – but he kept this latter idea strictly to himself – and he entered upon those ten halcyon days with a grim determination to make himself indispensable to Susan, even if it meant being a temporary 'Mrs Doings' and included cooking. But he wasn't afraid of that. He'd camped and looked after himself too often. He'd been more than satisfied with his welcome. He had no rival – of that he was sure. It might be hard work to win Susan, but he fully realized that until the war with Japan was over and the door of every eastern prison camp thrown open, he must be patient, and at the back of his mind the nagging thought that, after all, Frank might turn up one day helped his decision. If that happened, then... He had liked Frank. Such a good chap. It would be too awful if he couldn't look him in the eye.

But Mark had some bad moments, such as the evening Michael turned up unexpectedly, and he himself went back to sleep at the 'Bugle' where he had retained his room. As Mandy had predicted, Michael lost his heart to the cottage at first sight, really in much the same way as Susan had seen him lose it once before to Mandy. It charmed him, and he determined to fly down as often as his duties permitted, if only for a few precious hours, or to spend the night, even if it meant leaving at daybreak. Mark longed for the same freedom, and wished with all with soul that he had the same right.

However, he enjoyed his leave to the full, and regretted the days he had been forced to spend in London, for the very necessary purpose of new kit, for the moths had been busy. His belongings were in a deplorable state.

It was glorious fun, and Susan realized that nothing could have been better for Mark at this juncture than a home and absolute freedom until he got rid of the sensation of being everlastingly on the alert, and the fear of betraying himself. And Mark proved to be quite a good housekeeper, although he did spend the majority of the precious points on treacle for waffles. He was never bored throughout the long days that he was alone. There were books in plenty, and he talked to the villagers, and said the cats were good company. Without analysing her feelings too deeply Susan was gratified that she had this hospitality to offer, and only wished she had more time to give to him.

Of his captivity Mark spoke little. To Susan he owned that even speaking of it made him smell the cowstalls again, but one sentence above all others gave her fuller understanding. 'I never got away from it. Nowhere to sleep was offered me, and I was glad. If in my sleep I spoke English the cows wouldn't split!'

'But it's rotten,' protested Susan, 'that after all that you aren't having a better time *now*. I mean doing chores isn't exactly—'

Mark laughed.

'I couldn't be having a better time. This is the war for me! "Men must cook and women must fly; he reads a book while she sweeps the sky!" How's that for poetry?' He broke off with another laugh.

Susan found herself thinking much of Mark. She was perfectly aware of the position between them, and of the strain he was putting on himself. She knew he loved her, even as Frank had loved her, and she never tempted him, but tried to keep him on exactly the same friendly footing as Mandy and Michael. Sometimes on long flights, or while waiting for the Anson or Fairchild, she let her thoughts drift, and owned that she was depending more and more upon him. Dependability – that was his attraction. Stability and truth. Cardinal virtues, he possessed them in full measure. The very fact that, when his one desire had been to come straight to her, he had set it aside and gone first to see Smith's mother proved it.

Thoughtlessly, that first evening, she had asked why he had gone straight away to Lincoln. His almost laconic reply had been characteristic. Softly he quoted: 'Smith, our brother... Only son of loving mother... Know that?'

Comprehending, Susan nodded. 'Yes. I bought that little book for its title. It meant something to *me* – *'Beyond this Disregard'*.

And Mandy, during those ten days, neglected no opportunity of leaving Susan and Mark together. She implicitly believed, with Susan, that Frank was dead; and there was that curious happening on the day of Susan's test flight. Mandy had thought a lot about that. It was not imaginary, and it could be no living person; and, just as intensely as Susan had wished for Mandy's happiness, so Mandy now longed within herself, when she yawned and feigned sleepiness, and finally gathered her long legs together and made disbelieved excuses for betaking herself to bed and leaving Susan and Mark to sit out of doors until the midges drove them in, or sprawled in the easy chairs of the 'Dolphin's' one-time bar.

It was then Susan and Mark had their most serious conversations. Sometimes reminiscent, sometimes wandering to many lands and subjects as well as to flying. It was then Susan learned Mark's history, absolutely unknown before. One of two brothers, whose parent had been one of two brothers, each had inherited a sufficient patrimony to follow his bent. By mutual agreement Mark's brother had taken over the uncle's wealth and extensive sheep farms, while Mark inherited his father's interest in a large business of import and export.

'It's a company nowadays,' said Mark, 'but I own most of the shares, and it leaves me free to fly, so we are both suited. You will like Jim—' he broke off meditatively, and the words gave Susan a qualm, making her realize no matter how she pushed the future out of her mind, it was occupying a large place in Mark's thoughts.

'Is your brother married?' she asked.

'Not as far as I know. Wasn't a year ago.'

The days sped swiftly and soon the feasts of hot lobsters and waffles were over, as was the cocktail party which Mark sprang upon them on his last evening. From whence he got the where-with-all was a mystery he would not divulge, beyond: 'Bribery – corruption – black market and back pay. Don't ask questions. Mary's husband is safe and we're celebrating. That's all.'

In the end, too, Mandy kept her promise, and found her 'Mrs Mop'. Before Mark left she got on the trail of Mrs Walters, but another three days elapsed before she ran her down, and yet another week before she could come and 'oblige'. However, she proved well worth waiting for, and Mandy laid down her duster with a great sigh of relief.

From then on all went smoothly, and in the weeks that followed many a lively party forgathered beneath the 'Dolphin's' hospitable roof.

And so August passed into September, and except when held up by weather, work never stopped, and Susan and Mandy's list of deliveries piled up and up. Not infrequently a day's flying took them the length and breadth of England and Wales, and oftentimes over the border to Scotland. September, however, was not without its moments. Susan had her own on the morning of the twenty-fourth.

Lying on the ante-room table that morning Susan found two chits made out for 'Third Officer Sandyman'. They both represented Spitfires, the first a Mark Nine from Lyneham to High Ercall, the second a Mark Sixteen to be collected at Cosford and taken to Tangmere.

'Lucky dog!' Mandy commented, reading the ferry chits over her shoulder. 'Just my luck to be doing the milk round on a day like this,' and she waved a full taxi sheet towards the window.

It certainly was a brilliant day, unusual too for so late in September, because there was not even a trace of ground mist. Perfect weather for enjoying a 'Spit' to the full, and Susan agreed with Mandy that she was indeed a lucky dog.

With the unexpectedness to which Susan never became quite accustomed, a voice from the tannoy broke sharply across the general hum of conversation in the ante-room.

'Attention please! Taxis off at nine twenty-five. Will First Officer Mackey report to Operations immediately, and Third Officer Barnes to the Sick Bay.'

As soon as the voice stopped the broken threads of conversation were picked up again. Several pilots made a dive for the dining-room to get a cup of coffee and a sandwich before starting the day's work, among them Mandy who, as usual, had been so late getting up that she had had no time for breakfast at the cottage.

On her way to the Met Office Susan looked to see if there were any letters in her pigeon-hole, but, as was usually the case, there was nothing. Her weekly letter from Grannie had come the day before and so had one from Mark. She missed her mother's letters more than words could say. As for her in-laws, both Frank's parents were dead and his only sister married to a Canadian and living in Toronto.

Four times a year, with the regularity of the seasons, Mrs MacKenzie, née Marjorie Sandyman, sent her sister-in-law a food parcel and an accompanying brief and utterly impersonal letter, relating the fact that she and her two children were fit and well, and 'Ed' was still with a training unit somewhere in Canada, and hoping that Susan herself was well. That any intimacy failed to grow between the two women was hardly surprising, for they had never met, and from what Frank had told Susan of his sister, who was ten years his senior, Susan felt very little desire to push the acquaintanceship.

'Lo, Sandy!' Toni, the Met Officer, greeted Susan as she stepped down into the little back room with the map-lined walls. 'Whither away?'

'Lyneham, High Ercall, Cosford and Tangmere,' was the laconic reply, 'OK?'

Susan's well-marked eyebrows rose questioningly as she scanned the slate which ran the length of the wall opposite the windows. For once there were no figures marked in red chalk; no belts of fog or ground mist, so common to an English autumn.

'Yes, all OK. Clear as a bell from here to PK, and from PK to Land's End. Most unusual, and not even a "front" coming in!'

Toni picked up a large square of white silk on which she was embroidering the signatures of all the pilots of Number Fifteen Ferry Pool, and drew a scarlet strand from the skein in her lap.

'Nothing much for a Met Queen to do today; almost wish I were coming with you, tho' the last time I went for a ride in an "Annie" I was sick as a dog!'

Reflectively she sucked the end of the silk thread and looked down at the piece of material in her hand. 'You know, it's funny,' she mused, 'but almost half these names are foreign, and when I'm working on them I keep wondering where they really came from, what events led up to their arrival here in England, and even more what will happen to them when this is all over. Will they all want to go back, or, if they want to stay in this country, will they be allowed to?'

Her needle poised before her, Toni screwed up her eyes and squinted slightly as she tried to thread it.

'What a sorting out there will—' she began, but stopped short as Nina, now a Hamble pilot, appeared in the doorway, and concentrated all her attention on her needle.

After four years in England Nina's accent was hardly noticeable, yet in a hundred little undefinable ways Susan was certain she would never have mistaken her for an English girl. Perhaps it was the skin, so taut and fine-drawn over the beautifully moulded features, which had obviously been nurtured in some less kind climate, lacking the soft, warm rains of English skies; or, perhaps, it was the way in which she wore her hair in a simply coiled knot at the nape of her neck, or even the tiny golden crucifix attached to the engraved identity disc on her wrist. Whatever this subtle difference might be, whenever Susan looked at Nina it never failed to strike her with disturbing clarity that here was an individual who had suffered and survived more, both mentally and physically, than anyone else she knew, and she was certain that if the story of the Polish girl were told it would make even her own sorrows pale into insignificance. But nothing much was known about Nina except that she was a countess, and before the war had been fabulously wealthy, and that now she lived entirely on her pay; that she had had a miraculous escape to France, which had somehow earned her a Croix de Guerre, and that it was quite impossible to draw her out to say more about herself.

Looking at her now as she leant against the doorpost of the Met Office, her graceful body indolently relaxed, the heavy eyelashes drooping a little over the slightly upward-slanting black eyes, Susan could not help wondering about the men in Nina's life, for obviously she must have had many admirers, and why she now so assiduously avoided all male company.

'Odd,' she thought, 'how many closed books both official and personal one handles in wartime, yet how few one can ever open and comprehend.'

'Weather OK in Scotland?' Nina asked.

'Yes, at least fifteen miles, and three thousand feet all the way. Light easterly wind, veering to south by midday. Going to PK?'

'Yes, Mossie up and a Lib. back to Thorney Island – my first—' she answered, rather absently, glancing at the chits in her hand. 'What about some bridge after tea?'

Toni nodded and Nina turned to Susan. 'You, too, Sandy? Will you be back?'

'Yes, I should be in by four easily if I am picked up at Tangmere on time.'

Toni laughed her fat, friendly laugh.

'That's easily fixed,' she said. 'Just ask Alison to be the fourth, and Ops will organize the Fairchild to be waiting for you – Alison loves her rubber!'

However, the proposed game of bridge was not destined to be played that evening for Nina's Liberator was US at Prestwick and she found herself making up a four in a small hotel in Ayr instead, while Susan sweated over what seemed to her far the worst part of her first crash – composing an Accident Report!

She sucked her pencil and gazed out of the writing-room window across the deserted airfield on which the mist already lay wispily. Her eyes, however, did not register it as mist but as a white sheet of glycol spouting from the nose of a Spitfire and viciously slashing at the perspex in front of her and above her head.

If only she had not taken that tiny risk! True, on take-off the oil pressure had been sixty pounds per square inch and normal lay anywhere between fifty and one hundred and forty pounds, but as she set off on course to the northward Susan had noticed it drop to fifty-five pounds and then five minutes later to forty-five – the emergency minimum! From then on things had happened so quickly that now she was having some difficulty in remembering the sequence of events and writing an accurate description of them.

As the oil pressure had sunk so the engine temperature and oil temperatures had risen at quite an alarming speed, so that Susan knew it could only be a matter of five minutes at the outside before the engine seized up – and as to what exactly happened when this occurred she was definitely vague.

Her one idea had naturally been to reach *terra firma* as quickly as possible, and as her mind registered the sinister story unfolding on the instrument panel so her eyes had automatically swept the ground beneath her for an airfield or some suitable forced landing ground.

A mile to starboard lay the ancient town of Cirencester, while to port stretched a large patch of woodland beyond which Susan knew lay Aston Down, a big airfield boasting long, wide runways, and, what was better, an ATA Ferry Pool.

After the initial shock of realizing that now only her own skill lay between her and certain death, Susan's brain had become as ice cold as the sweat streaming down her back, and clear as the brilliant September day itself.

There had been no thought of Frank or Mark, or of anyone else, only the sensation of stark fear and the violent instinct of self-preservation which accompanies it – the sky above her head was blue, the earth beneath basked in the warmth of a kindly sun, Susan, at that moment, realized how very much she wanted to live – but all her family had gone – was she to be the last? – her blood ran cold.

She made for Aston Down immediately, but over the centre of the wood the speed had begun to fall off, back to one hundred and ninety... one hundred and sixty... one hundred and forty – and she was losing height fast.

'Don't try and make the airfield, it's just too far – you've got to do a belly landing—' her brain had told her. 'There's a big field straight ahead and it's only stubble. The wind's behind – but it's very light – and well – it just can't be helped.'

It had been at this moment of decision that the escaping glycol had struck the perspex and quickly switching off the engine Susan had trimmed the machine to its gliding speed of one hundred and ten miles an hour.

In the few remaining seconds she had somehow turned off the petrol cock, jettisoned the hood, made certain that the Sutton harness was locked and finally pulled down her goggles from her forehead over her eyes. Her actions at this time had not been instinctive but the result of a training so thorough that even naked fear could not now uproot it, and if any of Susan's erstwhile instructors could have seen her at this moment they would have counted their time well spent.

The ground had come up to meet her with a sickening rush, and as the hedge swept by Susan tried to hold off as if for a normal landing, and braced her feet against the rudder bars to meet the force of the final impact.

It had come with remarkable smoothness, and apart from the showers of earth and stones, the tips of the propeller flying off and a spray of oil, the actual touch-down and subsequent belly-skid had been the least alarming part of the whole affair.

However, Susan had not stopped to consider her luck, for she had heard of too many machines bursting into flames, or exploding, after successful crash landings, and with the two almost full ninety-five gallon tanks less than a yard in front of her nose, she was taking no risks, so that by the time the Spitfire had come to a complete and juddering standstill, Susan had drawn the locking pin from her harness, released her parachute straps and was climbing out.

From then on she had moved as in a dream, for it was the first time she had had to take 'Accident Procedure', and the whole thing seemed very confusing.

The ambulance and the fire-tender crews had been very kind and helpful, had collected her parachute, overnight bag and log books from the wreck, and had driven her into the airfield and round to the huts which were the Headquarters of Number Twelve Ferry Pool, ATA.

There had been endless data to collect, reports from two eye-witnesses, which were of course both completely different, contradictory and highly dramatized; a sketch or plan of the scene had to be made or committed to memory, damage to the field to be noted and the name and address of the owner to be discovered.

Such details as organizing a guard for the aircraft, and notifying the maintenance unit at High Ercall that their machine would not be delivered today after all; telephoning Hamble and arranging for a taxi machine to pick her up later in the day; all these had been coped with by the efficient and cheerful Operations Officer who assured Susan that she could not possibly be held responsible for the loss of the machine and that there was absolutely nothing to flap about.

Although these words cheered Susan considerably, she could not help feeling guilty. 'If only I had circled Lyneham a few times just to make *quite* certain that the oil pressure was OK this would never have happened,' she told herself: and then another part of her mind cut in and argued, 'Well, you were within the normal limits so there was no reason why you should have waited!'

Yet there lay one more battered Spitfire, representing five thousand pounds of the country's money, and, even more important, representing hundreds of man-hours and precious labour – one more victory in the enemy bag as surely as if it had been shot out of the sky by their own fighters.

Apart from a bruised leg and a torn jacket Susan herself was none the worse for her crash, and, when examined by the RAF Medical Officer at Aston Down, had shown no signs of shock.

'Strong nervous system,' he had commented. 'All the same I should give flying a miss for twenty-four hours, and when you get home lie down and take this.' He gave her a small pill which she knew, from her hospital experience, must be a sedative.

'Don't be surprised if you have a spot of delayed shock later today; I find it often happens with the boys. Probably feel a bit dizzy or sick, but don't worry, it's quite usual, and as long as you rest you won't come to any harm.'

The doctor's words proved correct, for although at the time Susan had felt quite normal and singularly calm, some hours later, after she had arrived back at Hamble, she suddenly felt faint and had been very sick, and so September the twenty-fourth became one of the dates engraven on her memory. She wrote it so many times on that report.

TWELVE

EARLY IN OCTOBER Mark was posted to Brize Norton, as a test pilot to Number Six Maintenance Unit, and Susan saw him frequently, because at this time Spitfires were being delivered there almost daily, by ATA pilots of Hamble, for testing and modifications, before being packed and shipped to the far eastern theatre of war.

Although Susan was not aware of it, Mark, when he had finished his 'Test Pilot's Course', was given the choice of being posted either to Brize Norton or to a big Spitfire factory in the Midlands. He chose Brize Norton for no other reason than the outstanding fact that it brought him some hundred miles nearer to Susan.

Neither did Susan know, nor guess, how anxiously he watched the arrival of each new machine which taxied into Number Six MU dispersal, or how his heart thumped when the propeller ceased to churn and a gloved hand pushed back the disguising helmet to reveal Susan's honey-coloured curls. During these months Susan somehow achieved, with success, the art of living from day to day. She looked neither backward into the past, nor forward into the future, and she spoke little of either. Her days off she spent quietly at Hazeley with Grannie. There was nothing else she wanted to do, and once the Memorial Service, which Grannie arranged for All Saints' Day, was over, unless some business affair had to be discussed she spoke little of her mother. Yet over and over again she re-read that last letter and remembered Lady Dalrymple's words.

Then it happened that suddenly Mandy needed comforting. Michael was ordered to Australia and sailed early in December. Mandy was inconsolable. Even Susan was shocked at the language she used towards the Japs in particular and the war in general. She looked white and lost weight during those days; and when one morning, after delivering a Spitfire at Brize Norton and the Fairchild was delayed in fetching her, Susan had time for a cigarette with Mark, and he asked tentatively if he might spend his next seven days' leave at the 'Dolphin', Susan first poked fun at him.

'Sure it won't be boring?' she asked with a smile, while her eyes belied her words. 'It's such a long day – besides I might, or Mandy might, be stuck out for nights on end at this time of the year.'

He answered in the same spirit. 'Oh, I think I could stand it at a pinch. Just leave a few good books about and I shall be quite happy,' and their eyes met and they laughed simultaneously. Susan finished:

'Honestly, Mark, I shall be glad if you'll come. Mandy's a problem just now. She's fretting – sometimes she's quite difficult. When does your leave begin?'

'Boxing Day,' said Mark.

'That's grand,' said Susan. 'I couldn't have you just at Christmas because Mandy and I have both volunteered to be two of the eight pilots left on duty – it doesn't matter to us, and I expect you have any amount of gaieties in the Mess. So come when you like and stay as long you like, and don't worry – I shan't be offended if you depart next day!'

But Mark did not depart on the next day. On the contrary, he stayed till the last possible moment, and by so doing let himself in for a tedious, ghastly cross-country journey back to Brize Norton, where he had to report by midnight on January 2nd.

As he jolted along on the last stage of this journey, lying back with his eyes closed in the ancient taxi-cab he had managed to dig out in Oxford, he let his mind wander back over the last seven days. He relived them all. The long, cosy winter evenings spent in front of the log fire, the discussions, which ranged over everything from books to aircraft, from religion to Mark's plans for starting a private flying club in Australia after the war, of the fun he and Susan had had while creating a curry together in the little kitchen, of the party which had just happened, on New Year's Eve, and had been such a wild success, the walks he had taken while Susan and Mandy were at work, the relief when his fears that one or the other might be stuck out overnight were squashed by the sound of the MG's horn. It had been the happiest week of his life, and he was fully aware of the reason. His love for Susan. Would it ever come to anything? Or had he to live out his days with this unsatisfied longing? That was the question he turned over and over in his mind.

For Susan also it had been a happy week, and when Mark had

gone she found herself missing him more than, even to herself, she would admit. It seemed that his presence had brought her a peace of mind that she had not known for over three years, and with his going some of it had vanished. Mandy, too, had come under his influence. She was more resigned to Michael's absence. Mark's quiet words: 'You aren't cut off. Mike isn't a prisoner, or wounded, and you have letters,' steadied her and brought home to her how blessed she was. She sensed the contrast of which Mark was thinking. Michael wasn't forced to hide in a cow-stall to ensure his safe return. Tactfully, after Mark had gone, Mandy did not refer to him too often. Instinctively she knew that it was a subject best left alone. One couldn't rag Susan as one would some of the others about more obvious and ordinary beaux. Susan had suffered too much.

It was during the first week of 1945 that there appeared on the ante-room notice board the news that Third Officer Sandra Cushing had been killed whilst ferrying a Mustang down south from Sherburn, in Elmet, and although Susan and Mandy tried not to let it depress them, a certain gloom did fall over the cottage during the next few days.

'Poor old Sandra!' said Mandy, as she flopped down exhausted in front of the 'Dolphin's' blazing fire. It was her only comment, and immediately afterward she turned on the radio full blast and retired behind the latest copy of *Flight*.

Susan remained silent. For the fourth time she was reading a cutting from the 'On Active Service' column of that morning's *Times*.

Cushing. On Jan. 5th, 1945, Third Officer Sandra Kay Cushing, Air Transport Auxiliary. Of New York City, USA. Killed while ferrying His Majesty's aircraft.

On the floor beside Susan lay an envelope addressed to Lieutenant Elmer Cushing, Sandra's son, but the sheet of notepaper on her knee was blank, as it had been for the last twenty minutes.

'If only I'd once seen him!' she was thinking. 'Will he really care, or won't it mean much to him?' So many times she had looked at the almost life-sized photograph of Elmer, which Sandra had kept in the centre of her dressing-table at Hopefield House; but somehow she had never been able to picture this golden-hearted, brassy-headed American in the role of a mother, and now she found it excessively difficult to write to her son.

On top of this the weather closed in. England lay frozen in the iron grip of frost and snow. Each day more and more airfields became unserviceable, until finally flying came temporarily to a standstill, and the pilots of Number Fifteen Ferry Pool were given forty-eight hours' extra leave.

Mandy said: 'Oh, damn! And no Michael! What a waste of a buckshee forty-eight!'

'What will you do?' asked Susan. 'Go home?'

For a moment Mandy did not answer but just stood with her hands stuck deep in her trouser pockets contemplating the giddy whirl of snowflakes outside the ante-room window.

'Yes, I think so,' she answered after a few minutes. 'Coming? We've got stacks of skis and an old toboggan up in the loft. Might be fun. How are we placed for petrol?'

'Petrol's OK. Mark gave me a couple of coupons last week. I'd love to come.'

Susan joined Mandy at the window and contemplated the weather. 'Looks as if it's going to stop,' she said. 'Roads mayn't be so bad. Wouldn't do to get snowbound.'

The fact that the snow might have drifted, and might be inches deep in some places, or cover a layer of sheet ice, worried Susan not at all, although the possibility did pass through her mind. After all it was a matter of comparisons. A three hundred mile flight in a ropey old aircraft in dirty weather conditions was far more hazardous than an eighty-mile run in a good car, even though roads were frozen and the temperature nearly down to zero, but the MG was good, and she had chains.

Well muffled up and wearing flying-boots and greatcoats, they started at dawn next morning and had a perfectly uneventful journey, followed by hilarious hours of tobogganing on the snow-covered slopes of Falcombe Park. The house was quiet, the Canadian soldiers being mostly in France.

The return journey the next day was not quite so pleasant. They had left it rather late. It was dark and the thaw had come; the roads were slushy and disaster awaited them at the cottage.

Susan had gaily given Mrs Walters two days off, and all of them had completely forgotten to turn off the water at the main and empty the cistern. The kitchen was awash, hall ceiling sagging and Susan and Mandy had their first experience of burst pipes.

The only comfort was the fire, which Susan got going, while Mandy, late as it was, fled for Mrs Walters, who came, scanned the damage and comfortingly promised 'Mr Finch, to see to it'.

Mr Finch, an erstwhile boat-builder, arrived early next morning and assured them that by the time they came back in the evening 'she'd be a right new ship'. Mandy gave a sigh of relief as she took her place in the car and said wistfully: 'I'm learning, Sue. Had no idea what ups and downs there could be in love in a cottage.'

But that morning both Susan and Mandy found three ferry chits awaiting them, with the result that neither got back that night to admire Mr Finch's handiwork, Susan being stuck out at Ternhill and Mandy at Moreton-in-the-Marsh.

For the next few days there was a formidable amount of ferrying to be done, as, in spite of the weather, the factories and the great maintenance units continued to turn out machines, although flying had practically come to a standstill.

Snow showers, freak storms, dangerous icing conditions and frozen or waterlogged airfields were the rule rather than the exception at this time of the year, and Susan, never forgetting Commander MacKenzie's stern warning away back in Barton days, took no chances.

On no less than four occasions in February, murmuring 'Paid to be safe' to herself, she lobbed into strange airfields on account of the weather, and even in March she was stuck out twice.

'Stuck out in the Midlands'! All the girls dreaded it. By the spring of 1945 Susan knew it only too well. In fact on more than one occasion she knew herself to be guilty of pushing on well after last landing time to some more salubrious neighbourhood where she could spend the night as the guest of the RAF, the Fleet Air Arm or the American Air Force.

Nothing, in Susan's estimation, was worse than landing after a long day's flying, cold, tired and hungry, to find that after seeing her machine safely bedded down for the night she herself must bus or hitch-hike into the nearest dreary, blacked out, provincial town and then start tramping the streets in search of a bed.

In anticipation of ferrying to the continent, some practices of dinghy drill took place in Southampton swimming-baths during the early months of 1945.

Dressed in a 'Mae West' over a bathing suit, and encumbered by dinghy pack and parachute, the drop from the high dive was made an occasion for great hilarity. Most of the girls were expert swimmers, and the 'Mae West' inflated itself as it touched the water, but inflating the dinghy and getting in to it required some practice, especially while one's fellows did their best to imitate a rough sea.

'All very well, safe in a swimming bath!' remarked Jackie. 'A rough sea would be another story. One would have to treat it with respect. I, for one, certainly hope this sort of excursion *never* happens!'

It was towards the end of March when Susan first noticed that Mandy, who used to be so restless, would now sit silently staring into the fire for long hours at a time, with her thoughts evidently far away. Sometimes she looked little sad, but at others a happy, enigmatic smile played round her lips. Susan, while wondering, made no comment.

Michael's letters came every few days. Sometimes two or three at a time and Mandy always gave vent to the same scathing words.

'Doing nothing! Simply nothing! Of course the Japs have jibbed. Might just as well have stayed at home.'

The next outstanding event of importance to both Susan and Mandy was their first 'ocean going' flight. The designation was Mandy's. One morning, early in April, their ferry chits bore identical orders. 'Barracudas to be flown from Eastleigh to the Isle of, Man'. Toni reported 'Clear weather to the coast', but she warned them that always somewhere over the Irish Sea there might be mist.

Mandy was the more excited, but Susan's eyes sparkled, and she laughed light-heartedly when Mandy said, 'Don't forget your dinghy rill!'

'Mae West', parachute, dinghy pack and overnight bag. It certainly seemed a lot of impedimenta. The 'Mae West' went on first and over that the parachute, the dinghy pack being attached by a cord to the 'Mae West'. Mandy set off first and waited in the circuit until Susan joined her, as was their usual habit when going to the same places to deliver the same machines. Toni had been right. It was a lovely morning and perfectly clear weather until they were over the Irish Sea. Then a wisp of cloud came up: beyond it lay an almost imperceptible mist, and Susan lost sight of Mandy. She scanned the sky and the horizon, and became a little worried. Mandy had been flying at a lower level about half a mile to port. Susan banked her machine in the endeavour to see if Mandy was below, but saw no sign of her. A little frightened, she flew on. If an accident had befallen Mandy there was simply nothing she could do but hurry on and report. She might only be hidden by the mist, which was now thicker. With the thought of the three-hundred-foot cliffs in her mind Susan kept steadily on her course, inwardly hoping that near the coast there would again be clear weather, and to her joy, about half a mile off shore, the mist lifted and straight ahead was the gap for which she was making. Once again she scanned sea and sky, and still there was no sign of Mandy. But, to her amazement and relief, as she flew in over the airfield and made her circuit, she saw Mandy's Barracuda landing, and as she herself touched down Mandy was being guided to a distant part of the airfield, and very soon Susan found herself parked alongside.

She called herself a 'first-class idiot', and resolved to say nothing of her fright. It was but one more instance of how large is the sky and how deceptive is mist.

But when Susan had collected her various impedimenta and reached the ground, Mandy was nowhere to be seen, although her parachute and overnight bag lay, apparently, where she had thrown them down. Susan looked up, wondering if she had climbed back for a forgotten object, but Mandy wasn't in the cockpit, and obeying some instinct Susan proceeded to walk quickly round the other side of the aircraft – the side turned away from the airfield buildings. Then she saw Mandy, tucked well in under the Barracuda's high wing, and she was bending over. Susan heard a sound and ran forward just as Mandy straightened up. Susan caught her arm and Mandy turned a wan face.

'Only been sick,' she said.

'So I see,' answered Susan. 'Are you ill?'

'No – no.' Mandy shook her head. 'It's only – must be – fumes – or atmosphere!' She grinned sheepishly.

'But—' began Susan. 'But—' and whatever it was she was about to say vanished from her mind as the suspicion dawned. 'Mandy!' she exclaimed. 'You're not—?'

Mandy grinned again. 'Could be – Come along. It's over. I'm all right now.'

Susan was overwhelmed. Mandy was pregnant and Michael on the other side of the world, and perhaps knowing nothing about it. There was no reason why Mandy shouldn't have a baby, of course, but the thought had not before entered Susan's head. If it had she would have casually dismissed it and only have told herself, 'Oh, no, they won't – not till after the war.'

It was not until the evening when they were back at the 'Dolphin' that either of them referred to the subject again. They had been taxied back from Ronaldsway by an Anson to Hawarden, and from there an awaiting Anson from Hamble had brought them home.

The April evenings were cold but Mrs Walters' fires always lit at a touch, and Susan's orders to Mandy were peremptory that night. She nodded to the most comfortable arm-chair.

'Park yourself, Mandy. And don't move till I get the fire going.'

Mandy did as she was told, and Susan knelt and used the bellows to such good purpose that in a few minutes the fire was blazing to her satisfaction. Then she turned, still on her knees, to find Mandy looking at her shaking with suppressed laughter.

'Sue, you're priceless! Like an old hen!'

'But why on earth didn't you tell me? Anything might have happened.'

'Just because I know exactly what you'd say. That I must tell Mummie and stop flying. I'm all right, Sue, really. Please don't tell.'

'Does Michael know?' asked Susan.

Mandy nodded. 'Yes. We are hoping he will get home before August. The war in Europe is ending so fast, Sue. I'd like to see it through.'

Susan was still kneeling on the floor. Mandy leaned forward and rubbed her head against Susan just as a puppy might.

'Sue, didn't you feel when your baby was coming – that it was all right? That – nothing could go wrong?' And now Susan nodded.

'And nothing did?' continued Mandy. 'Well – that's what I feel about' – she hesitated – 'Richard.'

'Richard?' Susan repeated.

'Yes. That will be his name.'

Susan was quiet a moment. She looked towards the fire and Mandy saw the teardrops glistening on her eyelashes.

'Sue,' she said softly. 'Let me have my way.'

'All right,' said Susan. 'Only promise you'll be sensible and say if you don't feel well?'

'I'll promise,' said Mandy. 'I won't be foolish.'

With the advent of spring Susan and Mandy, except when they were away on leave, rarely found themselves absent from the 'Dolphin' at night, and towards the end of April, as the war in Europe moved relentlessly towards its climax, Susan felt less and less desire to be away. She had many friends, both in Ramble and old Bursledon; she loved the villages themselves, and the old cottage, and she realized that it could not be long now before they would become part of the past and she would have to think seriously about the future. And Susan did not want to think about the future. It might be years before the war with Japan was over, and meanwhile she would have to make another fresh start, more new faces and new scenes, and the inevitably painful farewells from people and a life she had come to love. There could be no job more satisfactory. How she would miss it!

Swiftly April gave place to May, and even more swiftly the allied forces pushed on into the very heart of the Reich.

The seventh of May dawned at last! VE Day! And, to celebrate, forty-eight hours' extra leave.

Mandy dashed off to Falcombe. The time had come when she must break her news. Susan spent her two days quietly with Grannie, where she was surprised by a visit from Mark, who also had some hours' leave.

It was his first visit. Old Mrs Ledgard repeated his name thoughtfully.

'Who is he, my dear? Are we "at home"?'

'He's a great friend of mine,' stammered Susan. 'He's the pilot who taught Frank and me to fly in Australia.'

'Oh!' said Grannie. 'Show him in, Rose.'

Mark paid Grannie a great deal of attention. He made a good impression. He stayed to tea. He told her how he had reached Hazeley.

'I've only half a day. I flew from Brize Norton to Odiham and hitchhiked.'

When six o'clock came Grannie rang for Rose and ordered champagne cocktails, saying, 'We must have something very special to celebrate tonight—' but she did not go into details as to what. She invited Mark to stay to dinner, and suggested that in the interim, the evening being pleasant, Susan should show him her garden.

After they had disappeared Grannie sat back in her chair and smiled to herself. Her aged cheeks were a little flushed, and her eyes were bright. This little unexpected event had given her more personal pleasure than even the wider issues of the day.

From the house Susan led the way across the tiny flagged terrace, but did not speak until she said: 'Come and be introduced to Grannie's beech tree. Isn't it glorious?' As she spoke she thought of that quiet, still afternoon last November when she had watched its dead leaves fluttering to the ground.

'It's all so lovely – so English,' said Mark. 'Like your cottage.'

He glanced at the house. 'It's what you call Georgian, isn't it? Or Regency? The back is even prettier than the front!'

'Georgian,' said Susan. 'Now, look up.'

The beech tree was not yet in full leaf. Its delicate leaves made a dainty lacework of intricate pattern against the sky. Mark gazed upwards, and an almost awe-stricken expression crossed his face.

'It's beautiful. How old is it? It's a curious colour.'

'It's a copper beech,' answered Susan. 'I have never seen another as big. The gardener says it's well over a hundred years old.'

Mark lowered his eyes and looked straight into Susan's.

'Has she – your grandmother – always lived here?' The words, and his expression of them, gave Susan the impression that was not exactly what he had been going to say, and her curiosity as to the purpose of his unexpected visit was aroused.

'Always in the summer – ever since I can remember,' she answered.

'But she has been a great traveller. Now come and see the rest of the garden.'

The garden was not over-big. A wide lawn lay about the roots of the beech tree, and then a wide path, broken at a little distance by a perfect specimen of a lime tree, almost as tall as the beech, divided a croquet lawn from a sunken rose garden, with a beautiful wrought-iron gateway. On either side of the path were flower beds, at this moment closely planted out with masses of polyanthus of every colour. A perfect carpet. Mark stared and stooped down.

'I've never seen anything more perfect. They're such sweet little flowers, so – so' – he hesitated for a word – 'so affectionate.'

The word pleased Susan, but she made no comment and Mark seemed not to expect any. He had straightened up now and was looking across the garden to where a grey stone seat on the far side, under the old rose-coloured brick wall, and set about with forget-me-nots of a vivid blue, and tall, late-flowering pink tulips, made another perfect picture. Again his eyes came back to Susan's and he took her hand.

'It overwhelms me. Come – let's go to the other end. There is something I want to ask you.'

Susan's heart missed a beat. Surely he was not going to spoil everything? She had been wondering ever since he arrived why he had come today. He must realize she couldn't – couldn't settle anything, not yet. Susan's thoughts were in a turmoil; she did not speak until they were seated on a bench half hidden from the house, and which overlooked the far end of the garden. Then one glance at Mark showed his thoughts at that moment to be very far away.

'What is it, Mark?' she said gently.

'I've been thinking things over,' he answered, and he half turned towards her. 'Sue, would it help you...' – he paused. 'Some chaps are sure to be sent east *now*. Perhaps I could worm myself in? Might be a chance for Burma, and eventually Malaya; perhaps I could find out for you.'

Again Susan's heart missed a beat, and she caught her breath.

'You mean...?' she began.

'Go and have a look for Frank.'

'No. No, Mark. No. I – oh – I *don't* know.'

Mark took both her hands. 'T'isn't only for your sake, Sue. I must be honest. If we knew—' He broke off.

Susan shook her bead vehemently. 'No, Mark. I know what you are going to say. *Please – don't say it*. Things must go on as they are until – until the war with Japan is over. It's to find out what *happened*. I *know* Frank is dead; but how – when – where? You can't bring him back. I know you would if you could, and if it happened in the ordinary sequence of events that you were ordered east, that would be different, but I'm not going to *ask* you to go, and you are not to pull strings. I *won't* have it.'

Exactly what she meant Susan would have found it difficult to explain. She longed for news – any news – but everything in her revolted at the thought of Mark deliberately seeking danger for her sake, or for his own sake, or for the sake of their mutual future.

'Very well,' said Mark. 'I came over just to ask you. It might have been difficult, but it isn't impossible.'

'And the alternative—?' began Susan.

'Dropping food supplies over Holland, at this minute. I was there yesterday. It was wonderful. People on the roofs, waving and waving sheets and things. They needed food so badly.'

'That is where you should go first, Mark. To see Ans. I pray she is safe.'

'And I too,' said Mark.

THIRTEEN

SUSAN STOOD ON the platform and scanned the carriage windows as the train puffed into Basingstoke station the next morning. She was wondering if Mandy would be there, and, if she was, would she spot her in time? The train was crowded, mostly it seemed with sailors, who, probably, had also had leave to celebrate.

But luck was in. Mandy was standing in the corridor and waved as she passed. Susan crowded in, and her first words: 'Can't you get a seat, Mandy? You shouldn't be standing,' brought Mandy's laughing answer:

'Imposs. Shouldn't have seen you, and the Navy is reposing in every seat.'

Susan piled their overnight bags one on top of the other and said: 'Perch on that.'

'Old hen!' said Mandy, and her eyes twinkled.

But it was not until they were in the car, which Susan had left garaged in Southampton, that they were able to talk. As soon as they were clear of the worst of the traffic Susan began:

'Now, fire away. Tell me your news.'

'Got to give it up!' sighed Mandy. 'Mummie is insistent. Will have me under her eye. As for Nanny—!' Mandy rolled her eyes heavenward.

'Good!' said Susan. 'Time you had a little discipline, if not for your own then for the baby's sake.'

'But it's awful!' groaned Mandy. 'No more flying! I've promised to tell Anna right away. Mummie didn't turn a hair. One would think she'd known all the time.' She broke off. 'Now – why that grin?' and she looked reproachfully at Susan.

'Perhaps she did,' said Susan. 'I told you once before that she was more practical than you think.' But Mandy made no answer. She remembered her own retort on that occasion.

'I hate leaving you, Sue. Like hell.'

'But Richard is more important,' said Susan.

'Yes, I know,' and Mandy heaved the deepest of sighs. 'What about the cottage, Sue? Will you keep it on?'

'I haven't thought about it yet,' said Susan. 'I'll have to get one of the others to come and live with me. Nina, perhaps. After all, she began with us.'

'Yes, do. You'll have heaps of offers!' and Mandy giggled.

'You'll find out what a popular girl you are!'

And so it came about that Mandy packed her belongings and departed. She was the first to go.

Nina was delighted. Since she had been at Hamble she had had no settled billet, and for years no settled home. She had been to many parties at the cottage, and, as had others, envied Susan and Mandy its possession. She could not of course take Mandy's place and Susan missed Mandy at every turn, but she was companionable and very well read and educated; and although sometimes she talked to Susan of her Russian childhood, she was absolutely silent about her later years. Sometimes Susan wished she would talk more. She was sure that Nina's must be a most interesting story. It wasn't exactly curiosity, and Nina, she knew, was not naturally secretive. It would do her good, Susan thought, on more than one occasion, if she could expand a little.

* * *

The Hamble pilots were a most interesting crowd. With Mandy's departure Susan got to know some of them so much better. Perhaps it was because the end was in sight that Susan heard much of hopes and fears for the future. Perhaps because there was not so much flying these days, and more time to sit about in the sun, on the grass plots outside, with nothing to do but sew and listen.

Chili she loved, but Chili was popular, and now she was a twin-engined bomber pilot. Then Jackie was always fascinating: and Jackie had hitch-hiked to South Africa, on two months' leave, to see her mother; but Jackie was married now and would soon be leaving. Then there was Ida, always to be found studying aircraft engines, and who had been, Susan discovered, an air hostess of the Royal Dutch Airlines before the war; and another, rather silent girl to whom Susan's sympathy went out because, like herself, she was, supposedly, a war widow from Singapore. Susan was never curious, but one by one she somehow won their confidence and got to know more about them. To so many the war had really been a wonderful interlude. It had brought colour and romance into what had been previously drab and humdrum lives. It had given ambition opportunity. And now so many had nothing to which to look forward but to return to the daily grind in offices and shops, while yet others hoped to return to their own distant countries, and others for re-opening of social life, travel, parties and gaiety. After all, there were the people of twenty-eight different nationalities in ATA. Now that there was more time to talk the ante-room often buzzed with stories of happenings, and Susan began to feel that time was growing short, but she was in no mood to relax. She hailed with joy the days when she had a long flight. The two hours and twenty minutes it took to reach the Isle of Man became somewhat of a treat. Susan loved flying over the sea, and, after that first time, neither mist nor cliffs bothered her. She looked upon those days as red-letter days.

The next happening of importance was the General Election. Suddenly it became the sole topic of conversation, and the first week of July dawned before Susan remembered that she was registered at Haddenham and must go there to register her vote. She seemed to be the only one, so her day was arranged by 'Ops' as conveniently as possible. Thame airfield was closed. She could not land there, so she was given a Spitfire for Cranfield, and decided she would land at Westcott, and hitch-hike the few miles to Haddenham. There were sure to be cars about on General Election day, Susan reflected.

It was afternoon before she set off. A sultry afternoon with big, midsummer, cumulus clouds banked up on the horizon, and if the Griffon engine of the Spitfire she was flying had allowed Susan would have heard distant thunder rolling round the hills. As it was she climbed up high above the Chilterns to avoid the bumpy conditions which she now knew, from experience, persisted over high ground in such weather. 'This must be unique,' she thought as she flew northwards. 'I expect I'm the first, if not the only, girl who has ever gone to the poll in a Spitfire!'

Soon she was flying over Thame airfield, or what had been Thame airfield. She knew ATA had packed up there some weeks before, but she was not prepared for the sight that now met her eyes. Her first reaction was one of incredulity. Could such a metamorphosis take place so swiftly? Was this hay field really the scene of those early thrills and trials and endeavours? Banking steeply in order to get an uninterrupted view, Susan stared again. Yes, sure enough, there were the School huts and the big hangar; the Ferry Pool building, the old snack bar and the First Aid Station – but how different they looked!

Grass and weeds had grown up everywhere, between the huts, over the perimeter track, and green tufts even sprouted from the tops of the blister hangars. Now no noisy training machines flew continuously round the circuit. No figures in the familiar dark blue uniform moved ceaselessly to and fro on the ground and, apart from the horse plodding patiently up the field, drawing a ladened hay cart, and a man at its head, there was not a living soul in sight. Somehow everything had shrunk in size – and in importance. 'Or is it,' thought Susan, 'that my own perspective has changed and grown?'

At least half a dozen times Susan circled the field, and when at last she headed westwards towards Westcott, a hundred memories crowded in behind her, and faces loomed up clearly with features she would never see again in the flesh – Gavin – Sandra – David – Leslie – and Susie – dear Susie Slade!

Susan pushed her goggles up on her forehead to let the wind brush away the tear which hung on the lashes of her left eye. She was in the circuit of Westcott now, and needed both her eyes and all her thoughts for landing.

It was strange to be in Haddenham once again. There were a lot of people about, but no one of ATA. Susan did not linger. She went no further than the School buildings where she registered her vote. She was not politically minded and had not followed all the reasoning as to why a General Election was necessary at this juncture of the country's affairs, but as she made her cross she thought to herself: 'That's my vote of confidence in the Chief Pilot. The battle for peace is safe in his hands.' She did not stay to visit the 'Elms' site, or Hopefield House, but found herself wondering what had befallen John Cherry. Then she saw a car turning in her direction. It looked hopeful for a lift. It was. And very shortly Susan was once again in the air.

The General Election had made an interlude in the slack days which Susan had found irksome. Luckily at this time she was given several new and more advanced types to ferry, among them the famous Tempest, with its economical cruising speed of three hundred miles per hour: and then, to her delight, towards the end of July, she found her name down on the list for the next Class Four Conversion Course at White Waltham.

Ever since January, when the girl pilots of ATA had first been allowed to ferry to the continent, Susan had wished that she had been a Class Four Pilot, for this was one of the necessary qualifications, as now it also was for flying 'jet' machines. Her one consolation was that had she been ferrying to the continent she would have had to leave the cottage, and been posted away from Hamble to one of the two Invasion Pools, which were White Waltham and Aston Down, and then – well – she would probably not have seen very much of Mark.

As it was, Mark spent any leave he had at the 'Dolphin'; also he wrote frequently, and when during the evenings the telephone rang, it was as likely to be Mark as Mandy, who always wanted to know all the news. In the same way she put off thinking about the future, Susan put off analysing her feelings for Mark, and yet she was perfectly well aware that nowadays it was only when in his company, or when she was flying, that she was completely at peace.

'I wish you weren't going to do this conversion course, Sue,' he told her about a week before she was due to report at White Waltham. 'Seems silly at this point of the war. The end can't be far off.'

'Why silly?' she asked. 'It's more knowledge—' and Mark lit a cigarette, which he did not want, before he answered:

'Oh, I don't know. Just a thought.' Intently he followed the course of a smoke ring he had blown until it vanished on a sudden puff of wind off the river. For some minutes they were both silent.

'When do you go?' he asked at length. 'Day after tomorrow. Tuesday.'

But neither Mark nor Susan knew, as they sat in the cottage garden that evening watching the sun fall into the sea beyond the Isle of Wight, that history was coming to one of its rare climaxes on the other side of the world, nor did they know that the next day, Monday, August 6th, 1945, would see the agonizing birth of a new age. The Atomic Age.

The first Susan heard of it was on the six o'clock news the following evening. She and Nina had both ferried Typhoons down to St Eval in Cornwall, and then had one very ancient Harvard to bring back between them. Nina having won the toss as to who should pilot it, Susan had sat in the rear cockpit, with her eyes on the midsummer beauty of the west country and her mind on the morrow and her plans. Should she, or should she not, retain the cottage, which she now had on a monthly tenancy, for at least one more month? That was the question in her mind. Mark would like it. It would be somewhere for Nina on her days off, and Mrs Walters would keep it ready and look after the cats.

Later, sprawled on the sofa in the almost deserted ante-room, with a glass of lemonade beside her, Susan's thoughts were on the weeks of training ahead, and she had fallen into a reverie in which she already saw herself in the cockpit of a Mosquito. She did not notice Jackie come in and cross to the radio.

Suddenly the room, which a few minutes before had been silent and empty, was filled with people. Susan saw Commander Gore and Nina come in from the dining-room, Rachel and Alison from Operations, four or five pilots from the Locker Room, and Ethel, the ever cheerful Assistant Adjutant, appeared as if from nowhere, and Toni from Met, and silence fell on the room while the impersonal voice of the BBC announcer relayed the momentous news.

The first atomic bomb had been dropped on Hiroshima, a town in Japan of which Susan had never heard, and which no longer existed. For a moment silence fell on the room until someone said:

'Gosh! That's done it!'

'Sounds like the final curtain,' she heard someone else say a few minutes later.

'And the end of Air Transport Auxiliary!' someone else said quietly.

Both were right. Three days later came the news of the second atomic bomb on Nagasaki, and at midnight on August 15th the announcement of Japan's unconditional surrender.

All conversion courses were cancelled, and from that moment rumours came thick and fast. On all sides it was said that ATA had finished its job.

But one thing was not rumour. One by one the pilots left. Third Officers first. Susan's services were no longer required – or Nina's – or those girls who had followed them.

Susan found herself thinking much of Nina, who was more silent than usual. What of Nina's future?

Sitting out of doors one evening after supper, Susan was tempted to broach the subject when Nina softly quoted, '"Among new men, strange faces, other minds..." That is your Lord Tennyson. I wonder if he wrote from experience?'

Susan shook her head. The previous line had flashed into her memory, and for a moment she could not speak. 'And I, the last, go forth companionless.' Was that what Nina was thinking?

'I don't know. Hardly, perhaps, I think. He lived during the best time of the Victorian age – for the rich, that is.' Susan paused and added gently, 'You're thinking of the future?'

'Yes.' Nina leaned forward and picked up a shabby cushion from the ground and put it across her knees. One of the cats had appeared from nowhere, and both were much attached to Nina. Susan thought it was because she always sat so still. 'Come along then,' she said, and the next moment Whiskey, the larger of the two cats, had firmly settled himself on her lap.

Susan smiled. 'The cats will miss you, Nina! They've learnt to behave beautifully since you came.' And then another thought flashed into her mind – a solution that might help Nina. 'Nina' – she said, and purposely she made her voice rather hesitant – 'have you got any immediate plans, or could you help me about something?'

Nina's head turned slowly towards her with a questioning glance in her eyes. 'Of course,' she said, 'if I can. What is it?'

'It may take some weeks,' said Susan.

'All the better,' said Nina. 'The end of the war has come somewhat abruptly for me—' and her eyes clouded. 'I envy Sandra – and the others. Such a waste too – people who want to live and have things to live for.'

'I think,' said Susan gently, 'we all come to times when we think there is nothing left, but we re-adjust – it's the philosophy of life.' Nina nodded her head slowly, but made no answer, and after a few moments asked: 'What is it? This thing I can help you with?'

'My house. I'd be so grateful.' And Susan went on to explain about King's Lane. 'My tenants leave at Michaelmas,' she finished. 'They are army people. I want to sell it, and meanwhile I must live in it, lest it be commandeered. I do not know if that danger is yet over. I can't alone, and probably there will only be daily help to be got. There is such a lot of heart-breaking sorting out to do. Mother packed so much away.'

Nina turned her head, and her large, almost almond-shaped eyes lingered on Susan's.

'You aren't inventing, by any chance, are you?' she asked.

'Honest Injun!' answered Susan: 'It won't be a holiday, but it will give you time to make plans. Let's give up the cottage and go on the first.'

'What about Mark?' questioned Nina.

'It's just as easy for Mark to get to Hazeley as to Hamble,' answered Susan. 'Is it settled, Nina? We can stay with Grannie until the tenants go.'

A slow smile spread over Nina's face. 'Thank you, Sue,' and she glanced down at her hands, where, as always, a lovely diamond and emerald ring gleamed. 'You are enabling me once again to postpone the eating of my ring.'

And so, on the first of September, the MG, loaded to capacity, and with Susan and Nina on board, left Hamble for the last time.

Everyone was going. One by one the Ferry Pools all over England were closing down. Thame was not the only one where grass and weeds had already appeared between hutments.

Susan and Nina, with very mixed feelings – relief that the war was over – regrets that flying also was over – made what they thought would be their last visit to White Waltham to hand in their kit.

But they went once again. On Saturday, September 29th, when for the first and last time White Waltham airfield was open to the public.

It was a lovely day, and Susan and Nina, now staying with Grannie, decided to have an early lunch and leave directly afterwards. The MG would get them there in little over half an hour. But during the morning they were surprised by a telephone call from Mark, who said he had the opportunity of flying over to White Waltham, and would meet them there.

It was more to see her co-pilots that Susan had wanted to go than for anything else. Some, she knew, could not be there – Mandy, for one. Baby Richard was six weeks old, and nothing would induce Mandy to abandon Falcombe, where she hourly expected Michael.

They found thousands of people on the airfield, mostly enthusiastically inspecting some of the many types of aircraft whose names were familiar through the daily press, and watching a display of flying which, Susan overheard someone say, 'paled a Hendon pageant of pre-war days'. Only neither she, nor Nina, nor Mark, had ever seen a Hendon pageant, so could not compare. It was a glorious afternoon. But the joy of it lay in meeting so many of one's old friends and talking with them, and hearing what they were doing and their plans for the future.

The only flying job that was open to the girl pilots seemed to be to become an air hostess for BOAC, and several had already applied. To Susan this seemed sad, and in a way purposeless, and she said so to Mark, but Mark's answer astonished her.

'Well, you have proved yourselves equally as good pilots as men. Wouldn't surprise me if the RAF found a use for women pilots one day.'

And to Nina he made a suggestion. 'Why not come out to Australia, Nina? When I get my flying club going?'

'If you mean it—? Glorious!' answered Nina.

It was late when they, all three, after squeezing together into the MG, arrived at Grannie's for supper.

To both Mark and Nina she was no longer 'Mrs Ledgard'. They both affectionately called her 'Grannie', and Susan strongly suspected Grannie had heard far more of Nina's story than she had ever told to anyone else.

And it was amazing what Grannie allowed Nina to do. Her snow-white hair was cut short and curled softly all over her head. Nina manicured Grannie's fingernails: and polished her ring. She seemed to know all about the cleaning of jewellery. She washed and re-strung Grannie's pearls, until Susan said laughingly: 'You're making her as vain as a kitten, Nina! But she looks lovely!'

'She *is* lovely!' said Nina.

But how Grannie's housekeeping was managed no one ever knew.

She had lived a very long time in Hazeley, and was, in a way, an institution. Susan always said, 'If there's anything going, Grannie will always get the first offer.' So, tonight, over cold chicken, and one of Grannie's remaining bottles of champagne, they were a quietly happy party. There was nothing over which to hurry. Rose beamed in the background and Mark was staying the night.

There had been some letters for Susan by the afternoon post, but Susan, after a casual glance, had taken them up to her room. Only the bank. 'Some more business,' she remarked. 'It can wait.' And she did not think of them again until about midnight, when, half undressed, she remembered them.

Two – both from the bank – one merely the acknowledgment of her tenant's last cheque, but the other had an enclosure, addressed in an unknown hand. Idly, with her mind on her departing tenants and King's Lane, Susan opened it, and glanced first at the signature. 'Dorothy Verner'! The room swam – was it – news – at last?

For a few moments Susan could not take it in – the words 'not good news, I'm afraid' seemed to stand out in letters of fire.

'Not good news—'

After a minute or two Susan sat down on her dressing-stool and, leaning towards the light, read calmly:

Dear Mrs Sandyman,

It seems a very long time since that wet morning when you so kindly let David and me share your taxi. But it is only now that I have news for you. Not good news, I'm afraid, and I am so sorry to have to say it.

We did as we said, and John, my brother, had your name.

John is so dependable. He is on the Flagship, so had an early opportunity to pursue his enquiries. By a miracle, he says, he traced your husband, and found that he died fighting, with the Australians, defending the Causeway. We've only had one short airmail letter. When more details come I will write again. John said to be sure to tell you that it would seem that he was killed outright, not wounded. I feel that may be a little comfort, and with all my heart I wish I could have sent better news.

My mother and my brothers join me in deep sympathy.

Will you, some day, come and visit us? We should be so pleased. If John gets home we will let you know.'

* * *

It was no shock to Susan – only confirmation. She had known all the time – but – before she knew it, she was on her knees beside the bed and her sobs came, heavily at first, then slower, as peace came to her. Almost she felt Frank close at hand. Felt the pressure of his hand on her shoulder. She longed to move but would not – if she moved that close feeling might vanish. His voice came to her. Things they had talked about – what they would do if either lost the other – she had been so startled when Frank had said: 'Marry again? Of course! The compliment would be to you. Just as I should expect you to make some other chap as happy as you have made me, It can't be the first time again – that is *ours* – yours and mine – but—'

Susan felt the room empty again, and she rose to her feet.

Afterwards, she had no remembrance of how she got there, but she had dressed again, and quite deliberately put on a warm coat. She heard Jason, who slept in the hall, move as she came downstairs. She called to him softly, and he came padding across and thrust his nose into her hand, but made no sound. A moment later they were standing on the flagstones of the little terrace. Grannie and Nina slept in the front of the house. Susan's room overlooked the garden, as did the one Mark occupied on the other side of the landing.

The hall clock struck the hour. One o'clock, and Jason pressed closer. A light still burned in Mark's room – Susan stood under the window.

'Mark!' she called softly, and again, 'Mark!'

Had he fallen asleep over his book? But in a moment Mark's head appeared at the open window.

'Susan!' The whisper floated down.

'Come down. I want you.' The whisper floated back.

It was a matter of moments only before Mark, clad only m a dressing-gown thrown over his pyjamas, and trousers, stood beside her. 'What is it, Sue? Are you ill?'

'No – but that letter – from the bank. There was one in it – from Dorothy Verner – you know who I mean?'

Mark nodded.

'I have news. Come to the top of the garden.'

The light of Susan's torch enabled Mark to read Dorothy Verner's letter, then, without a word, he folded it and put it gently back into Susan's hands and switched out the torch, and then, still without a word, his arms went round Susan, and he drew her close – the next moment she was sobbing on his shoulder.

Mark kissed and comforted her, patting her and stroking her hair, as one would a child. As her sobs subsided he asked, very gently:

'Susan – does this mean that you will marry me?'

'Yes – but I'm so afraid – so afraid that I can't love you as I did Frank.'

'I haven't asked you to, darling. Give me what you can, and some day—' He held her still closer. After some time Susan lifted her head, and for the first time Mark's lips met hers, and again, after an interval, he said:

'We will buy a machine of some sort and fly to Australia. Shall we?'

'Yes.' Susan lay in his arms at perfect peace, and Jason stood up and nuzzled his nose between them.

'Nice old boy!' said Mark. 'The first to congratulate me.'

A late moon rose over the garden. They sat talking quietly and watching it until the first coming of dawn.

A bird twittered.

'Sunday!' said Susan.

'A new day – and a new life!' said Mark.

ISBN 9781912423071
£8.99

'Alexander Baron's *From the City, From the Plough* is undoubtedly one of the very greatest British novels of the Second World War and provides the most honest and authentic account of front line life for an infantryman in North West Europe.'

ANTONY BEEVOR

ISBN 9781912423163
£8.99

'Few other novels of the war describe the grinding claustrophobia, violence and lethal danger of being in a tank crew with the stark vividness of Peter Elstob... a forgotten classic that deserves to be read and read.'

JAMES HOLLAND

ISBN 9781912423095
£8.99

'Takes you straight back to Blitzed London... boasts everything a great whodunit should have, and more.'

ANDREW ROBERTS

ISBN 9781912423378
£8.99

'A highly unusual war novel with several confluent narratives; moving, interesting and of great literary value.'

LOUIS de BERNIÈRES

ISBN 9781912423156
£8.99

'When a man has been a soldier and seen action, he writes of war with true understanding, and with authority. When that man writes with, elegance and imagination, as Fred Majdalany does in *Patrol*, he produces a military masterpiece.'

ALLAN MALLINSON

ISBN 9781912423088
£8.99

'A tremendous rediscovery of a brilliant novel. Extremely well-written, its effects are both sophisticated and visceral. Remarkable.'

WILLIAM BOYD

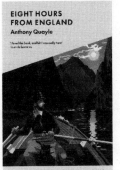

ISBN 9781912423101
£8.99

'Much more than a novel'

RODERICK BAILEY

'I loved this book, and felt I was really there'

LOUIS de BERNIÈRES

'One of the greatest adventure stories of the Second World War'

ANDREW ROBERTS

ISBN 9781912423385
£8.99

'Brilliant... a quietly confident masterwork'

WILLIAM BOYD

'One of the best books to come out of the Second World War'

JOSHUA LEVINE

ISBN 9781912423279
£8.99

'A hidden masterpiece, crackling with authenticity'

PATRICK BISHOP

'Supposedly fiction, but these pages live – and so, for a brief inspiring hour, do the young men who lived in them.'

FREDERICK FORSYTH

ISBN 9781912423262
£8.99

'Witty, warm and hugely endearing...
a lovely novel'

AJ PEARCE

'Evokes the highs and lows, joys and
agonies of being a Land Girl'
JULIE SUMMERS

ISBN 9781912423491
£8.99

In 1943 John Foley is posted to command
Five Troop and their trusty Churchill tanks
Avenger, Alert, and Angler – thus begins
his initiation into the Royal Armoured
Corps. This intimate and detailed account
follows the fate of this group of men in the
latter stages of the Second World War.

ISBN 9781912423507
£8.99

George Bunting, businessman, husband
and father, lives a quiet life at home in
Laburnam Villa in Essex, reading about the
progress of the war in his trusty newspaper.
But as the War continues into the summer
of 1940, this bumbling 'everyman' is
forced to confront the true realities of the
conflict. He does so with a remarkable
stoicism, imbuing him with a quiet dignity.